I0653452

FANTASTIC JOURNEY

The Soul of Speculative Fiction and
Fantasy Adventure

Azalea Dabill

Dynamos Press

Coeur d'Alene, Idaho

Copyright © 2020 by Azalea Dabill

Dynamos Press
2705 N Howard St.
Coeur d 'Alene Idaho/83815
www.azaleadabill.com

All rights reserved. This book remains the copyrighted property of the author, and may not be redistributed to others for commercial or non-commercial purposes. No part of this publication may be reproduced, distributed or transmitted in any form or by any means, including photocopying, recording, or other electronic or mechanical methods, without the prior written permission of the publisher, except in the case of brief quotations embodied in critical reviews and certain other noncommercial uses permitted by copyright law. For permission requests, write to the publisher, addressed "Attention: Permissions Coordinator," at the address above. Thank you for your support.

Publisher's Note: This is a work of non-fiction that quotes fiction. Most names, characters, places, and incidents are a product of the author's imagination. Locales and public names are sometimes used for atmospheric and citation purposes.

Book Layout Copyright 2020 BookDesignTemplates.com

Cover Designer: Derek Murphy at creativindie.com
Editor: Jennifer Leo

Fantastic Journey: The Soul of Speculative Fiction and Fantasy Adventure/Azalea Dabill, 1st ed.

ISBN 978-1-943034-13-0

This book is for those who love the mystery and magnificent allure of new worlds, including all who are weak in body and yet love bold and beautiful adventure, and for my Dad and Mom, who showed me gleaming facets of the wisdom and love of the Creator of the world.

—Azalea

"The author who benefits you most is not the one who tells you something you did not know before, but the one who gives expression to the truth that has been struggling in you for utterance."

—OSWALD CHAMBERS

What people are saying about
Fantastic Journey

"It will be treasured by fantasy fans, and also be an informative intro-duction to the genre . . ."
–Jenny Leo, Editor

Falcon Heart

"Exciting, engaging, rich. Adventure, intrigue, battles, all the elements of a good tale."
–Lynn Leissler

Other Books

The Falcon Chronicle:
Falcon Heart
Falcon Flight
Lance and Quill
Falcon Dagger*
Poetry Companion: Falcon's Ode

Coloring Books:
Trencher and Board
Nightshade and Knitbone

All books are available on Amazon.
Books with an asterisk* are coming soon.

CONTENTS

The Sword, the Ring, and the Chalice • Bonemender's Choice is a Heart-thrilling Quest for Genuine Love

Who Can Put a Price on Daring Love, Loyalty, and Swordsmanship? • Every Guy's Dream—Terrific Inventions, Fantastic Beasts, and Killer Adventure • Get Hooked on a Fantasy Character Kaleidoscope • Don't You Need the Startling Truth of Genuine Dragons? • Where Narnia Reveals Hard-hitting Good and Evil • Rousing Fantasy Adventure is Wondrous Easy to Follow • The Romance of the Glittering Treasure of Shahrazad

Encounter the Rare Vision of Your Proven Soul Mate • Devastating Abuse Comes Unexpected but Rise Unvanquished • Deerskin Retells How a Wounded Heart Can be Healed • Dream of Warrior Love in The Blue Sword* • Prove Your Love Through Fire in The Crown of Eden • The Surprising Attraction of Faithful Relationships in A School for Unusual Girls • A Rare and Magnificent Love on Treacherous Ground • The Reverse Romance—Love Refused Creates Conflict—or Character • Discover the Best Fantasy Romance in The Bonemender

Amazing Fantasy Tactics in The Deed of Paksenarrion* • Medieval Unarmed Combat Secrets in Falcon Heart • Unmatched Fantasy Tears and Training in the Arena • Brave Principles and Weapons Protect the Seeking Heart in Divided Allegiance • Why Paranormal and Visionary Warfare Blows Your Mind • The Shocking Supernatural in Legends of the Guardian King

Do You Crave Pixies, Dragons, and Secret Trysts in a Wild World? • How High Fantasy Paints Inspiring Elves and Fairies of the Light • Come Join an Epic Journey to The Iron Tower • How Do Rich Gnomes and Imposing Dwarves Make Spectacular Fantasy? • How to Find the Best Fantastic Beast, from The Griffin Mage to DragonSpell • Do Wizards, Witches, and Tyrants Make War on Authority? • Magicians and Good Versus Evil in The Blood of Kings

Foreword

Few great adventures are accomplished alone. This book is no exception. Here is my shameless endorsement.

CJ and Shelley Hitz's Christian Book Academy, Derek Murphy's CreativIndie ideas and courses, Nina Amir's blogging advice, and Derek Doepker's audiobook and marketing training took this book places I never dreamed.

But the idea began much earlier.

At first I didn't know what was at the back of my sense of something missing in so much of the fantasy on library shelves. At twenty-two, I loved the adventure, the overcoming, the beautiful places, and the sense of being in the skin of a person saving the world, with the power to change things.

But I began to sense a difference among the fantasy books I enjoyed. For example, the fantasies of C. S. Lewis, J. R. R. Tolkien, George MacDonald, and Kathy Tyers, among others, left me filled with hope, looking beyond myself in a kind of wonder, in awe of what they saw in other worlds, with delight in the relationships they found. Other fantasies by authors like Ursula K. Le Guin, Robert Jordan, Robin Hobb, and some of C. J. Cherryh's work were grand adventures, with characters and worlds I loved, but they also left me with a sense of dark futility about the purpose of life in the worlds, immorality on many levels, and an inward-turning self-reliance. Though there were threads of good in them, in the end, everything narrowed to the darkness of self without hope beyond ourselves, which is no hope at all.

We will become like our friends, and books we love are friends of a kind. What desires are our friends stirring in us? What do our best friends admire? What are they drawing us toward? Beauty and joy and mystery and hope and courage? Or a desire for love, led astray? Or do some of our friends whirl us through a grey landscape of self unending, ultimately turned inward, then through an exciting world of danger and daring, but without true purpose? Does the story whisper in our ear of tainted power, illicit pleasure, and compromise with evil to achieve a good end? Does it tell us knowledge ends with our hearts?

This kind of fantasy started to poison me until I regretfully changed my bookish diet, limiting some, and cutting others. Now I am thankful I did. It is important to note, not necessarily all the above mentioned authors' books were the sort that darkened my mind and heart. Some of C. J. Cherryh's fantasies I enjoy still, but the immoral fantasy was a problem that had to be addressed. That problem led to this book.

I am no expert beyond what extensive reading and experience have taught me. I am learning still, as we sail along our journey together through the world of fantasy adventure. Please forgive the mistakes, which are mine alone.

It is true that the best human-authored books are a mix, with either some error or other drawback mixed in with good adventure and great storytelling, but that does not let us off judging whether it is *predominantly* true or false. And though someone may say, to avoid bad fiction we would have to go out of the world, we must decide whether a story is inspiring us toward greater heights and the light, or greater depths of darkness.

Embark on a fantastic journey into the soul of speculative fiction and fantasy adventure. Stories have a soul, a central meaning in each. Let us travel the fantasy realm of earth, wind, and wave to hunt out gems of great story.

Note: "We" includes some thoughts of the author and various others, some passed from this world and some still living, who have given so much wisdom, insight, and general fantasy lore to our world. This book of collective knowledge would not exist without many before me who have appreciated good fantasy. "We" seemed appropriate. In cases where "I" is used, this is solely my personal experience, opinion, or decision as the author of this book.

An asterisked title contains a reference or mention you may wish to skip, and authors with an asterisk have written other titles than the one *we quote, which you may wish to avoid, depending on your definition of clean fantasy. (*) Means read with caution.*

Dive 0.0

The Soul of Imaginative Fiction and Fantasy Adventure

Take a deep breath before our first plunge into the sea of fantasy.

In worlds near and far, beauty can be true, mystery can be found, and battle can be praiseworthy. The beauty, the mystery, and the adventure are vital to our spirits. Fantastic journeys invite us to search beyond what we see for truth, to dig deeper for courage.

The soul of fantasy adventure, speculative and otherwise, benefits us on three levels. In the spiritual arena, the wide world of ideas, and the sphere we breathe in.

What difference does it make? Why do the quest and the hero's journey draw us all? How do we find the best epic fantasy?

To discover these answers and more, we bring up select jewels from the deep and explore mountain troves to whet our appetite for the riches of imaginative fiction. Our aim is to clear away the creeping muck, the destructive ideas, and the flawed gems that beset every treasure seeker in the realm of fantasy.

If we show readers how to ferret out false, deceptive jewels and spread before them the gleaming wealth of morally brave story, our quest will be complete. Our goal is to show every hunter of fantasy the epic adventure of clean fiction and its rewards.

This is a joint venture. The seventy authors and their inspiring adventures we explore are beacons of extraordinary story. Most of them are lights by contrast, guiding us to enchanting lands of danger in the ocean of fantasy. With them, we learn how to identify true gems and sell them not. How to discern enemies, friends, and endless possibilities with our inner eye: to touch and to taste the truths of life in realms near and far.

Never underestimate the power of anything we invite inside our minds and hearts, in our world or elsewhere. False or true, foolish or wise, corrupt or clean, what we welcome inside transforms our inner world and our ideas and colors all that we become. We must take heed, for our journey, though fantastic, is full of danger.

From birth we carry a journal of knowledge, waiting for us to fill its pages. But knowledge can cut both ways. It can protect or destroy. For our book of knowledge to be a blade of truth that divides bad from good, we must temper it with understanding gained from experience—experience written in our hearts with the living, willing ink of our blood. The experience, the wisdom, our blood and breath and book—all begin in our Creator.

Before we embark upon the perilous realm, read what the wise who have gone before us have written in our book in bold, glimmering hue of opalescent green, pink, and blue.

THE HIDDEN GEMS

A Treasure to sail for:

We will open many books of fantasy to find the elusive gems. The journey is dangerous, hunting by land and sea, but such jewels leave us with a greater grasp of truth, hopeful of life, with deep empathy and a sense of wonder over treasures heaped on endless shores.

A Diamond to steer by:

The best fantasies are about change by conflict, where powerful truth transforms the familiar. As we walk among jewels of clean fantasy, we find ourselves beckoned "higher up and further in," as C.S. Lewis so aptly says, to another world. A liberating world of transcendent beauty, mysterious wonder, and adventure beyond compare.

A Zircon to know:

The secret of purely great fantasy, stories that are not utterly boring—is contrast. How evil is portrayed and for what purpose creates soul-destroying or soul-inspiring adventure.

An Emerald to watch for:

Our definition of "clean fantasy" is that evil is not glorified, is not subtly admired by the story as a whole, is not wallowed in for shock value. Good and evil, beauty and ugliness are drawn into battle in great fantasy, and there they show their differences in a way that makes us want to stand up and cheer or knuckle down and fight with all we are.

A Topaz to see by:

Morally base fantasies that glorify deception, ugliness, and futility leave us wanting to cry. The beauty of truth, the conflict of good versus evil, and the sword of justice weave through the best imaginative fiction, calling us to leave desolation behind. Though these bright threads may wind through strongholds of deepest evil, it is never a journey of deception, muddling through injustice to exalt despairing fate. Rather, they call us to fight desolation in the light of a sure hope. Great fantasy on a spiritual level helps remove the cloud of hopelessness from one lens through which we see life—our imagination. Goodness shines the clearer as it beats back darkness.

A Thought of Gold:

Fantasy is a weaving of power that transforms a tapestry into a tale, a mirror into a portal, a string of runes on a page into a living, breathing world. Where do we gather great fantasies so we don't waste time on fool's gold and fatally flawed stories? How do we sort adventurous, inspiring fantasy from the insipid, the bad, and the destructive? We dive into the waves of the sea and explore the mountains of fantasy, but read a page or few of our prospective wealth before we bring it home or on deck.

Silver to seek:

Every good fantasy holds vast secrets for brave hearts. Listen to those who sail the waves, to experienced salts who search the epic depths and chart the islands. They will be the first to tell there are undiscovered ocean vaults beneath the surface. Entire islands of mystery and danger await every adventurer seeking riches, yearning for jewels of strong and precious story. When the dive is done and the fight is fought, what precious things will we bring to light?

A Pearl to hold:

The alluring glamour of the forbidden, which promises life-giving water but offers a goblet of hemlock, will not draw seekers to their deaths on this *Fantastic Journey*. The fantasies we depict do not paint scenes of immorality, where the sweetness of stolen water conceals death. There *are* battles, perils, and conflicts of every description, but true intimacy stops at the chamber door, where we leave it with a nod, a knowing smile, and respect for a precious thing.

A Ruby to remember:

Epic fantasy adventure benefits us on three levels: the spiritual arena, the wide world of ideas, and the sphere we breathe in. The realm of fantasy touches all three. It conveys life deeper than sand and sea, breathes into being lands nearer than we know, shows us the adventure of love in all its facets, and transfers truth from thought and experience to our heart's grasp.

The ocean of fantasy adventure broadens our horizons and enthralls our hearts with crystal joys and enchanting beauties on a voyage across a perilous realm. Will we discover that which is the wealth of souls?

Note: Each chapter dives for jewels in its subchapters. Chapter 1.0 has 11 such dives. For example, subchapter "Dive 1.11".

Chapter 1.0

Discover the Irresistible Beauty of Truth in Fantasy

Who does not wish that at least one moment in a beautiful epic fantasy were true? But some of those moments are true, and some of those places. The mystery of beauty, and sacrifice, the brave call of loyalty, and the torch of true relationships make us yearn for something we often cannot name. But we feel it in epic fantasies of courage, perseverance, and friendship that illuminate selflessness. We behold spiritual heights, physical depths, and in far realms we learn to refuse evil and choose good until it influences our adventures in our own sphere. Fantasy relates to deep reality.

Some people may say there is little truth in the ocean of fantasy. They claim the very words *fantasy fiction* are a double negative of reality. Others say that fantasy involves Wicca, witchcraft, magick—at the very least, it means New Age muddled thought. They claim fantasy is not for serious Christians because it does not encourage spirituality and faith. They say idealism or fantasy doesn't apply to real life, and abstract ideas in fantasy rarely touch real things.

In truth, real things and the ideals we hold are as closely connected as our body and spirit. Abstract ideals are intertwined in the physical and spiritual in every occurrence in the spatial universe. Every idea we believe, experience, and come to understand moves the breath, blood, and bone we call our body—*because* ideals first move our heart and spirit.

Fantasy mirrors reality, showing the abstract in sharper facets. It casts reality back at us in a thousand reflections, penetrating deeper into our souls at times than any physical blade on this earth.

Andrew Peterson puts it wonderfully well in *Adorning the Dark:*

> *"But instead, I experienced something much deeper.*
>
> *The reintroduction of fairy tales to my redeemed imagination helped me to see the Maker, his Word, and the abounding human (but sometimes Spirit-commandeered) tales as interconnected. It was like holding the intricate crystal of Scripture up to the light, seeing it lovely and complete, then discovering on the sidewalk a spray of refracted colors. The colors aren't Scripture, nor are they the light behind it. Rather, they're an expression of the truth, born of the light beyond, framed by the prism of revelation, and given expression on solid ground."*

–*Adorning the Dark* by Andrew Peterson, pg. 70

Fantasy grows on ideas, it thrives on abstract ideals that drive the world we are part of, good or bad, false or true. Good fantasies on the solid ground of the world depict evil incisively, the better to identify and destroy it, as light inherently banishes darkness, however slow its inexorable advance. For instance, a great fantasy can reveal the very human wish for vengeance and, in the end, its antidote, as *The Traitor's Heir* does so well. (The second quote below contains a slight spoiler, if you wish to skip it.)

> *It was not fear of death that moved him but the cutting words, the gait, the laughter, the dead body on the ground, and the terrible, unbearable thought of Hughan's face delighting in his death.*
>
> *He pinned burning hands about Giles's throat. The man was caught off guard, and Eamon bore him to the ground. Arrows hissed past his shoulder; one seared past his arm, drawing blood. He heard Cathair's voice behind, and from the corner of his eye*

he saw a red light arching outwards. A moment later one of Giles's archers screamed, consumed in a bloody glow.

But Eamon had no interest in the Hands or the archers; all his thought was bent on the winded man beneath him. Giles lashed back. Eamon swerved to avoid a crushing blow. He knew that Giles was stronger than him and that he was a fool to think he could take the villain down. But dizzying rage coursed through him, leaving room only for vengeance. He gleefully pressed flaming hands down on his enemy's throat.

–*The Traitor's Heir* by Anna Thayer, pg. 387

...

Giles watched him carefully. "Sir—"

"You have heard of breachers," Eamon told him quietly. "I was one, and I opened your mind, Giles, but I did not mean to breach it; I meant to break it." Giles looked hard at him, surprised, and gave a low breath. "Where there is something that you do not recall, you do not recall it because I took it from you," Eamon said. It seemed long ago and yet so very vivid still before his mind. "I am sorry for what I did. You must know also," he added at last, "that I knew I had done wrong, and that I had no peace thereafter. When I destroyed your mind I saw how much I had become Edelred's servant. It was then that I resolved to turn back to the King."

"Then good came from it," Giles said simply.

"That still does not excuse what I did to you," Eamon replied. "I am sorry, Giles. Whatever wrongs you had done to me..." He trailed off. "I should not have done it to you. But I was angry, and I was blinded, and I hated you. I do not now."

–*The Broken Blade* by Anna Thayer, pg. 563

The beauty of bright, strong lands set against darkness, where heroes hunt down those who would inflict their painful will on others, are commonplace in fantasy and sometimes the stories that most closely border our own world. And in the more mind-bending forms of fantasy, we are intrigued by the maze of the human mind and spirit, the tangle of desire for good things and for evil, where it is possible to see the shades of our own hearts, and shiver.

So moral, well-crafted fantasy does fit abstract ideals into our real world, and real hearts. But can fantasy and faith even exist together, let alone thrive? Do belief in God and enjoyment of fantasy cancel each other out?

By "faith" I mean the Creator's gift of belief, however small, in the power and goodness of the God of the Bible. My other senses of faith, like faith in friends, in water being wet, that the sun will rise, in the end are fed by that wellspring of faith in him who created all worlds. Faith that he gives good things and made good laws upon which all the worlds stand, including those of fantasy. Though fantasy worlds exist in a different sense.

And even if some believe God himself is a fantasy, can't they still see bravery, self-sacrifice, and love—a desire to live well and make a difference in the world—in great fantasy stories? Moral fantasy adventure genres encourage the best from us, including belief in the possibility of goodness, of truth, of joy.

Even though we often fall short of the shining moments of our heroes that fantasies portray, heroes and heroines draw us to admire greater heights of character and to reach for it ourselves. They whisper that somewhere, perfect joy, truth, and goodness do exist. We hear that call, and seek the gems of epics hidden beneath the waves and the wealth concealed in the mountains. Are we not seeking the beauty we have tasted somewhere, that strength that came to us at some time, that moment when a scent drifted past, as if it were a touch or a thought from another world? That time we were reading and a whole universe opened up, which had never existed for us before?

Reading great fantasy expands our horizons, inner and outer. But know that each fantasy mirrors the world as the author sees it, and can be as clouded as the author's sight—or as clear. It will reveal truth or falsehood, usually both, to greater and lesser degrees.

But what we see is also as clear as our own inner sight as we read. The lens of belief that we see through frames fantasy stories—with our clouded desires or with the truth. Yet strangely, the soul of clean fantasy can pierce and change our desires, can sharpen our sight, and our perception, even our enjoyment.

As we voyage in the ocean of fantasy, we add to our journals of knowledge with the pen of experience.

Are our adventures not real? We treasure the knowledge we hunt down in books, but even more, our understanding of that knowledge and how it fits into our world.

For fantasy *can* mean Wicca, witchcraft, magick, and New Age muddled thought. These fantasies promote evil: our desire to be the center, to manipulate every shred of acknowledgement we can snatch to our own ends, the pursuit of inward-bent power and pleasure.

Or true epic fantasy can weave a picture of the shining heart of the Person and power at work in the worlds. And seeing a glimpse of him, we draw near that life and light and power—in fear or in joy, but always in anticipation.

Because each work of fantasy reveals the spiritual perception of the author, fantasy *is* for serious Christians—unless we wish to abandon the battlefield to the enemy of all light. For fantasy can reveal facets of the greatest spiritual things in the cameo of the small and the unusual. As a genre, fantasy tends to silhouette the hero's spiritual growth toward darkness or light, toward the ugly and vile or the beautiful and good. It reveals the enchanter, the enchanted, and the one who breaks the enchantment. It cannot hide those dominated by unlawful power, or the one who refuses to serve it.

If we give clean fantasy half a chance, it proves itself amply strong. Far from insipid, sanctimonious, or blasphemous, excellent fantasy adventure is an experience not to be missed. "Fantasy fiction" mirrors reality and absolute truth in the deeds of daring hearts. Taste for yourself.

In the following subchapters of *Fantastic Journey* we invite you to dive into adventures from the sea of fantasy, such as Jaye L. Knight's the Ilyon Chronicles, where there are treasures beyond dragons. Open M.I. McAllister's *Urchin of the Riding Stars* and be enchanted by a brave little squirrel who risks all for his king and his land in the mist. Cross swords with orcs at Aragorn's side in the battle against the dark tide in *The Lord of the Rings*. Confront utter darkness of soul in Patrick Carr's *The Shock of Night* and be emboldened to fight your own demons. And always, always follow the light in such fantasies as George MacDonald's *The Golden Key*. Whether tried by time or new on our horizon, clean fantasy adventure pours light, knowledge, and understanding into our lives.

Paths of fantasy, under water or over wold, take us to interesting places and wondrous spaces, not to mention introducing us to fascinating people, where every character is involved in the battle we all fight. If we live, we must choose. On which side will we lift a blade? Whether we know it or not, the light and the darkness draw us. These realms and this battle are what fantasy is all about.

Come and feel the meaning of the mountain under your feet in *Princess Academy,* and speak with telepathic animals of forest and plain in *Kayndo—Ring of Death.* Spend a fantastic *Summer at Castle Auburn,* then meet a thief of wit intent on stealing a kingdom and peace in The Queen's Thief series. Explore *The Floating Islands* above an ocean of grief, and in *Waterfall* combat vile intrigue. Discover belief in *The Shock of Night,* and find experience sharper than a blade in *The Princess and the Goblin.* Follow Drizzt Do'urden into unrivaled fantasy combat in *Exile.* Become a Dragonback companion in *Dragon and Slave*—then storm space itself with *Dakiti* and *Firebird.*

We anchor our vessel first in the bay of a faraway land. In the next subchapter, disembark and follow the rocky path from shore up the mountain, where we first discover magic, mountains, and Miri. Our adventure is real.

Note: Some subchapter "dives" into epic fantasy adventure began as posts for my blog at www.azaleadabill.com, but morphed into this book.

Dive 1.1

Fantastic Meanings of the Mountain in Fantasy

Is a fantasy a mountain in the sense of an insurmountable obstacle, a mountain of danger, or a mountain of refuge? What do you think of when you hear the word *fantasy,* as it applies to a book? Do you think *unrealistic, dull plap,* or *magick and witches?*

If you think *unrealistic,* you might try looking a little deeper. All fiction is "real life with the boring bits taken out," as someone wise once said. Fantasy, in particular, takes the boring bits out and adds beautiful settings, fascinating looks at characters we'd love to meet—or run from—and contrasts the familiar with the unfamiliar, giving it a new spice of enchantment.

If fantasy makes you think *magick and witches,* there is truth to that, though not for the fantasies we recommend. At least not in the sense that *magick* with a *k* means.

Richard Abanes wrote several wonderful and intriguing books on fantasy and family, and how the *k* indicates real witchcraft teaching. As he relates, *magick* is a meaningful spelling, in common usage among witches in their own circles. But not all magic in fantasy contains that meaning. In *Harry Potter, Narnia, and The Lord of the Rings,* Abanes says,

'"What we see in Lewis is how certain objects or practices in fantasy, even if they are not changed enough to make them totally unrecognizable, can still be arranged within an entirely different system, thereby taking them far away from any real-world context. Consequently, such objects and practices need not pose a problem for religious parents worried about any direct links to the occult. In other words, because fantasy often takes place in an alternate reality, different definitions, meanings, and laws of existence apply"' (pg. 57).

In *Fantastic Journey*, I'm primarily concerned with magic as it represents a given or gifted power—either assumed, implied, or stated, under different laws of existence. Good power is not gained or wielded by manipulation of spirits, spells, or anything of that sort. Magic that is a part of the created order in the hero or heroine's world is a gift, just insofar as it is given by the Creator where different "laws of existence [do] apply."

Again, never is good power gained by evil spells, chants, or any form of witchcraft, which at a basic level is unlawful manipulation. Though Lucy read the spell to make the Dufflepuds become visible, it was neither an evil spell nor witchcraft, for the authority behind the magician in *The Voyage of the Dawn Treader*, his magic book, and every spell in the story *is* under a different law of existence. The magician, a retired star, lived in a different realm, under other laws of existence: Narnia under Aslan's rule. As Aslan said,

"I have been here all the time," said he, "but you have just made me visible."

"Aslan!" said Lucy almost a little reproachfully. "Don't make fun of me. As if anything I could do would make you visible!"

"It did," said Aslan. "Do you think I wouldn't obey my own rules?"

–The Voyage of the Dawn Treader by C. S. Lewis, pg. 135

Reading a book of spells belonging to either the White Witch or Uncle Andrew would be another matter entirely. Their unlawful, manipulative power comes from someone quite different from Aslan.

In the fantasy stories I give you in this book, witches are never good. *Good witch* is a confusion of terms. Either the supposed witch is not using unlawful power, in which case he or she is not a witch or warlock, as we commonly understand it, or unlawful power *is* being used, thus goodness does not enter the equation. *Good witch* is a true oxy-moron, a contradiction of terms.

Many books use *witch* as a term for someone displaying a power that another character is not used to seeing, an unusual or strange ability, which may have nothing to do with witchcraft. Just because someone is called a witch does not mean they are. And someone may actually be a witch without ever bearing the name.

Leaving the definition of *good witch* behind, if you are entrenched in the idea that reading fantasy is as hard as climbing a dangerous mountain of *dull plap*, I don't think *Fantastic Journey* will be much help, unless you're willing to open a fantasy book and taste a few words. Then you might be hooked before you know it. Fair warning—it may not be what you expect.

Dennis McKiernan's clean earlier books, such as The Silver Call Duology, show us mountains as majestic barriers, awe-inspiring homes to dwarves and practical places of ambush. In Karen Hancock's *Arena,* mountains are walls that force characters to face mystery and new ideas of themselves. Then the mountains in Shannon Hale's *Princess Academy* are home to Miri.

Peasant daughter of a quarry village, Miri sees mind pictures and hears whispers through a special stone called *linder.* Things get more interesting when the lowland king declares every village girl will leave her home to enroll in a newly-built Princess Academy, to learn things Miri never dreamed of, where one of the girls will be chosen to marry the prince. Of course, since this is an adventure, nothing turns out like that.

First there are angry villagers, then kidnappers ... then skeptical, practical, brave, and romantic Miri.

> *Linder. It was the mountain's only crop, her village's one means of livelihood. Over centuries, whenever one quarry ran out of linder, the villagers dug a new one, moving the village of Mount Eskel into the old quarry. Each of the mountain's quarries had produced slight variations on the brilliant white stone. They had mined linder marbled with pale veins of pink, blue, green, and now silver.*
>
> *Miri tethered the goats to a twisted tree, sat on the shorn grass, and plucked one of the tiny pink flowers that bloomed out of crack in the rocks. A miri flower.*
>
> *The linder of the current quarry had been uncovered the day she was born, and her father had wanted to name her after the stone.*
>
> *"This bed of linder is the most beautiful yet," he had told her mother, "pure white with streaks of silver."*
>
> *But in the story that Miri had pulled out of her pa many times, her mother had refused. "I don't want a daughter named after a stone," she had said, choosing instead to name her Miri after the flower that conquered rock and climbed to face the sun.*
>
> *–Princess Academy* by Shannon Hale, pg. 13

For me, the word *fantasy* evokes ancient, pristine, or future worlds in peril, fantastic creatures—from ugly to breathtakingly beautiful, enthralling quests, and enchanting peoples that sweep me far away to a welcome hour after work. There I set off on an adventure to learn of sacrifice, deeds of kindness great and small, to overcome in battle, and then return inspired to love the good things in our world a little more.

Books are mountains of promise, beckoning forests of adventure, heights of joy, palaces with rooms of endless imagining, and always the mountain's roots extend into the sea, plunging below the surface into meaning. What treasures yet lie undiscovered!

I often travel among my mountains of refuge, gazing over the ocean of fantasy, anticipating diving for a new treasure I will never forget. On some forays beneath the waves I find a flawed gem and must dive repeatedly to gain a worthy jewel, but a true gem never disappoints. Then I take my treasure, sail to shore, and move up the mountain, where ruby and pearl and jet, crystal and gold, glisten under the sun, each fitting into a place in the walls of my imagination in a palace yet unfinished, smelling of the fresh adventure of the sea of fantasy.

So, now we have journaled in our book of knowledge several meanings of *mountain,* among many. A mountain as an obstacle, a danger, or a refuge, has many shades of implication and purpose. One of the beauties of fantasy is that the meaning of the mountain in many stories may even be metaphorical and vary as much as the fantasy the mountains inhabit. The fantastic realm is a great place to find simile, metaphor, and plain down-to-earth meaning. For we all recognize mountains, and enjoy climbing them as well as traversing the ocean of fantasy.

But many other extravagant spaces involved in the conflict between familiar and unfamiliar, the *real* in fantasy, awaits us.

Dive 1.2

Animal-speakers on the Plains Within a Ring of Death

Plains of fragrant grass, whispering under the wandering wind, as far as the eye can see. The occasional piping bird around the track before our feet, the rustle of breath in our ears, the thud of our hearts—and the sudden rise of an enemy from the grass, his spear drawn back to throw.

And the magnetism of the plains is clear. The great open spaces are featured as obstacles, as places of meditation and peace, as fields of battle, and as ground for crops and villages to grow on. Epic fantasy uses plains to great effect, such as Tolkien's home of the horselords in *The Lord of the Rings*, Dennis McKiernan's Hel's Crucible duology, and John Flanagan's *Plains of Gorlan* in Ranger's Apprentice, where the monstrous Kalkerra hunt in the ruins. In nearly every realm, plains are a vital part of kingdoms and communities.

Talking animals on those plains add enticing spice to adventure. Have you ever wondered what it would be like to be a horse whisperer? To speak to an owl?

In *Kayndo—Ring of Death* by Terri Luckey, we learn of Wolf Mountain Pack history, in which the man who became the Kayndo could speak to every animal and bird, though most tribes after the great war that destroyed technology and drove civilization back to rudimentary shelters could only speak with one kind of animal—that is, if one were lucky enough to be chosen by that animal. For animals saw human hearts, heard human thoughts, and judged a human worthy—or not.

Dayvee faces his first choosing. He desperately wants to become a full member of the Calupi tribe of Wolf Mountain Pack. If only his father could see he is not afraid, not a failure. But then Dayvee is chosen to bond with a wolf who is training to serve the prince of a kingdom that does not esteem animal companions, and Dayvee's adventure begins. Becoming who he was born to be will lead him across continents and plains, through love and loss, and will either kill him or prove his heart. For if Terra is to survive, it needs a Kayndo at any cost.

The owl seemed much larger than normal as it flew to the next tree and landed. Those big yellow-orange eyes sparkled with intelligence as it returned Dayvee's gaze—not fearful, but curious.

"That's a companion," Elayni said.

"Yes." Dayvee scanned the area. "If we can find its chosen, maybe we can ask if the owl's glimpsed any herds."

"Good idea. They say owls see and hear for huge distances, but I don't see anyone."

"Me either." Dayvee sighed.

I saw a buffalo herd last night, *a voice sounded in Dayvee's mind.*

That wasn't Jaycee. Was he going crazy? Or could it be? Dayvee twisted around to Jaycee—the wolf studied the owl. Jaycee, did you hear that?

Jaycee cocked his head. Yes, it's the owl speaking.

I'm not bonded yet. *The owl's thought rippled through Dayvee's consciousness.*

–Kayndo: Ring of Death by Terri Luckey, pg. 198

What bond might an owl believe you worthy of? And what good inside you might it strengthen? If animals could speak in our world, what a boon that would be. How many forests would they lead us into, I wonder? To show us a nest, a den, a gathering of intrigue?

Dive 1.3

Fantastic *Summers at Castle Auburn* in a Mysterious Forest

Spiritual growth in fantasy is uncertain. A deadly fairy forest across a river, populated by enigmatic fey beings that men hunt as slaves, is a different take on a fairy tale than we've run across before.

The prince who will become king is also a type of villain not often seen, demonstrating the uncertainty of growth. As does the heroine, Coriel, or Corie, a young healer's apprentice with blinders on. Will she cast them off in time to save the aliora, the kingdom, and herself from destruction?

The summer I was fourteen, my uncle Jaxon took me with him on an expedition to hunt for aliora. I had only seen the fey, delicate creatures in captivity, and then only when I was visiting Castle Auburn. I was as excited about the trip to the Faelyn River as I had been about anything in my life.

I had been surly at first when Greta insisted that I could not go alone with my uncle such a far distance from the castle. "People will say things," she pronounced in her hateful voice. "A young girl and an older man gone off together for three nights or more. It will cause talk."

"He's my uncle," I pointed out, but Greta was not appeased. She did not like me, and I assumed her ambition was more to thwart my glorious adventure than to protect my reputation.

However, when I learned who my traveling companions were to be, I stopped complaining and began dreaming. Bryan of Auburn was everything a young prince should be: handsome, fiery, reckless, and barely sixteen. Not destined to take the crown for another four years, he still had the charisma, panache, and arrogance of royalty, and not a girl within a hundred miles of the castle did not love him with all her heart. I did, even though I knew he was not for me. He was betrothed to my sister, Elisandra, whom he would wed the year he turned twenty.

But I would be with him for three whole days, and say clever things, and laugh fetchingly. I expected this trip to be the grandest memory of my life.

The others who were assigned to us I accepted with passable grace, though only one had come my way often. Kent Ouvrelet was Bryan's cousin, a thin, serious young man whom I had known since I first began visiting the castle eight years ago. Damien, a peasant's son, was Bryan's food taster, and never more than three feet from the prince. However, I could hardly say I knew him since he almost never spoke. The last member of our party was a young guardsman, tall, sandy-haired, lanky, and freckle-faced. He was new to the castle since my last summer there, and I did not even know his name until we set out.

–*Summers at Castle Auburn* by Sharon Shinn*, pg. 3

This is a story about discernment, growing up, and complex people, all bundled into grand adventure. In other words, it illuminates the truth of our motives, the consequences of right and wrong, and subsequent growth.

This tale pulls at our heartstrings. And the fey forest is as much a character as Coriel. A mysterious place, dark and shadowy, it holds the scent of growing, green things, always concealing a possible glimpse of an aliora.

What girl has never wanted to see a fairy, never hoped such beings of grace and beauty are real? We're not talking about dark-hearted fairies, sprites, forest spirits and the like, though those exist in some tales.

Forests can shape the fey as much as the fey shape forests, in our imaginations. Fantasy and fairies touch each other, and the forest in its many guises of spring, fall, and winter also impacts our world, our reality. A forest is always growing, as we are, toward darkness or light.

In *Falcon Heart,* the autumn woods around Kyrin's stronghold in Britannia call to her spirit. Their sense of mystery pulls at her from beyond the walls, signaling the beginning of her adventure from slavery to freedom, and a search for the truth of her heart on a quest that spans sand and sea, from Oman to the King's court.

Her mother's grey gaze sharpened. "It is a godfather's duty. Why are you wary of him? He is a good man."

Yes, but it had been thirteen summers since he heard her first cry, and to be first-daughter of Cierheld and of age was to be caged. She did not need another cage and keeper.

She had no sisters—and no brothers. No brothers was worse. A brother would take the mantle of inheritance and release her to the woods and the wild wings of the falcons. It was not likely she would hunt again after she had hand-fasted. Truly hunt, that is— astride Aart—unless she found a lord she could meld to her will.
...

Father was not here to tickle her mother's ear with a kiss and a low laugh on the morrow—to seal her freedom for a day in the woods, thick now with yellow-clad willow and birch and green pines. He could not tell Mother she would be safe outside Lord Fenwer's stronghold despite the sea-mist and the cliffs, flying her hunters of the air. The sea-thunder boded ill. The moaning wind around the tower would batter any hawk or falcon to a bolt of wet feathers hurtling to ruin under the trees.

"What do you think, Kyrin?"

Kyrin started and turned, with a swift smile.

Her mother's tunic, the rich ochre of autumn, flowed to the tips of her doeskin shoes. The saffron sleeves of her over-tunic brushed her girdle, and from the braided linen swung the key of Cierheld. A beautiful, handspan-long, angular piece of iron.

Kyrin stared at it grimly. Before many more sunrises she would hand her own key to a lord. And she had not yet found him.

–*Falcon Heart* by Azalea Dabill, pgs. 2 and 11

Forests in fantasy shape our experience of color and scent and other aspects of quests of the heart to a large degree. They bring home the truth of a kingdom delightfully outside us, made with insightful attention to the most delicate flower, the tallest tree, the greenest of moss, the clear, chuckling stream, and the raging river. In other lands, those waters often run with clear truth and the force of desire. Even the desires of a thief, who is more than he seems.

Dive 1.4

Can a Thief of Wit Steal Peace for a Kingdom?

Waterways in fantasy often conceal strong beauties of faith and truth beneath the surface. So if someone wanted a thief to steal something, why would they take him straight from prison to a river? But that is exactly what one ambassador did with a mysterious prisoner.

The panic grew stronger. At the first locked door I spilled my tools out of their leather wrapper. The false keys, the awl, the tumbler jams—everything scattered on the stone floor, and I had to kneel down to gather them up. My hands shook. I nearly dropped everything again before I worked the lock open and stepped through the door into a puddle that hadn't been left by the receding river. It was the first sign of the Aracthus's return.

Panting with haste, I rushed to the next door and forgot my lamp behind me. I went back for the lamp, then turned again to the exit. It had swung closed sometime during the night, pushing my shoe ahead of it. Water poured through the grill in its bottom, washing toward me. Frantically I worked the lock. As it released, the door leapt open—I narrowly avoided being hit in the face— and the water behind it surged in, pushing me backward.

I swung my arms for balance, dropped the pry bar, and let it go. I waded upstream to the barred stone door between me and the antechamber to the maze where the water came in through the ceiling. Waves sloshed in the tiny room.

I lifted the locking bar on the door and opened it, then edged my way along the wall of the antechamber and down the stairs. The water was still only five or six inches deep, but it had backed up against the door at the bottom where its path was restricted to the narrow slits in the door. With the strength that comes from terror I pulled the door open, against the force of the water; then the water and I both rushed out over the threshold. The door slammed behind me with force enough to break bones.

–*The Thief* by Megan Whalen Turner*, pg. 166

Water is strong, strong with secrets. But are those secrets stronger than the desire in Eugenides' heart for his kingdom's peace? Rivers are dangerous things, as I remember from my childhood experiences with a creek in flood and a more recent rafting trip.

Rivers can be beautiful, and often offer the quickest route to a destination for our heroes and heroines, even as they are an endless source of mishap. But more than a peaceful place to cool off on a hot day, rivers and waterways can hide unexpected truth and reveal unseen treasure.

A long shape glinted in the water under ripple and shadow. Kyrin tucked her hair behind her ear with a wet hand and reached down. It was thin, with two equal sides. She lifted it out, scrubbing it with a handful of sand. She wiped the blade dry on her chemise, then held it high in both hands. Its long, clean length reminded her of Hyl and his wolfship. And his ravens, gathering about death and darkness. Like a swirling cloud of the birds, men gathered against Cierheld. Samson was gone, her father like to follow.

Staring at the bright edge, somehow the gathering dark did not seem so black. Samson kept his heart to the end. Fierce cry in the sky, wild and high . . .

"Kyrin, what are you doing?"

Kyrin spun, and fell with a splash. Spluttering, the blade in her hand, she rose. Esther stood looking over the bank with Talik beside her, her arm in his. He loosed Esther and leaped lightly

down the bank, a falconry glove on his right arm. "We were look-
ing for Samson. Cernalt said he should have been back last even.
But you found a sword—in the stream?"

"Yes. Catch." Kyrin tossed it to him and he caught it expertly
with his gloved hand.

–*Falcon Flight* by Azalea Dabill, pg. 362

Waterways wend through almost every fantasy, historical and futuristic, then and now. They hold as much life and possibility and
challenge as an ocean in the realm of story. And oceans can hold untold
depths of feeling.

Dive 1.5

The Floating Islands Inspire an Ocean of Imagination and Magic

Oceans in fantasy captivate us, from the ships that sail them, to the men and women who rise to the challenge of the waves, to the isles of mystery that the waves nurture and surround. Oceans can also mirror our feelings, even to grief.

> *Trei was fourteen the first time he saw the Floating Islands. He had made the whole long voyage south from Rounn in a haze of loss and misery, not really noticing the harbors in which the ship sometimes anchored or the sea between. But here, where both sea and sky lay pearl-gray in the dawn, the wonder of the Floating Islands broke at last into that haze.*
>
> *A boy high in the rigging called out in a shrill voice, pointing, and then the deeper voice of an officer rang out and the ship smoothly adjusted it heading. Before them the Islands rose shimmering out of the dawn mist. They stood high above the sea—too high, even in that first mist-shrouded glimpse. Then the early sun, rising, turned the air to gold and the sea to sapphire and picked the Islands out of the mist like jewels. In that light, they seemed too beautiful to hold terror or despair or anguish. Trei could hardly bear to look at them, yet could not bring himself to look away. He gripped the railing hard and bit his lip almost till it bled.*
>
> *–The Floating Islands* by Rachel Neumeier*, pg. 1

Oceans are almost inescapable in fantasy. Fantasies that don't mention them are fewer than we can count on one hand. Oceans, the last frontier of creatures and continents unknown, fire our minds and souls and ignite epic, world-spanning quests in many hearts. They are the wings beneath many an adventure.

Umar yanked, and Kyrin stumbled to her feet again. She felt her tower rising behind, empty. The yard, hours ago holding children, servants, and contented hounds, was wind-swept, dark and slick with puddles. Umar forced her through the yard gate, the oak bars yet whole, and over the endless killing ground to the forlorn, flapping side gate. Without the great out-wall, the sea growled. Kyrin looked back, wind thrumming in her ears.

Against the grey clouds tipped with dawn her godfather's stronghold crouched like a powerful beast, fallen, its heart ripped from it. Umar cuffed her again; her head rang. At the cliffs' edge she faltered.

Pink from the east blanketed the fog spreading away at her feet. A thin path went down into the mist, toward the thundering ocean. Muddy and scratched from falls, she at last reached the bottom. She scrambled down to gravel and the sea that swirled inside a protecting curve of rock. A gaggle of boats rocked and spun on the foam-flecked swells. Round marsh-boats.

Umar tossed her inside the nearest and stepped over her to the woven withe bench. Seawater slapped over the side and soaked Kyrin, cold and bitter on her lips. There was nowhere to run—water left no tracks for Father.

She levered herself up on her bound hands, panting. She could not swim. Her wool cloak pulled on her aching throat, and she wriggled her shoulders until it eased.

Mist fenced her in on a spinning island of skin and wood. It beaded on Umar's black hair. She stared at his back while he paddled. By his breadth of shoulder and cast of face he had at least twice her summers.

A wave welled toward them, and the skin boat rushed up it and fell, to swoop up another mountain and smack down at the bottom with a jolt. Kyrin rolled, and shoved her feet wide, wedging her toes against the boat's curving sides. Thin hide rippled under her shoulders, the cold water outside squeezing her against Umar's bench. She gulped.

Umar paddled harder. The boat spun, and her stomach with it. Kyrin closed her eyes, swallowing. A solid thump against the boat and raucous hails roused her from stupor.

She squinted through gouts of spray at the wall of a ship, and up, and up. Grinning brown-skinned men, many beardless, peered down at her through patches of mist from a deck above. A fat man with a silver hoop dragging at his ear bawled an order. Men tossed ropes to Umar.

He knotted a thick rope around her middle, and his gesture sent her sliding up the slimy side of the ship. Batted by the waves, she swung and bumped to the top, her middle sawn near in two by the prickly rope. They dumped her on the deck.

Kyrin lifted her head. The last breaths of the storm chilled her. Her bound hands were stiff, her skinned elbows and stomach burned. She rolled over and laid her cheek on the wet wood. The mist wisped away. Dawn spangled the deck with red and silver drops, as with blood and water.

–*Falcon Heart* by Azalea Dabill, pg. 29

Beautiful and perilous, fantasy oceans mirror our moods as often as those of wind and sky. The waves bear on their crests pirates, traders, travelers, and exiles, and are home to a multitude of awe-inspiring underwater creatures. Oceans are stirred by whatever touches them, and so they can reflect many a truth. They are the lifeblood of trade to ports and cities, rife with the ugly and vile, the treachery and intrigue of men.

Why Cities of Intrigue are Deadly in the River of Time

Fantasy conflict is often between the vile and noble, leading to cities of intrigue and mystery.

Cities. I've never liked them. You may. Crowded they are, with danger at every turn, dangers we often cannot see until they are upon us.

He whipped out his hand so fast I didn't even realize it was his hand until I felt it pressing cruelly into the sides of my throat. I heard the slide of Luca's sword, as well as the massive knight's, but my eyes remained locked on Lord Vannucci's. "You think me a fool," he ground out. "You are lying."

Lia cried out as he turned me around and rushed me to the stone wall, knocking me against it. I could see Luca doing his best to battle the massive Paratore knight, but he was not faring very well.

"What deception is going on here? Tell me now, and you may just survive this night."

He released the pressure on my throat a little, and I hunched over, gasping for breath. I eased one hand under my cape, as if holding my chest, still trying to recover, but as I did so, I unsheathed my knife and then sprang away, raising the dagger between us.

"You little deceiver," he snarled, advancing upon me as if he wasn't scared at all.

"You are the deceiver, pretending friendship, alliance with the Sienese, supping with them, and then betraying them to the Florentines." I pulled my sword from the back sheath, even as I dodged a swipe from the Paratore knight, who was aiming for Luca.

–Waterfall by Lisa T. Bergren, pg. 279

Whenever power is up for grabs, especially the power to rule a city, predators circle a war-ground. When individual power is held by the right of succession or strength, the struggle is constant. Someone with a vile heart would bring the existing authority down and rule many hearts in its stead—though never his own; the noble spirit would defend many hearts inviolate, while ruling his own passion. A high house in Oman is one such nest of intrigue.

Framed by the arch of the Blue Flower room, Sirius turned his head. "It is done. Let nothing be heard in the men's quarters." He spun on his heel. "Bring her."

The weasel guard nudged Kyrin between the shoulders with his blade, amusement tugging one side of his mouth. Wordless, Kyrin followed the wazir's straight back.

Sirius ignored possible ambush in the passage and strode toward the guest room. He would not be so cheerful if he knew Jachin was about, as Jachin must be, and Umar. Kyrin's heart sank. Or did Sirius know that Jachin was dead, and did Nara and the rest lie still somewhere in the rooms they passed? It was so quiet.

Sirius had ordered no noise to be heard from the men's quarters. He might have lied to Tae, killed everyone . . .

The wazir stopped, and the guard's weapon forced her through the guest door ahead of Sirius. Her foot caught on the hem of her thawb, and she stumbled inside; the door creaked shut behind her and latched with a click. Sirius stood in front of it.

Kyrin pivoted to conceal her right side. A stool and a small table sat beneath a window that looked over Ali's fields. A brazier flanked the table. Opposite the window, near the door, a crisp kaffiyeh hung from a peg. Under the peg a long pallet held baggage, bound with cord. He was leaving, soon.

Kyrin dragged in a harsh breath. There was no time for quiet removal. Buried in her sash her small blade lay hard against her side. Sirius had been a warrior all his life. Likely he cut his teeth on a dagger. She would use the dagger and the stool, then if those failed—the baggage and the brazier—but first she must find out where he held Tae and Alaina.

–*Falcon Flight* by Azalea Dabill, pgs. 39, 41

Anywhere people gather, in a city or in a house, intrigue and mystery are the binding glue of a fantasy. A tale skillfully penned holds a reader in thrall, as many fantasies have enjoyably held me, not least Patrick Carr's *The Shock of Night,* where a sleepwalker searches for the truth of murder done among children. As cities spawn the power of intrigue, one man seeks justice, a scent from another world.

Dive 1.7

Why Spice Historical Fantasy with Mayhem, Murder, and War?

Murder, war, and mayhem. Such do spice fantasy, across many genres. Some may argue such depictions are not necessary. But they are, at least to tell the kind of story that spans the human soul, because the desires we fan to flame in our spirits, holy and unholy, are truths of our human existence. This does not mean we must rub our minds in dirt.

It means we must deal honestly with every reality we face within and without, or twist ourselves into untruth. Fantasy brings out what we believe about justice and mercy. In *The Shock of Night*, Lord Dura pursued the truth of murder wherever it led.

> *I tried to face the speaker. "I'm the king's reeve, and what I do is up to him." I ran my tongue over my front teeth and spat on the floor. "Your potion tastes like manure." Two people on my left made sounds of distaste at my coarseness, and I made a note. At least some of those who held me were highborn.*
>
> *"Someone is killing children in the poor quarter." I tried to give the appearance of seeing through the hood and traced an arc, looking left to right. I forced disdain into my voice, past the fear that made my mouth dry. "Unless you've got information that will help me . . ."*
>
> *I stopped and took a breath as I shook my head. I was about to get really insulting. "No, I don't suppose the deaths of pickpockets and whores or children matter much to the four orders.*

Funny. When the Chief of Servants was talking at me, not once did she show concern for Robin's death, only Elwin's. I don't think I care much for you people. So get to the point and let me get back to my work."

Silence. I'd hoped for yelling and screaming to verify my thrust in the dark, but I heard nothing. Then I heard a sharp intake of breath.

"You dare to accuse us?"

–The Shock of Night by Patrick Carr, pg. 85

Two people may honestly come at the same truth from opposing sides, but in the end, only one side is right, if both truly oppose each other. *Oppose* has to do with opposites, and opposites can never mean the same thing. But an opponent can change, can align with the truth. In this way, honorable opponents can show themselves worthy. For following truth brings respect—at least, it does in the eyes of him whose verdict matters.

Every desire, for truth or not, begins in the heart, and mayhem and war may trace their seeds to the smallest things.

Lord Jorn's gate guard admitted Hal without demur when he gruffly stated he was Hal Loring. Celine followed at his heels, through a wood and iron gate wide enough for two horses. Behind him, the gate and the stronghold's wall rose from the steep hill-shoulder. Nothing grew between him and the rampart but short grass. They crossed the yard toward the hall. Before the porch and along the path to the step lay a bed of flowers, sere with winter dress.

Jornhold had been built on a right angle, the double-story wings joined at the center. The angle of the courtyard running between the north and south wings made a quarter of a pasty pie, divided again by another low wall into eighths, one of which was a garden. Hal grunted.

Only the inner-facing walls, between the house wings, had ground-floor windows. Archers in the south wing could decimate anyone attempting to reach the iron-hinged, thick door of the north wing, and the same in reverse, supposing by some miracle an enemy made it across the bare expanse of the killing ground, over the wall, and across the yard.

The farthest walled court held a bench for visitors, while the closer garden was bare rock and weeds. Hal shook his head. Poor Myrna. He could not help being glad for her sake that Kyrin had beaten him, though he would never hear the end of Jorn's champion—not until he learned Lady Kyrin's skill, defeated her, and stilled Thorgil's tongue—at least while he was in earshot. Hal grinned. Her skills would earn him coin with those who could hire him.

If only his foster daughter was more willing. Celine had wanted to learn how to use a staff since she came to his Breanna for help two years agone, but she emphatically hadn't desired to learn from Jorn's champion. Here was a better teacher, and she dragged her feet. "Celine! Follow on, girl; follow on. She's a warrior, but she does'na bite, and you'll learn a thing or two."

—Falcon Flight by Azalea Dabill, pg. 213

Warring hearts find a home, or at least a den, in the castles and strongholds that dot the pages of fantasy. Warriors are also made and destroyed atop walls, fighting across every manner of castle ground and in many a hall, while lives ride on the quality of the defenses. Enemy strongholds bring adventure and caution.

"With these, any warrior can climb wood and stone, provided a wall has the smallest crack."

Kyrin hummed to herself and handed Talik another thong, weaving her own through the claw's oblong frame to hold it to her foot. There. The ones for her feet were done, now for the hands.

The first thong on the claw tied about the wrist or ankle, a second slipped over the hand or toe of a boot, while the thongs woven as a web over the frame limited noise.

Talik fingered the finished claws. "The leather will be stronger and quieter than cloth."

"Unless it gets wet—then it may slip. I'll roughen the layers."

"We'll pray there's no rain. Noise is a bigger thing, since I have not your training. I would certainly give us away, on stone or wood." He grinned. "It has a chance of working," he said more thoughtfully, turning a claw over in his long-fingered brown hands.

"They will." Kyrin tested hers to the size of her feet. She could walk without pain this even. They left prints as of a strange beast.

"All plans are risky," Talik said soberly.

–Falcon Flight by Azalea Dabill, pg. 252

In the dark, Kyrin followed Talik across the meadow and a wide, dry moat, careful of her ankle and shoulder, though only soreness was left. Midway between the gates, they climbed the wall. No one would expect to see them there, facing their enemy head-on. Trembling with tension, Kyrin's claws scratched lightly on rock. They reached the top.

She and Talik slipped across the walkway as a guard's steps echoed around a corner. They slid over the inside edge of the wall and hung silently by their arms, hoping the guard missed the iron tips of their claws clinging to the stone at his feet. The guard passed, humming quietly. They crawled to the ground. Kyrin's tunic, damp all over again, clung to her. She worked her shoulder, relieved it had held up, and put on her shoes she'd carried tied around her neck.

They trotted in the shadows from one building to another, toward the north gate. Four guards stood duty around Lord Keffer's prisoners, seventy-five paces from the gate and the tower that extended above. The square tower above the gate had windows for eyes. For strength, wide buttresses straddled the wall on either side.

Torches flanked the north entrance in wrought sconces, while another flickered near the guards in the yard, near burnt out. The light moved across bodies curled together on the frosted ground under a tattered blanket, with two more in another heap a length away. Ropes led from them to four tall posts, above their reach. The guards leaned quiet against the posts.

Talik touched Kyrin's arm and turned into the shadows.

–Falcon Flight by Azalea Dabill, pg. 254

In halls and holds, in war and peace, right and wrong rest on our choices and our response to the choices of others. What we believe moves our blood, breath, and bone. Do we leave the oppressed to fight alone, or do we seize courage and take the fight to the very den of evil, even underground?

Dive 1.8

Amazing Fantasy Caves in *The Princess and the Goblin*

Fantasy casts experience back at us in sharper facets than in our own world.

Some may ask how that is possible. It is possible, even certain, because good fantasy gives us a safe place and time to explore motives, aspirations, consequences bad and good, and the crannies of our own hearts' desires. George MacDonald's books have been around a while, but they are in danger of being forgotten by the generation flying up behind. I loved *The Princess and the Goblin* as a kid, and read it aloud to my brothers and sisters. Recently, I read it again. I found myself in tears several times, sometimes laughing, always led to a deeper belief in things that matter.

Coming to greater faith in things we cannot see leads to deeper courage to face the unknown, to a renewed determination to persevere, and to an aching feeling in the midst of it that we are catching a glimpse, an elusive scent, of somewhere beyond this world.

That is what George MacDonald gives us in his tales of danger, unbelief, derring-do, and simple but profound faith in the power and goodness of God. Someday I will be able to tell him what hope he birthed in me, what stars in a dark place his books have been. His *Phantastes* is a higher level yet, a clean, spiritual adventure for adults. And though we read Curdie's adventure in relative safety, Curdie was in danger of many things.

> *He was at the entrance of a magnificent cavern, of an oval shape, once probably a huge natural reservoir of water, now the great palace hall of the goblins. It rose to a tremendous height, but the roof was composed of such shining materials, and the multitude of torches carried by the goblins who crowded the floor lighted up the place so brilliantly, that Curdie could see to the top quite well. But he had no idea how immense the place was until his eyes had got accustomed to it, which was not for a good many minutes. The rough projections on the walls, and the shadows thrown upwards from them by the torches, made the sides of the chamber look as if they were crowded with statues upon brackets and pedestals, reaching in irregular tiers from floor to roof. The walls themselves were, in many parts, of gloriously shining substances, some of them gorgeously coloured besides, which powerfully contrasted with the shadows.*

–*The Princess and the Goblin* by George MacDonald, pg. 63

Of course, there are many more adventurous parts in the story: wondrous caves of jewels, vengeful goblins, snooty housekeepers, and Curdie, who risks his all for his people, his king, and his princess. But this setting forecasts Curdie's quest, of a deeper, wilder, truer sort than we find in many books. Sniff out Curdie's adventures in *The Princess and the Goblin,* and, of course, the rest of the story in the sequel, *The Princess and Curdie.*

In our next trove we find a cave the likes of which we have probably never seen—even in the wildest imaginative books. *Exile* highlights the conflict between evil and ascendant good, even when good starts out buried alive.

Buried Alive With Drizzt Do'Urden

"Buried alive" has a ring to it, does it not? The savor of long, desperate days of slow death. But this tale is anything but slow. Often in fantasy, weapons are more than physical, and wielding them affects the soul as well as the body. Never say all fantasy action is shallow. This trilogy ends in triumph, where weapons are wielded well.

With some experience in martial arts, we love fantasy fight scenes if they're competent. If the author has never done martial arts themselves, that lack of experience usually becomes apparent. But however much R. A. Salvatore personally knows of martial arts, Drizzt is convincingly and utterly delightful. Salvatore's not-so-dark character's sword work is unmatched, in our opinion. Don't start reading *Homeland* unless you're prepared to be hooked.

I've read this trilogy four or five times. The growth in Drizzt as he battles evil in himself, across the underground world of his people, and at last in the sun-brightened air, is phenomenal. The Dark Elf trilogy goes far beyond a more-or-less shallow action story. The inherent meaning is layered into unavoidable moral conflict between Drizzt, who reveres life and light, but is born into an entire society living in a dark city, and most of his kin, who gleefully sacrifice goodness. When a situation, a person, or an authority will force us to go against what we know is right and true, then we must flee. Some realities must be fled, even in fantasy, as Drizzt is forced to do—or watch himself become a monster worse than the direst life in the deepest cavern.

The Monster lumbered along the quiet corridors of the Under-dark, its eight scaly legs occasionally scuffing the stone. It did not recoil at its own echoing sounds, fearing the revealing noise, nor did it scurry for cover, expecting the rush of another predator. For even in the dangers of the Underdark, this creature knew only security, confident of its ability to defeat any foe. Its breath reeked of deadly poison, the hard edges of its claws dug deep gouges into solid stone, and the rows of spearlike teeth that lined its wicked maw could tear through the thickest of hides. But worst of all was the monster's gaze, the gaze of a basilisk, which could transmutate into solid stone any living thing it fell upon.

The creature, huge and terrible, was among the greatest of its kind. It did not know fear.

The hunter watched the basilisk pass . . .

–Exile by R. A. Salvatore*, 1

Drizzt, driven by conscience from his own kind, is going mad, becoming a creature of instinct, of kill or be killed, with no higher thought. He knows it, and runs again, into the hands of the gnomes, enemies of his people, thinking his own death better than mindless killing. The gnomes recognize his honor, besides what he means to them. The right use of blade and heart creates great heights of character.

But what happens when enemies catch a benevolent dragon between them in space, leaving him nowhere to run?

Dive 1.10

Who Could Say No to a Clean Space Adventure?

Is space even a place in fantasy? We think it is. At least for all who are adventurously young at heart, in years or in the way they look at the worlds. Think of this young thought: evil identified is set up for destruction.

Jack Morgan, a 14-year-old thief with a trained gift for safe-cracking, meets a symbiotic dragon who morphs from 2-D to 3-D form—on Jack's back. Jack is an unwilling host, but finds the dragon growing on him. Almost literally. Taken for a tattoo by most, the dragon named Draco leads Jack to far more than a plan to save his symbiotic race in Timothy Zahn's Dragonback series.

Doing the right thing and being brave in spite of oneself, and in space—what's not to like? Draco tells Jack there is always a way to live with honor, and to die with the same, if necessary. But Jack's Uncle Virge, a cynical virtual personality left in the ship's drive when Jack's real uncle died, won't look out for anyone but number one—not without a fight.

Torn between his admiration for Draco's unearthly fighting prowess—a gift curtailed by the hours the dragon must spend on Jack's back—and Draco's generous ideals, Jack knows Uncle Virge wants the last word. But will any of them have the last word, with the Valahgua out to destroy all who bar their way to a star system?

The Dragonback series has immense heart. Timothy Zahn has a gift for slipping the reader inside Jack's shoes. Jack, who seeks to keep his word to Draco to help save the dragon's people from the Valahgua, who wiped out Draco's home world. The Valahgua have allied with mercenary humans and will blow the last of Draco's ships out of space if he and Jack cannot discover the traitors and beat their enemies at their own high-stakes game.

Grib made a sniffing sound. "One of those," he muttered to his brother.

Greb nodded. "See you tomorrow, Jack," he said, taking Grib's arm. Circling the table, they headed to a pair of empty cots that had been pushed together and lay down on them.

Jack frowned toward Maerlynn. "One of those what?"

She shrugged, looking uncomfortable. "They were born here," she said. "Slavery is the only life they've ever known."

"So was I," Noy spoke up.

"That's different," Maerlynn said. "Your folks never accepted this life the way Greb and Grib and their parents did. Yours never gave up hoping for freedom."

"Are they still here?" Jack asked, glancing over his shoulder at the other slaves.

"No," Maerlynn said gently. "They're . . . "

"They're dead," Noy said, an odd note of defiance in his voice. "My dad was beaten to death after he tried to escape. After that, my mom got a fever and she died, too."

Jack grimaced. "I'm sorry," he said, wishing he'd kept his mouth shut. "I didn't know." . . .

–Dragon and Slave by Timothy Zahn, pg. 52

Evil sets itself against a thief who does not want to be a thief, vowing to kill Jack if he does not steal again. This series packs a fist-wallop of life lessons in a hair-raising adventure where Jack explores good without compromise.

Taste forgiveness, and the shades of our own hearts, and shiver. It's a rousing good space adventure if we don't mind mixing star-bred sci-fi with a bit of fantasy. After all, our definition of fantasy stretches among the stars.

Dive 1.11

Firebird and Space Adventure Makes for Star Entertainment

We often fall short in shining moments, despite good intent. And then learn to shine indeed.

For example, take Ziva, who seeks redemption in spite of herself. Drawn to Aroska, though he hates her for the mistaken assassination of his brother, Ziva must work with him to outwit a hidden force determined to take down civilization across more worlds than one. A mystery, a difficult love, with goodness shining through . . . what more could we desire in a space fantasy with EJ Fisch's heroine?

The growth of relationship—if Aroska lives to take that chance.

> *The look on Ziva's face had expressed genuine shock and pain, but she recovered quickly. She caught his arm, digging her thumb into the pressure point above his elbow, then spun him around, pinning him against the glass in return. "You have no idea who you're dealing with." She hesitated a moment. "You know, I honestly thought you knew what you were doing, but this? This could get you killed."*

–*Dakiti* by EJ Fisch, pg. 70

Acknowledging the truth of our failure and changing leads to great things.

And then there's *Firebird*. A discarded third princess wants so badly to shine in her people's eyes. Despite the worst betrayal, Firebird experiences the human journey into rapture with our divine Maker, drawn to her destiny by romance and a heart-expanding love.

> *... a sudden music so incomprehensibly magnificent that the universe exploded into existence, every particle and energy wave singing praise at all frequencies, an exultant harmony that condensed into billions upon billions of brilliant stars and their attendant worlds. He was the ultimate otherness, the omniscience beyond . . . If the Eternal Singer existed, who was Phoena to frighten her?*

–*Firebird* by Kathy Tyers, pg. 266

Firebird—Mari, for short—radiates joy when she is fully persuaded how deeply she is loved. To be loved by the Creator, and to accept it, is to be eternally safe in all the ways that matter. Then Firebird begins to rise indeed, when she leaves her reputation to pursue the safety and good of her world.

If you enjoy space adventure, empaths, royal intrigue and romance, this story is for you. In the fantasy realms, those set among the stars hold a sense of awe, of new beginnings and new peoples. Maybe when we gain heaven, that farthest world, we will become able to explore the stars in a whole new way.

For now, dreaming of them and working towards everything they represent is a worthy engagement of our faculties. *Firebird* and the rest of the trilogy are not strictly fantasy, but they're too good to leave out of the reading realm on our farthest frontier, where they take space by storm, and rise to shining moments.

But in every fantasy jewel we have dreamed of, what of the heroes and heroines in them? Our horizons expand in *Fantasy Avatars—are Strong Heroines and Intelligent Heroes Enough?*

Chapter 2.0

Fantasy Avatars—Are Strong Heroines and Intelligent Heroes Enough?

We all need heroes and heroines. But are strong heroines and intelligent heroes enough to overcome the obstacles they face? Are they enough together? It's in our internal makeup to learn from others' greatness.

No, you say? Tell me you have never admired anyone—then we may part ways. But let us go on together as friends instead, knowing two heads *are* better than one, however heroic or powerful or wise. But there is even more to greatness.

To live well in the ocean of fantasy let alone in our own world, we require mercy, forgiveness, and love for when we, or the hero or heroine, are *not* so great. There is also the physical conflict, which requires strength of body and mind, whether our hero is in company or alone. Strangely enough, all qualities of strength require the so-called gentler virtues of compassion and forgiveness to achieve their potential, though love, fiercest of the virtues, is the force that drives them all. It covers a multitude of wrongs, in more ways than one.

Let's look at greatness in the ocean of fantasy. Specifically at the facets of greatness that shine in *Shades of Milk and Honey,* The Falcon Chronicle series, Tolkien's *Lord of the Rings (LOTR), Rose Daughter* and The Deed of Paksenarrion trilogy.

Dive 2.1

Fantasy at Its Best Creates Intelligent Heroes

Fantasy is great indeed, where differences between the sexes are not denigrated but understood, and heroines and heroes complement each other to the advantage of both. Often in our time the reversal of historical roles is played up as a battle of the sexes, showcasing the weaknesses of one character and their sex against that of the hero or heroine.

In our past, the focus of fantasy has been on beautiful or intelligent heroines and strong heroes as types of greatness worthy of emulation. Now we see a swing toward the reverse: strong heroines and intelligent, handsome heroes, though usually not in equal leading parts in one story.

But I've seen a few books that reveal our heroes' and heroines' weaknesses and strengths in a complementary way, which, not surprisingly, becomes complimentary to all concerned, if you can stand a play on words. But the wisdom to act in a manner that complements or completes others is rather more than play. The ability and will to work together becomes a credit to the characters, a point of honor between them both, and an inspiration to the story and to the reader.

We enjoy our heroes and heroines, handsome and beautiful or not, whether they overcome together or are pitted against their enemy alone. Their spirit, their strengths, and yes, sometimes even their weaknesses, endear them to us—when they show themselves human, yet with a capacity for greatness. Things we all wish for.

We all wish to be brave, to overcome wind and wave and monster—to be a hero to someone, even if only in the ocean of fantasy.

Greatness grows, and this is manifested in various ways in *Shades of Milk and Honey*. From the complementary angle in her Glamourist Histories, a Jane Austen-like magic fantasy series, Mary Robinette Kowal depicts excellently well how men and women complete or round each other, growing through conflicts to find great love.

"Act as though you trust me."

With an almost animal snarl, he released the door and stalked into the other room.

Jane closed her eyes, swaying. She had pushed him too far. Even if every word she uttered had been justified, a wife could not speak so to her husband.

"Actions." Vincent stood again in the doorway. He held his battered writing desk. "Sit with me, and I will explain all."

Now that she had won her point, Jane doubted the wisdom of her course. "What of the Prince Regent's command?"

"I am not married to him." Vincent tried for a smile and succeeded only in curling his lips. "Please, Muse. I have no gift with words."

Jane nodded and followed him into the sitting room, but she took no triumph from her victory, for she could not help but feel that she had used emotion as a weapon. Beneath that unease lay another, deeper fear: that Vincent had been right she would give him away by some change in her countenance, and her husband's life would be forfeit to her pride.

–Shades of Milk and Honey by Mary Robinette Kowal*, pg. 216

(Please remember that some authors have written other books than the ones we recommend. Anytime you see an * asterisk beside an author, know that not all books by that author are morally clean. We also mark titles with an asterisk if they have a very slight scene or word you may wish to skip.)

In *Falcon Heart*, the first book in the Falcon Chronicle series, Kyrin has two friends who challenge her to greatness, despite the fact all three of them are enslaved.

> *Kyrin pulled her hand away. "You are not my servant."*
>
> *"I did not seek to be." Alaina's heart thudded. She dared much, but to not be alone . . .*
>
> *"What do you mean?"*
>
> *"We mean to rise together, to stand, bound to each other's good," Tae broke in.*
>
> *"He has said it—sister." Alaina dared to loose the word to the waiting air.*
>
> *"But you know what I did, my mother fell because I feared—I'm not . . . worthy." Desolation choked Kyrin's voice.*
>
> *"Oh that," Alaina said airily, and held her close. Kyrin cried, drawing a shivering breath in her arms. Had Kyrin never had a sister? Alaina hugged her hard.*
>
> –*Falcon Heart* by Azalea Dabill, pg. 66

Besides the complementary relationships of heroes and heroines and their friends, there is the pure attraction of seeing an antagonist's pride, greed, and desire for world domination fail when they face off against sometimes the smallest person, whose heart is bigger than the frame that holds it, who are determined to fight evil no matter the cost. And that great heart must either die, grow enough to sustain its purpose, or receive unlooked-for help.

Dive 2.2

How do Our Souls Compare to the World of Characters in LOTR?

Love is courageous, and a facet of greatness in itself.

Just as our physical frame must grow to sustain our earthly heart, so in the spiritual realm, the inner heart sustains the soul. And how do these three—body, heart, and soul—reinforce each other? What sustains a heart in the hour of desperate need, at the end of all? When the monster must be faced, and greatness is lost or won?

Tolkien's *Lord of the Rings* has a splendid picture of this outworking of heart.

Frodo is willing to take on the burden laid before him. First for necessity, because there is no one else to bear it to Rivendell. Second, he carries the ring on from there because he would not see every chance of peace and freedom destroyed. Third, he faces the burden's challenge because it tempts him, and he would see it destroy none of his companions. Here are planted seeds of love, compassion, and forgiveness. How they bloom we all know.

Sam is loyal. And what drives his brave loyalty? Love—which goes deeper than a mere brother's—to the deepest friendship. He is also practical and down-to-earth, using whatever weapon comes to his hand, whether a frying pan for an orc's head, a dish of rabbit stew for Frodo's strength, or an encouraging word to lighten a dark hour.

And the elf Glorfindel—I have always admired Glorfindel, and was disappointed he was not in the movie. Here Frodo speaks of him with Gandalf.

"What about Rivendell and the elves? Is Rivendell safe?"

"Yes, at present, until all else is conquered. The elves may fear the Dark Lord, and they may fly before him, but never again will they listen to him or serve him. And here in Rivendell there live still some of his chief foes: the Elven-wise, lords of the Eldar from beyond the furthest seas. They do not fear the Ring-wraiths, for those who have dwelt in the Blessed Realm live at once in both worlds, and against both the Seen and the Unseen they have great power."

"I thought that I saw a white figure that shone and did not grow dim like the others. Was that Glorfindel then?"

"Yes, you saw him for a moment as he is upon the other side: one of the mighty of the First-born. He is an elf-lord of a house of princes. . . ."

–The Fellowship of the Ring by J. R. R. Tolkien, pg. 294

All through the trilogy there are further hints of what sustains a heart—and Frodo's and ours—indirect allusions to the Blessed Realm and to the one who rules all worlds and gives us facets of greatness. These books carry food for the heart and soul, and so also, in a way, support our bodies by showing us better how to live—with honor and courage. These stories pierce far deeper than the screen. I could go on about the *LOTRs* multitude of admirable characters, but let glimpses of these be enough to convince you to taste the heroism, the gritty adventure, and the laughter in these pages for yourself.

Then share Kyrin's joy in the ocean of fantasy in yet another facet of greatness in *Falcon Heart*:

The dolphins were free and beautiful. While they wove through the water the slaves were taken out of themselves, caught up by that power, that beauty. Winfrey smiled, floating on her back, and Tae nodded at something she whispered.

Did they feel the surge of sweetness, the almost-sorrow of long-ing, as if something here would dance in them forever? It stirred in the depths of her, surged into her throat.

The flip of a grey-blue fin, water running from its edge, drops sparkling in a joyful swathe under the beast's leap—somehow it all mingled with the softness in Tae toward every person in pain, with Alaina's mischievous grin that lit her face, with the falcon blade, the edge sharp against evil, fighting for goodness and courage…. Everything all suddenly mattered intensely, though Kyrin could not shape it in words. Purpose was all around her; every moment a part of eternity.

–*Falcon Heart* by Azalea Dabill, pg. 96

Fantasy's ocean widens before is. Besides beauty, compassion, and strength, the sea draws storms of conflict. Clouds of metaphor and emo-tion billow, and the physical stabs like lightning—displayed across the waves in terrifying beauty. Consider how *Rose Daughter, Sheep-farmer's Daughter,* and *Falcon Heart* each demonstrate the emotional, the physical, and the metaphorical aspects of fantasy in the heart's transformation into the loyal gold of great courage.

It takes daring to dive for great riches of illuminating metaphor, de-spite sharp emotion under a dangerous sky. Do we dare to explore these facets of greatness in the stormy dark?

Dive 2.3

Do You Crave Fantasy Combat and the Illumination of the Mundane?

At first glance, fantasy mirrors reality as simple parts of a whole. But layers of conflict expand into a threefold metaphorical, emotional, and physical flower, illuminating the mundane. Reality may not be what it seems.

Robin McKinley's *Rose Daughter* brings together reality in a great picture of metaphor and emotion, where the heroine, Beauty, strives to piece facets of the mundane, her desire, and her struggle together, to make sense of her inner and outer world. Beauty traces a thorny rose's petals, staring into a mirror of reality, joining each facet of meaning to the next.

> *If he had sent her father's illness to beat them into acquiescence, she would hate him for it.*

> *The bitterness of her thoughts weighed her down till she had to stop walking. She looked again at the beech trees and, not waiting for a gap this time, fought her way through to the nearest and leant against it, turning her head so that her cheek was against the bark. The Beast is a Beast, even if he keeps his promises; how could she guess how a Beast thinks, especially one who is so great a sorcerer? It was foolish to talk of hating him—foolish and wasteful. What had happened had happened, like anything else might happen, like a bit of paper giving you a new home*

when you had none finding its way into your hand, like a company of the ugliest, worst-tempered plants you'd ever seen opening their flowers and becoming rose-bushes, the most beautiful, lovable plants you've ever seen. Perhaps it was the Beast's near presence that made her own roses grow. Did she not owe him something for that if that were the case? It was a curious thing, she thought sadly, how one is no longer satisfied with what one was or had if one has discovered something better. She could not now happily live without roses, although she had never seen a rose before three years ago.

–*Rose Daughter* by Robin McKinley*, pg. 96

First we are caught with Beauty in the mundane moment of emotion for her father, then in her desperate desire to break free of the Beast, and later in the story we enter the conflict within her heart, where love and compassion struggle to grow deeper and higher.

The unexpected complexity of these facets of true story becomes more apparent the longer we linger before the mirror of this fantasy, pondering the words written. The pieces of reality, reflections that form strong shapes, regal and true in the glass, reveal the extraordinary hidden in the mundane. And we find our own struggle taking shape, as the beast turns to stare into our eyes.

For every bit of truth, every reflection of reality in the mirror, holds a spark of the extraordinary beyond the mundane—because of the one who made it. Even in a fairy tale, those mundane and not-so-mundane pieces make up the truth of the story. Since they *are* true in themselves, they reflect what is real. They reveal underlying lies that cause unfathomable harm, they show essential truths, solid foundation stones on which to build trust, to grow a garden, a city, a world, a universe, a life. But do we truly see?

What if the mirror, meant to convey truth, is twisted instead, showing a lie necessary to navigate life, that love is never true, and that taking a rose, just a rose, does no harm where none is intended? Then what do we see? The whirling confusion of a dying rose, an embittered mind, a blackening heart, and a shattered shard whose cracks spread through the entire mirror. And worst of all, a monster stretching sinuously in its shadows.

The inner story of that fantasy, skewed by such flawed glass, will never meet the outer world of the living in a way that brings meaningful good. If meaning does break through, it will likely be a creature of distorted horror, emerging into the air a monster indeed.

We all see the same reality in front of our noses. But we gaze into different mirrors, and see different things *in* reality. If we allow the mirror of truth in fantasy and elsewhere to reveal what is hidden, that sight, and the choices we make afterward, will change us within the revelation of the mirror of truth, for good. If the shattered mirror is used, and gazed into often . . . the result you can imagine.

Against evil, physical combat becomes at last inevitable, and brings its own results, as *Sheepfarmer's Daughter* in The Deed of Paksenarrion trilogy demonstrates so well—overcoming evil and showing the rewards of good, with touches of emotion and metaphor within the mundane.

When the last of Cracolnya's men had stepped back, the Duke turned to Paks's cohort.

"You have no captain to speak for you," he said, "Nor sergeants, nor corporals. Yet your deeds speak aloud without their aid. I cannot pick and choose among you; I will have made for each of you, from these spoils, a ring to commemorate your deeds. But those to whom you owe your lives, who brought me word of your peril: even among such honor, they deserve honor. Three started: Canna Arendts, Saben Kanasson, and Paksenarrion Dorthansdotter. When they were attacked by brigands near Rotengre, only Paks was able to win free. We do not know the fate of the others; be assured that search will continue until we know. But now—Paksenarrion, come forward."

Paks felt herself blushing, and could hardly tear her eyes from the ground. She limped forward.

"Here is a ring," he said, "that I think best represents your deed. Three strands, for the three who started together, braided into

one: the one who succeeded, the message, for returning to the place you began. And imperishable gold, for loyalty."

–*Sheepfarmer's Daughter* by Elizabeth Moon, pg. 301

This book shows the extraordinary within the ordinary.

The reality we see, and the reality we experience in the mirror of another story as we follow a heroine into physical conflict, impacts our spirit in the unseen realm and resonates through the metaphorical and the mundane in *Falcon Heart:*

Kyrin stepped back and spread her arms wide as Seliam's sword whispered from his sash. "I do not desire to fight you." She gestured at her bronze falcon dagger. "This contest is not in honor. Ask a blade for me." She would use every dragging moment.

Seliam tossed his head, raising his sword. "They told me you could do more than speak, fearful one." His two-handed grip whitened his knuckles.

The thin blade held sun and shadow and burning-cold crystals that crept toward her heart. Kyrin willed her gaze past the edge to his contempt. "I am not afraid, but a trial of skill lies between the strong!"

He blinked and laughed, and his mouth fell into habitual lines of petulance. "I will gain a beautiful gazelle, and your blood will flood these stones, loosing her to me. You, Nasrany, will beg of Allah."

She took a breath and slid the falcon free. "I would sooner plead with a djinn!" The ice shattered.

–*Falcon Heart* by Azalea Dabill, pg. 377

Fantasy at its best grows at least a threefold triumvirate of reality: the reflection of conflict in its glory of sharp-held metaphor, the lightning-strong struggle, and the emotion as deep as death and life. Inspired by heroes and heroines, the reality of the facets of greatness are restful, and the mirror brings us back to our world better able to fight what we find here. We have monsters enough that have not come through the glass.

Our heroes inspire us to dare again the vastness of wind and wave under a bright sun, with the taste of salt on our lips, and to discover *How the Best Fantasy Tests the Hearts and Souls of Men.*

Chapter 3.0

How the Best Fantasy Tests the Hearts and Souls of Men

It is amazing how people—that term including all sentient beings—can speak at cross-purposes under pressure. Of course, that's what makes a fantasy interesting, the cross-purposes and the pressure.

"Think before you leap." It's still true. In either world, seeming good or beauty can hide dire evil where purposes diverge.

If we throw different cultures into the uncertainty of cross-purposes, with different beliefs they are willing to die for, or not—including humans with their mixed motives in a struggle for power—then we've got an enticing stew.

Why is it hard for living hearts and minds to meet in amity? Can it be we are that selfish, that we will not suffer another's gain at our expense? Why is it so much easier to discern whether a thought, word, or deed is moral in a fantasy as opposed to our often confused state over the same issue when we face it in our world?

Is it possible that in fantasy we have just enough emotional distance from what is going on that we make a better decision than when our anger is shaking us like a rag doll, or fear looms before us like a chilling monster, or the other side of the fence looks safe, and spreads tempting riches of all sorts for our delight?

Just so, story tests us, as well as the hearts of the men and women through whom we perceive the world. In as many ways as there are tales, we are tested as we go together past the physical realm into the spiritual, into other minds and hearts, into empathy with other beings.

Find yourself *Astray* in an urban fantasy, caught between *fasgadair* who hunt for blood and a stranded human in a racial war for survival, feel how a half-dragon outcast torn between two races fights despair in *Seraphina*, and in the Hel's Crucible Duology join all free peoples in an epic battle against an evil determined to rule. In The Dark Elf trilogy an exile is hunted by his people for daring to be different, and in *The Queen's Poisoner* a boy, hostage to a king, struggles to save his estranged family from a plot-filled court.

Dive 3.1

Why the Spirit, Mind, and Body is a Fantastic Battleground—from *Astray* to *Seraphina*

Different motives and different goals pit us against those who traffic with demons. But, one may say, who is to say which is right? There is the question. Who will make the call? Who can make it? If we refuse rightful judgment and say anything we want to do is right for us, what happens when my right and yours come into opposition, and a conflict is born? Both of us cannot be right when we contradict each other.

Well, someone may say, surely we can meet in the middle if we seek peace with all our hearts. Doesn't it depend on the peace terms, and on what we seek to negotiate, whether it is a principle of true and fair dealing, or merely a step toward our desire?

What if the stated goal of our terms of peace included working together at the side of a vampirish race of *fasgadair,* to supply them with our own people for food in exchange for immortality for a select few? Dare we deny the truth of a living hell worse than death, if we accept the terms? Dare we call it right to sacrifice others on the altar of our life? And who may call us to answer for that choice?

Fallon faces just such a struggle of contradictions in a growing knowledge of right and wrong. Cross purposes are not always a bad thing. Accepting a bad peace can mean no peace.

"This is your last chance to change your mind. I can give you immortality." Aodan secured my hands behind my back. "Or you will die today."

For the first time in my life, puking seemed like a good idea, if only to release the pressure in my gut. What was I doing? Part of me wished my friends would come storming in to rescue me. Another portion wanted to accept Aodan's offer and free my mother. I tried to force those thoughts away, focusing instead on my God.

But doubt seeped in. What if I'd been tricked? What if I had failed a test? Hadn't I already taken things into my own hands by abandoning my friends and coming here alone?

They told me not to listen to Le'Corenci. I'd believed the words of one of those demonic beings and a silly dream over my friends—believers. Then Ryann died. Because of me. My choices. I had no way to rescue my mother. Were those parts of God's plan or proof of my error? And I had trusted Wolf. What if he'd been using me all along just to get me to this point? To die?

I had to stop torturing myself. Right or wrong, nothing could change the choices I'd made. It was too late.

As of this moment, I already had immortality, maybe not in this life, but who'd want to stay here, with Aodan and his irrational mood swings, for eternity?

–Astray by J. F. Rogers, (ebook edition)

Eternity in a good world, for Fallon and for us, hinges on a right choice, and the true purpose of peace.

As far as fantasy and cross-purposes go, *Seraphina* flies directly into a familiar yet alien universe. Here, dragons are thinking beings who can morph from flying form to a more human-like, scaled form. They are feared by humans, and both races are bound by an uncertain truce. Half-breeds are anathema.

Being such a part-dragon, with her telltale scaly bits concealed, Seraphina finds herself at cross-purposes with a prince. Placed high up in the king's court, with a gift for music that touches souls, Seraphina is tested to the edges of her being.

I suddenly found myself warm from the exertion of climbing and cold at this reminder that he was so observant. I needed to be careful. His friendliness notwithstanding, the prince and I could not be friends. I had so many things to hide, and it was in his nature to seek.

My right hand had wormed as far as it could under the binding of my left sleeve and was fingering my scaly wrist. That was exactly the sort of unconscious habit he would notice; I forced myself to stop. ...

I waved the last white flag I had: "I don't wish to talk about my mother. Please excuse me."

His brow furrowed in concern; he could tell I was upset, but not why. He guessed exactly wrong: "It's hard that she left you so young. Mine did too. But she did not live in vain. What a wonderful legacy she left you!"

Legacy? Up my arm, around my waist, and scattershot through my head? The hooting memory box, which I feared would burst open at any moment?

"She gave you an ability to touch people's very souls," he said kindly. "What is it like to be so talented?"

"What is it like to be a bastard?" I blurted.

I clapped a hand to my mouth, horrified.

–Seraphina by Rachel Hartmann, pg. 151

Beyond her anger and the cross-purposes that pit Seraphina against a prince, when races converge, questions are raised and the battle is fought on spiritual, physical, and relational ground. Differences must be put aside in favor of truth to find peace. Without strong central truth in a society, there is no peace.

Dennis McKiernan* portrays this in his Hel's Crucible Duology, but comes to differing conclusions than we do about the nature of the universe. The testing of our ideas and beliefs only strengthens truth, since we have to mine it out, seeking it as gold among the dross of what is said within a rather vague system of philosophical thought.

Fantasy universes explore other minds, which lead us to fascinating hearts and a mix of beliefs in *Hel's Crucible,* where evil and good people are both willing to die to achieve their goals.

Dive 3.2

Explore Fascinating Cultures in the Astonishing Hel's Crucible*

Culture is not truth. Truth supersedes culture. On Mithgar, among the races of Elves, Trolls, Dwarves, Baeron, Men, Mages, Pysks, and Warrows, beliefs can be very different, or interestingly similar. It is what we would expect if there was one central truth they all, consciously or unconsciously, saw with varying degrees of muddled sight.

But, some may say, aren't we all muddled in our view of truth to some extent? Yes. Thankfully, our less than perfect perception does not negate the truth we do see. Far less him who is truth, the Creator of all, who brings us to ever clearer sight as we follow the light.

Though sometimes we try to create our own reality, our own truths, real truth constantly intrudes, disproving our false beliefs. Truth is absolutely real.

But, someone may say, everything we call reality is a figment of our imaginations. I would not agree, but I could respect such an honest person, if to prove their point they never ate again, since food is not real. That is an example of the end result of that person's thinking; truth has most uncomfortable ways of getting past our false fantasies.

People growing up around central beliefs in Mithgar, including truth, half-truth, and untruth, act on what they believe, and those actions spread through every area of life until they solidify into what we call culture. But culture is not truth, rather an amalgamation of beliefs, from true to false. Culture must be challenged and measured against truth, whether in Mithgar or our own world.

Before we are reconciled with our Creator and pass from spiritual death to life, at any point in our earthly life we are either acknowledging what we do see of truth, or going our own way. And until the fateful moment when all choice is gone, if we see bright glimmers of truth in the dark sea of partial truth and lies in our own culture, and struggle toward it, we are also testing the minds and hearts of others and what they call true. This does not end when we begin to live in our Creator's love of truth. Our blade is merely honed and sharpened for a battlefield we see ever clearer.

Small people like Warrows who are drawn into battle in their culture contain just as great or withered a heart as those of larger stature. The degree of withering or greatness depends on the amount of truth each of them holds to, and whether they are seeking more truth or denying it.

Rael turned up a hand. "The pith of the debate was that Adon argued for the right of all peoples to freely choose the paths they would follow, whereas Gyphon spoke for the domination and control of those he named 'inferior beings.'"

Beau now stood and stepped to a different portion of the tapestry and climbed upon a chair, and Tipperton said, "I take it then that these Black Mages side with Gyphon, for as you have said, they seek dominion, control, power over others."

All the Lian nodded in agreement, and Loric said, "They have become allies of Gyphon, yet should Gyphon himself gain the upper hand, he will utterly dominate them as well, much to their everlasting sorrow, though they believe it not."

Beau, standing on the seat, peered at the figure representing Gyphon. "Why, he isn't a pure single color at all, but instead shimmers like oil on water."

"Aye," responded Talarin. "'Tis because he is the Great Deceiver, showing a given person or people whatever face need be

until he has them in his grasp. Then and only then will his true nature show, and it is monstrous."

Hurriedly, Beau drew back from the tapestry, clambering down and resuming his chair.

"And this Modru in Gron, the Black Mage fighting against High King Blaine, he's been deceived by Gyphon?" asked Tip.

–*Into the Forge** by Dennis McKiernan, pg. 105

This fantasy duology has a couple mentions of immorality and a mixed view of truth, which I've overlooked. This story has much to recommend it. We would be the poorer for not reading this tale.

In Mithgar, Gyphon and Modru's deception led to worldwide war and the testing of many comrades in friendship and love and the crucible of life-and-death loyalty. And those decisions withered the heart or made it greater, truer than it had been before.

The testing of the Warrows' beliefs lead to their greater knowledge, and to our own. Honest, logical questions about why we exist, even in fantasy, need answered. The next most important question is whether the knowledge we gain progresses to understanding—do we rightly act upon the knowledge we wrest from the war-ground of culture? Truth supersedes culture. Will we follow it?

Such is the journey of one elf against his race. Can we challenge an underground world of terrible morality and actively object against the mob?

Dive 3.3

Will You Challenge a Subterranean World of Terrible Ethics and Elves?

Wrong suffered tests the heart and soul by fire, pushing us beyond knowledge to understanding. Or to our refusal of understanding, if we count the cost of aligning ourselves with right as too high. Knowledge does not guarantee understanding.

Thankfully, Drizzt the elf enters many tests—passing from knowledge to understanding—with all his heart, two swords, and a determination to be different. He is set on living well despite his utterly corrupt society.

The Academy.

It is the propagation of the lies that bind drow society together, the ultimate perpetration of falsehoods repeated so many times that they ring true against any contrary evidence. The lessons young drow are taught of truth and justice are so blatantly refuted by everyday life in wicked Menzoberranzan that it is hard to understand how any could believe them. Still they do.

Even now, decades removed, the thought of the place frightens me, not for any physical pain or the ever-present sense of possible death—I have trod down many roads equally dangerous in that way. The Academy of Menzoberranzan frightens me when I think of the survivors, the graduates, existing—reveling—within the evil fabrications that shape their world. They live with the belief that anything is acceptable if you can get away with it, that self-gratification is the most important aspect of existence, and that power comes only to she or he who is strong enough and cunning enough to snatch it from the failing hands of those who no longer deserve it. Compassion has no place in Menzoberranzan, and yet it is compassion, not fear, that brings harmony to most races. It is harmony, working toward shared goals, that precedes greatness.

Lies engulf the drow in fear and mistrust, refute friendship at the tip of a Lolth-blessed sword. The hatred and ambition fostered by these amoral tenets are the doom of my people, a weakness that they perceive as strength. The result is a paralyzing, paranoid existence that the drow call the edge of readiness.

I do not know how I survived the Academy, how I discovered the falsehoods early enough to use them in contrast, and thus strengthen, those ideals I most cherish.

It was Zaknafein, I must believe, my teacher. Through the experiences of Zak's long years, which embittered him and cost him so much, I came to hear the screams: the screams of protest against murderous treachery; the screams of rage from the leaders of drow society, the high priestesses of the Spider Queen, echoing down the paths of my mind, ever to hold a place within my mind. The screams of dying children. –Drizzt Do'Urden

–The Dark Elf trilogy by R. A. Salvatore, pg. 113

Though not yet as bad as Menzoberranzan, our world is close. There is much barbarism to fight. Injustice, laziness, greed, passivity, lack of compassion—in a word, self-centeredness under a veneer of civility. We need taken out of ourselves, to dive beyond our narrow insides—then when we return with a jewel from the ocean we will see both ourselves and everyone around us more clearly. We will have gained a little light to see by, as Drizzt gained light to guide him through the dangers of the Underdark.

Why do we cheer for Drizzt? Is it only because he is one against the world, so to speak, and we wish we had the same courage? Or is it that we behold the same choices before us, watch the same dangers in our world, sense the same dire monsters stalking us—and wish to keep our society from becoming another collapsed civilization? A world of roaming bodies whose souls are dead, who have killed every shred of their hearts—willingly?

For that is what happens when right and truth are rejected. Evil starts with the smallest things, though the principle behind them is never small, and spreads like plague through the largest. In every instance where truth is abandoned the result is death, separation from the life inherent in reality. As light signifies life, and darkness death, so to be separated from life and light is to cling to darkness and to die. It makes one shiver.

In his journey, Drizzt goes only so far as to refuse to do evil as much as he can, and so he pursues the light and the life-giver, though in his story he does not yet fully know what and who he yearns for. Though he has caught sight of the path of right, to cross the abyss of the wrong he has done will take more than he ever dreams, more than he possesses.

For as the wisest has said, "The heart is deceitful above all else." The motives of our hearts are the deepest waters of all. A fantasy gem rescued from the sea, *The Queen's Poisoner* makes this abundantly clear, set amid tempting riches of power.

Dive 3.4

Can Fantasy Master the Motives of the Human Soul?

What can be more dangerous in the mountain heights of the fantasy realm than the fog that conceals a cliff and a sheer face to be scaled? Bad motive is the thickest mist. Worse, a lack of truth, directing that motive, can be more deadly than the clammy, creeping cold to a climber.

Like a lancing shaft of dawn, truth strikes the frost in our hearts and pierces the fog, giving us light to avoid the cliff, warming our blood so we may scale the face with confidence that our muscles will hold.

In the palace of Kingfountain are cliffs of deception and the slick, sheer faces of many schemers and their intentions. High loyalties of right are torn, torn by those who know better, who inflict terrible pain upon a child. A perceptive child, who must navigate the dangers of his own heart and a king's to save his family.

"But everyone says . . ." She lifted her gaze to meet his eyes, and his voice trailed off. He swallowed. "But everyone says he did it, so it must be true."

Ankarette smiled, but it wasn't a pleased smile. It was almost a smile of pain. "It's been my experience, Owen, that when everyone agrees on some point of fact, it tends to be the biggest deception of all." She reached out and tousled his hair. "Remember that. Never trust another person to do your thinking for you."

–The Queen's Poisoner by Jeff Wheeler, pg. 121

How right Ankarette is, Owen soon discovers.

We must go beyond our knee-jerk reaction to the core of the matter. Why would we tell a partial truth or seek a respected person's favor illicitly? And what reason will we find to tell the truth instead and seek favor lawfully, using what is true to direct our motive and not what is false? The rise and fall of many may depend on our decision. Motive touches the will, and the will, decision.

The will—how delicate and how tough—at times a desert flower in bloom or an unbreakable Damascus blade.

The will can transform from one into the other as needed, especially with training. For sometimes it is good to be a flower, yielding to another the sweet perfume of friendship or love. At other times any yielding is perilous, and we must hold our purpose as strong as steel.

The testing of our motive to do right, of our will and our spirit is the toughest training, a hard course in how to truly live. Such testing pushes us beyond the mere motions of living—which is the coward's way—to living with vigorous purpose, in steady knowledge that what we do makes a difference.

Maybe that is another reason we love the adventure of voyaging in the fantasy realm. For the magic and mystery of discovery, where choices matter and we impact everything we touch.

Do not mistake learning about the truth for living it out. Truth that is known and not lived is worse than truth not yet known. Unlived truth is like a path to mountain riches, riches hidden from our eyes, wealth that we will never discover because we believe we have already gathered those jewels. When we live out the truth we have learned, we stop in excitement over a gem that appears by the will of a benevolent power under our feet, larger and more beautiful than our dreams, and of a depth we had not imagined.

For in fantasy the lie is not so often told that everything is relative, and so of no real effect. In fantasyland things of no effect find it very hard to breathe, ephemeral as mist, while the ground of choice, watered by acts of will, produce all manner of living things that stretch our spirits toward understanding, knowledge, and power. In fantasy you *can,* in fact you *will,* save a kingdom or lose it by what you *believe,* which drives what you *do.* And when you return to our world, what you did there touches here, the sphere we breathe in. At the very least you impact a life, my life—and far more probably you will proceed to direct a kingdom aright, even if it is only your own.

Fantasy's testing and training leads us to questions and quests in *Questioning Spirits and Questing Souls—Are You One?*

Chapter 4.0

Questing Spirits and Questioning Souls - Are You One?

Questions come to us in many forms, often at unexpected or inconvenient times, as do quests. But it is good to be a questioner, seeking the truth of life. If we don't question the unknown thing rising in our view, if we assume we know what it is, we are blind to it, not fully seeing what it is—or isn't—and so we are blind to its possibilities.

Come, you who say it is better not to question, not to open a container of worms. We need bait for the monstrous fish in the ocean trenches, for we need sustenance even while we search for riches beneath the waters. Often we must search and dig in the realm of the unknown after fat worms of question, before we descend into the abyss in search of fish, however fantastic or common. Both question and fish feed us well. And the right question is also the beginning of a good quest, serving as both bait and a light for the deeps.

Why are we here? What is our purpose in the kingdom of fantasy and can our world be restored? Can there be accord between cultures near and far? How can a small sigil or talisman lead to heroic things and peace? Is love even real?

Have we not all wrestled with these questions and started quests of our own to find the answers?

No matter the date written in our book of knowledge, or how far along we are on our journey, it is delightful work to follow the paths of heroes and to hear the answers they have found.

Let's dive for *The Door Within*, on a "why am I here" quest, then risk our souls to restore the world in *The Shock of Night*. We quest for purpose with *The Seer and the Sword*, and bridge culture in *Shaman's Fire*. Searching for more than a talisman in The Sword the Ring and the Chalice, we also quest for true love in *The Bonemender*.

The following dives may change the course of our lives.

Dive 4.1

Discover the Key to the Quest of *The Door Within*

The realm of Alleble calls Aidan from our world to a place where young men and women fight for freedom. He finds a key to another world that leads into his own heart—and out again—higher up and further in. A question of purpose and a key of hope.

Aidan looked up through a haze of fears, but the eyes of his Captain, like beacons for a lost ship, penetrated deep into Aidan's heart. In Alleble, there was meaning and purpose. Things happened for a reason. To leave, to turn his back on it all, would be to abandon everything he ever wanted. It would mean throwing away his dreams forever.

Staying would not be safe—that was clear. But, Aidan decided, it was the right path. And so, with courage swelling within, he cried out, "Aye!"

The crowd of Glimpses erupted in cheers, whoops, and hurrahs! The Captain's snowy mustache curled on one side in a proud smile, and he nodded.

Finally, when the roar diminished, Captain Valithor gently tapped each of Aidan's shoulders with Aidan's new sword and announced, "Then, by the heartfelt confession of your lips, I now dub thee Sir Aidan, Knight of Alleble and Servant of the one true King!"

The next thing Aidan knew, he was at the bottom of a massive pile of joyous Glimpses. He felt squashed, but he didn't care. And though he couldn't see anything through the jumble of arms and legs, Aidan heard thunderous deep hurrahs and huzzahs above all the other din, and he knew it had to be Mallik. I have friends here, Aidan thought.

–The Door Within by Wayne Thomas Batson, pg. 124

That is another reason gems of fantasy call to us. Each book is a friend, the spirit of someone we come to know in some small ways. Especially when we cannot get out very often in our world for our own adventures due to peculiar confines of our bodies, we treasure friends like these. Within fantasy we find adventure, beauty, new worlds, and friends we cannot reach elsewhere. Nowhere, that is, but through the door within.

Every world has its own purposes, questions, answers, and a way within peculiar to itself.

In one such, a reluctant reeve we have met once before struggles to find answers and preserve his life while those in power strive to take even his memory from him, a commoner elevated beyond his station to the king's court.

Dive 4.2

An Amazing Quest to Save the World in *The Shock of Night*

What will we risk to restore justice to the world? Willet Dura takes the full risk, and soon finds himself beyond his depth. The vault of night will swallow him along with the rest of the world if he does not find the right answer to a lethal riddle locked away in his mind.

Generally no quest to save the realm is begun with full knowledge of what lies ahead by any hero or heroine. But the questions we pursue through many dangers tend to have satisfying answers if we carefully discern our way. At times, we may even differ from our hero as to the right answer, and that is as it should be. Our choices are our responsibility, though we may take counsel from others

> My response left my mouth before I had time to stop it. "I don't care to be a part of your group, Pellin."
>
> The tone of my voice alone should have roused some ire in him, but he chuckled as if I'd assayed some mild jest. "I think I remember feeling the same way, once. Your gift may make you a part of us whether you will or not. How long you share our company is up to you, of course. If you wish to be rid of us in short order, I must say you've gone about it the right way. At this rate you'll be dead in a matter of weeks."
>
> I'd been threatened several times over the course of the months since I'd been raised to the nobility, and a few times those doing

the threatening had tried to back it up either in person or by proxy. None had carried the casual certitude of Pellin's statement.

I tried to moisten my lips. "I'm listening."

He nodded once, short and sharp. "It's about time. Lord Dura, you have a gift, a gift everyone in the Vigil shares, to see into the minds and hearts of any you touch. You're not the first to attempt to bring justice to the world overnight. We've had others."

–The Shock of Night by Patrick Carr, pg. 109

What will Lord Willet Dura do to foil the dangers of his past, injustices which have crept ahead of him, into his future, to threaten all the known world if he cannot face a time of peril he does not even remember? This is his question.

For others it is a question of escape. Sometimes a heroine must run in order to save more than herself.

Dive 4.3

Share an Enthralling Quest in *The Seer and the Sword*

What if we knew something bad was going to happen to those we loved but we were powerless to stop it?

Questions whose deadly answers force us to run from our castle and everyone we know lead to a soul searching. Learning that most of those we love are dead behind us, killed by a traitor's hand—a trusted traitor who remains masked as all that is worthy—is a crisis most of us would decide to hide from. But there is an end to hiding, especially when the people suffer, and the traitor hunts the only one who can unmask him.

> *She stood and paced restlessly. It seemed impossible to live another day in such sad and hidden loneliness. She wondered what the people she had once known would say if they could visit her. What would her mother tell her, or Gramere?*
>
> Gramere would want me to find a way past my troubles. And she would understand. My dear, tender mother? She would love me, love me, but she would not understand. My father? He'd fight his way through and stake his chances on victory. Landen? What does it matter? He's gone.
>
> *Torina opened her door and looked into the thick trees she had somehow stumbled through during her escape from Vesputo.*
>
> *Escape! That was what she had to do. She'd escaped Archeld, but never left it behind. She must create a future and live again.*

–The Seer and the Sword by Victoria Hanley, pg. 185

In fantasy there are many kinds of kingdoms to be won: the kingdom of a crown, the kingdom of the soul, the realm of a loved one's heart, the animal kingdom, or sometimes even a metaphysical land. But what of the kingdom of purpose?

What is our purpose, and what do we purpose to do about it? And then there are other cultures.

Cultures are a kingdom to win in the sense of our bridging wary hearts and different mindsets, of coming to understand one another. Even to highly value another culture's unique insights. Such is Sayla's quest to bridge cultures in Sandy Cathcart's *Shaman's Fire*.

Dive 4.4

A Remarkable Quest of Wondrous Cultures in *Shaman's Fire*

Is not fantasy about making the impossible, possible? Indeed, pursuing it? Not always.

But, one may say, aren't you just splitting a pin feather, setting two sides of the same coin against each other? No. There may be good reason not to pursue a power to achieve the "impossible".

Any attempt at a meeting of minds between two peoples calls forth and strengthens the inherent qualities in both. In a successful bridge where cultures meet in truth, the unique talents of mind and spirit are clarified and developed and what was named impossible is overcome in a right way.

On the other hand, add a path where we seek spiritual power at all costs to an unsuccessful attempt to bridge a culture, and we're in a near-impossible situation.

Spiritual knowledge must be pursued carefully, with understanding. Because some paths of knowledge must be run from, for our lives. In both worlds—the seen and the unseen.

A river still runs beside me, the forest is quiet and still, but the shaman and fire are gone.

Hearing the sound of heavy breathing I spin around, but see nothing.

There! Between the trees darting, a shadowy shape I know too well. Slanting yellow eyes stare. When I hear the growl, I turn and run, splashing through water until the waves catch me in their grip. This is not the calm river of Sacred Mountain Ranch; this is a wild, angry river full of danger. The waves pull me under, swiftly moving me downstream. Gasping for air, I gulp one clean breath before being pulled back under. Stone scrapes my legs and arms. Too late, I think of Gran's warning and wonder if my own life will be the price of this most recent gift.

–Shaman's Fire by Sandy Cathcart, pg. 285

Truth and the reality of rightful authority and deceitful powers does not change with culture. Their trappings may appear different, but truth transcends every culture, and the Creator remains himself.

In a perilous situation, we have to feel our way toward what is right by using our minds and hearts and the truth we already know. Above our own knowledge we must seek the Creator, who knows our fallen moments and yet loves us. The one who gives knowledge and feeling and truth will lead us onto the right path again if we are willing to listen.

There is a difference between unintentional blindness and not wanting to see what something is when it stares us in the face. Especially when it is a gift of power. Sometimes a gift horse *must* be looked in the mouth. Gifts may be given for many purposes, and the smallest gift, when we esteem the giver, may lead us far into good or evil.

But the impossible bridge between hearts, once right motive and truth is established and acted on, becomes a right solid possibility between peoples. In navigating fantasy, as in our world, small things lead to great.

A talisman is another small thing that may represent truth, or hold meaning, or a secret far bigger than itself.

Dive 4.5

Join an Ultimate Quest in The Sword, the Ring, and the Chalice

Some talismans lead the heroine into a quest, and some quests lead the hero in search of a talisman, while the talisman often teases us with secrets in either case. I am not talking here of the talismans of superstitious power in our world, named charms, but of sigils or symbols, like the falcon dagger in The Falcon Chronicle series.

> *A sheathed dagger lay on her [mother's] breast, tangled in her hair.* She reached for this when she fell. *Kyrin freed the weapon and slid the blade from the leather. She opened her hand, and blinked. The brazed dagger was a cunningly shaped falcon.*
>
> *Torchlight played over the bronze feathers. Beak open in a defiant scream, the falcon's eyes penetrated hers, amber lurking in the ebony depths. The falcon's body and shoulders formed the haft, etched wing-tips brushing the reddish blade. The reaching talons and fanned tail formed a down-swept hand guard on either side. The blade was straight, sharp and clean. Kyrin shivered, drawn again to the falcon's far-seeing eyes.*
>
> *It saw her ugly shrinking, her fear. Where was the hunter of the woods? But unfaltering warmth enfolded her: the falcon gently called her to fly higher. Kyrin's tears came in a rush.*
>
> –*Falcon Heart* by Azalea Dabill, pg. 24

The sigil of the fearless falcon leads Kyrin to courage and the hidden power of a questing heart. The secret of the falcon dagger will save a kingdom of the soul and a crown.

Follow another talisman of fantasy into the realm of The Sword, the Ring and the Chalice, where all three aspects of talismans adorn one epic trilogy. Dive into a story where a talisman can be different things, with differing meanings. Such a little thing, to have so great an impact on the hero and everyone around him.

If not for the recovery of his bard crystal, Dain would have believed himself completely the loser of this battle of wills.

He tucked the pendant even farther beneath his wet tunic, patting his chest in comfort at having it back again. He felt stronger now, more confident against the dark forces beyond the walls of this hold. The crystal had no special powers, no magic other than how it made song. But it belonged to the side of nature unsullied by the Nonkind. If he fell into trouble, the crystal's presence would help him keep a clear head. Besides, it was his talisman, his only legacy.

–*The Sword* by Deborah Chester, pg. 347

Dain noticed that tonight Lord Odfrey's weapon was not the usual utilitarian blade that he wore into battle but instead one longer and very old. It was not fashioned of magicked steel forged by dwarves but instead of some metal equally mysterious, ancient in fact, with a resonance that traveled along Dain's senses. He had never seen such metal before, and he could not get a clear look at it with the cloth draped across the blade, but he closed his eyes and listened to the hum of it.

"I am Truthseeker," it said within the hum. Great power flowed inside the blade. Long ago, many battles had it fought. Images of blood and death mingled with war cries in tongues that Dain had never heard before. He shuddered and opened his eyes as the

draped sword was pointed straight at his heart, then turned side-ways and laid at Dain's feet. Gold wire was wrapped around the two-handed hilt and a row of fiery emeralds studded the straight edge of the guard. Glittering and gleaming, Truthseeker lay on the floor in humility, but even the cloth could not mask its great-ness.

Wide-eyed with awe, Dain stared at Lord Odfrey, and his entire image of the man changed to something new. Of what lineage was this man that he owned a sword made of god-steel?

–*The Sword* by Deborah Chester, pg. 376

Clothed in mystery and secrets, or revealing a double-edged power to impact the physical and the spiritual realm, talismans are often met-aphors of something else. A talisman can also be an animal or an ornament, or a token of common use with a special meaning to the one who holds it. It then becomes essential to us as readers, diving for jew-els as we are in the ocean of fantasy.

It is also essential to writers. If you are a writer or reader wanting to craft jewels that hold extraordinary talismans, be sure to get *The Fan-tasy Fiction Formula.* It is a gem for all who are interested in crafting inspiring fantasy adventure. Some may name it speculative fiction, or another genre name. Whatever its moniker, a skillful tale pulls us in and take us places we have never been. To inspire us, it must whirl us away with dexterity on ventures of the spirit as well as forging new paths in our imaginations. When a story does this well, there is always a rea-son—the meanings within, the story behind the story—the absolutes that anchor worlds even though they are supposed to be only *natural laws.* Whether some name them *conscience* or *ethics,* all form bounda-ries that shape freedom.

This freedom rises within the boundary law of forgiveness, breathes in the unbreakable draw of the lodestone of mercy, and lives in the ex-plosive potential of a talisman lying inert in the blast-powder barrel of meaning.

Though the deck of our ship creaks, frail against the might of the worst storm, as the ropes groan and we smell the sweat of fear, there is one who can bring us through. No storm of life is proof against *his* star of forgiveness and power. The lodestone points true. The talisman reveals hidden things. In our wild and wet course through the fantasy realms, the laws of life enrich our spirits.

Whatever monsters of the deep we face, Helarms or dragons dire, or whether we find merely the hilarious, like *The Marvelous Misadventures of Sebastian,* we seek always the craft to master the danger and to experience the wonder and the beauty of our mysterious adventures, there and in our own world.

That ability and that experience is the goal, the end, the aim of every great fantasy. For both the writer and the reader.

As a reader we bring our imagination to shape what we read into life, and as writers, we craft the facet that will yield the truest shape. A shape to hold the living breath, that usually comes from we know not where, and surprises us.

There is a mystery in this, in our crafting. We cannot shape a jewel into something we have never seen. To every fantasy gem a writer crafts or shapes, we bring a large part of ourselves, and build on it. And if we are looking outward, the facets cut and shaped will bring joy and riches to both the writer and the reader, who will treasure it.

If we writers work in the power of the greatest Craftsman, we will escape the narrowness of our own minds, feel the thrill of our stony hearts becoming flesh, and teach our grasping souls generosity. The light will banish the darkness that was our life. We love, because he first loved us.

For us as readers, no talisman leads to greater things than one that is a sign or sigil of love. Love is kind, and patient, and hopeful. It is not arrogant, and it endures, seeking the ultimate good of the one loved. The quest for love—between man and woman, or father, mother, with daughter or son, between brother and sister, or the deepest affection of friends—is a quest unrivaled in its risk and its reward.

True love is worth everything it costs. Both to be loved truly, and to truly love another. These may seem like small things, these talismans of meaning, but they affect us all. Gabrielle is a healer on an unwitting quest to the ecstatic heights, the bitter depths, and the bliss of genuine love.

Dive 4.6

Bonemender's Choice is a Heart-thrilling Quest for Genuine Love

Love is deeper than an ocean, more enduring than a mountain, more real than a fantasy. Oh yes. If you have never experienced it, or have experienced the opposite of a loving relationship and, because of that, say there is no such thing as true love, we encourage you: don't give up!

This series is one of our favorite fantasy romances, right up there with *The Blue Sword*, though it is also an adventure. Is not the quest for true love always an adventure? And the love we seek so often not what we thought, but different in a delightful way? And is not the one we love often unlike the person we pictured in our dreams?

Love in all its forms has many pitfalls to navigate, for our hearts are not yet true, not to anything or anyone. Either we are not ready to embrace the love that comes to us in the common form it appears in, or we mistake something else for it, or we foolishly refuse the love we find (hopefully only until we gain better sense), or we accept someone's love and betray them, or they betray us. That is when the bond between two spirits is utterly tested, by the fire of betrayal, intentional or not. Love endures and overcomes.

> *Now she stood at the castle gate with her family, ready to bid their guests farewell. She squared her shoulders, grasping at the shreds of her composure and knew it would fail her.*

Danais had kissed Solange, thanked Jerome gravely and bear-hugged her brother. Now he came to Gabrielle, soft brown eyes filled with gentleness.

"You will be in our hearts always."

Tears welled up and she could do nothing to stop them. Danais opened his cloak and enfolded her, pulling her close. An un-looked for sense of strength and peace stole into her. A gift, from him to her. In her need, she did not wonder or question, but simply accepted. In a while she stood and gave him a shaky smile.

"There, beautiful healer. One small thing I can do for thee." Danais touched his breast and turned to his horse.

Feolan. He stood before her, eyes dark with sorrow. I cannot hold you, Gabrielle thought, or I will never let you go. Feolan put his hand to his heart and then held out his palm. Her hand reached out to meet his, and in that gesture were all the words neither one could say. Feolan reached into his pouch, pulled out a folded parchment and tucked it into her hand. "If you ever need me," he whispered, and kissed her lightly on the brow.

Gabrielle stood watching the riders until they were out of sight. The tears flowed unheeded down her face as the urgent beat of her heart pleaded with her to follow, now, before it was too late.

–*The Bonemender* by Holly Bennett, pg. 57

There is only one love that has never failed, and it is not our human love, but the love of the one who made every love. Every great thing, every act of heroism, every worthy sacrifice, every life lived for good, traces its roots back to the love of the one who loved us truly and did not fail. Echoes of that love resonate between us and bring forth children, bits of ourselves to whom we yearn to show the greatest love. Our book of knowledge grows, marked by experience.

We have yet to scribe our adventures to our children so they may find the fire of clean romance, and walk inside the conflict of spirits and kingdoms at war, in loyalty and lore. *Never to be Forgotten—Experience the Wonder with Your Children.*

Chapter 5.0

Never to Be Forgotten—Experience the Wonder with Your Children

Reading with kids, or to them, is one of my best memories. Great fantasy is as much for kids as for adults. We never know what wonders we'll open for them until they can explore the vast waters on their own, what steadying comfort our presence will give them for later rainy days, what unfolding word will find its way into their book of knowledge, or what essential training they will gain from talking over fantastic books with us. Clean fantasy carries the magic of making memories that outpace time. And the best things are those we enjoy together.

As the oldest of five intrepid adventurers, I read a lot to my brothers and sisters. It was a blast, though my throat wore out too soon—it got a little raspy and Darth Vader-ish. But the best, the very best, was when Dad would read to us—or Mom, when she wasn't busily taking care of us all.

As a child, those warm hours curled up by the fire, on the couch, or in a pile of blankets, brothers, and sisters listening to a story, was the stuff dreams are made of. The coziness, the warmth of spirit, the sense of safety, and the grand adventure coming alive in Dad's voice—today, hearing him read anything at all evokes that time.

Whether it was *The Wind in the Willows* or George MacDonald's *The Princess and the Goblin*, or another adventure, we loved every one.

Though we were mostly good readers, we still loved to experience new worlds and wonders together.

Avid witnesses add power to our experiences, however deep and rich an experience is alone. Togetherness adds a further dimension to tastes, places, and people—to adventure in this world or any other. And worlds designed for younger readers still somehow deeply appeal to us older readers—maybe because we're young at heart. I'm not sure why, but the story of a youngling exploring something new, learning about bravery and selflessness and the wide world, never tires me. In fact, such stories are like a rain shower bringing the freshest, brightest spring I can remember, with all the smells of earth and flower . . . .

Such a tale is Urchin's, a series about a squirrel born on a night of shooting stars, then fallen into the sea and washed ashore, destined to change the lives of all those he lives among. Isn't that what we dream of, for ourselves and our children? That we may bravely create lasting change for good?

Fantasy and the soul of imaginative fiction impacts us as a rock dropped in the pond of our heart, the ripples expanding through our outermost skin, demanding we act. In light of that call to courage, let us make good memories with those who are our closest and dearest.

And for that we need the bravery of The Monster Blood Tattoo series, the wit and wisdom to trust carefully on *The Edge of the Dark Sea of Darkness*, and the truth about *The Dragons of Chiril*. We need to see the crown and the claw of good and evil in *The Lion, the Witch and the Wardrobe*, watch the courage of a slight archer pitted against battle school bullies in *The Ruins of Gorlan*, and see the determination of a crippled storyteller who would rescue a princess in *Shadow Spinner* before she loses her head in a kingdom of shade and sand.

Dive 5.1

Who Can Put a Price on Daring Love, Loyalty, and Swordsmanship?

In *Urchin of the Riding Stars,* Urchin's world is the island of Mistmantle, eternally surrounded by fog no islander can cross and return, unless they return by another way. Visitors are few, but welcome.

In the peaceful and industrious island kingdom of Mistmantle, Urchin yearns to be a tower squirrel, to work near the king and his family. At last he is chosen, but then the king's son is killed, and the traitor threatens the peace of Mistmantle, the safety of every loyal animal, and the love of the Heartstone that binds the king and the kingdom together.

Urchin didn't often use tunnels. Trying to remember what Padra had taught him about them he found an entrance in a corner of the wall. The frightened hedgehog voice was closer, and so was cruel laughter, and then, to his horror, the rasp of a sword being drawn. Urchin tore toward it.

The tunnel opened out so suddenly that Urchin wasn't ready for what he saw, and had to pull himself together. He was in some sort of guard room, where a platter lay on a small table, a lamp glowed on a wall, and two moles, who neither looked nor sounded like Mistmantle moles, had their backs to him. They were pointing their swords toward a hedgehog so small, so scruffy, and so brave in its terror that fury fired Urchin.

"I'll fight you . . ." the hedgehog was saying, though his voice was thin and his mouth trembled. "I'll fight you. One at a time. But you'll have to lend me a sword, or it's not fair."

Soundlessly, Urchin sprang onto the table and picked up the platter for a shield. If the hedgehog had seen him, it was wise enough to keep quiet. The entrance was free, so the moles would probably escape rather than fight.

"Captain Padra will be very cross," Said the hedgehog, trying very hard not to cry.

"Aah! Poor ickle hedgehog!" Said a mole.

"Aah!" said the other, and was turning away as Urchin sprang from the table. "Aaaarh!"

There was no need to fight. The moles had seen, not a young squirrel, but a raging armed warrior. The first fled, and the other followed as the flat of Urchin's sword skimmed across his flank.

–Urchin of the Riding Stars by M.I. McAllister, pg. 263

Urchin was young at heart but not small at heart. To become a true creature, be he a captain, a prince, a king, or merely a squirrel like no other, one must learn many things.

Bravery alone can sometimes defeat an enemy. At other times it takes perseverance and hard fighting. And the thing worth fighting for, kept clear in our mind's eye, is vital to winning the battle. Hold high before your heart the shield of faith in the goodness of the one who made the world, wield your sword for the downtrodden you defend, and in the end right will be done.

If we do not know what we risk our lives for, giving up seems a logical option when the fight grows long. For family, for friends, for law and order, for the apple pie on the table—in a word—we fight for the freedom of goodness. For justice, for love, for mercy, for knowledge and for truth itself.

And how does a young squirrel learn to do these things? By serving first among the lowest ranks, growing in knowledge and skill, and rescuing those he loves. As Urchin moves upward in sword-wielding and people-watching, he comes to know what he needs by feeling it, touching it, doing it. Making mistakes, of course, but fewer and fewer.

Until at last the time comes and a young squirrel and a king are ready. They contend for merry feasts of gathering under the oaks, for the right of an otter to swim in the sea about a tower, for a disturber of the peace to be brought to justice, and for a king to come into his own, one who cares for all creatures under the Creator's uplifting hand. Urchin sees a true king who is the first to go hungry when necessary, the first into a just fight, the last to retreat from enemies, and the last to sit down at a feast of plenty.

Here is an adventure of a lifetime, filled with triumph, tears, and trust. We journey with wise words gained from the pages of those who have traveled the sea of life before us, who watch us with unseen eyes full of glad expectation.

And how to join this journey to such places where such heart-knowledge is written, with more revealed every day?

Cracking on full sail, speed across the waves, the wind fresh in our face, and dream of lasting change, terrific inventions, fantastic beasts, and killer adventure on the ocean of fantasy. Dream of true greatness, all who are young at heart but great in spirit, while your deeds send ripples ahead of you. It's all there in DM Cornish's *Foundling,* Book 1 of the Monster Blood Tattoo series.

Dive 5.2

Every Guy's Dream—Terrific Inventions, Fantastic Beasts, and Killer Adventure

The snatched quill of a daring gull scratches the page of our book of knowledge, leaving a trail of reddish ink, much like the spilled blood of a monster of the sea. And the story of the monsters that we're reading come alive.

What makes a monster a monster? Is it strange and scary looks or smells, or pain, or cruelty or fear of harm?

In D. M. Cornish's Monster Blood Tattoo series, Book 1, we dive deep into what a monster is—and is not. Wasn't it Tolkien who said that not all that glitters is gold, not all those who wander are lost? An apt metaphor, in this case. A monster may have a true heart of gold underneath the most horrible skin, and a skin soft and clean may contain the most terrifying monster of all, as we discover with Rossamund. What will he unearth about the soul of monsters?

Rossamund held up his almanac. "I can't find it in here either."

"Well, that ain't surprising," Fouracres chuckled. "There's more kinds of monster than many a book could catalog."

He quickly became sad and serious. "Not that most folks think they're worth a-cataloging anyways. Most folks would rather just see them killed and that be the end of it or at most see a list of glaring faces tattooed ter the limbs of a teratologist. Still, worth a look."

Rossamund returned the book to his lap. "Uh . . . Mister Foura- cres, have you . . . ever killed a monster?"

"Unfortunately, Mister Rossamund, I have been forced ter do so, yes." The postman looked sad. "Yer see, if it's a choice 'twixt they or me, I choose me each time."

"Does that mean you have monster-blood tattoos, then?" Ros- samund could not help asking.

Fouracres hesitated, then frowned. "Well, no, actually. I don't go a-glorying in killings my hand's been forced to do. It's just part of getting the post ter where it needs ter be."

–Foundling by D. M. Cornish, pg. 239-240

On his journey to be a lamplighter on the edge of the empire, Ros- samund finds many delights and dangers: a lady teratologist, or monster-killer, whose inner health of cogs and organs he finds himself in charge of tending with organic mixtures—despite his secret sympa- thy for the monsters she pursues. Caught between his regard for both of them, and then swirled up in even wider tides among monster prince- lings, Rossamund must decide who is worthy of trust, and whether he will be worthy of it himself. Choosing requires all his wit and wisdom, if his brave courage is not too late.

Speaking of courage, most characters are a kaleidoscope of things they've done and seen and dared to overcome. But what happens when the three main adventurers in a story are two daring brothers and a crip- pled sister? With normal feelings of "the youngest," "the oldest," and, "I'm never as good as them"? No, this is not Narnia; there are three, not four children. But it is another scrumptious place full of peoples and creatures who come alive in their own right.

We'll laugh like never before, we'll run for our lives from the black carriage of Dang, and we'll stare with our mouth hanging open. Like the toothy cows of . . . but let us explore the irresistible Wingfeather saga in the next subchapter.

Get Hooked on a Fantasy Character Kaleidoscope

With laughter we enter the land of Anniera and the Wingfeather Saga, but in a different way than usual. We enter on the wings of the keen humor and wit of those who look ahead for their children with the understanding to encourage them to grow into the knowledge and experience they must have to grasp their destinies. To take hold of that for which they have been taken hold of.

"Are you crazy?" Janner interrupted.

Tink stared blankly at his brother, who looked at the door and lowered his voice.

"No way." Janner shook his head.

Tink's eyes twinkled. "You're the crazy one. How can you find a treasure map and not want to find the treasure?"

"It doesn't say 'treasure' anywhere on this map! In two days we've been in fights with two Fangs, thrown in jail, and almost taken for a ride in the Black Carriage. You've stolen a map, and Slarb's informed us that he means to kill us all! And now you want to follow a map to a haunted house near the forest because of a riddle that says that it leads to pain, woe, and sorrow?"

Tink grinned. "Yes."

Janner let out a wail.

"Shh!" Tink grimaced. "I'm just saying there's a lot more to this little town than we thought. Our mother has a hidden stash of jewels that we didn't know about. Mister Reteep gets an Annieran journal in a crate from Dang. He has a hidden map. And some mysterious person with perfect aim saved our lives yesterday."

Janner cocked his head. "You're right," he admitted. "I heard Podo and Ma say they think they know who saved our lives too."

Tink's brow creased.

Janner looked hard into Tink's eyes. "And there's something else. Something about our father."

Tink was silent.

"His name was Esben."

"Who told you that?" Tink asked softly.

"I heard Mama say it yesterday. I don't think she meant to."

"Esben," Tink said to himself.

–On the Edge of the Dark Sea of Darkness by Andrew Peterson, pg. 102

A father they have not seen and who is almost never spoken of, a kingdom of peril, and three children who are its future. When rivalry tears at them worse than the beast-shape Tink dooms himself to wear, what will they become? Can they overcome their jealous rivalries that would unravel their world?

That is a question that faces us all. What will we find? Treasure that holds their memories which fantasy tells best. Besides their stories, fantasy also holds the unexpected. Dragons fit that definition.

They are the more delightful—the good dragons—the more they surprise us. For dragons, startling and otherwise, make our spirits grow.

Don't You Need the Startling Truth of Genuine Dragons?

But, you protest, there are no such things as dragons. Try telling that to Eve, or Adam, when next you see them.

From *Eragon* and his good dragon Sapphira to evil Smaug in *The Lord of the Rings,* from creatures as small as dragonflies to those larger than houses, from nearly invisible beasts of air to those sleeping in mountains, the wit, guile, pleasure and power of dragons draw us like a lodestone. They have a propensity for involvement with matters of the heart and the kingdom, from peasant and king, to stolen princes and princesses. One who clothed himself in a dragon's skin is involved with the fall of the entire human race in our world. Wherever we face dragons, large or small, we do not come away unchanged.

Tipper could name most of the plants, but at the far end of the walkway, one unusual shrub caught her attention. The beauty of this bush fascinated Tipper. Tiny dark green leaves provided the backdrop to large, brilliant blooms. She had never seen a plant that put forth flowers in such a variety of colors.

She hurried down the path to examine it and stopped in shock as the blossoms uncurled and flew away. "Minor dragons!"

Dozens of minor dragons inhabited the foliage. She wandered the intertwining lanes in the expansive garden. Birds, butterflies, and dragons flitted from hedges to stands of miniature trees to flower beds.

–*The Dragons of Chiril* by Donita K. Paul, pg. 175

Who wouldn't love a dragon like that? Small enough to fit in our hand, delicate but strong of heart—as they are later shown to be.

But evil dragons in other tales—they are a fit companion of our enemy, named *dragon* or *serpent* in our world, from when he first conceived our fall. Bad dragons are patterned after him.

Such creatures are what they are to the core, and rightly make us shiver. Never believe them, though they whisper words we wish were true. Beware of our own hearts. We are all *lesser dragons* of the same ilk as Eustace was. Only our inner skins show it, until we are undressed and transformed. But take heart. If we're alive, change is always possible.

There is an order to the world that will not be denied. Though evil *dragons* of many kinds appear to reign in our world, they can be defeated. Good will win in the end—forever.

And dragons such as Sapphira, little Gymn, and even the sea-dragons of Anniera are indispensable to those of us who are happy to see good dragons in far worlds. The truth of dragons, good or bad, always calls us to courage.

In Narnia we face the same hard-hitting crown and claw of good and evil.

Dive 5.5

Where Narnia Reveals Hard-hitting Good and Evil

The crown and the claw of good and evil: those words right there would draw any lover of adventure to a new fantasy. And well they should, if we want to grow. Not grow *up*—grow inside. Do we know the difference? What grows besides our bodies and bones?

There are many points in Narnia where the crown and the claw of good and evil become clear. Though to many this is not a new fantasy to most of us, we have picked two points to savor.

> [The witch] *stood by Aslan's head. Her face was working and twitching with passion, but his looked up at the sky, still quiet, neither angry nor afraid, but a little sad. Then, just before she gave the blow, she stooped down and said in a quivering voice,*
>
> *"And now, who has won? Fool, did you think that by all this you would save the human traitor? Now I will kill you instead of him as our pact was and so the Deep Magic will be appeased. But when you are dead what will prevent me from killing him as well? And who will take him out of my hand then? Understand that you have given me Narnia forever, you have lost your own life and you have not saved his. In that knowledge, despair and die."* . . .
>
> *"It means," said Aslan, "that though the Witch knew the Deep Magic, there is a magic deeper still which she did not know. Her knowledge goes back only to the dawn of Time. But if she could*

have looked a little further back, into the stillness and the darkness before Time dawned, she would have read there a different incantation. ["Deep Magic" and "incantation" are metaphors here, or possibly the only name the witch had for what she would have seen.] *She would have known that when a willing victim who had committed no treachery was killed in a traitor's stead, the Table would crack and Death itself would start working backwards."*

–The Lion, the Witch and the Wardrobe by C. S. Lewis, pg. 152

The crown and the claw—the crown of goodness is the fact that it works against every evil, from the smallest unkind word to our greatest enemy, death. The claw of evil we know well—the darkness that hides behind a mask of desirable light, to destroy us. The struggle between the claw and the crown none can deny. There is no question between them of balance; between light and dark, the crown and the claw.

Evil and good are utter and un-reconcilable opposites, not two forces that feed each other in a natural order as Eastern yin-yang beliefs would have it.

The good planted in us, tainted though it is, calls our souls to grow, to admire the true hero and heroine in every fantasy and follow them in such small ways as we might. And in particular, we are drawn to heed the only hero in our own history who defeated death, calling us to follow him to victory.

The crown and claw of fantasy story affects us all. If we take heed, our spirits grow.

Most of us cut our teeth on the Chronicles of Narnia at some point. Don't miss the movies. The older three put out by BBC are good, and of the more recent movies, *The Lion the Witch and the Wardrobe* with Andrew Adamson is best. In the latest two movies, *Prince Caspian* and *The Voyage of the Dawn Treader,* the truth has been watered down. Yet good remains.

In preparation for our next dive, few of us deny bullies are one claw of evil. Unless we are bullies ourselves, of course. Friends are made for the fiery forge that bullies bring into play against us. But what if the friend who could save us was an enemy?

Fantasy adventure is wondrously twisty, especially when it involves a slight archer named Will against battle school bullies and his enemy, Horace, another of the bullies' victims. Until Will and Horace band together.

Dive 5.6

Rousing Fantasy Adventure is Wondrous Easy to Follow

We all know bullies, don't we?

The Ranger's Apprentice series is a great work in nine books. A light, quick-stepping, but deep story with similarities to Robin Hood, if we picture him a young orphan raised by castle folk and employed by foresters to become a defender of the kingdom.

In *The Ruins of Gorlan*, Will, a scrawny underdog with plenty of scrappiness, learns the right road is not always what he thinks it is. Doing the right thing is not always easy, but it is worth every blister of training to become a true ranger's apprentice. And an enemy won is a friend who sticks closer than a brother when bullies come to call.

> *Horace looked at his long-time tormentor, then at the sword in his hand. "I don't need this," he muttered, and let the sword drop.*

> *The right-hand punch that he threw traveled no more than twenty centimeters to the point of Alda's jaw. But it had his shoulder and body weight and months of suffering and loneliness behind it—the loneliness that only a victim of bullying can know.*

> *Will's eyes widened slightly as Alda came off his feet and hurtled backward, to come crashing down in the cold snow beside his two friends. He thought about the times in the past when he had*

fought with Horace. If he'd known the other boy was capable of throwing a punch like that, he never would have done so.

Alda didn't move. Odds were, he wouldn't move for some time, Will thought. Horace stepped back, shaking his bruised knuckles and heaving a sigh of satisfaction.

"You have no idea how good that felt," he said. "Thank you, Ranger."

Halt nodded acknowledgment. "Thank you for taking a hand when they attacked Will. And by the way, my friends call me Halt."

–*The Ruins of Gorlan* by John Flanagan, pg. 164

United we stand. And not just the strong. For the strongest of us have at least one weakness, usually several. And it only takes one weakness, yielded to once, to bring us down. In fact, we are usually down, at least in small ways, more than we are up.

Weak people may also have this advantage—they know their weaknesses so well that they admit them, and accept help when they cannot rescue themselves, and build good habits to guard against them. Humility is truthful—and so it is exceedingly hopeful. Change is always possible—and just around the corner in fantasy. To create lasting change we may have to stand as fixed as ivory marble and be persistent as flowing water, like queen Shahrazad.

Dive 5.7

The Romance of the Glittering Treasure of Shahrazad

Just as we sail the sun-sparked sea of fantasy, drop anchor, dive and then return to an unexpectedly gathering storm, so change is inescapable to a hero or heroine. For are not stories supposed to change us?

Do you not think so? If you believe yourself unchanged by fantasy, just think back to the last story you read where you felt something strongly. It can be anything you felt deeply. What thoughts went through your mind? Then tell us you believe yourself completely unchanged, and we may concede the point. Though we say with a laugh, that our journey is not yet done, and we hope to enchant you thoroughly!

The greatest storyteller of them all lives in the palace, where the Sultan no longer kills his wives of one night. Marjan discovers that her heroine, who inspired her to spin her own stories, desperately searches for tales to tell the Sultan that he has not yet heard. She enters a world of daring and danger, where integrity does not live in the same breath with intrigue. But they must in Marjan, if the gems of stories, especially the gleaming facet of a new tale, are the price of life and death, laid down to buy palace-shaking change. Marjan can spin the shadows of stories to reflect change *and* bring it about. Though the change may be difficult, it is the same for a princess, as for a mother, a daughter, a girl in our world.

My heart stood still. The rest of it. *I didn't know any rest of it. I groped back through my memory, trying to remember the name of Julnar's son—trying to remember* anything *about Julnar's son other than the things I had already told, about how he was taken down into the sea as an infant, about the magic that made him able to breathe there. I was* certain *I hadn't heard his name.*

Shahrazad was still smiling at me. She looked eager, happy—so different from the day before. I didn't want to tell her that I didn't know what she needed to know. I didn't want to watch her face, how it was going to change.

"Marjan?" She looked puzzled.

I took a deep breath. "My lady," I said. "I am so very sorry. Truly I am. But . . . I know nothing of Julnar's son other than what I've told you. Neither his name nor anything that happened to him after his uncle brought him back from the sea."

A breeze rustled in the curtain that draped the lattice. In the distance, I heard a tinkling of chimes. Shahrazad's face did not change, but rather froze, as if time were no longer flowing, but stood in a quiet pool.

–*Shadow Spinner* by Susan Fletcher, pg. 43

One scarlet thread winds love and jealousy and death closer than lovers, soul to soul. Of the many forms of love, that between man and woman draws endless bright threads through fantasy. Love must grow, and deepen, if it is not to die. In *Shadow Spinner* love will either sink into evil and jealousy, or rise through the pressing depths toward light and life. And we will bring one of the grandest adventures of all aboard. True love is something we must grow into.

When the made-up cultural mask of romantic pretense and the dirt of cheap lust are seen through, first by child-like curiosity and then by our earnest search for romance as the years pass, we are at last grown ready for our heart's blooming into the red rose of true love's passion, sacrifice, and sweetness. For those of us who have fallen to lust or pretense, there is cleansing and hope in the next chapter. *Can You Claim the Passionate, Fiery Heart of Clean Romance?*

Chapter 6.0

Can You Claim the Passionate, Fiery Heart of Clean Romance?

Yes, we can. In forgiveness of past mistakes and wrong, hope is sown, and it blooms in good, right choices.

For most of us, the passionate fire involved in romance—in our dreaming of our loved one and in courtship—is a given. But how does "clean" come into it? And rare as clean passion is in fantasy, what does it even mean? What does it mean for our love, and what does it mean in our stories?

"Clean romance" simply means honorable contact between us and the one we love—in touch, in mind, and in spirit. It means we love and respect the other person enough not to harm them and ourselves by the flawed, fallible, false "compatibility gauntlet" of sleeping or living together before we're married. As for needing *experience*, good things only grow in the honorable doing of them.

Sex and love do not always mean the same thing. Sex in its rightful place is only one expression of love, and utterly holy. Tosca Lee relates this in *Havah: the Story of Eve,* where she contrasts sex as love versus lust, as an act of glorious giving versus insatiable devouring. Our goal is not the practice and experience of lust, but love. And that comes at the proper time, grown sweet and powerful with the waiting and the trust.

I have not quoted *Havah* in case young eyes that parents believe un-ready are eager to add to their book of knowledge. Younger readers, this is one place wisdom comes in. Remember that understanding must be paired with knowledge.

But Tosca's story of Eve never makes us blush with shame because of dirty details. It's a good example of how human love should be treated, in our world and that of fantasy, unveiling the relational world of the heart, spirit, and body, and the cosmic struggle between sin and holiness, wrong and right, evil and good, moral and immoral.

In fantasy, clean romance means not having to sift through mind pictures of intimate things to be cherished between lovers at the right time, by them alone. It means not having to wade through filth thrown on a beautiful thing. Though no one ever succeeds in making love itself ugly, only themselves by their twisting of it.

Stolen fruit rots as it is eaten. Waiting, an action that seeks the other's good and not its own desire, bears the sweet perfume of love's unfolding bloom. There it reveals its heart. A treasure that grows, and gives, a living gem.

True love in fantasy is an ocean in itself, with a myriad mysteries and precious things to be found in its depths. Unavoidable storms come to romantic fantasy, as they come to every love in every world, but they may be weathered, and the sun usually shines all the brighter on the other side for the cleansing rain of conflict.

We freely acknowledge we are but wayfarers on the ocean of ro-mance.

In *Tahn* a kidnapped baron's daughter finds that her vision of a soul mate navigates dangerous shoals of truth and lie, then in *Shadowed Eden* a time-traveler's soul rises unvanquished under abuse. A prin-cess's wounded heart in *Deerskin* is healed as she learns to risk love again. Romance between warriors is sweet to the soul when they com-plement each other in *The Blue Sword*. A betrayed, captive love is proven through the fire of warring kingdoms in *The Crown of Eden*, and the faithfulness of young love in near-Regency England in *A School for*

Unusual Girls is the kind a soul can long for. In *A Posse of Princesses* the treachery of princes cannot kill love, and in *Falcon Heart* a love broken for the sake of another creates a love deeper yet. A gentle healer discovers strength and fire in her soul in *The Bonemender*.

Fantasies all, here true love rises above war, death, dreams, and life itself. We will dive in exotic waters, sail farther, and discover rich, uncharted lands to scribe in glory in our book of knowledge.

Dive 6.1

Encounter the Rare Vision of Your Proven Soul Mate

There is a common phrase, "soul mate." We hear things like "Ohhh—he must be your soul mate," or "If she did that, there's no way she could be your soul mate." This idea seems especially prevalent in shape-shifting fantasy.

The idea implies that when our lover fails to meet our pleasure or expectation, the love between us was not meant to be, or was not true. This usage of *soul mate* overlooks the fact that we are *all* flawed jewels, and that as we are shaped by our Creator, we are becoming less flawed. None of us is a perfect soul mate. *We* say soul mates are not born, but created. Some may say that is ridiculous.

Can we not agree that we are born with the natural *feeling* of affection? But when affection fails, as it does quickly, what then? Love works through purpose, our Creator's and our own. Love *purposes* that no contrary feeling, no unloveliness, will stand in its way of loving another. Our goal is the absolute best for the one for whom we care: we desire a communion of souls, to enjoy each other and the heights and depths of our hearts, and to grow together, for good.

And there lurks the problem, in our heart, that bright castle high on a cliff above the sea. In our highest garden of delight and in the ocean of our heart's depths below the parapets wait monsters from the darkest deeps of fantasy, circling our hidden treasures. The one-eyed giant of self-will, the cold sea-dragon of selfishness, and the whining imp of self-love.

Their fierce, yellow gazes are focused on one thing, our opened vaults under castle-pave and sea wave. When we who keep our castle troves yield to the myopic, one-eyed giant of self-will with rending nails, when we hesitate before the selfish, cold sea-dragon that whips its coils about us quicker than thought, or if we pet the whining imp of self-love who bites so cruelly in the end, leaving jagged and gaping wounds, then the bitterness of death will cast a pall over our joined souls. The treasures we once shared with smiles and laughter when we opened our vaults or dove for jewels together can turn to loss and hate.

But love is stronger than steel, harder than diamond, more enduring than gold. It lives and breathes to defeat these deadly creatures seeking our very lives.

Two hearts *become* soul mates when they defend their castle gardens and dare to laugh in them, and kill their marauding monsters—together; as they dive for precious gems and hunt their dragons—together. Loss and hate can turn again, into a deeper, truer love.

Though our enemies infect us by pain and strangulation and deadly bite, we can seize the hate and loss and step inside our Creator's glowing smelting pot. We emerge unhurt, but not unchanged. The dross of evil destroyed in stinking black smoke, we can hold the shape of love in our hands and hearts, and with our Maker's wisdom, forge a blade between us far stronger than steel, harder than diamond, more enduring than gold.

But the sword of truth and love is not created or wielded without sweat and tears. The labor may be long, to hone the glittering beauty of the weapon and the skill to protect our homes and hearts.

So in a fantasy story, when a girl secure in her castle is overcome by assassins of murder and ambition from without, and one assassin leaves her with a vault of confusion, loss, and hate, how does she see that vision of her soul-mate change?

Torn by inner monsters, this assassin may turn again. For her dese-
crated vaults are nothing to his, though both are haunted by fear and
doubt. But love will always prove itself, as the furnace is for gold.
Strong, warm arms, living, and loving, and sharing—are the rarest
treasures of any realm.

*The following evening, Netta finally got an opportunity to speak
to Father Anolle as they both entered the sanctuary alone.*

*"Father, I am troubled," she began. "I need to speak to you
about Mr. Dorn."*

"Yes?"

*Netta fidgeted with a dress ruffle. "I—I respect what he's done
for us. And I rejoice at his salvation."*

*The priest looked confused. "Then why are you troubled, daugh-
ter?"*

*She burst out with the words before she could think better of it.
"I don't want to think too much of him! It concerns Jarel. He
feels I could become too attached. Am I being unwise to care
about him?"*

"You would be un-Christlike if you did not care."

"But do I care too much, Father? Or inappropriately?"

Anolle smiled. "You'll find your heart."

*"Jarel says he could be dangerous. And I had such a fear of him
before. But I don't see it now. What do you think? Is he yet dangerous?"*

*"I have no doubt, daughter, that if you were in peril, he would
be dangerous to your assailant."*

*Netta shook her head. "Not only me. He would help you or any-
one else, surely. You don't think he has a special care for me, do
you? Vari thinks he does, but Vari's a bit of a dreamer."*

"It will take him some time, Netta, to know his heart and accept it. He does not see himself in the light others see him."

"What do you mean?"

"We see the lives he's saved. But he sees himself as a man struggling for a footing in faith, with no special virtues to his credit."

Netta stared at him. "No virtues? He has such strength! To survive, and to reach out—"

Father Anolle smiled.

"Oh!" She shook her head in embarrassment. "You must think Jarel right, how I talk! But I never expected to find good in such a nightmare."

"Peace, child. There is no harm in gratitude nor in admiration."

"But—"

"Love is of God, Netta. You'll have to sort out your own heart and trust what you find there. And that is not Jarel's job to do. Your father would appreciate you sharing your feelings. But he will not be too greatly troubled, I think. He accepts Mr. Dorn as an honorable man with a captive past."

–Tahn by L. A. Kelly, pgs. 246-248

"A captive past." Is that not what love does? Kills our monsters, binds their corpses with ropes of forgiveness, and puts bitterness and hatred to the blade, releasing us to deeper and higher love? May we be such lovers, and free the 'soul-mates' in each other.

Then when we travel through time, and abuse comes unexpected, we can learn to rise through it with a heroine, un-vanquished, on wings of healing.

Dive 6.2

Devastating Abuse Comes Unexpected but Rise Unvanquished

Abuse can come with a blow or a word. Aren't abusing words insidious? They are sometimes hard for us to acknowledge because they leave no visible mark, and we somehow feel they should not pain us, though they pierce us like a spear. So they are all the more deadly, as we do not staunch the blood flowing from our hearts.

When someone treats us as if what we want, and need, and do, and dream of are as worthless as ourselves who hold them precious, they can destroy us drop by bloody drop. We can come to believe what their abusing words say about us if we do not fight back.

We must learn to wield the sword of truth and love in our minds. We cannot allow anyone to tear apart our true self, given by our Creator. Entering the fray, we must deflect the flashing spears of cruel, untrue words. For to love ourselves means to defend who God made us to be, in the outworking of his salvation, holding high the shield of faith in the new creation he has made us.

Young Avery travels on the ocean of fantasy in the current of time, learning the ways of the sword in Katie Clark's *Shadowed Eden*.

"Should we try to find it?"

Luca shook his head. "After all that? No way. Maybe you should talk to him, Aves."

She gnawed on her lip as she walked. "Daddy won't listen to me. He never has." The realization wasn't a nice one. He didn't care what was best for anyone except himself, not even when it came to his own daughter. He wanted her going away, finding her own life, and he'd pay good money for it. If she stuck close to home, he'd feel responsible for her. She might expect things of him.

The truth hurt.

–*Shadowed Eden,* Kindle excerpt, by Katie Clark

Yes, truth can hurt. But when it identifies and removes evil, the blade makes room for healing.

Wounds of the heart and soul can be healed as well as those of the body. Healing takes the burning of cleansing time and the struggle of painful growth, leavings signs of the wound, but it will close if we dare to love again. *Deerskin* tells how one young heart was wounded under most awful abuse, but found healing among friends. Friends undreamed of, along with a friend who draws closer yet, and shows her clean passion is possible.

Deerskin Retells How a Wounded Heart Can be Healed

After being hurt almost to death by another's lust, it takes extreme courage to love and to accept love again. Is it not part of fantasy's purpose to show us the road to overcoming?

In the unconditional devotion and protection of her regal dog, Ash, who accompanies Deerskin in her escape from horror, healing begins. This retelling of *Donkeyskin* contains love's courage, to risk the hope it holds dear and to give all that should be given to another who is worthy. Even when new love's capacity is wrapped in strangling memories of betrayal, pain, and destruction, love can step out and dare to call the memory and the present what they are. It dares the moment and holds out both hands to offer and take true love.

Deerskin is betrayed in her body by her father, who ought to have been her defender against all things unholy, and she struggles to recognize a friend who is strong enough to love her as she should be loved.

She remembered the three days and nights of her life as a princess; remembered the draining away of that life, and the last violent act that she believed had killed her. Even now, her body's wounds healed by time and Ash and snow and solitude and Moonwoman, and six puppies, and the friendship of a prince and a stable-hand; even now the memory of that act of violence would shatter her; she could not contain the memory even as her body had not been able to contain the result of its betrayal.

"Deerskin," said her friend. "What is wrong?"

–Deerskin by Robin McKinley, pg. 222

Just a fellow traveler asking that—being there—concerned, may be the hand that holds us back from the pit, may be the heart that gives us leave to seek joy, that pushes us out on the waters of love to sail again. Loving includes vulnerability to some degree.

We must arm ourselves with outward-looking love and prayer and our sword on the adventurous road to overcoming, knowing that only our Creator always loves us perfectly. We love because he first loved us, and we must love in all our ways with all our strength as he grows the priceless bloom within our wounded spirits. What a destiny of marvelous mystery beyond our imagining!

In the oceans of fantasy there are many who seek romantic love. Some are warriors of heart and body, and when they meet, bound by the steel of a blue sword, honor becomes a precious thing.

Dive 6.4

Dream of Warrior Love in *The Blue Sword**

Humor. It can defuse tense situations, add perspective to too-serious hearts, and lift the spirit to unrealized heights. *The Blue Sword* has a wry sense of humor that fits Harimad-sol extremely well, adding laughter to the human story of warrior love in a way no other fantasy we have ever explored has done.

Life is not easy, in fantasy or our world, still less is love. Moving to a strange land, an unknown people, unsure of how one fits in one's own head and heart, not to mention being kidnapped by the king of the hills of Damar, is enough to try the mettle of any soul. And being the bridge to peace between two kingdoms is a fire hot enough to melt any blade and forge it anew.

Angharad or Hari is no exception, earning her new name, Harimad-sol, from the people who take her by force into the desert and the hills of the North. Foremost among them, the king, Corlath, regards her as a rather prickly inconvenience to both his conscience and his plans. Until Hari strikes out on a doomed journey to stop a threat to the kingdom she has come to love as well as the kingdom she left behind. Each must trust the other, or lose their lives, their lands, and their love.

I am not sure why I overlook the mentions of "goddess" and magic in this book. I do know it is at least partially because the magic in the land of Damar is more of a birthright, like sci-fi telepathy, a created gift rather than the power of the evil one which hides behind the mask of magick; magick that a person takes and wields to his or her own ends through spells and consorting with demons and dangerous inner desires for power. Power of any sort, magical or otherwise, certainly never came in any way *from* us unless it was first *given*. And the question is, given by who?

The 'who' determines the source of the magic—whether it is the simple powerful word of The Emperor over Sea—or the magick incantations of the dark one, hiding his designs behind pretensions of a being of light who wants to help us find our inner power. We know the tree by its fruit.

Love can also be proved by the blade. The moment of decision sometimes arrives almost unnoticed.

Corlath grinned down at her, and she could not help smiling back. "There have been more graceful kings and Riders since the world began, but we'll do," said Corlath to her, quietly, below the roar around them. "Take your sword, and mind you treat her well. You will have Aerin's shade to answer to, else."

Harry's fingers closed round the blue hilt and she knew at once that she would handle this sword very well indeed—or it would handle her. For a moment she found herself wishing that she had been carrying Gonturan the day of the trials, and at this a slow sly smile spread across her face. She raised her eyes to Corlath's face—he had taken his own sword back and sheathed it, and one of the Riders was tying the napkin around the wounded hand and saying something sardonic; but Corlath only laughed, and turned back to watch her. Such was the slow sly smile he offered her in return that she rather thought he knew just what she was thinking.

–*The Blue Sword* by Robin McKinley, pg. 138

The goodness in *The Blue Sword,* remnants of morality from the age the author was born in, though not sustained by conviction of biblical understanding beyond that brief acknowledgement, still upholds doing what is right because it *is* right. Bravery, humor, mercy, tenacity, truth-fulness—all find their way onto the path Hari carves with her blue sword, which has a personality of its own. Beyond Hari's trial of her love by the blade, in fantasy there is also the trial by fire. Love is proved through the flame—beyond dreams and in an enemy's court.

Prove Your Love Through Fire in *The Crown of Eden*

Fire is known for its purifying power, even in our world. It kills disease, melts away untrue substances, gives a heart blazing strength when it needs it most, and warms all who gather to its light. And however low the flame of love flickers, it cannot be hidden.

When love between two royal houses is foretold as a meeting of starfire of gold and silver in the heavens, two hearts are plunged into a fiercer proving than most.

> *"The prophecy is too great a matter for me to comprehend fully, but I believe in you, Father, and on the strength of that, I willingly obey the terms of your vow."*
>
> *The heart of the king leapt for joy at his daughter's promise, but he choked back the pride that swelled in his throat and said, "The grace of heaven is that such commitments are credited as if they were dedicated to their proper object. In time you will come to know more fully the higher power that guides me and will place your trust directly in him, but for now, your commitment to my commitment is enough.*
>
> *"Now listen well, my daughter. There is one thing you must be very careful to remember. Whatever the cost, you must not marry the crown prince until the terms of the prophecy are fulfilled— until the Crown of Eden rests upon his head and the golden comet*

blends with the silver star. If you wed before these events occur, disastrous results will surely follow."

–*The Crown of Eden* by Thomas Williams, pg. 88

There are always consequences when a single path divides around the double-edged blade of choice. He who chooses wisely will find a treasure, though it be hard gained, he who does not will find a sea-nest of horrors. It would be well to explore the depths and heights of every realm, especially our own, with our eyes open and our heart ready.

The wisdom of being faithful to the one we love, in ways far beyond the simple physical sense, brings a wealth of adventure and a growing strength. We even find the faithful relationships of gifted students in a school for unusual girls surprisingly attractive in numerous ways.

Dive 6.6

The Surprising Attraction of Faithful Relationships in *A School for Unusual Girls*

One small point of faithfulness is often the point from which our reach expands in ever-widening rings to touch others, far beyond our knowledge. In fantasy especially, the sphere of the spiritual touches ideas, and ideas touch the realm we breathe in.

Four talented girls cast to the doubtful mercies of an 'unusual' boarding school in a near-Regency alternate world of fantasy where Napoleon is taking over the seas and their land's borders must learn to rely upon each other, and the men they love. And be faithful to them, in every way needed. A girl cannot be fragile, blown about by every traitor who whirls her around the ballrooms, or overcome by the vapors of perfumed treachery.

I was stumbling and panting for air when Tess caught up with me. Her expression looked grim. That meant I'd failed. The nightmare was still in place. I wanted to scream in anguish. It was grotesquely unfair. Cruel. How could so much rest on one failure? One mistake? And dear God in heaven, why must it be my mistake?

My stride faltered. I wanted to collapse right there on the street, wanted to crumble into tears of regret, wanted to scream at the perverseness of the universe. But I couldn't. My lungs burned like

*the fires of hell and my heart felt heavier than a fieldstone, but I
knew if I gave up now Sebastian would die. That lone thought
drove me forward. The whole continent might sink into ruin because of me, but the truth is I thumped each bruised foot, one
after the other, because of Sebastian. Call me selfish, I could not
bear the thought of living in this muddled world without him in
it. He would surrender his own life to save all those thousands of
strangers. I could do no less, to save him.*

–*A School for Unusual Girls* by Kathleen Baldwin*, pg. 270

Trust is a risk, but it is worth every pain to give the one we love this
priceless gift: that we believe them capable of faithfulness. Faithful love
trusts despite risks. We can help each other grow into this high calling
and continue in it. The treasure to be won is vast.

But learning about love inevitably brings treacherous acts to light.
Some by design and some without ill motive. And how hard might it be
to discern treacherous design when we cannot see our heart's unmean-
ing betrayal? But we must never trust the heart consistently set on
treachery, for that risk is an entirely different thing than a heart struggling to find its way. Discerning between the two treads dangerous
ground.

Dive 6.7

A Rare and Magnificent Love on Treacherous Ground

What happens when the one we love has put in motion a most perfidious plan? Then our love is tested by the ability, or the lack of it, to see through another's eyes. At a getaway ball for all the heirs of the kingdoms, where the crown prince will choose one princess, how far will one girl go against what is expected to see right done? Can she remain herself in the conflicting tides of others' approval and disapproval, amid weaknesses and strengths, the intrigue of the self-sacrificing and the self-serving? Even to the rise and fall of kingdoms?

Why didn't she want to face Dandiar? Too many thoughts all yammering for her attention. Shera—Glaen—Lios—Iardith—Yuzhyu—even Taniva, and her odd attitude at breakfast.

Dandiar. Why did it upset her so, to find him kissing Yuzhyu's cheek? Whether that 'brother and sister' talk was true or not, Rhis could understand why Yuzhyu had come to see her about it—she didn't want gossip. The thought that Dandiar was prowling this empty hall, maybe looking for her to get reassurance about Rhis not blabbing it around, made her tense with disgust. No, more than disgust, with anger.

Why? She blinked rain from her eyelashes, rambling faster down the pathway as her thoughts galloped along. Dandiar. How much fun he was! And interesting. She liked him better than anyone else. Oh, he wasn't handsome like Lios or that grim, tough Jarvas, or powerful and wealthy, like half-a-dozen others easily named, but he was so very much . . . himself.

She'd never met anyone like him. She'd felt, without even knowing it, that she could talk to him forever, that she would search every corner of her mind for something interesting to say, just to see that sudden smile with the shadowy quirk at the corners of his mouth, and the way his eyebrows rose in a sort of rueful humor, like a silent sharing of a private joke, just between Dandiar and Rhis. She liked the way he'd looked so appreciatively at her the night of the masquerade, admiration making his gaze linger. Nobody else's admiration made her feel outlined in light.

–A Posse of Princesses by Sherwood Smith*, pg. 146

Light. The way we look at others, and what we see in them, what we persist in seeing, has immense power. Love seeks and sees the other's good.

If we choose to see clearly the mix that most of us are, yet encourage the good, much can be done to protect our love against the blows of the world—and self-condemnation. For even our inner, just condemnation against ourselves should always bring us to the seat of mercy, where *forgiven* is a word unending—if we accept our Creator's gift. Then with that restoring elixir of sure, oxygenating hope, we can dive deep into the ocean to fight the monsters we find there, indeed, anywhere, and return to our ship with treasure untold, fully justified, forever. To be forgiven and to extend it is a large part of love; to seek the other's good and not our own, as Rhis did for Dandiar.

But how can one discover such rich, uncharted places when a love will bring destruction?

Dive 6.8

The Reverse Romance—Love Refused Creates Conflict—or Character

We may refuse love for many reasons. "Refuse love?!" Some may gasp. Yes. It is not safe to follow everyone of royal blood to their realm, even in fantasy.

What if instead of bringing up a hidden chest of imperishable gems from beneath the clear ocean waves of a bright reef, some instead choose to dwell in the cold deeps—forever. And so transform into something less than human. They offer for love what is most precious to them—a drowned enchanted lair where an iron anchor binds them to a sandy golden bed, and their throne commands a myriad creatures of the abyss.

Though we all have more than a bit of the monster about us, still we cannot sanely choose to make ourselves more beast-like by joining ourselves to someone who is. Sometimes we must make a difficult choice, even if the beastly one turns out to be a prince or princess. They may be heir to the under-realm. We must discover which realm calls them ruler, the one above, or the one below.

Before the feast Faisal walked past her tent on his way up from the Twilket camp. His grandfather's tents spread from the spring down along the wadi, a black flood into the desert. He saw her, lying on her back, open-eyed beside Alaina. His eyes were hot coals, then he averted his stony gaze and went inside the tent—his no longer but Tae's—and yanked the flap closed.

Kyrin rolled over, burying her face in her cushion. So Gershem Salin agreed with her and Tae. It was not a fit handfasting.

What might it have been like to walk with Faisal in the majesty of the desert, unbound, on her way home. To go before her father as a bride; to hunt rabbits and Wudhaihi, to laugh at each other's shots, to eat hot gazelle, drink sweet tea, and paint her hands with bright henna flowers? What would she give to see Faisal's smile light his face, to feel his kiss like the desert wind over her skin? Faisal would come to see their Father, he had goodness in him—and when his anger forged him to a brittle blade, they would destroy each other.

He must let love in, before he can love me. I wish I had never seen him. No, no I don't.

–Falcon Heart by Azalea Dabill, pg. 268

Sometimes a prince must be left to his choices. Either his own anchor will devour his bones at the last, or love will draw him above the waves to life. In the unavoidable storm of love torn or challenged, he must choose: love or hate, God or devil.

However much our heart weeps, hoping and believing the best of a beast-man or beast-woman is not enough. They must be given space to think, their choices made clear by time and action. Which is growing stronger, self-love or true love?

Which do they feed? That is the question, and on the answer hinges their destiny. And mayhap ours, if we choose to bind our heart to theirs.

The best fantasy romance bears this out in *The Bonemender,* where love grows from shallower considerations to the deepest triumphant conquest of themselves.

Dive 6.9

Discover the Best Fantasy Romance in
The Bonemender

In waiting for her love, often in stories the woman exhibits great patience. But for an elf to wait for a human woman? That is far rarer. Feolan's patience, gentleness, and strength call to us on a million levels.

> *"Gabi, I'm so sorry to have hurt you." He had never called her that. No one but Tristan had ever called her that. "But I don't understand. I know this is a shock, but is it so impossible?"*
>
> *"Of course it's impossible."*
>
> *"But why? I mean, why for you? We could still have a lifetime together—one of your lifetimes. How is that different from what you would have with another Human?"*
>
> *Gabrielle stared at him. He didn't see it. She had told him to spell things out for her. Now she would have to do the same.*
>
> *"Feolan, think about it. I will not be like I am now until the day I die. I am twenty-seven years old. In thirty years I'll be gray and stiff in the joints. For the last twenty years of my life I'll be a wrinkled, bent, frail old woman, and you will be in the full flush of youth. You won't be my lover—you'll be my nursemaid."*
>
> *Feolan bowed his head. He sat in silence for a long while, and when he looked up, he did not hide the wetness on his cheeks.*

"Yet would I walk with you to the end, if you would have me."

–The Bonemender by Holly Bennett, pg. 55

Love rises above self-interest. In many ways Feolan and Gabrielle's story is a clear drink of water in a desert. The loving relationships that grow between their races, between the king and his daughter, between Gabrielle and her mother, sister and brother, friend and enemy—they're all here in a depth we've rarely seen in fantasy. This gem is worth diving for, and the treasures we find in it will surely fill a page or two of our book of knowledge.

Leaving the emotion of new, true, and tried love in fantasy, our vessel gains the waves beyond. Those of combat—from weapons and tactics to the supernatural and visionary—in *The Groundbreaking Conflict of Spirits at War in the Worlds.*

Chapter 7.0

The Groundbreaking Conflict of Spirits at War in the Worlds

Some may say fantasy combat is always very unrealistic. We see their point. *If* they mean stories where a sudden miracle out of story context saves the day, or the hero gains an illogical, unstoppable power, or the heroine performs flying martial arts, though beautiful in grace, which would never stop an enemy. Don't think we don't like Wushu. We love the action in *Crouching Tiger, Hidden Dragon.* But we do recognize it is not humanly, physically realistic.

But there is one place where combat is utterly real, always—inside the mind, heart, and spirit where the ground is set for any conflict to be won—or lost. If we lose there, we lose outwardly, no matter our fighting method or weapon. The inner fight determines the results of the outer. For the inner fight is a moral one, either a wrong choice or a right choice fought and decided in the core of our beings.

Warfare in the inner and outer realm takes training, as any skill does. Aspects of both are usually taught together for strength of mind, spirit, and body. In Ji Do Kwan Tae Kwon Do the five tenets are courtesy, integrity, perseverance, self-control, and indomitable spirit. Becoming a warrior is not learned overnight. We can train a few weeks in unarmed combat, but then we are more a soldier with a little training than a warrior.

Becoming a warrior from the outside in takes years of sweat and perseverance until the particular methodology is ingrained in every pore and every heart-fiber. Spiritual warfare, which began the moment we were born, requires directing and honing from the inside out.

We fight with what we are born with in the inner arena, with tactics and weapons on the sands of the outer arena, and combine the knowledge gained in mind and body. But in the next dimension, the spiritual world beyond the bright blue waves of fantasy books and the clouds we see on our horizon, we discover we may win some battles with courage, strength, and indomitable spirit alone, but that we are losing the moral war.

It is the invisible war that spills constantly into the visible world. In the war of right against wrong in our inner arena, our small weapons of courage, truth, and will avail little, for they are flawed. Until, that is, we change allegiance and follow the only person who won his moral war, aligning our will with that of our Creator's son. In his victory, his conquering of our greatest enemies, our victory is assured. Then, every good thing is possible to us.

Most often, rather than casting fire upon our enemies in a miraculous blast, our Creator transforms, empowers, and trains *us,* enabling us to rise to the groundbreaking conflict of spirits at war in the worlds. Nothing is impossible that fits the peace or danger of the moment, which we are willing to put our hand to at his command. He wants us to learn moral warfare from the inside out, where all battles begin. In him we are indomitable at last.

The war is deeper and wider than we dream, and we see but a small part of it at any one time, whether we voyage through our own world on the physical and spiritual planes, or in the world of fantasy. But that we may become fit for our part in the fight—that takes training. We learn our warfare from the inside out, and the outside in.

He trains us for that war—on both planes—that visible conflict that we have always known and the invisible battle we are coming to know deeper. To trust in the rock above ourselves and our limited knowledge—that is the secret of our strength. Wisdom gives us the wit and will to rely on our only enduring source of power.

By training in the inner arena, our Creator also arms us for every outer battle, whether we rise to victory or fall within the ranks of right, whether we win in this world or pass in the final fight to our high home. At every moment wisdom is the key to knowledge, and understanding is a treasure chest holding weapons both old and new. The discipline of endurance in pain, and sorrow, and defeat are lessons just as important as the triumph of skill in times of strength, and joy, and victory.

So while we search out fantasy adventures, and fight alongside the struggle for good in their pages, remember our true strength and ability and training, and the moral battle. And whether we are strong or weak in body, winning our battles first lies in the unseen realm. Then that war spills into the seen. We should be ready to fight as best we may in both worlds to defend the right.

Study fantasy tactics in The Deed of Paksenarrion, and search out the hidden strengths of early Tae Kwon Do in unarmed combat in *Falcon Heart*, and train far more than your body in *Arena*. Fortify seen and unseen defenses of a kingdom in *Oath of Gold*. Inner vision leads to war in *Falcon Flight,* and the supernatural hits with an edge of the real in Legends of the Guardian King. Fight well from the outside in—and the inside out—on every plane, in every sphere.

Dive 7.1

Amazing Fantasy Tactics in The Deed of Paksenarrion*

Fantasy follows the rules and realities of warfare in our world in many ways. We believe everyone will admit that people who have been in battle situations tend to have the knowledge, the skill, and the feel for what is necessary to overcome their opposition—such as gathering all the tactics they can from others' experience.

We need to know our objective, the stakes, and the best way to gain the goal.

Along with all this, they were introduced to tactics. Paks had thought that after mastering the intricacies of drill, nothing remained to learn about engaging the enemy. She was wrong.

"But I thought that we just ran at them and started fighting," said Vik, echoing her thought.

"No, that's the way to get killed, and quickly. None of you will make these decisions now, but you all need to know something of tactics. You can do your job better if you know what you're trying to accomplish." They were gathered around Stammel in the messhall between meals; he began to set out apples on the table. "Now suppose this—here—is the Duke's Company. And this over here is the enemy. Look at the length of lines."

"Theirs is longer," said Saben, stating the obvious. "But we—"

"Listen. Now suppose we engage just as we are. What happens on each end of our line, on the flanks?"

"They can hit the side too," said Vik.

"If they have enough, they can go all around," Paks put in.

"Yes, that looks bad, doesn't it? But it depends on why their line is so long, and what they're fighting with." He added more apples to the array. "Suppose they've only as many men as we have, so their line is long and thin. We form the square, and we engage one on one all the way around. With our depth, we actually have them outnumbered at each position. If they're fighting with swords, they won't have a chance. We have concentrated our strength on their weakness—or rather, they have stupidly chosen to make themselves weak all over."

Effa frowned at the table. "So it's better to make the square?"

"Not always. We can't move fast or far in the square—you remember—" They nodded. "Mobility is important, too. So is terrain—where is the good ground?" Quickly he showed them how slope, water, and such hazards as swamp and loose rock could change the choice of tactics. "It's the commander's responsibility to choose the best ground—for our side, of course. The Duke's famous for it. But you need to know how it's done, so you'll know what to watch out for, and which way to move—"

"But we're under orders, aren't we? We just do what we're told—"

"Yes. But sergeants and corporals get killed—even captains. In battle, there's no time to send questions to the Duke. If the regulars don't know what to do and why, the cohort will fall apart. ..."

–*Sheepfarmer's Daughter* by Elizabeth Moon, pg. 91

Tactics include relying on our captain, obeying our commander, and fighting with all we are and every weapon we hold. On some level, everyone drawing breath in our world or that of fantasy is part of the war that darkness wages against the light, no matter how young or old we are. Are we ready to stand up in our Creator and be counted? Certain victory comes through courage, strength, and indomitable spirit. The warriors who have gone before us, men and women of swift strength and gentleness, welcome us to stand among them.

In each battle we either take ground, or let the rush of conflict carry us where it will, as a boulder spinning in a dark river at night, destroying ourselves and others in our path. Know the objective, the stakes, and the best way to gain the goal.

In Kyrin's journey to find courage and defend her stronghold against treachery in the Falcon Chronicle series, I use some of the lesser known secrets of unarmed combat. I've been trained in the art of fighting with heart and hand and foot, not with steel, though I admire the way of the sword and would love to learn it. And yet other tactics I use in the unseen war in our world. Indomitable spirit, courtesy, self-control . . . perseverance . . . integrity: such things or their lack can spell *lost* or *won.*

The secrets of war have always held my intense attention. We'll discover why in our next surprising adventure, while we briefly hold our breath below the surface of the sea, and walk the sandy floor of the fantasy arena in unarmed attack and defense.

Dive 7.2

Medieval Unarmed Combat Secrets in *Falcon Heart*

Unarmed combat—that seems a contradiction to anyone unfamiliar with English, or who sees those words from a slightly different perspective. After all, we say, we must have our arms in order to fight effectively! Unarmed combat appears a play on words, but history reveals otherwise.

Arms and *armed* are older terms for weapons and the state of carrying them. Below its surface meaning, *unarmed combat* holds a feeling of mysterious power that human and inhuman minds have used in all the long ages in their struggle of right against wrong, though the thought of trying to fight with arms separated from the body leaves us with a chuckle. In unarmed combat, when one has nothing else, of course we use the arms we have. And sometimes using what we have is the most effective weapon of all.

> *Alaina blurted, "You protected me!" She turned to Kyrin, her words flowing fast, eyes shining. "He is a warrior, and with his hands and feet he is terrible. He and my brother, Owin . . . Well, when Owin and the baker's son fell, it took more than three of Ali's men to hold him. He killed one of them after they knocked his sword away."*
>
> *Kyrin flinched. Oh, Alaina. Tae could not save her brother. But killing without a weapon? That was curious. She had grown up*

with warriors and their tales, and she had never heard of anyone but wrestlers or tumblers fighting without a blade, be it but a spear or a two-handed sword.

"Feet and hands do not have all power," Tae said. "A sword gives much advantage, and a spear or a bow, more. The mind gives most."

That was something Father might have said. Kyrin stared at Tae. He was shorter and slighter than any warrior she knew, muscled as a hart. He had walked up with their bread and fish quiet as a fox; she had looked around when she smelled the fish. His brown feet were short and broad, callused, and not unmarked. The white scars on his hands said they knew many things. She shivered at his slow, sure smile, but not for herself.

Any who opposed him would not find what they wished. There was more to him than a simple warrior . . .

–*Falcon Heart* by Azalea Dabill, pg. 49

Our mind is one of our best weapons. It guards whatever treasury or treasure we fight to protect, directed by our heart.

Every warrior worth their salt knows the discipline of sweat and pain, but not every warrior cares to discipline their mind and spirit by allowing truth to guide them to strength of heart, equal to or surpassing that of their body.

All forms of learning require the humility to accept we do not yet know what our teacher holds in his heart, mind, and hands for us. And that gift of humility and gem of learning, the realization that we do not know, but we *will* know, are beyond price.

We must discover that power, beyond the arms of body or blade, which is our foremost weapon. Here our training truly begins, with experience in the inner arena.

Dive 7.3

Unmatched Fantasy Tears and Training in the Arena

As we have said, there is always some kind of pain in training: from that of tearing, expanding muscle, to rigorous trial of spirit, to heart-pain that makes room for compassion or which turns that which is weak inside to steel. Can we agree that is true? Hence forging forces are needed in the inner arena.

The training arena, the gladiatorial arena, and the liberating arena of ideas where spirits strive through the ages—all have served this purpose. When a fantasy story combines the external elements of training, the contest, and the gaze of witnesses with the high inner stakes of the moral war, we have a great story and fly through the pages, forgetting to record in our book of knowledge, we are so absorbed. That is as well.

In entertaining conflict, we absorb nuances of understanding and purpose, and our spirits tread places higher than we knew before. After walking there in that sweet, bracing air, when we return to our world, we acknowledge evil more readily in ourselves and recognize good more easily in others, widening our horizons and scribing our book of knowledge in more than flesh. In fantasy, the battle is fought on more planes than one.

"Well, we've had our training, babe. Years of it. I don't think we need any more."

"Actually we haven't even begun," Pierce said.

Startled, Callie turned to find him standing behind the sectional to her left. He held a dark book in one hand, and his face wore a pinched expression that made her stomach tighten with sudden concern.

No one said anything, not even Rowena, until John broke the tension in his oblivious way. "Pierce buddy! You missed the grand tour. Not that we saw much of interest, since most everything was locked, but—"

"Those are armories and shooting ranges," Pierce said.

His statement took John aback. "How would you know that, bud?" He glanced at the others, smiling indulgently. "I mean, you haven't seen—"

"We're going to have to be in prime shape, mentally and physically," Pierce went on, ignoring him. "Because the Exit is at the middle of the Inner Realm in a Trog city called Splagnos. The route will have to be worked out from information in the manual along with direct guidance from our Benefactor." He drew a deep breath and let it out. "It's not going to be easy."

By now Morgan was standing, Rowena beside him, all of them staring at Pierce.

Morgan said, "How do you know this?"

Pierce's face was expressionless as his eyes flicked over the gathering. Callie looked again at the book in his hand, and understanding dawned. "He can read the manual," she said softly, her voice clear in the silence. "He's the Guide we're supposed to wait for."

–Arena by Karen Hancock, pg. 186

Our guide is wisdom—or should be. When we see danger looming before a protagonist in fantasy and we're screaming for them to pay attention—don't you see the lie?! Don't you see the enemy waiting for your next step to kill you? Or we urge them to trust the person who has shown himself worthy—and they don't—well, we learn right along with them the price of choosing wrong, and find pain or wisdom. For in great fantasy we also find the reward of right.

Our weapons of choice on all planes also make themselves known. In every arena, if we don't choose a weapon to effect change, we recognize that we *are* choosing another, even if we wield empty hands, or the envy, anger, fear, or love in our hearts. Principles, or their lack, drive the blade in every world.

Dive 7.4

Brave Principles and Weapons Protect the Seeking Heart in *Divided Allegiance*

Someone may ask: How can brave principles protect anyone?

Without them, there is no motive but self-interest to protect anyone at all from an attacker. When self-interest is conflicted, it always caves to expedience. Our castle may have the strongest walls, but if the strength of principle is not part of the mortar between the stones of our freedom, our right to life, and our pursuit of happiness, those walls will fall at the most inopportune moment in the heat of battle. Many may die—for our lack of principle.

The interesting thing about training the body is that it paradoxically tends to make us more aware of our principles and ideals and where we stand, or don't, inside. Physical training shows us where we need to become stronger in spirit. And how much we have to learn in both arenas.

"Now, what sort of training did you look for?"

Paks could hardly believe her ears. "You mean—you'll let me stay?"

"Let you! By Gird, I'm not likely to let someone like you wander the world unconvinced without giving my best chance to convert you. Of course you'll stay."

"But if I don't—"

"Paksenarrion, you will stay until either you wish to leave, or you give me cause to send you away. When—notice that I do not say if, being granted almost as much stubbornness as you, by Gird's grace—when you find that you can swear your honor to Gird's fellowship, it will be my pleasure to give and receive your strokes. Is that satisfactory, or have you more conditions for a Marshal-General of Gird, and Captain-Temporal of the High Lord?"

Paks blushed. "No, my lady. I'm sorry. I—"

"Enough. Tell me what you thought to learn."

"Well—everything about war—"

The Marshal-General whooped. "Everything? About war? Gird's grace, Paksenarrion, no one knows that but the High Lord, who sees all beginnings and endings at once."

"I meant," muttered Paks, ears flaming, "weapons-skills, and things about forts—things the Duke's captains knew about, like tunnels—"

"All right," said the Marshal-General, wiping her eyes on her sleeve. "I see what you mean. Things about forts. Honestly! No, sorry, I see you're serious. Well, then. I'll assign you to the training company. Many of them are younger than you . . .

–Divided Allegiance (The Deed of Paksenarrion) by Elizabeth Moon, pg. 303

Indeed, we all have much to learn, always. In both the world of fantasy and in our own, where the spiritual arena is driven by the wide world of ideas, and touches the sphere we breathe in.

The genre of spiritual or supernatural fantasy is often shunned because of the bad reputation it has gotten from theological mishandling and manipulation in tales that lean toward horror. The Lamb Among the Stars series is very different.

Where things of the spirit are handled well, the soul of fantasy becomes a flaming light that leads every seeker to joys unknown, to the surety of victory, where no good thing is impossible.

Dive 7.5

Why Paranormal and Visionary Warfare Blows Your Mind

Paranormal and visionary or spiritual fantasy is a vital part of our world, reflecting, even if inaccurately, at least the reality we all sense but sometimes disavow: that there is an arena beyond our physical senses among the worlds. The players within it are far from neutral, as we have seen. Evil is a real force, with marshaled troops, even a general.

Caution is necessary here. Going into battle without reconnaissance is not wise. So we must be able to tell good from evil, friend from foe, truth from deception. We must use our inner and outer vision and all the weapons at our command of heart and hand to ward us.

In fantasy books, as everywhere else, evil's favorite masquerade is harmlessness or goodness. We so often blind ourselves because we wish things to be good enough we needn't trouble ourselves about them—or even that the evil might be small enough it does not spoil the whole. But any compromise with poison will kill us. Right *cannot* be compromised without becoming un-right. There may be an avenue we have not seen that is a compromise *in a situation,* but which does not compromise what is *right and just,* which is something altogether different. Often enough, there is more than one right solution to a conflict. Sometimes what carries the day is something far different than the steel of bullet or blade.

The board of visionary fantasy is spread richly, sometimes with dishes of dreams, or portents and dangers, and wound through them all, truth and adventure. Dreams can be a kind of inner vision.

Kyrin turned on her side by a warding fire. Flame shadows leapt across the sand, and she gripped a sheathed blade. Her nemesis threw back his head with a savage snarl, ears pinned to his skull. She yanked frantically on the sword, drawing the beast closer. The blade did not budge.

Above, a falcon cried. She circled, screaming. Then she dived, crying down the wind.

Kyrin's heart dove with her. "No!"

Her queen of the air was an attacking blur, wings swept back, beak open, talons extended.

The tiger lunged, reaching up with a massive paw. He swept the falcon from the air. Her defiant cry broke off in an explosion of feathers.

Kyrin could not leave the falcon to his mercies. She stepped from the light. Tears wet her face as she whirled the sheathed sword in a humming arc. But it was too late.

Ignoring her edgeless weapon, the tiger kept malevolent eyes on her, hunching over the bundle of grey-blue feathers with a throaty growl, cracking bones in thick jaws.

The falcon fell—she should not have come! Not for me.

Amber and gold danced in the watching eyes of the tiger's collar. They seemed to gaze at the stars, at a sky of distant light and a cold silver moon. Where was their Master and hers, who governed all? But love is loyal. And I know he wills good.

Kyrin edged back to the fire and sank to her knees, wiping at her face. Glinting in the moonlight, the watchers about the tiger's neck gazed at her, at peace. And another eye winked into existence among them.

Kyrin stared in wonder. The falcons were not caged and wingless, but were part of a cloud of witnesses from ages past, of whom her mother was one, and the falcon dagger another. Kyrin's skin burned with cold. Would they witness aught but a fallen first daughter? She must get up, must learn to draw the sword in her hand against the beast, must fight it.

–Falcon Flight by Azalea Dabill, pg. 285

Evil must be fought, for the sake of all. That courage, that determination to fight the wide war is admirable. Moral principle drives all fantasy, *especially* the visionary and paranormal, or supernatural fantasy. There, the principal actors have cast off their cloaks.

The Shocking Supernatural in Legends of the Guardian King

The supernatural does shock us, when we first realize it involves an all-powerful being who is without spot, who dwells in unapproachable light. The Lord of the supernatural is master of all, and he tells us to look up—that there is hope, far beyond our common meaning of the word.

In fantasy, this looking to hope comes in many guises.

Meridon pushed weakly against his ribs. "Let me go, then. And get back."

"But . . ." Abramm swallowed his protest and complied. The other man crawled onto his pallet and collapsed face down in the crackling straw. A faint buzzing filled the chamber, building to a mellow hum. At the same time Abramm's skin prickled as of lightning about to strike, and Trap's body began to glow.

Abramm leapt to his feet.

The glow intensified, hurting his eyes, though he could not look away, held by fascination as much as by fear. It thickened around the Terstan's form, a bright, white cloud, flashing with silver-and-gold coruscation.

Footfalls down the corridor broke the spell, and he snatched the blanket from his own pallet, draping it over the other's body, fearing the blaze might burn through it as the stone had burned his tunic back in Qarkeshan. But though the light was so strong it shone through the weave and blared up under the folds, it did not harm the fabric itself.

–*The Light of Eidon* by Karen Hancock, pg. 189

When we look to hope, and the refuge above ourselves, we have joined the cosmic war. Our training has begun.

And the entire rightful aim of training for war is peace—when evil will be no more in the cosmos. Until that time of complete healing, we can but bind the world's wounds after groundbreaking conflict, when the seeds of peace are sown in peace by the makers of peace between the worlds.

In the sphere we breathe in, our hearts are forged in battle-fire, where we plant seeds of peace in every realm, and find that forgiveness and friendship may at least heal personal wounds between those who were once hostile. So, in any world, how do enemies reach that peaceful ground? *How Do Unique Races Become Best Friends?*

Chapter 8.0

How Do Unique Races Become Best Friends?

Different beings may start their relationship as enemies or friends. They may be as similar as the many colors of humanity, or as distant in origin from us as those who live on another world and look like nothing human. Does not deep relationship usually contain conflict? Working through that conflict ends in knowledge of each other, for example, between human and Atevi in the fantasy *Foreigner,* by CJ Cherryh.

For a nation to defend or attack against an invading race is good. Sometimes defense and attack are synonymous to our survival. This mind-bending fantasy takes these ideas and stands them on their heads, as humans are the ones invading.

In our world, if alien human invaders come peacefully to live in a better land than their own as lawful citizens in our country, then they are no longer perceived as invaders, and all is well. If they come to plant a colony with the same tyrannical rules of the land or society they left, they are invading us by guile, and must be fought by law, and force of arms if it comes to that.

After peaceful freedom is hard-won, a continuing peace does not mean appeasing the invader, however friendly or fascinating. They may keep their differences—as long as they do not impose them on us—and abide by the law of our land.

Which means an ambassador with a healthy dose of understanding is needed even in a time of victorious peace. Negotiating peace between two cultures is enough to give anyone a massive case of "I can't do this!" For *understanding them* does not necessarily mean capitulation to an invading culture, allowing it to absorb and overcome the land by slow degrees. Or why did the invaders come to our country in the first place, if they meant to leave their own, and not extend it?

Such is the mind of the Atevi toward the humans forced to land on their world. The former invader also has the expectation of a fair adherence to the just treaty and laws of the land where both have chosen to live.

When someone like Ambassador Bren Cameron comes to the Ateva capital of Shejidan in good faith, with truth, justice, and a code of "if you want to live in their land follow their laws" attitude, real friendship and a meeting of Atevi and human minds has a fighting chance.

So whether it is on Earth, or we have met an alien race on their soil and in their space, if such fair conditions are met, mutual respect, strength, goodwill, and truth may progress to trust.

But long ago human and Atevi began on a friendly footing and then fell out, and so traveled a harder road to trust. The subtle differences between human and Atevi minds flouted just expectations on both sides, which became visible later with disastrous results. We always tend to think others are like us in basic essentials beyond our small, skin-deep differences and language, in spite of varied thinking patterns, goals, and beliefs that color all we see—or don't see.

In fantasy, the more we get to know other intelligences the more we find out how astonishingly different minds are, even among humans. As for other worlds and aliens, though they are a reflection of our imaginations the gap between us is wider yet. But there are surprisingly realistic aliens at large in fantasy, very worth getting to know. Such as the Ateva.

For the voyaging traveler interested in discovering new races, hearts, and minds, as we are, the struggle is much the same as Ambassador

Bren's. We must battle prejudice in ourselves and others, even enmity, perhaps defend our people, or uphold justice for both sides before a true meeting of minds on equal ground can be approached.

Curiosity helps an ambassador, and in *Foreigner*, it's good the cat has nine lives. Peace-keeping is a dangerous business in any realm, either by force of defending arms or skillful wile and wit. So how do unique races in the middle of conflict become the best of friends?

By wit and wile, force of hand and friendly guile. And as often as not, a smile or its equivalent. By shared danger, shared dreams, shared life, even if humans and aliens oppose each other at times. Conflict *can* be worked through and lead to a relationship deeper yet; if both parties desire it.

These aliens of the space-ways, particularly CJ Cherryh's humanoid Atevi, the cat-like Hani, and Timothy Zahn's dragon-like Kd'a, stand tall in the ranks of good fantasy. These three in particular have a large impact on our perception of decent aliens. CJ Cherryh's *Foreigner* has a few sentences that need skipped to be a clean read, but *The Pride of Chanur* has only slight mentions, and Zahn's *Dragon and Thief* is completely clean.

The great stories like these let us live for a time in another place as another being, and in fantasy especially we may find ourselves in quite a foreign body, mind, or world. But *foreign* is not synonymous with *bad,* and much good can come from our sojourn in another's shoes. Exploring other creatures' lives can become a pleasant and profitable addiction. We are glad witnesses to that! Those of our own race we know and understand best, of course, for in a sense their hearts beat within ours. Since good beasts and beings of many descriptions have made their way into every corner of my soul, I am blessed.

As we sail to mysterious lands of fantasy, in addition to aliens we find ourselves enamored by the wildness of edila in *Perelandra,* the risks of a *Dragon and Thief,* and the humor of pixies in *Numin U'ia.* Grasp courage in *Knife,* the inner beauty of elves in *The Lord of the*

Rings, the charm and brave loyalty of halflings in *The Iron Tower,* intriguing gnomes in *Divided Allegiance,* and fantastic beasts in The Griffin Mage series. Hobbits, dwarves, gnomes, and halflings each have their own charm, however rustic or rough their exteriors.

Not all intelligent beings will let us have goodness and plenty in peace. The record is clear. If wizards, witches, or tyrants throw off rightful authority they must be opposed, or evil will rule. Yet the tyrant's defeat is coming in *DragonQuest,* wizards and witches are sorted in *The Blood of Kings,* fabulous biomechanics delight us in *Foundling,* and Feechies stir up hilarious fun wherever they go with *The Bark of the Bog Owl.* New friends gather to meet us but dives away!

Dive 8.1

Do You Crave Pixies, Dragons, and Secret Trysts in a Wild World?

We will find all races and kinds of beings in the waters of fantasy, from C. S. Lewis' eldila of *Perelandra* through Zahn's noteworthy good dragon, to trysts with A. A. Radda's pixies in *Numin U'ia*. "But," someone protests, "such races and beings are too strange for us to relate to." Should we not even *try* to relate to them?

How far will we reach for friendship? To share the fears and hopes of another soul? Savor the wildness, the risk, and the humor of meeting another mind.

The wildness is unmistakable in *Perelandra*:

> *On the other hand, all those doubts which I had felt before I entered the cottage as to whether these creatures were friend or foe, and whether Ransom were a pioneer or a dupe, had for the moment vanished. My fear was now of another kind. I felt sure that the creature was what we call "good," but I wasn't sure whether I liked "goodness" so much as I had supposed. This is a very terrible experience. As long as what you are afraid of is something evil, you may still hope that the good may come to your rescue. But suppose you struggle through to the good and find that it also is dreadful? How if food itself turns out to be the very thing you can't eat, and home the very place you can't live, and your very comforter the person who makes you uncomfortable? Then, indeed, there is no rescue possible: the last card has been played. For a second or two I was nearly in that condition.*

Here at last was a bit of that world from beyond the world, which I had always supposed that I loved and desired, breaking through and appearing to my senses: and I didn't like it, I wanted it to go away. I wanted every possible distance, gulf, curtain, blanket, and barrier between it and me. But I did not fall quite into the gulf. Oddly enough my very sense of helplessness saved me and steadied me. For now I was quite obviously "drawn in." The struggle was over. The next decision did not lie with me.

Then, like a noise from a different world, came the opening of the door, and the sound of boots on the door-mat, and I saw, silhouetted against the greyness of the night in the open doorway, a figure which I recognized as Ransom. The speaking which was not a voice came again out of the rod of light and Ransom, instead of moving, stood still and answered it.

–*Perelandra* by C. S. Lewis, pg 19

The risk in meeting another mind is high in *Dragon and Thief*:

The same pattern as the vanished dragon.

A horrible thought struck him. Pulling the shirt free from his jeans, he slid it all the way off his right arm so that it was hanging on his left arm and shoulder. Twisting his head around, he looked down at his right shoulder.

To find himself gazing directly into the dragon's face.

"Ye-oup!" He yelped, jerking his head back and jumping three feet to his left.

It was like trying to jump away from his own body, and about as successful. The picture of the dragon didn't disappear or slide off or anything like that. It was still there, as if it had been painted on him.

Then, to his utter astonishment, the face rose slowly out of his skin, like the top of an alligator's head rising up through the surface of the water. The long upper jaw opened slightly, giving him a glimpse of sharp teeth—"Don't be afraid," a soft, snakelike voice said.

Jack screeched loud enough to hurt his own ears. His tangler was in his left hand, though he had no memory of having drawn it, and with all his strength he slammed the short barrel down on the dragon's head.

But the beast was too fast for him. It sank flat onto his skin again, and Jack's screech turned to a howl of pain as his attack succeeded only in bruising his own shoulder. Ignoring the pain, he struck again and again, stumbling sideways in a useless attempt to get away. Through the noise of his own panicked babbling, he was distantly aware that there were two different voices shouting at him.

–*Dragon and Thief* by Timothy Zahn, pg. 39

But the humor is worth the attempt in *Numin U'ia:*

"GIIIIILMAAAAAR!" The squeal rang through the clearing. Millilent screamed in reaction, and Gilmar jerked upright. Taeyain shook his head, either in reproof or to clear the scream out, Gilmar couldn't tell which. Leith, wrapped in his cloak under a fourth tree, sat up straight, his dagger ready. Taeyain rose, and Leith pushed himself to his feet. Gilmar groaned and sank back on his elbows.

The three of them glared at Millilent.

"What was that?" Millilent panted in terror.

Gilmar glanced around again. The embers of their fire sent amber glows in occasional flickers through the trees, and where these faded the stars provided enough light to see by, but he couldn't spot the object he knew had begun the disturbance. "Only a pixie. Go to sleep," he told Millilent.

"I can't. Someone screamed." Millilent turned from one to another of them until she saw Taeyain in the shadows. She stared at him, and screamed again. "That! There it is! It screamed! What's that thing? It has wings!" She shrieked and closed her eyes tight. Looking at her, Gilmar realized with misgiving that she was one of those who wake up only half-way at night, and

remain completely unreasonable until morning. Or after it, in her case.

"That is Taeyain." He enunciated every syllable. "He is my friend, and he arrived after you were asleep. He did not, and would not ever, scream."

"Something screamed."

"Yes. You screamed," said Leith. After taking a shrewd glance at Gilmar, he had already curled back up in the warmth of his cloak.

–*Numin-U'ia* by A. A. Radda, pg. 360

Wildness, risk, and humor, if they are of the right kind and in the right dose, add meaning to our experiences in any land. I like to think that to gain friends we will navigate the shoals of differing ways of thinking to meet on the bright sands of truth, navigating amid reefs and havens of belief, to carefully examine the various things we hoard, such as time and empathy, to see if they might be given more profitably as gifts to our new friend.

How far will we reach for friendship, for the clear diamond of wildness, the living emerald of risk, the glittering sapphire of humor? To this beguiling mixture of adventure, high fantasy adds inspiring fairies and elves, the very best of friends. As all excellent creatures do, they take us out of ourselves.

Dive 8.2

How High Fantasy Paints Inspiring Elves and Fairies of the Light

Personal knowledge of other hearts can inspire courage and bestow the gift of peace between two who are entirely different. Possessing the honor to do what is right, no matter the cost, inspires us deeply. The courage to sacrifice when necessary attracts us to stories as honey does a Narnian bear. Because of stories like these, I hope and pray when my time comes I will have that courage. The courage to make a difference. Selfless love can overcome great wrong.

> *Paul toppled out of the chair and hit the oily water with a splash. His legs were dead weights, and he made no effort to move his arms. He simply relaxed into the pool ...*
>
> *...and was gone.*
>
> *Knife stared at the ripples spreading outwards across the gloomy water, the last flurry of bubbles as Paul's bright hair sank beneath the surface. Her throat closed up, and a dull pain spread beneath her ribcage.*
>
> *There was nothing she could do. With her crippled wing she couldn't fly for help, and she was far too tiny to rescue him by herself...*
>
> *Knife's shoulders slumped. She turned away, took one step – then spun around, hurtled down the slope, and dived straight into the pool.*

...

His cheeks puffed out in a last, weak cough; he stirred, and opened his eyes.

'Aaaah!"

Alarmed, Knife let go of him and leaped back. Only then did she realize what had made him cry out, and she stared at her filth-spattered hands in disbelief.

'You,' croaked Paul. 'You're—'

'I'm big,' said Knife blankly.

'You're human,' said Paul in a voice husky with wonder, and his cold fingers brushed her cheek.

Blood surged into her face; she jerked away from the touch. 'I am not!'

'Your hair,' he lifted a strand. 'It's blonde, instead of white. And your eyes look...lighter. Sort of grey.'

'Stop it.' She slapped his hand away. 'I may be your size, but I am not human. It must be a trick of the light.'

'Then where are your wings?'

–*Knife* by R. J. Anderson, pgs. 140, 142

This fairy had wings of the soul: an inner strength of compassion and courage and the will to do beyond what she thought she could. And her act of will changed her and her people for the better. RJ Anderson's *Knife* strikes deep, as do her other fantasy stories. Open *Knife* for the rest of her adventure, and find courage.

As for elves, of all that we have met in different lands, those in Middle Earth stand out in a wisdom that matches their inner beauty. Knowledge of such hearts as these coax forth our bravery, and makes room for the gift of peace to invade our souls.

"And what gift would a Dwarf ask of the Elves?" said Galadriel, turning to Gimli.

"None, Lady," answered Gimli. "It is enough for me to have seen the Lady of the Galadhrim, and to have heard her gentle words."

"Hear all ye Elves!" she cried to those about her. "Let none say again that Dwarves are grasping and ungracious! Yet surely, Gimli son of Gloin, you desire something that I could give? Name it, I bid you! You shall not be the only guest without a gift."

"There is nothing, Lady Galadriel," said Gimli, bowing low and stammering. 'Nothing, unless it might be – unless it is permitted to ask, nay, to name a single strand of your hair, which surpasses the gold of the earth as the stars surpass the gems of the mine. I do not ask for such a gift. But you commanded me to name my desire."

The elves stirred and murmured with astonishment, and Celeborn gazed at the Dwarf in wonder, but the Lady smiled. "It is said that the skill of the Dwarves is in their hands rather than in their tongues," she said; "yet that is not true of Gimli. For none have ever made to me a request so bold and yet so courteous. And how shall I refuse, since I commanded him to speak? But tell me, what would you do with such a gift?"

"Treasure it, Lady," he answered, "in memory of your words to me at our first meeting. And if ever I return to the smithies of my home, it shall be set in imperishable crystal to be an heirloom of my house, and a pledge of goodwill between the Mountain and the Wood until the end of days."

Then the Lady unbraided one of her long tresses, and cut off three golden hairs, and laid them in Gimli's hand. "These words shall go with the gift," she said. "I do not foretell, for all foretelling is now vain: on the one hand lies darkness, and on the other only hope. But if hope should not fail, then I say to you, Gimli son of Gloin, that your hands shall flow with gold, and yet over you gold shall have no dominion."

–The Fellowship of the Ring by J. R. R. Tolkien, pg. 486

That is a gift indeed. One heart calling to the other. Strong, gentle goodness ushered in a brave peace between two hearts and two races where none had been before.

Fantasies that become classics do so for good reason: their meaning impacts us far beyond the hour they are written. As well as inspiring us as readers, such excellent fiction influences yet more of us to craft great works of fantasy. Take note: all of us authors plagiarize in one sense— we write while under the enchantment of everything we have ever read. And most good authors at one time or another imitate the great story-tellers as a way of studying under a master. One series well and honestly done in this manner is *The Iron Tower* by Dennis McKiernan*, where halflings show us how to find the fire in our hearts.

Dive 8.3

Come Join an Epic Journey to *The Iron Tower*

Relationships sometimes involve the longest journey. Don't you think?

In *The Iron Tower*, Warrows inhabit a parallel world, Mithgar. Like Hobbits, Warrows are yet their own race. All the better to show us how truth and skillful wit can help us make relationships right. Are not relationships the same in every world, except for the outer trappings of what we quarrel over?

Full of adventure, comradeship, and discovery, Mithgar is a world worth visiting. Its only drawback is that it portrays a rather confused, vague knowledge of its creator. Yet, as far as we can remember, those who live in Middle-earth do not speak of their creator much, but his immutable existence is everywhere taken for granted, framing every judgment and action of every person, for good or for evil.

Elsewhere, Tolkien speaks of the Creator under the name Eru Iluvatar. As Creator, he is the bedrock of existence in Middle Earth, of who they are. But in Mithgar, the question we all face about why we exist is not answered satisfactorily. The question is only raised, and that creator is made to appear a lesser being than God. *God* defined as a being uncreated; who is the origin of all things. But *The Iron Tower* does raise the question, along with a grand adventure.

With a final burst of speed, the young buccan Warrow raced through ankle-deep snow, his black hair flying out behind. In one hand he carried a bow already nocked with an arrow, and he sprinted toward a fallen log, clots of snow flinging out behind his flying boots; yet little or no sound did he make, for he was one of the Wee Folk. Swiftly he reached the log and silently dropped to one knee, quickly drawing the bow to the full and loosing the arrow with a humming twang of bowstring. Even before the deadly missile had sped to the target, another arrow was released, and another, another, and another—in all, five arrows were shot in rapid succession, hissing through the air, striking home with deadly accuracy.

"Whang! Right square in the center, Tuck!" cried Old Barlo as the last arrow thudded into the mark. "That's four for five, and you would'er got the other, too, if you'd'er held a bit." Old Barlo, a granther Warrow, stood up to his full three feet two inches of height and turned and cocked a baleful emerald-green eye upon the other young buccen gathered on the snowy slopes behind. "Now I'm telling all you rattlepates: draw fast, and loose quick, but no quicker as what you can fly it straight. The arrow as strays might well'er been throwed away, for all the good it does." Barlo turned back to Tuck. "Fetch up your arrows, lad, and sit and catch your breath. Who's next now? Well, step up here, slowcoach Tarpy."

Tuckerby Underbank slipped his chilled hands back into his mittens and quickly retrieved his five arrows from the tattered, black, Wolf silhouette on the haycock. With his breath blowing whitely in the cold air, Tuck trotted back through the snow to the watching group of archers at the edge of End Field, where he sat down on a fallen log, standing his bow against a nearby barren tree.

As Tuck watched little Tarpy sprint toward the target to fly arrows at the string-circle mark, the young buccan sitting beside him—Danner Bramblethorn as it was—leaned over and spoke: "Four out of five, indeed, Tuck," Danner said, exasperated. "Why, your first arrow nicked the ring. But Barlo Stingy won't give you credit for it, mark my words."

"Oh, Old Barlo's right, you know," replied Tuck. "I hurried the shot. It was out. He called it true. But you ought to know he's fair, Danner. You're the best shot here, and he says so. You're too hard on him. He's not a stingy, *he just expects us to get it right—every time."*

–*The Iron Tower* by Dennis McKiernan, pg. 3

Every time—and by the time we reach Tuck's words, his story has pulled us under a spell. In relationships, truth and skillful wit can help us get it right. We need the ability to laugh at ourselves if we are to escape the megalomania that plagues our earth.

We enjoyed this jewel of fantasy with its facets of loyalty, endurance, and charming inhabitants with delight. The fact that ugly people—in spirit and appearance—also dwell in Mithgar simply makes the appeal of those who stand against them all the greater. Wherever they are found, Men, Hobbits, or Halflings, if a person stands for good, their hearts are great indeed.

Even when races differ, quarrel, or cultivate less than cordial dealings with each other, like dwarves and elves, yet when the chips fall at last, as individual people they often take a stance far better than their words. At the last, they discover themselves friends.

We have touched on dwarves in our journey, but what figures do gnomes cut in fantasy when strength and code of law seem to oppose each other?

Dive 8.4

How Do Rich Gnomes and Imposing Dwarves Make Spectacular Fantasy?

We know somewhat of the stalwart nature of dwarves, quite formidable in ways apart from their height-challenge, taught to us by Tolkien, McKiernan, and others, but gnomes—what are they like? Are you not curious, however strange they may be?

Fairness and logic are the codes they live by. At least in Tsaia, where there are many forms of strength, and admiration leaves the door open to friendship. Sometimes called sly tricksters and devious inhabitants of gardens, or forests, or denizens underground, at other times gnomes are a race with a sense of law unsurpassed, though slight of frame and with a curious formality in their speech.

> *The gnome bowed from the waist, and met Paks's eyes as he stood upright. "It shall be that you have the reward of the Aldonfulk, lady. For this indeed shall value be given. It is that our partner of Lyonya is eaten by that monster, true?"*
>
> *"We haven't seen him," said Paks, thinking of the armring with a shudder. "Is that what you think happened?"*
>
> *"It took him. It seemed hungry. We heard cries. We have not knowledge, but that is logical."*
>
> *"Is your friend hurt?" The gnome on the floor had not moved.*

"Only slightly—he was hit by arrow of robbers. He sleeps to gain strength."

Paks was surprised by the gnome's composure. Despite days of imprisonment in a dark cell, the death of one companion and the wounds of another, the gnome was calm and matter-of-fact. He turned to the other gnome, and spoke loudly in gnomish. Paks could not understand a word of it. She looked around to see if the others did, but they looked as blank as she felt. The gnome on the floor stirred, and opened his eyes.

–*Divided Allegiance* by Elizabeth Moon, pg. 259

A closer look at these people makes us examine what we believe is fair and courteous through the gaze of someone who lays ten times as much weight on fairness as we do. Gnomes feel a sense of obligation far deeper than we, for things we often take for granted, like someone doing us a simple favor.

We can respect the gnomes' take on fairness, even if we do not always think they are right. We admire their sincerity as they honestly stand by what they believe is good to the best of their ability. And admiration leaves the door open for friendship. As for logic, we agree with it as far as it makes sense in the realm of understanding—but some things like faith and the unseen cannot be grasped by logic alone, though logic points in their direction, as unerring as a lodestone.

But are we not forgetting how good fantasy beasts impact us? What of Griffins, Talking Animals, and Dragons? For starters, we'd far rather meet any one of them in a field of conversation or friendly contest than in a battle. But that might not be our choice—they have their own purposes, after all.

How to Find the Best Fantastic Beast, from The Griffin Mage to *DragonSpell*

Intelligent beasts we make friends of in fantasy tend to create a boundary line on our journey, to be a visible marker of our inner direction. Depending, of course, on which beast we let into our hearts, whether we ally with a good one or a bad one. So how to find your own best fantastic beast?

A beast can be a friend, an enemy, or something in between. They can be as dangerous and intriguing as griffins, who bring the grandeur and stark beauty of the desert to touch our lives in The Griffin Mage series, or as endearing as *DragonQuest* and its minor dragons. Or as deadly as the stalking Kalkarra of *The Ruins of Gorlan*, or as strangely fascinating as the monsters, good and bad, found in *Factotum* by D. M. Cornish.

We never tire of fantastic beasts. They are each their own being, worthy of study as an interesting creature, owed the dignity of one who bears with us the stamp of creation. Though if they have turned to evil, whether dumb (non-speaking) or intelligent, we may be forced to fight them, for we cannot let them destroy innocent lives unchallenged. But the good ones are more than worthy companions.

Especially in the land of Amara, where every being on the side of good may become a companion, even a miniature dragon with a talent that outweighs itself.

Kale wanted to speak, but her tongue had grown dry and too big for her mouth.

Maybe I don't feel so well after all.

Lebrettowit, there's something wrong.

The tumanhofer rose quickly and clambered up the last few steps.

"The poison is already past the arm. She's mute." He glared at them all. "Bardon, pick her up before she falls over. Gymn, ride on her chest and see what you can do to help. We must get her through the gateway and to Fenworth."

Bardon sheathed his sword. He scooped Kale into his arms as if she weighed nothing and charged up the metal steps. The clatter of his boots hurt her ears.

Gymn landed on her. His feet bore down as if he were digging his claws into her skin. Kale knew he weighed less than Toopka. The minor dragon wasn't causing the pain. It was the poison.

She felt Gymn's sympathy and concern coming through to her mind, but she couldn't feel the soothing effect he usually had on her nerves. He lay down and stretched out, covering as much of her as he could with his tiny body.

I can't feel it! The panicked thought circled in her brain. I should be able to feel his healing. He's trying to heal me, and I feel nothing!

–*DragonQuest* by Donita K. Paul, pg. 42

Even a good beast can go through hard times in their relationship with a human. Both may fail, then forgive each other, and mend their relationship, making it stronger than before. Hearts become truer as they stand the test, un-breaking.

Yet other beings that draw us outside of ourselves, a healing we are nearly always in need of, also broaden our souls in inexplicable ways. Greater sympathy, higher aspirations, a stronger will to do the right thing: all these come when we make time to be with another mind and soul that is aligned with good, no matter their shape or skin. That beast becomes a boundary line, a visible marker, one who gives us strength.

Iron sharpens iron, and that is not applied only to weapons and battle. Iron sharpens iron as it warms us, feeds us, and makes up things of beauty: as in a stove, a fork, and a decorative fire-screen, where beauty itself holds strength, and imparts it to our hearts.

Bad beasts act on us like rust, their cunning self-service, their disregard, their hate for others, eats away at all that is strong and worthy in the beast and in the one who allows it inside their mind. But we are seeking a good beast: one who strengthens and delights and grows our heart.

The good beasts are all "best" in a sense. Without any one of them, we would not be the same. So step out with a smile and walk with a beast you have not met before. It is all right to have more than one best beast!

Dive 8.6

Do Wizards, Witches, and Tyrants Make War on Authority?

If someone acknowledges no authority but their own, this pits them against every other authority. Gaining peace with those of this ilk costs heavily, when wizards are sorted by good and ill in long, hard struggle. But to choose to let the *ill* have their way is more costly still.

In varying degrees, most wizards, witches, and tyrants make war on everyone who dares say they are wrong. They are an exception to the minds and hearts we enjoy getting to know.

Some wizards, like the wizard Fenwer in *DragonQuest,* have discerned where they lawfully fit in their world. Under the authority of Wulder, the Creator of Amara, a wizard may lawfully use the Creator's laws for good, much as a scientist does the laws of God's order in our world. This is one wizardly scientist we would like to meet.

> *"I don't understand all of this," she said.*
>
> *"We don't have to," explained Regidor. "Fenworth says Wulder does all the work anyway. Being a wizard means understanding His creation and working with His universal laws. Fenworth says Wulder has systems for everything, and they always work."*
>
> *–DragonQuest* by Donita K. Paul, pg. 72

We would hesitate to call Fenwer a wizard. At least, not in the usual, common sense of the word. In our world the definition means a man who uses spells, incantations, or forbidden power from spirits or the occult to manipulate our world in ways God has not sanctioned.

But this is fantasy, another world, where the word *wizard* carries the possibility of another, better meaning. In Amara, a wizard, at least a good wizard, is a man, woman, or other sentient creature who works with Wulder, under his authority and within his creation.

Kale nodded her head but had no idea how this related to the three very small things Fenworth said made everything in the universe.

"Wulder took three ingredients and made the world," continued the wizard. "Of course, He also created the three ingredients. One is ozoic, the second is azoic, and the third is ezoic."

The picture above them changed to three round dots, one red, one blue, and the other white.

"In the first element we will examine, we have one ozoic and one azoic."

The bowl reappeared, and the red dot and blue dot fell into it much as the eggs had.

Except he didn't crack them on the edge. Kale suppressed a giggle.

"Don't let your mind wander, Kale," the wizard's voice entered her thoughts, reprimanding her.

"Yes sir."

The bowl disappeared, leaving the two colored dots suspended in midair, clinging to one another. The white dot circled the pair.

–*DragonQuest* by Donita K Paul, pg. 93

Such hearts as those above bless us with profitable addictions to knowledge and quirky characters. It seems rather curious that evil wizards are usually rebels against all established authority because they are seeking ultimate authority for themselves. World domination is a goal they have in common with tyrants.

Of course, sometimes the established governmental authority is a tyrant itself, not serving the people, and then those aligned with good must defy it. Good struggles with evil in many forms and ways, and the battle never ends. Until the end of the world.

Good and evil are opposites, opposed to each other from their roots. Hard-won peace is worth the cost when wizards, witches, and tyrants are sorted. The alternative is unthinkable.

Magicians and Good Versus Evil in The Blood of Kings

What is the key difference between a wielder of virtuous power and of wicked power? None, some may say; the only difference is what the wielder does with their power. We disagree.

The source of power determines the goodness or badness of the result. Listen with your heart's ears to why people act toward others as they do. Learn why power reveals us, and how it transmogrifies us into an insatiable monster when we are controlled by none but ourselves.

A bad magician or wizard seeks power over others, sometimes even seeking rigid control over himself so he may order his destiny. He is doomed to failure, certainly at least as far as mastering himself goes. It is interesting that those who hold the most power over others often exert the least control over their own passions. But none of us can gain that mastery alone.

Though we wish it were different, until we are overcome by Love, and acknowledge his authority, we are at the mercy of our tyrannous desires. Our feelings and passions dictate to us.

A tiny pinch started in the base of the back of her skull. The sensations grew slowly until it felt like a fist had reached inside and squeezed her brain. She let out a ragged breath and swallowed again. A tear trickled down her cheek, into the place where his thumb touched her chin. Her limbs trembled. She fought to steady them. Her arm twitched involuntarily and slapped his. He did not flinch. He did not release her.

Vrell uttered a small cry, sucked in another breath, and steeled herself against the ferocious pain. Her forehead grew damp with sweat. She glanced down to her master's storming, enlarged pupils, and her knees buckled. She pulled back to catch her balance and severed his grip.

Master Hadar hummed. "Excellent! Your tolerance is incredible. Had you not met my eyes you'd have lasted longer. I could get nothing from you. Nothing at all."

Vrell couldn't stop shivering. She did not want to last longer. She never wanted him to touch her in such a way again. What horrible magic did this man wield?

"What are you called?" Master Hadar asked.

"Ffff . . ." Vrell paused and sucked in a deep breath. "Vrell Sparrow," she whispered.

"You may go, Vrell. Join me here for breakfast tomorrow morning."

"Ye-y-yes, Master."

Vrell turned and strode as fast as she could without looking like she was in a hurry. Once the door clicked shut behind her, she fled down the stairs and back to her chamber. She pulled back the covers of her bed, climbed underneath, and sobbed.

–*By Darkness Hid* by Jill Williamson, pg. 246

Power, if uncontrolled by more than self, violates others. Wicked magicians inspire fear by their power for at least two reasons. First, because they use the power of evil beings to gain evil ends, and second, because evil in any amount, used in any way, always births more confusion, twisted results, and agony than a magician or wizard began with.

Though we may not be a wizard good or bad, any evil or good idea, acted on, becomes a kind of power in itself. We energize it with the power of choice we've been given; the power to will and to work.

We also have the power to choose our salvation from self-tyranny in the energizing, purifying power of the one who works within us, to will and to work of his good pleasure in love. We also have the power to do evil. Neither good nor evil is static. One or the other is always growing or diminishing in us, winning at a particular moment or going down in defeat. Though if we have chosen our Creator the outcome of our war is certain, still the battles between this moment and our certain victory are not set in stone. We hammer either evil or good into our lives and out in our actions.

Here, good magicians, wizards, and bearers of power come into the story in all their glory.

Think of these four opposites in pairs: Sauron, a wizard or sorcerer, and Gandalf, also a wizard; think of the White Witch and Magician Coriakin in Narnia. Think of the telepathic Shuhr and the Sentinels who opposed their megalomania in the Firebird trilogy, think of the villainous Right Hand of the Throned and the First Knight who stood against him in *The Broken Blade*.

What makes four of them good and four of them evil? Who their power comes from, and who they revere, for that reverence leads to their predominating evil or good actions.

Sauron seeks dominion over every living thing with every shred of power he can gather—*except* for the intrinsic, rightful power of Eru Illuvatar, who created Middle Earth, who gave Gandalf his wizardly position as an overseer and protector, though Gandalf is not perfect.

The White Witch aligned herself with all who opposed Aslan. Aslan, the son of the Emperor over the Sea, who said, "Do you grow weary, Coriakin, of ruling such foolish subjects as I have given you here?"

"No," said the Magician, "they are very stupid but there is no real harm in them. I begin to grow rather fond of the creatures. Sometimes, perhaps, I am a little impatient, waiting for the day when they can be governed by wisdom instead of this rough magic." (*The Voyage of the Dawn Treader,* pg. 137)

When we love the one who first loved us, then we can love the one who walks beside us. When we kneel to Love's power—then we can share that care and kindness and laughter with our neighbor. In many ways, love is the greatest power that exists, though it does not always seem so. It is the driving force behind every good word and deed, though at present it appears often overcome by the forces of evil.

This is borne out in the space fantasy *Firebird*, by Kathy Tyers, where Shuhr and Sentinel face off as opposites with the same genetic and empathic abilities. The Shuhr seek to part the veil of the future and close their iron grip around events to become a super race, while the Sentinels seek the freedom of the Eternal Speaker and work every moment for the good of their fellow beings, and the future of all worlds.

In The Knight of Eldaran trilogy, the Right Hand of the Throned seeks Eamon out to destroy him with every wile of seduction, of darkness and deceit, marked by the scarlet light of pain and rending. The hidden, blue-white light of the King enfolds Eamon as his First Knight with truth, kindness, and the creative energy of goodness. Eamon infiltrates the stronghold of the Throned and the cadre of Hands who serve him with various powers: to breach minds, foresee, shift locations, and break wills with red fire, the color of torment. Eamon learns that a traitor can turn, and turn again. So Eamon, a mind breacher, at last lays down his power in the service of his rightful King, and takes it up again with his mantle as First Knight, protector of the people.

Sauron, the Witch, the Shuhr, and the Throned seek power and glory, opposing Gandalf, Aslan, the Sentinels, the true King—and all those they represent in our world. Sauron and company oppose every ultimate authority outside themselves.

Those good few—magicians such as Coriakin, wizards like Gandalf, and bearers of lawful power like Eamon—seek to rescue us all from the domination of those who pursue power outside law.

I think the confusion about good and evil wielders of power sometimes arises because of their names: *magician*, *wizard*, and others like these. *Wizard* can mean something other than "evil power wielder." It depends on whether the power is from the evil one or our Creator, or in fantasy, from their representatives.

Be cautious. Some names do mean exactly what they say, in any world. *Fortune-teller* means someone who uses the spirits of the dead in their black trade on human curiosity and grief. *Spiritist* and *palm-reader*, *sorceress* and *sorcerer*, meaning those who deal with evil spirits, also belong to this category.

Magician, wizard, witch, telepath, gifted, seer, prophet—these names also often carry very similar meanings, and depend on the context of the story (or history) they live in for final definition and meaning. Was the power they possess given to them lawfully by the rightful authority of whatever star-system or world they inhabit?

Sometimes when a character has power we are unfamiliar with, we do not know what name to give them, other than the name *magician*, or a similar one. The connotation and meaning of *magician* or *wizard* or *seer* change in different stories, depending on whom they serve. Are they using their power under rightful authority, seeking every good thing, or are they pursuing their own selfish ambitions? And not all names given to a person are true. A prophet may be called a witch or wizard or a dabbler in sorcery by his or her enemies.

Our Creator's power is greater than all evil, and will swallow up wizards, sorcerers, and witches if they insist on opposing him, as the Egyptian sorcerers who tried to imitate his power discovered. After he transformed Moses's staff into a snake, using their dark arts, they turned their own staffs into snakes, but their evil beasts were literally swallowed by a greater good.

This is not smoke and mirrors.

What are the key differences between a bad wielder of power and a good one? How do we know which they are? It comes down to who the power comes from, and how it is used.

And because a person's real position is defined by the authority behind their power, all fantasy essentially identifies both that world's authority and the bearer of power clearly by the way they act in sum total.

As for us, do we side with magicians like Hadar and the dark Hands of the Throned, who wield power to imprison others in pain, sorrow, and servitude? Or will we defy them with Vrell Sparrow and Eamon? Will we follow the one with the power to free us—from evil in all its forms and faces? When, instead of a sorcerer's hard visage, evil bears our own face?

Will we plant the tree of life with Digory in *The Magician's Nephew,* in *Oath of Gold* pick up a sword beside Paksenarrion, and take up the call with the Longtreaders, "The Green Ember burns; the seed of the new World smolders. Healing is on the horizon, but a fire comes first. Bear the flame. ... My place beside you, my blood for yours. Till the Green Ember rises, or the end of the world." (*The Green Ember* by S. D. Smith, pgs. 364,191)

Worlds beyond our own have such great impact on us because we pay attention when we are drawn into them. There, the numbing drug of familiarity cannot dull the blazing aliveness of truth.

One world revealing such piercing light is *Foundling,* where fabulous biomechanics strike the heart with awe. Here, deep relationships between races begin in conflict. And good and evil wielders of power are found out.

Dive 8.8

Fabulous Biomechanics Take *Foundling* Out of This World

Hearts that fight together find it hard to disguise themselves from each other. On the other hand, biomechanics, or the fusion of a living body with mechanical parts, is a growing part of fantasy these days, and D. M. Cornish's trilogy is exceptional, and undisguised.

A treat for monster-lovers everywhere, as well as those who enjoy steam-punk and Regency type adventures, this appealing story of an orphan, Rossamund, details dangerous fulgars, or monster fighters, monsters both deadly and delightful, and the importance of courage, compassion, and standing up for what is right under threat of death.

Having discovered a secret that may destroy him, that touches all he is, Rossamund walks a thin line between destruction and the hope that his monster-slaying employer will extend him her protection. But their enemies are many, and before the end, monsters on both sides shed their disguises.

Stepping lightly off the half log, the Branden Rose advanced through tufts and stumps toward the sapperling once again. At her approach, the worm-thing bent its head as if to regard her properly. After all the desperate mayhem, the scene seemed oddly tranquil in the failing light.

Europe raised her arms, holding them up and out to her sides.

What is she doing? Rossamund paced as far as he dared to the right, seeking a better view.

Without any alerting reflex or countermotion, the vermid thing shot out a grasping limb, snatching the unresisting fulgar about her waist and yanking her in to engulf her just as it had poor Agitis.

"NO!" Rossamund shrieked a second time. Instantly he was to action, hurling both potives to detonate yellow-green and blue about its shoulders.

The sapperling tried to reach out and grasp him too but shuddered, the half-fashioned arm twitching, hesitating, retracting. Its sides appeared to flex and bloat.

Rossamund finally stood still.

The tapered head began to whip about violently. The saps that formed it wilted and fell. The legs collapsed, and the bulk dropped into the filth with a loud squelch. Flickers of static forced their way through the mutual grip of the remaining worms, lighting the bog with a dazzling, strobing brilliance. Of a sudden, the distending mass of worms sucked inward. An almighty deafening bang, like the cracking of the back of the world, a stupefying flash and the entire creature was flung apart, its bits thrown wide, Europe's fuse flying to strike the ground shudderingly not one yard from Rossamund. A subtle growl like the echo of distant thunder rolled about the sink as a drizzle of orange muck and particles of black hide fell all around.

The sapperling beast was no more.

In its place, amid a mess of worm-parts, stood the Branden Rose, arms akimbo, fists clenched, head down, hair loose and hair tine missing, ruffled but unharmed. She looked up to Rossamund, his cheeks smeared with unabashed tears of relief, then down with vague irritation at the messes that smeared and tearing that dulled her once-sumptuous coat.

"My best Number 3 ruined," she said.

–*Factotum* by D. M. Cornish, pg. 355

We often try to mask our reactions to events and people and put forth various guises of sophistication, or cynicism, or strength. But funny stories have ways of getting at the roots of things and tearing our carefully crafted appearances to shreds. The heat of peril and the quick illumination of humor, reveals hearts beyond the ability of disguise to conceal them. Even more, when hearts fight together.

Happily it is better so, and few are stronger in heart or quicker of wit than Feechies.

Dive 8.9

Feechies Bend Hilarious Imagination in the Wilderking

One word of humor can illuminate an entire moment, reveal a wealth of meaning, and pierce the mask of supposition to reveal a realm of layered truth in a grand adventure. But even on such a great journey, one must sojourn in another's shoes to see the humorous.

Aidan was terrified. His hands and feet were still bound, so he could neither run away nor defend himself. And gagged as he was, he couldn't even beg for mercy. He steeled himself to receive whatever punishment this fierce she-feechie had in mind for the civilizer who had corrupted her son.

Dobro's mother stood directly in front of Aidan, that strange light still in her eyes. Looking intently at the civilizer, she reached her right hand toward Rabbo. "Give me your knife, Rabbo."

Rabbo hesitated. He didn't want to see the civilizer killed without a proper trial. But Mrs. Turtlebane kept her hand outstretched. The intensity of her mother-love finally bent Rabbo's will to her own, and he handed over the stone knife.

Mrs. Turtlebane pointed the blade in Aidan's face, three inches from his chin. Aidan did his best to breathe evenly and not to whimper; he was the only civilizer these people had ever seen, and he didn't want to give the impression that civilizers were a tribe of whiners or cowards. "I don't want no civilizers around my boy," she said, sneering at the prisoner.

Mrs. Turtlebane made a quick upward thrust with the stone knife. Aidan closed his eyes and offered up a quick prayer, sorrowful that his life was ending so early and so suddenly. He felt no pain. But on the other hand, he didn't feel dead either. Opening one eye, he saw the vine gag lying on the ground, cut in two. Opening the other, he stared at the she-feechie sawing away at the vines that bound his hands.

"I don't want no civilizers around my boy!" Mrs. Turtlebane re-peated. Then she broke into a greenish grin. "But for them what saves his life, I can make an exception."

–The Bark of the Bog Owl by Jonathan Rogers, pg. 112

The bits of humor tickling us here bring the savor of clashing wills, a glimpse of what love is, and that the unexpected can surprise us with hope. Good humor is full of hope, and that hope does not disappoint.

Laughter, at least a grin, creates for us a warmth of joy, much needed in our world where pure humor is so seldom found. Walking in another's larger shoes brings us to laughter, to clean, sparkling humor. And all creatures growing toward goodness know how to laugh, or at least want to.

Peoples of wisdom can laugh at one another's oddities without offense. For they recognize it as the unexpected in themselves. Evil persons take offense at the most innocent laugh—imagining it a slight to their intelligence. The opposite is true, if they only knew it. But they kill humor with their cynicism, believing the worst.

Cynicism is often a weapon of those who oppose our champions. These evil creatures, tyrants, and villains, believing the worst, quite against their will often mold our heroes into the great hearts they become. The most intriguing and *The Best Evil Creatures, Tyrants, and Villains Defeat Themselves.*

Chapter 9.0

The Best Evil Creatures, Tyrants, and Villains Defeat Themselves

Evil characters—in fantasy or otherwise, tend to sow the seeds of their own destruction. Is it not so? Though they win at times, even prosper, their end is sure. Cunning or dull of wit, sooner or later they fall and their judgment comes. The smarter they are, and the greater their temporary gain, the more they lose. And the more dangerous and desperate they become, sensing their end approaching.

We have noticed that the people these villains, creatures, and tyrants hurt as they force their way toward their goal by whatever means they think necessary, are often the same people who see justice done upon them, directly or indirectly. They either live to see their antagonists fall or, if killed by the villain, they act as a catalyst that draws together the winds of change to overthrow them.

Through the clashing tides of strife and goodwill, of cunning villains and persevering heroes in the ocean of fantasy, some hearts die, some live, and right never despairs for long; it remembers that justice *will* be done, even if it comes after our earthly eyes close.

For evil characters tend to defeat themselves, refusing the mercy of love, payment of their debt, and the freedom of changing masters. They love the tyranny of bowing to themselves. There is no harsher master, when all softening traces of goodness are gone, and all that is left is a kind of endless devouring, the hunger that swallowed the self they called their own. They are instruments of their own demise because of the royal law that declares what is sown will be reaped.

When any of us believes we can become what we will in the face of moral law, the falsehood we embrace with determination blinds us with the belief that we can do what we will with impunity or a mere rap on the knuckles. We become a villain on our own journey, destroying those around us. Even if we later turn from evil, there are consequences to some extent. Better never to begin on such a road. However small or large a part we play on our voyage, let us leave the villain's selfish ways to tyrants and evil creatures.

Dine with dire dragons in *Heartless* in the Tales of Goldstone Wood. Behold wicked magic wielders in *Homeland,* find dwarves dangerous and deadly in *Prince Caspian,* and outwit Trolls and other nasty customers in *The Silver Call.* And never forget that villains are *not* always stupid, as *Airman* proves. Yet know that all villains carry the seeds of their own destruction. It is not possible to escape the law of the King in *A Princess of Wind and Wave.*

Dive 9.1

Have You Eaten With Dragons in the Tales of Goldstone Wood?

A bad dragon must be stopped, or it will devour forever.

Sometimes we unwittingly invite a villain in. We've seen it again and again, in our world and elsewhere. This is a particular trick of the evil dragon. He pretends to bring goodness and wisdom, but we are blessed to escape with our life if we strike a bargain with a bad dragon, who deceives.

Only the king and the young prince were at the table that evening, seated in the glow of tall taper candles. Nurse bobbed a curtsey to them when she opened the door before scuttling off into a corner, where she crouched like a hunted animal.

"Ah, Una," Fidel said when his daughter entered. "I was wondering—" His voice died when he saw upon whose arm she hung.

"Good evening, Your Majesty," the man with the white face said, bowing deeply. "Your daughter has invited me to dine."

A candle sputtered.

The king's wine glass shattered on the floor.

Fidel grabbed a carving knife and lunged at the man.

Quick as thought, the man grabbed Fidel's wrist, twisted him around, and slammed him facedown into the table. Plates and cutlery fell and smashed. Felix leapt to his feet, shouting, "Guards!"

The man with the white face silenced him with a look. Felix fell back in his chair, his mouth shaped in a silent scream even as footsteps sounded in the hall. Guards burst into the room.

"Stay back," the man with the white face said, turning slowly on the ten armed men who crowded the doorway.

He smiled, and they fell away, one of them crying, "Heaven shield us!"

"Well, Your Majesty," the man with the white face said, leaning down to whisper in the king's ear. "That wasn't very friendly of you."

"Monster!" the king barked. "Demon!" Wine from an over-turned cup ran into his beard, staining his face like blood.

"Sticks and stones, dear king," the man laughed. His grip on Fidel's wrist tightened until the king's fingers went blue and he dropped his knife. The man in the black cloak hauled him upright and turned him to face his guards, who shifted and growled, hands on their weapons.

–*Heartless* by Anne Elizabeth Stengl, pgs. 173-174

Fighting a dragon to win our heart is the part of a true prince. For a bad dragon must be stopped, or it will devour all and leave nothing but ash.

Evil creatures are also a vortex of winds of change, and call heroes and heroines of all races to combat. Even a dark elf from the heart of the earth.

How Does Magic Affect Evil Elves in The Dark Elf* trilogy?

Evil and good are far more than skin deep. We think most of us agree that skin color has never determined the purity of the heart beneath, and never will. Two of equally black skin may show themselves entirely different, as The Dark Elf brings to light.

> *"Impossible," Masoj muttered when he found his breath. Could the young Do'Urden actually defeat an elemental? Masoj scanned the rest of the area. Several drow and many gnomes lay dead or grievously wounded, but the main fighting was moving even farther away as the gnomes found their tiny escape tunnels and the drow, enraged beyond good sense, followed them.*
>
> *Guenhwyvar was gone. In this chamber, only Masoj, the elemental, and Drizzt remained as witnesses. The invisible wizard felt his mouth draw up in a smile. Now was the time to strike.*
>
> *Drizzt had the elemental lurching to one side, nearly beaten, when the bolt roared in, a blast of lightning that blinded the young drow and sent him flying into the chamber's back wall. Drizzt watched the twitch of his hands, the wild dance of his stark white hair before his unmoving eyes. He felt nothing—no pain, no reviving draw of air into his lungs—and heard nothing, as if his life force had been somehow suspended.*
>
> *The attack dispelled Masoj's dweomer of invisibility, and he came back in view, laughing wickedly. The elemental, down in a*

broken, crumbled mass, slowly slipped back into the security of the stone floor.

"Are you dead?" the wizard asked Drizzt, the voice breaking the hush of Drizzt's deafness in dramatic booms. Drizzt could not answer, didn't really know the answer anyway. "Too easy," he heard Masoj say, and he suspected that the wizard was referring to him and not the elemental.

Then Drizzt felt a tingling in his fingers and bones and his lungs heaved suddenly, grabbing a volume of air. He gasped in rapid succession, then found control of his body and realized that he would survive.

Masoj glanced around for returning witnesses and saw none. "Good," he muttered as he watched Drizzt regain his senses. The wizard truly was glad that Drizzt's death had not been so very painless. He thought of another spell that would make the moment more fun.

A hand—a gigantic stone hand—reached out of the floor just then and grasped Masoj's leg, pulling his feet right into the stone.

The wizard's face twisted in a silent scream.

. . . Drizzt snatched up one of the scimitars from the ground and hacked at the elemental's arm. The weapon sliced in, and the monster, its head reappearing between Drizzt and Masoj, howled in rage and pain and pulled the trapped wizard deeper into the stone.

With both hands on the scimitar's hilt, Drizzt struck as hard as he could, splitting the elemental's head right in half. This time the rubble did not sink back into its earthen plane; this time the elemental was destroyed.

–The Dark Elf trilogy by R. A. Salvatore, pg. 215

One heart was set on murder, and the other on defending that murderer, at the double risk of his life. Imminent death has a way of drawing lines between truth and lie, of forcing us to deal with our corruption, on the side of darkness or light.

Evil and good are far more than skin deep. We all carry blackness in our hearts, no matter our outer color, and either the evil is killed, or it kills us. And though we think the cure may kill us, the blackness must be dealt with.

Dive 9.3

Is There a Time to Die When Men Are So Easily Corrupted?

What wrong will we die to today? What right will we live to?

Dying and living can *both* be dangerous and deadly. That is the nature of choice in life. Whenever we live to one thing, we are dying to another. But some things are worth dying *for*.

Dying for the sake of hope often brings life, as it does in *A Time to Rise*. It is odd that it is often necessary to die, sometimes literally, in order to truly live.

> *I am Parvin Blackwater.*
>
> *Where is Skelley Chase, the Council member who helped kill me? Where is Solomon? Did he escape? He can't possibly know the Council buried me alive.*
>
> *I'm alive.*
>
> *With this thought comes a rerun of the emotions that abducted my heart the last time I was awake. Hope that my friends escaped. Peace in the sacrifice of my life for their sakes.*
>
> *"I'm alive!" I laugh and then clap my lips shut. There goes more oxygen, but I'm not afraid. I should be dead, which means God had different plans. And that means . . .*
>
> *I'm escaping this coffin.*

This is the second time in my life I've willingly embraced death, and both times God responded with, NOT YET. Giddy excitement fills my heaving chest with a thousand mini bubbles. What does He have in store for me?

I squirm in the space. It's roomy—not made for me. My feet hit something lumpy. Ugh, not another body! No, it's too small to be a body.

How does one escape a buried box? I don't have a nanobook to send a message for help. Besides, I have no idea where I'm buried. Help would be too late, NAB or not. I'm not strong enough to lift the dirt, but the Council probably buried me with haste to get rid of the evidence, so they might not have buried me down all six feet.

The Council. They think I'm dead. Once I escape, I'll be invisible to them.

–*A Time to Rise* by Nadine Brandes, pgs. 8-9

Dying is not easy if we have time to watch it come, if we have time to choose between the dangers of death and life, as Parvin did.

Villains are often desperate, and we find with Trumpkin in *Prince Caspian* that dying or living is perilous in another way.

Dive 9.4

Why Are the Dwarves in *Prince Caspian* Dangerous and Deadly?

Villainous characters deal in dangerous, false ideas. Don't false ideas, when we know they will bring about evil, force us to act, if we count ourselves an honorable person? One such idea is that the boundary of right action is expedience.

Thoughts that are not true are poison, and villainous ideas often creep in slowly.

> "Yes," said Nikabrik very slowly and distinctly, "I mean the Witch. Sit down again. Don't all take fright at a name as if you were children. We want power: and we want a power that will be on our side. As for power, do not the stories say that the Witch defeated Aslan, and bound him, and killed him on that very stone which is over there, just beyond the light?"
>
> "But they also say that he came to life again," said the Badger sharply.
>
> "Yes, they say," answered Nikabrik, "but you'll notice that we hear precious little about anything he did afterwards. He just fades out of the story. How do you explain that, if he really came to life? Isn't it much more likely that he didn't, and that the stories say nothing more about him because there was nothing more to say?"
>
> "He established the Kings and Queens," said Caspian.

"A King who has just won a great battle can usually establish himself without the help of a performing lion," said Nikabrik. There was a fierce growl, probably from Trufflehunter.

"And anyway," continued Nikabrik, "what came of the Kings and their reign? They faded too. But it's very different with the Witch. They say she ruled for a hundred years: a hundred years of winter. There's power, if you like. There's something practical."

"But, heaven and earth!" said the King, "haven't we always been told that she was the worst enemy of all? Wasn't she a tyrant ten times worse than Miraz?"

"Perhaps," said Nikabrik in a cold voice. "Perhaps she was for you humans, if there were any of you in those days. Perhaps she was for some of the beasts. She stamped out the Beavers, I dare say; at least there are none of them in Narnia now. But she got on all right with us Dwarfs. I'm a Dwarf and I stand by my own people. We're not afraid of the Witch."

"But you've joined with us," said Trufflehunter.

"Yes, and a lot of good it has done my people so far," snapped Nikabrik. "Who is sent on all the dangerous raids? The Dwarfs. Who goes short when the rations fail? The Dwarfs. Who—"

"Lies! All lies!" said the Badger.

"And so," said Nikabrik, whose voice now rose to a scream, "if you can't help my people, I'll go to someone who can."

"Is this open treason, Dwarf?" asked the king.

"Put that sword back in its sheath, Caspian," said Nikabrik. "Murder at council, eh? Is that your game? Don't be fool enough to try it. Do you think I'm afraid of you? There's three on my side, and three on yours."

"Come on, then," snarled Trufflehunter, but he was immediately interrupted.

"Stop, stop, stop," said Master Cornelius. "You go on too fast. The Witch is dead. All the stories agree on that. What does Nikabrik mean by calling on the Witch?"

That grey and terrible voice which had spoken only once before said, "Oh, is she?"

And then the shrill, whining voice began, "Oh, bless his heart, his dear little Majesty needn't mind about the White Lady—that's what we call her—being dead. The Worshipful Master Doctor is only making game of a poor old woman like me when he says that. Sweet master doctor, learned master doctor, who ever heard of a witch that really died? You can always get them back."

"Call her up," said the grey voice. "We are all ready. Draw the circle. Prepare the blue fire."

Above the steadily increasing growl of the Badger and Cornelius's sharp "What?" rose the voice of King Caspian like thunder.

"So that is your plan, Nikabrik! Black sorcery and the calling up of an accursed spirit. And I see who your companions are—a Hag and a Wer-Wolf!"

–Prince Caspian by C. S. Lewis, pgs. 163-165

All disguised villainy becomes apparent with time, and then it must be fought or it will take the day without a blow struck. Clean story fights evil ideas on the battleground of the heart and mind. The hero in fantasy usually joins the spiritual fight to drive the blade of truth home, and cuts off the poison at its physical root, defeats its full-flowering plan, and scatters its poison flower before innocents can eat the lethal fruit. So a black dwarf can be deadly and dangerous at once, with deadly ideas and dangerous strange friends.

Or a dwarf can simply be dangerous and deadly, as Trumpkin was; dangerous to disloyalty, and deadly to ideas proved false. Even his own ideas. Though he did not believe in Aslan, once he had evidence he could trust, he believed indeed.

Nikabrik's mistake was thinking he could lure or force his companions to his way of thinking. Evil creeps in at every opportunity, but hearts cannot be forced, only persuaded. Whether for bad or for good, paths divide and hearts choose.

Faisal shrugged. "Allah says to convince unbelievers with whatever must be. If they do not come willingly, the sword shepherds them to knowledge."

"Yes, Allah says so." Kyrin forced her thick tongue around the words. "Our Father says not. A sword convinces no one's heart, but his body alone. Our Father's power comes from his love—he will have the best for us. Though he lets those who wish choose their own way."

Faisal's brow wrinkled. "Why do you speak of love? Love is for women. Loving is a part of their nature, for children. The joy of the sword is for men." He tapped his stick against his knee and smiled, a quick quirk. "Let us rest this hot hour, and in the morning Cicero will chase us rabbits to shoot."

Kyrin wished her lips could lock closed over what lay in her, a burning, heavy stone. She whispered, "Faisal, falcons must fly with the same wind to fly together. We do not. My Father opposes Allah. Allah, who feeds you other peoples' blood and takes you where the wind of mercy is not."

Faisal's brows slammed together.

Kyrin slid the falcon dagger from her sash and touched the point, forcing her tears back with the prick. She held up the blade and looked at him over the edge. "If this threatened to draw your life away, would you believe my Father?"

His mouth flattened and he looked aside. Then he took the falcon, tugging it free of her fingers with a wry smile. "Will you wait to see if we might enjoy the journey together, and fly to the same eyrie in the end?"

That Faisal. "You do not hear. Our path divides."

–Falcon Heart by Azalea Dabill, pgs. 266-267

Every heart takes one path or the other. Either the false or the true. Paths divide, and hearts choose. Dying to one thing and living to another. Truth leads to joy.

Persevere in the clash of tides, of ideas, of actions. Be dangerous and deadly in a good way. Follow truth into the world of the spirit, through the realm of ideas, and into the sphere we breathe in.

Dive 9.5

Learn How to Fight Trolls and Nasty Customers in The Silver Call

How do our heroines and heroes combat nasty characters, terrible villains, and the evil subtly working in themselves and other good people? We look to our Creator and our books of knowledge.

They do it as any warrior does: with a weapon. And much help from trustworthy companions. Whatever sphere we breathe in, weapons for our warfare are vital, and also a staunch companion who has our back.

But the Rūck numbers were many and the Squad but seven strong, and it would be only a matter of moments til the comrades would be overwhelmed.

Perry was still on the ground amid dead Spawn, grasping in the dirt for Bane; and Barak, above him, fought for both of their lives.

The Hlōk leader jumped forward with his curved scimitar slashing, and Barak engaged the larger foe. There was a clanging of axe on blade, and Perry was kicked aside. The Warrow glanced up and saw that Barak was pressing the Hlōk back; yet a Rūck from behind smashed a long iron cudgel into the Dwarf's skull, and Barak fell. The Hlōk leapt over Barak's still form and grabbed Perry by the front of his tunic, jerking him up off the ground, feet flailing and kicking. And with a slobbering, leering laugh, the huge Hlōk drew back his scimitar, preparing to back-handedly lop off the Warrow's head.

Just then a loud, venomous oath barked from the dimness beyond the firelight: "Hai, Rûpt!" At this cry the Hlōk's head snapped up, and with fear in his eyes he looked frantically into the gloom for the source of the challenge, the Warrow dangling from his grip momentarily forgotten.

At the moment the Rūcken leader jerked up to see—Sss-thok!— an arrow hissed out of the blackness and struck the creature be- tween the eyes . . .

–Trek to Kraggen-Cor by Dennis McKiernan, pg. 203

Journeying with companions who care is essential for every hero, just as choosing the right weapon brings failure or victory to the field of battle, in the arena of earth or the realm of fantasy.

Cotton, his eyes locked upon the massive War-bar, stepped back, and his foot came down upon the edge of the great split. He tee- tered and gasped in fear, his arms windmilling. And the vast dark gulf gaped blackly, and waited. Yet with a twisting motion, the Warrow managed to fall forward. And as he had been trained, Cotton rolled as he landed, to come back to his feet in a balanced stance with sword in hand to again face the foe. The great Cave Troll snarled in anger, yet its eyes took on a look of evil cunning, for it still had the wee Warrow trapped; and the monster swooshed the bar in a feint followed by a swift overhand stroke.

Crack! *The iron pole just missed the dodging Warrow, so close it ticked a golden scale.*

Again Cotton leapt to one side and then lunged forward; and the blazing rune-jeweled Troll's Bane flashed up as Cotton plunged it into the Ogru's kneecap: the stone-like skin that easily turned aside axes and swords yielded like soft butter to the flaming El- ven-blade; the point sank through the cap and into the knee joint, plunging nearly to the sinews at the back of the leg. Cotton jerked Bane out and twisted aside; black blood dropped from the bitter blade to the stone floor, and where it fell a reeking smoke coiled up from the hard rock.

The great Troll roared in agony and clutched at its pierced knee, and stumbled with a sliding crash to the stone at the lip of the great black abyss, to slip over the edge, grasping frantically but in vain at the smooth floor. And with a bellow of terror and its eyes wide in fear, and still gripping the massive War-bar, the huge Ogru fell howling beyond the rim and down into the bottomless black depths.

Cotton stared for a moment at the place where the Troll had gone over the edge; then the Warrow scooped up the Atalar Blade and ran back to Perry, who was conscious again.

–*The Brega Path* by Dennis McKiernan, pgs. 134-135

A staunch companion is a beautiful thing, even as the right weapon is fearsome. Given to our hand, that weapon can bring down the designs of the vilest creature, while a loyal friend may confound the worst villain and the strongest tyrant.

We have won. But our greatest heroes have their weaknesses, as we all do, and evil leaders are seldom dull of wit.

Dive 9.6

A Smart Villain Faces Off Against the *Airman*

Just because a person is evil does not mean they are stupid. True, the indiscipline of badness tends to corrupt the mind into a fat and flaccid state, but evil people are often intelligent, or cunning at the least. They will not easily flee the battlefield of the spirit, the battleground of ideas, or the arena of earth, but fight upon all of them. At the least, they order their henchmen to fight.

We must use all at our disposal. A physical weapon, spiritual weapons of knowledge, perseverance, and the strength of an indomitable heart, or friendship, allies, or help unlooked for.

Sometimes in battle a weapon works best as a distraction as we bring our larger arsenal to bear—the knowledge and the will that drives that weapon effectually. In our world or that of fantasy, at times our mind and heart can determinedly fire ideas on an effective path against evil swifter than our hands can bring the first blow. So a feint with our physical weapon is necessary, as we loose every lawful power against the evil that has risen. Because our enemies are not stupid, in mind or body.

Conor Broekhart might be a genius, but Hugo Bonvilain was ingenious. This situation was a test of his mettle. It would involve some quick thinking, but already the germ of a new plan was sprouting roots in the marshall's mind. There would be murder involved, but that was not really an issue, except it could very well be murder at a high level; and when indulging in such murders, one must seem completely blameless. European royal families did not approve of commoners disposing of their monarchs. And royal disapproval generally took the form of approaching warships and annexation. Hugo Bonvilain did not intend to share his diamonds or his seat of power with anybody, especially not with Isabella's close friend Queen Victoria of the British Empire.

The Bonvilains had been striving for too many centuries to reach the very position that he was in now for him to pack his satchel at the first sign of worthy opposition.

Bonvilain remembered the night his father died. He had been raving from the leprosy that he had picked up on a pilgrimage to Jerusalem, and much of what he had said was gibberish, but there were moments when his eyes were as clear as they had ever been.

We have been pruning, *he'd said to the young Bonvilain.* Do you know what I'm saying to you, Hugo? For centuries we have been pruning the Trudeaus. They breed like rabbits, God blast them, but we have set the crown on the right head, keeping the Saltee Islands independent. You must finish the job. You are the last in the line of servants, and the first in a line of Bonvilain masters. Promise me, Hugo. Promise me.

And the dying man had clutched at his son's forearm with bandaged hands.

I promise, *Bonvilain had said, unable to look at the wasted remains of his father's face.*

It occurred to Bonvilain now that he had been rocking in his seat, knuckles to forehead for several moments, which might appear strange. He leaned back, tugging straight the red-crossed, white Templar stole over his navy suit. "That's my thinking position, Arthur. Any objections?"

–*Airman* by Eoin Colfer, pgs. 332-333

After a tyrant's ingeniously nasty ideas have been discovered, still the villain remains to be defeated, his plans to be dismantled. At this point, a determined hero can bring the power of moral law to bear against a villain of high genius. And his end looms.

But take a breath of light and truth and dive into the stormy waters of special powers in fantasy. Lying beneath the waves, hidden enticingly, are they talent, gift, or magic? And should magic ever be used? Whether special powers are true diamonds or false glass remains to be seen.

Dive 9.7

A Princess of Wind and Wave—and Magic

Should magic ever be used?

"Yes, always. If you have the power, why not use it," some say. "Never, magic is evil," others say. We say, "It depends."

On the face of it, the solution is simple. If magic is a power for goodness, yes, it should be used to defeat evil—with the caveat never in our human world, where magic is never lawful. But since it is never good in our world, how do we determine if it is lawful or good in a particular fantasy story?

First, by going to the highest authority in that world's universe, as long as that Creator is not a puppet fabricated of human thought or directed by demonic influence, but is an honest reflection of our King, whether the story has a few facets relating to him or many.

One such story, reflecting clear facets of truth, is the mer-people's undersea kingdom of Merrita, where they answer to the High King and his kingdom's servants, the godmothers.

My hand reached forward instinctively, but my father pulled the chest back.

"Don't touch it," he said sharply. "This is my most valuable and dangerous possession."

Carefully he lowered the lid back down, re-locked the chest, and returned it to its hiding place. When he turned back to me, his face was set in stern lines.

"You wish me to believe that what you did back there was merely rash thoughtlessness." He gestured back toward the ballroom. "Well, now is the chance to prove it. I have trusted you with my greatest treasure—you must never breathe a word of its existence to anyone."

"Father, I wouldn't—"

He gripped me by both shoulders, his hands firm and his eyes boring into me.

"No one, do you understand me, Isla? No one can know of this shell or its hiding place."

I nodded, hesitated, and then spoke. "Of course I won't say a word to a soul. But ... Father ... what is it?"

He sighed. "That is the royal conch. Royal blood, royal conch— that's what the godmothers told my ancestor." He looked tired again. "It is my responsibility to bear, and mine alone. As it will be Oceana's after me."

"Does it ... do something?" I asked, no less confused than before.

My father stared at me blankly for a moment, as if he didn't understand the question.

"Yes, of course it does something. If I blow into that conch, Merrita will rise again from the sea and take her place among the kingdoms of the land."

I fell back, gasping, my hand flying to my throat.

"You! You hold the power to restore us to the surface with our entire home intact?" I raced forward and gripped his arm with both hands. "But Father, that is wonderful! This is the answer to all our problems. You must blow it before our barrier fails us."

"No." He spoke sharply, frowning down at me. "We have no proof the barrier is failing. Our Family has been tasked for generations with keeping our people safe until it is time to rise again."

"But surely now is the time," I cried, letting my hands drop. "The High King has sent us warnings, just as he did before Merrita sank. Here is the proof that we were always meant to rise—I don't understand how you've been denying the warnings all this time when you knew about this artifact."

"It is time you finally accepted that you are the one misinterpreting the message," my father said. "I can see now that it was foolishness to keep the truth from you—even though it was motivated by love and a desire to shield you. You're far too stubborn." His voice dropped. "Just like she was."

–*A Princess of Wind and Wave* by Melanie Cellier, pgs. 54-55

Moral principles in any world, pursued to the uttermost, bring us to light, which comes from the Person who brought every truth of reality into existence. All law springs from our Creator, including the moral law within us. As part of his creation in this world, we are divided into those who follow his laws and those who do not. This fact extends to our stories, where magic may be good or sorcerous.

Other lands where some kinds of magic, or power, are lawful, with honest representation of our Creator, include *Narnia*, Donita K. Paul's DragonSpell series, Andrew Peterson's Wingfeather Saga series, Karen Hancock's Legends of the Guardian King series, Anna Thayer's Knight of Eldaran trilogy, Anne Elizabeth Stengl's Tales of Goldstone Wood series, Jill Williamson's Blood of Kings series, Jeffrey Overstreet's Auralia Thread series, and S. D. Smith's The Green Ember series.

Many lands portray lawful magic with shadowy glimpses of a higher power who does not represent the Creator as accurately, either because of lack of details or vague theology. These include Middle Earth, McKiernan's *The Iron Tower,* Elizabeth Moon's Deed of Paksenarrion trilogy, and Megan Whelan Turner's The Queen's Thief series. Though these fantasies do not portray the Creator as well as some stories, they excellently depict the people, their quests, and underlying moral principles. Moral principles that drive these heroes to fight oppression and dishonor to their last breath, using every lawful power at their command.

But some fantasies merely call unlawful magick *power,* and make no distinction between good and evil besides the ends gained, whether they are expedient. Why is this dangerous? Because if we follow that line of thought we are in danger of becoming the villain, using evil means to gain an end that may not even be good. As Frodo discovered, the ring of power led every user into doing evil, because its power *was* evil.

Yes, lawful magic *should* be used, and every good power. From the everyday power of Sam's generous, loyal heart, Frodo's compassion and courage, and their companions' humor, to the magic Gandalf bore with authority, to the powers of wisdom and armed resistance of the elves.

To fight evil effectively, we must know who and what we're looking at. Is who we see an ally, or a dark lord's underling? Is the power they wield magic or something else? Is what they call *good* really so?

We and our heroes and heroines bring various kinds of power to bear against characters who align themselves with oppression, selfish ambition, and sorcery in moral fantasy. From our heart's courage to every physical tool, weapon, or mental gift and beyond, the abilities we do have lead us deeper into a conversation about magical power and the abilities we wish we had. *Special Powers in Fantasy—Are They a Talent, Gift, or Magic?*

Chapter 10.0

Special Powers in Fantasy—Are They a Talent, Gift, or Magic?

Are the powers in fantasy that characters use inherent talents and learned skills, or a gift, and are they associated with good magic or dark magick with a "k"? Sorting which is which ultimately comes down to three things: who the power is from, which world it is used in, and how a person uses it. These give us clues to the truth.

Witches and wizards get their power from evil spirits, ergo, demons, however their power is disguised as coming from a passed loved one, Mother Earth or Gaia, a form of the Force, or supposed gods or elemental spirits.

Magic, as the word is used in our world, carries the connotation of manipulation of unusual power by using certain rituals or spells. In fantasy books, magic is often used to define both good and bad power. To most people, magic itself is neither good nor bad, it is simply power. But that is not true.

The magic many fantasy stories often contain portrays some of the methods of real magick that witches pursue in our world, magick with a "k". Things like mediums who consult the dead or tarot cards, arranging words and saying them a certain way as a spell of power, tapping or honoring the powers of elemental spirits, opening your mind to channel the voices of the universe and hear their messages, using crystals for a focus, scrying as a form of foretelling, etc. If this magick is pursued only by the villains of the fantasy story, without the author going into too much detail, all is well and good, for their evil is shown as evil, as the White Witch is revealed. A distinction has been drawn.

For a distinction there is. Good power comes from our Creator, always, the shaper and maker and giver of life. From *good magic* or power, to the power of inherent talents and skills or gifts, all are given by the Creator as tools for good.

For we possess power in both worlds, in different senses. In fantasy, we bring the power of our own mind and spirit to bear alongside the heart and eyes of the character we see their world through. In our world we have the power of our mind, heart, and spirit to inspire others, and the ability to do things with our own hands. We most definitely hold this power, in both worlds, in a different spirit than a fantasy villain. To us, every power carries privileges but also responsibility. Those who become villains desire the privilege without responsibility.

Even though every story in other worlds is a mental extrapolation, what we *habitually* engage within our minds and hearts exists for us in some form, as a kind of lesser reality, and eventually impacts our real world. What we focus on in fantasy becomes real to an extent, even if only in our own minds, which affects how we perceive our world and how we act.

We constantly check our experience of everything against real reality, which is where truth comes in. If we don't allow truth to show us what is really real, we have nothing to stand on, no ground to fight from, no reason to act in either world, no reality to base action on. We are simply falling through air, endlessly scrambling after a solid hope within deception. Until we hit bottom, and death, the last curtain between us and true reality.

This is why reading great adventures of right against wrong, why thinking brave thoughts, and why doing what is good, out of a heart of love, is vitally important. So that everyone may see the truth, and come to the Creator who gives us the solid hope and certainty that enters within the veil.

Everything in our mind builds on what came before it. It is imperative that we see those fighting for good in the spiritual arena as well as those seeking to undermine goodness, it is vital that we keep a watch on the ideas in the wide worlds that grow truth, courage, and perseverance, and those that foster lies, discouragement, and despair. The battle in the spiritual arena is real, the fight is raging between world ideologies, and we are called to be a warrior in our own sphere. This is why what we read, though it is but facets of the real in the imaginary, heavily impacts the sphere we breathe in.

Only in our Creator do we live and move and have our being.

So there can be lawful magic, and we thoroughly enjoy stories with magical power set in worlds like Donita K. Paul's Amarra. There, the general definitions of *good magic* and *wizard* are completely different than sorcerous magick with a "k". In *DragonQuest* sources of good and evil power and character motives are delineated and not confused in the least.

> *Again, everyone in the room turned as one to see a third cake, which had appeared out of nowhere.*
>
> *Regidor harrumphed. "That still doesn't mean Kale and I can make cakes appear all around the room."*
>
> *"It doesn't?" Fenworth tilted his gray head to one side as if considering the matter. He stood that way for almost a minute, long enough for a vine to shoot out a tendril from his beard. "Are you sure, Regidor?" He considered the young meech dragon. "Have you tried?"*
>
> *Regidor's eyes narrowed in suspicion. He shook his head slowly.*
>
> *Fenworth clapped his hands together, a smile breaking across his wrinkled face. "That does it, then. You must try. Tut-tut. Can't say you can't until you've tried. Kale, come here and stand next to Regidor."*
>
> *Kale hurried across the room and stood shoulder to shoulder with her fellow apprentice.*

Now he's going to teach us! *She grinned at Dar across the room.*

"Close your eyes, both of you, " commanded Fenworth. "Picture in your mind the milk and eggs being stirred into the flour and baking powder.

"A batter forms. Since this is one of Wulder's principles, there is nothing you can do to stop this particular combination from turning into cake batter. "

Kale heard Bardon come to stand behind her. She inhaled the citrus smell of another o-rant. All her people carried the same tart fragrance.

Do all my people have an innate ability to perform wizardry? Could Bardon be an apprentice too?

"Tut-tut, your mind is wandering, Kale. "

Kale squelched the annoyance she felt. Bardon's presence had distracted her. She paid strict attention to Wizard Fenworth's deep, rough voice.

"Imagine pouring the mixture into pans and placing them in the oven. Yes, yes, that's right. The heat causes the batter to rise and solidify, another handy edict from Wulder.

"Think, think, children. What comes next? Oh dear, oh dear, don't jump ahead to the frosting, Regidor. Cool your cake. "

Kale heard Bardon expel a breath of air and felt the hair on the back of her head stir.

I will *not* let that bothersome lehman get me in trouble. I *will* pay attention to my teacher.

"Wizardry is all a matter of appreciating Wulder's creation, taking the time to understand the intricacies of the universe and then applying that knowledge. Quite simple, really.

"Slowly, slowly, step by step. Wulder has established what will go together and what will not. You are merely following His directions. "

Toopka's high-pitched squeal pierced the room. "Oh! Look! Look!"

Kale opened her eyes. Two more cakes sat on the table beside the first.

"Excellent!" Fenworth beamed and clapped his hands. "Enough wizard's cake for company, I should say. Unless Paladin sends us more than one urohm."

–*DragonQuest* by Donita K. Paul, pgs. 85-86

The heroes of Amarra are half scientists, half wizards, as they manipulate atoms within a framework of natural laws, though they bring their results about by words and thought instead of direct physical action. A knowledge and a power given to them by Wulder, the Creator of Amarra.

See how a definition can get fuzzy when it is used to describe two widely different or opposing things? Like a *wizard* who derives his power and knowledge from an evil spirit, and a *wizard* who gains his power from knowledge of his Creator's laws, physical and spiritual? Or a *magick* that manipulates a spell to call up an evil being, versus the power gained by seeking the face and law of the Life-giver of all things?

In many fantasy stories, definitions of good magic are pointedly stated in that world, or they may be implied by threads of context that they are different than sorcery, like the magic of Coriakin in Narnia, or of Uncle Andrew's rings in *The Magician's Nephew* governed by some kind of natural magnetic laws. And then, sometimes *magic* is used in fantasy synonymously with *gifting* or *inborn talent,* like in Rachel Neumeier's The Griffin Mage trilogy.

Amnachudran shrugged. "You were face down. I didn't see the brand at once. By the time I did see it, I knew you might live. Once I knew that, I couldn't leave you." He didn't ask, Are you glad or sorry I saved your life? But his eyes posed that question.

Gereint stared back at him for a moment in silence. He said at last, "That desert is not the place I would choose to leave my bones." Gathering up his line and hook, he went down to the river.

By full dark, the soup was boiling and two small fish were grilling over coals.

"I didn't think you'd catch any," Amnachudran admitted, turning one of the fish with a pair of twigs.

"I was lucky."

"That was a good hook. Nor would I have thought you could make a decent line out of that cord."

"It's a knack." Gereint turned the other fish.

"You're a maker."

And Amnachudran was far too perceptive, and far too difficult to lie to. It hadn't been a question. Gereint said merely, not looking up, "It makes me a valuable slave, yes."

–*Land of the Burning Sands* by Rachel Neumeier, pg. 31

We're not talking here about the innate ability to explore our spiritual side, claimed by witches, neo-pagans, and spiritists, who choose to twist spirituality apart from rightful authority. We are talking about a Creator-given power or gift, approved by him in another world. There are many skills and talents in far worlds, such as the telepathy in Kathy Tyer's *One Mind's Eye.*

So *magic* is sometimes a synonym for a talent, a gift, or a lawful power without reference to spirits or witchcraft of any sort. Or it may be spawned by the deepest pit of unlawful magick, used to awful effect by beings whose eyes are locked on our destruction. How better to do that than get us to drink of their poisoned power? For power holds an almost irresistible and an unreasoning attraction for us.

For that is where magick arts with a "k" come from, our seeking power which we have not been created to hold. Not yet.

This makes for interesting diving in the waters of fantasy, and careful examination of every treasure chest brought up, to sort false glass and flawed crystal from the diamonds. So, in answer to the question: are the powers in fantasy merely inherent talents and learned skills, or are they gifts, or are they dark magick? A story can hold all three.

Behold the cunning skill of our enemy to put good to wrong use in *The Two Towers,* define magic and the ways of power through The Chronicles of Narnia, sift pearls from sand in *The Iron Tower,* and find a lawful dreamwalker in *Flight of the Raven. The Prodigy* is a story about how the supernatural ties into inherent talent or gifting in our world, though again, some might call it magic. The power is real. The author of that power, we challenge you to discern.

Then we face the allure of magick in The Sword, the Ring and the Chalice series and learn of motive and method and gifts in another world, and the clouded thought of paganism. We also find that inherent laws of magic are not necessarily paradoxical in *DragonQuest,* and discover how telepathy and other powers are pivotal to *One Mind's Eye.*

Explore how rightful power transforms a *Cloak of Light*; watch dreams call forth secrets of the soul in *Falcon Flight,* discover thrilling prophecy by vision that brings victory in *The Shadow and Night*. Watch all three powers—gifts, dreams, and prophecy intertwine in Chris Walley's The Lamb Among the Stars trilogy. In these worlds there may also be sorcerous villains, where power is dark magick.

Dive 10.1

Fantasy Power can Easily be Sorcerous Dark Magick

Our enemy is cunning. It is even more challenging to sort evil powers from good in fantasy when other terms appear interchangeable, such as the name *seeing stone* or *crystal ball*. Both are beautiful polished lumps of clear, hard carbon, but serve vastly opposite purposes in their use.

Tolkien's "lost seeing stones" were not used in connection with spirits of the dead, or demons, though Sauron did use one as a tool to see across distances, much as we use Skype in our world. The seeing stones were not evil in themselves. Though that stone was still dangerous, serving the same function as a remote camera to pinpoint a target.

Tall ships and tall kings

Three times three,

What brought they from the foundered land

Over the flowing sea?

Seven stars and seven stones

And one white tree.

'What are you saying, Gandalf?' asked Pippin.

'I was just running over some of the Rhymes of Lore in my mind,' answered the wizard. *'Hobbits, I suppose, have forgotten them, even those that they ever knew.'*

'No, not all,' said Pippin. And we have many of our own, which wouldn't interest you, perhaps. But I have never heard this one. What is it about—the seven stars and seven stones?'

'About the Palantiri *of the Kings of Old,' said Gandalf.*

'And what are they?'

'The name meant that which looks far away. *The Orthanc-stone was one.'*

'Then it was not made, not made'—Pippin hesitated—'by the Enemy?'

'No,' said Gandalf. 'Nor by Saruman. It is beyond his art, and beyond Sauron's too. The Palantiri *come from beyond Westernesse, from Eldamar. The Noldor made them. Feanor himself, maybe, wrought them, in days so long ago that the time cannot be measured in years. But there is nothing that Sauron cannot turn to evil uses.*

–*The Two Towers* by J. R. R. Tolkien, pg. 258

A crystal ball, on the other hand, is used for the express purpose of conversing with spirits, and without the spirits would be nothing but a pretty rock.

Demons masquerade as spirits of the dead, which should be rather easy for them, since they *are* spirits. And as the Word says, why should we even try to consult the dead for counsel on behalf of the living? Who wants to ask a demon, a being who follows self-interest to its horrifyingly complete end, for advice?

Remember, there *is* magic in our world, dark magick. There are no forms of *white magic,* no lawful ability to move things with our minds, to use words to short-cut natural processes, like making a cake. Not for us. And I am glad there is no magic, after I thought about it a bit.

Magic in our world (as it is portrayed in fantasy) would add another, astronomical level of difficulty to our struggle against evil, especially in ourselves. Imagine being able to destroy or create even the *smallest* thing with a word.

There would be good done, yes, but the destruction wreaked would outweigh it by far. Some humans, probably most of us, would misuse it at one time or another. It would be another dimension to handle, and don't we have enough to do training our body, mind, and spirit in the ways of justice, love, and mercy? Or rather, letting our Creator mold us for our warfare in the physical and spiritual realms?

Though we *wish* we were fit for a power like magic. Or that we had the will to be heroic, to *change* things for good, no matter the cost. That's partially why we enjoy fantasy so much. There we dream of possibilities, and transformation, and see beauties often hidden in our world. There, by means of magic and heroic will, we learn change in any realm is possible, indeed, is inevitable in the end.

In this world, there is God's immeasurable power, which formed every good thing and every flower, and also Satan's power, which he twisted from its purpose, and that God has allowed him to keep for a time. And he is cunning. He entices us to turn from truth and embrace "all paths are equally true," even when we stand in the middle of a path that stretches on either side of us in opposite directions, leading to very different destinations.

Rather than tie magic to direct worship of himself in most cases, our enemy disguises it as latent, innate power, gained by worship of any of the gods and goddesses, whichever calls to the seeker. And we too often fall to that siren call, in spite of the fact we possess far greater power in our Creator. Real power, that won't fade away or fail.

The power to choose to align our will with God, to choose his life-giving Spirit, leading us to true individuality, at last free to do right, with no end in sight, as he created us to live richly. In our Creator, change is our destiny, and our final, perfect *change* is coming.

Our enemy would have us lose ourselves in destructive pride, as Sauron did, and twist every good to evil.

Though there is no lawful magic in our world at this time, there are hints in our Creator's Word that the laws of power may be different in heaven and in the new world after our earth. In his risen body our Creator's Son walked through walls, and among his other acts of power before he rose from the dead, on water.

Now *there* is the Master of the dead and the living. Glory be! If we are his, it might be in our future that these things we now call *fantasy powers* will not be the *magic* of a fantasy story, but inherent powers or gifts in a new body. There will be no danger then of our misusing them.

Only glorious days of play: building great and good things, gazing at the Giver of all, laughing in the beauty, the joy, the creation. Basking in his presence, in the warmth of Love and Life himself. But that is speculation on my part.

Of one thing we can be sure. Love is the strongest power of all, and we possess that now. May we grow and be trained in its greatest uses.

Of all the terms of power that may be horribly, ironically interchangeable at times, praying and spell-casting are two of them.

Dive 10.2

Prayer Has No Power in Itself But it Can Be Magick

Can a prayer be magic? We have heard rumor that some of us think prayer is powerful magic. For prayer can, it has, and it does play a large part in bringing about great acts of power in our world. But some of us treat prayer with certain words or names in it as magical, as a formula or rite, even chant that will grant our desires, though when we treat prayer so, it is doubly powerless.

For prayer has no power in itself, though (this might startle us) it can be magick with a "k". And very unlawful. Again, sorting power as wrong or right depends on who the power is from, how a person uses it, and which world it is used in. So it depends on what kind of prayer we are engaging in.

Prayer to who, and in what spirit, name, or nature? Are we praying to a tree, Buddha, a random spirit, or the Christ and who he is? In him, power and name and nature meet with authority—and if we pray to him, we must pray in spirit and in truth. When we pray, the power actually lies with the thing or person prayed to, ranging from the powerless and inanimate tree, to the dead, to the deceitful power of a random spirit, or the unlimited power of the I AM.

A note here to those of us who use prayer as a magic formula, seeking to compel or control by the use of any certain word, name, or arrangement of words—who, even among us, wants to be treated like a genie in a lamp?

True prayer does not coerce or command, it asks. It is opposite all magic in this respect: it does not manipulate by force or formula. All the power lies with the Person we ask for help.

Strictly defined, power in prayer never lies in a certain *way* we ask. Or a certain how, or when, or where: *our* strength, will, and determination have no bearing on "the power of prayer," for prayer has none. *He* considers our requests, our motives and methods; *he* decides his answer and decrees it in power and love. And mercy, since we often don't know how to pray.

Don't misunderstand. He *has* laid down ways we should approach him, in spirit and in truth, with thanksgiving, good motives, and sincere love among other things. His power flows in return, as he decrees. We *can* hinder our prayers by flippancy, or stubborn wrongdoing, or repetition for the purpose of manipulation. Our strength, will, and determination *do* affect the outcome of prayer in a sense. He has given us those things to enable us to reach out.

But all the power loosed and directed depends on his never-failing mercy and loving-kindness. Not on us, on how hard we pray or when, on our *feeling* of holiness or rightness or earnestness, or our lack of feeling them. When we take our feeble strength, our faulty will, our unstable determination, and kneel in the presence of his Spirit, then— then we become giants.

What name and nature and spirit are we of when we fall to our knees, down to our last weapon, which should have been our first?

Our Creator puts his endless power to work on behalf of those who are his, though we are so blindly familiar with it that often his power does not look glamorous, seem particularly special, or feel extravagantly powerful. We do not often look closely enough to see the new springs in dried up hearts that burst their bonds in living rivers under the influence of his power.

He has bound himself by solemn oath to perform what is best for us who belong to him. Thus the gift of restrained power, in some ways—like protecting us from being destroyed by full sight of his glory, power, and purity, until we are changed and enabled to see him as he is. Then the gift of his power loosed beyond what we dream, as he gives us the ability to walk aright. The power to change a heart, even our own, is beyond us. It is his daily work.

Many powers are his alone. Trying to force such powers to work for us apart from himself in any way, aka by magic or magic with a "k", or by wrongful prayer, is both laughable and flies in the face of all that is good, against the very well-springs of all life and love and laughter. This is why we agree with C. S. Lewis.

> *". . . we might draw a circle on the ground—and write things in queer letters in it—and stand inside it—and recite charms and spells . . .*
>
> *. . . now that it comes to the point, I've an idea that all those circles and things are rather rot. I don't think he'd like them. It would look as if we thought we could make him do things. But really, we can only ask him."*
>
> –*The Silver Chair* by C. S. Lewis, pg. 6

To come back to the idea of magic in fantasy worlds, yes at times other ways of power are lawful, and necessary, even delightful, because they bear no relation to magick with a "k." And yet . . . there is something better, something bigger, something that will eventually contain all good power and leave the word *magic* and its connotations behind, as the butterfly leaves the chrysalis.

That bright ability is the change that will bring control to our present powers of mind, body, and spirit, where magic is superseded by the heart to rule ourselves aright, by our Creator's grace. *Then* we will rightfully wield any power we contain or are given. Our old nature will be gone, never to rise again.

"Do you grow weary, Coriakin, of ruling such foolish subjects as I have given you here?"

"No," said the Magician, "they are very stupid but there is no real harm in them. I begin to grow rather fond of the creatures. Sometimes, perhaps, I am a little impatient, waiting for the day when they can be governed by wisdom instead of this rough magic."

–The Voyage of the Dawn Treader by C. S. Lewis, pg. 137

For now, we dream of good use of special powers, through "might have been," and "what if," or fantasy. By seeing our small, lawful local powers applied to mind-bending and soul-expanding horizons of fantasy, in ways magical and mundane, we learn to focus on the pivotal moment of truth, of choice. Because of that training, that clearer picture, we learn to use better the powers we hold in our world.

Prayer has no power in itself, it is a container offered under the thundering, life-giving waterfall of the loving power of our Creator. And his sparkling, clear power fills it to the brim, though it does not always hold the answer we wish. Yet in it is life. This should soon cure us of thinking of prayer as powerful in itself, or of treating prayer as formulaic magick. If we think of it "logically," as Peter would say.

Though our world is devoid of most special powers mentioned in fantasy, there are a couple that populate our world like colorful coral reefs. Our world is where they were born. One of them is prophecy.

Dive 10.3

The Power of Foreseeing in Fantasy as Prophecy

We have come across two very closely associated powers or gifts that span our world and fantasy. That of foreseeing and foretelling: or prophecy. Has prophecy or the power of the seer bloomed best among the reefs of our world? It was certainly born here, though it is now less common than it was. This mystery intrigues us.

In the realm of fantasy, most often prophecy is a tool of plot transplanted under the sea, where it may yet bloom prodigiously.

Some foreseeing is a mystery not understood at first telling, but a foretelling rede or missive that becomes clear at fulfillment. Other prophecy is quite clearly understood at the moment it is given, though its fulfillment is not clearly recognized, especially by those who oppose it. And sometimes the prophecy is neither understood at its beginning, nor fulfilled until much later, but both become clear.

Where does the power of prophecy come from and what is its purpose? Our Creator's Word is the best place to follow that path through history. Prophecy has been popular in our world since its creation. But not all prophecies are true.

Remember the three ways to tell if a power is associated with magick or if it is lawful? First its source, then whether it is authorized, and lastly, how and why it is used?

Foreseeing or foretelling is not necessarily, at first glance, either clearly magick or a gifted power, whether spoken by an oracle, a prophet, or by a seer (another name for a prophet or foreteller). Prophecies can be challenging to discern.

The power of prophecy at times has been given to us by God, and also to some among by our enemy. Prophets and oracles claim the power of prophecy even to this very day. How can we tell if the foreseeing or foretelling is good or evil, either in our world or fantasy?

The effects of all prophecy seem to be the same. Take prophets, foreseers, and fortune-tellers—they all claim to tell the future, to be given special insight beyond the veil of space, place, and time.

Our Creator has given us two keys to solve this riddle so that we can know which prophet, foreseer, or foreteller uses lying magick or hack sensationalism or plain lies, and which holds the true and rightful power of a God-given gift, to speak his Word.

The first key is obedience or disobedience, threads of context that run straight to the authority they serve.

Fortune-tellers directly oppose our Creator by disobeying his law and consorting with evil spirits. At times they do have partial glimpses of the future, and that's logical, since demons have been around our world some 6,000 years longer than we have, given our life-spans; with a wide history of experience with men, geography, and the natural and spiritual worlds. So they can predict partial truths, mixed in false foretelling.

A true prophet obeys the Lord, as Elisha and many in the past have, who made iron float in water, brought the dead to life, foretold the downfall of kings, and for-saw the outcomes of great battles. Even more, they were given glimpses of the time-line of our world, from its beginning to its end. And the glorious kingdom to come.

The second key to discern a true prophet from a false is if a foreteller's prophecy meets certain conditions—and then comes true. If the prophecy, its intent and scope, aligns with God's Word, the prophet claims power from him, *and* what that prophet says comes to pass, that prophet is empowered by our Creator.

God has allowed false prophets who oppose him to predict an event at times, though their prophecies as a whole do not align with his given Word, to test our hearts, whether we will be true to what he has already said.

So prophets may be legitimate messengers of God, or false dreamers and deceivers, pursuing their own glory and gold. There are many false prophets in fantasy and our world. We have seen no true prophets, in the old Testament sense, in our days as yet.

If we read his Word aright, it appears there may be two more seers coming in these last days of our world. And prophecy as a blatant power will bloom here again. But there are many reliable prophecies spoken long ago that have not yet come to pass. They will—some of them are shaping under our eyes. The Jews have returned to their land, and the temple plans are ready.

As it has enriched our world, prophecy has certainly added to fantasy. The greatest stories are those that reflect the mystery and power of true prophecy, and leads to foretelling and adventure in The Lamb Among the Stars series by Chris Walley.

But aren't there stories that use foreseeing, or prophecy by dreams, crystals for focus, spells, enchantments, or scrying and such things for good, against others that use the same things for evil, such as Andre Norton's *Crystal Gryphon?* And doesn't the power come from a source that is at times vaguely good or falsely mixed with Gaia, or which displays tangled human motives or intent so ill-defined it is nebulous?

In other words, are wrong methods to the power of foreseeing treated as right in fantasy, coming from a creator who is not a true picture of the universe's authority? Yes, there are many fantasies like the *Crystal Gryphon*, where the picture of power and authority is clouded or twisted. Reflected awry. Words used to shape mis-reflected meaning make a messy stew.

Most of us who love fantasy have read at least some of these.

One such reflection is The Iron Tower trilogy, by Dennis McKiernan. In cases like these, each diver into fantasy must use their best judgment whether to sift the sand from the spilled pearls, or throw the lot, if they must sift half the sea bottom for one gem of truth. It might be better to dive again in another fantasy, and find a whole silver casket of pearls. In our opinion, *The Iron Tower* yields numbers of pearls, worth the occasional grits of sand.

On the third evening Laurelin, looking down at Tuck, asked the small Warrow, "Do you have a beloved? Oh, I think you must. Do I see a sweetheart's favor around your neck?"

Tuck fumbled at Merrilee's silver locket, lifting the chain over his head. "Yes, my Lady," he answered, "only, in the Boskydells a sweetheart is called 'dammia,' er, I mean, I would call her 'dammia' while she would call me 'buccaran.' That is what we Warrows name each other, uh, Warrow sweethearts, that is. And yes, this is my dammia's favor, given to me on the day I left my home village of Woody Hollow." Tuck handed her the locket and chain.

"Why, this is beautiful, Tuck. An ancient work. Perhaps from Xian, itself." Laurelin pressed a hidden catch and the locket sprang open. Tuck was dumbfounded, for although he had touched the locket often, he had not known that it actually opened. "My, she is very pretty," said Laurelin, looking closely. "What is her name?"

"Merrilee," said Tuck, his hands atremble, yearning to take the locket back to see what face it held.

"A lovely name, that." Laurelin glanced to the brooding north. "My Lord Galen wears mine own golden locket at his heart, but no portrait has it, just a snippet of my hair. It must ever be so, that warriors in all times and all Lands have carried the lockets of their loved ones upon their breasts. If not lockets, then other tokens do soldiers bear into danger, to remind them of a love, hearth, home, or something or someone else dear to their hearts." Laurelin clicked shut Tuck's silver locket and handed it into his trembling hands, and turned once more to look beyond the abutment and across the winter plains.

Tuck eagerly fumbled at the locket, discovering at last that it opened by pressing down upon the stem where attached the chain. Click! The leaves of the locket fell open in his hand—mirrored silver on the left, and a miniature of . . . it was Merrilee! Oh, my black-haired dammia, you are so beautiful. *As he stood upon the cold granite rampart, all of his loneliness, his longing for quiet evenings before the fire at The Root, and his love for Merrilee welled up through his very being, and his vision blurred with tears.*

"Ah, Sir Tuck, you must miss her very much," said the Princess.

Blinking back his tears, Tuck looked up to see Laurelin's sad grey eyes upon his blue ones. "Yes, I do. And, you know, I didn't realize just how much until I saw her portrait just now." Tuck shuffled his feet, embarrassed. "You see, until you opened the locket, I didn't know she was there, all the time secretly next to my heart."

Laurelin's laughter had the ring of silver bells chiming in the wind, and Tuck smiled. "Ah, but Sir Tuck, did you not know?" asked the Princess. "We Women and dammen do practice our secret arts to remain in the hearts of our Men and buccen." And they laughed together.

–*The Iron Tower* by Dennis McKiernan, pgs. 102-103

The Iron Tower holds pearls of love, and bravery, loyalty, and honor, besides grand adventure and foreseeing.

But to complete our conversation: about magic or power or gift— and whether it is good or bad—a person in another world who follows the laws of a creator who clearly represents God, and who has been given powers like a kind of sixth sense, or foreseeing, or the ability to use water, wind, fire or any other thing, has lawful *magic*, if you will. Like the dreamwalker in Morgan Busse's *Flight of the Raven*. Though we think they are more accurately called gifts.

Selene sat in the chair to the right, her hands folded across her lap. "Just one?"

"Yes. You shared that house Ravenwood has been using their gift of dreaming to steal secrets and kill others." Her face blanched at his bluntness, but he went on. "However, when you had the chance to kill me, you didn't. Your words were, 'I couldn't do it.'"

She raised her chin. "Yes."

"Then you want nothing to do with house Ravenwood or your past?"

She wavered, then looked down. "No matter what, I will always be a Ravenwood, and I will always have my past."

Damien rubbed the back of his neck. "What I mean is, who do you want to be? Do you want to follow in your mother's footsteps? I've received letters from the other houses. They confirmed what you and your father said happened. Your mother murdered Lord Rune and his sister and lied about their deaths. Is that the kind of woman you want to become?"

Selene stood to her feet. Her nostrils flared and her hands tightened into two tight fists. "No."

Damien felt like all the air had left his body. He sagged against the side of the fireplace and rubbed his face. "I hoped you would say that."

"What?"

He looked over at her. "I had to know. It was eating at me from the inside."

–*Flight of the Raven* by Morgan Busse, pg. 176

A gift, and desire, and choosing destiny. There you have it.

Definitions are words that attempt to define meaning, and they can be squirrely hard to pin down entirely. The warp and woof of context gives the tapestry of meaning a clear voice and life. The gift of foretelling by dreams, the gift of walking through walls, the ability to be invisible, the power to know another's mind, as well as the power to name things what they are—these gifts must be used with skill and wisdom. This implies training for heroines and heroes of all levels.

So skill and gifts of power go together to make up great fantasy, and magic must be carefully watched. Abhor evil as a shark's toothy smile; cling to good as tenaciously as living coral. Prophecy has bloomed extravagantly best in our world, at least from our perspective. Our Creator is generous beyond our meaning of the word, warning and encouraging us to many things.

Dive 10.4

Is the Supernatural in *The Prodigy* an Inborn Gift, Talent, or a Magic Spell?

How does supernatural fantasy fit in the universe?

Alton Gansky weaves a daring, adventurous riddle of a modern-day tale. A story rife with dark forces intent on human destruction, a boy who must discover the truth of power before it's too late, and a rude awakening for some who think they are wise, this book is a prodigy all its own. We have not seen the meeting of power and truth in our present day revealed better in any other chest of jewels drawn from the sea of story.

> The words came out in a rush, Thomas unable to hold himself back any longer. "Toby is real, Dr. Pratt. Wellman may be a crook, but Toby is as real as they come. I've spent hours with him and he's a true genius—a prodigy in every sense, but he goes beyond that. Miracles happen around him."
>
> "I'm sure it might seem that way—"
>
> "It's true, Dr. Pratt. I've seen it with my own eyes. It was because of him that I went in search of you. He saved your life. Haven't you wondered why I was out there in a boat?"
>
> Pratt thought for a moment, then replied, "Not really. I was just so glad to see you. I had assumed God had sent you our way."

"I'm sure he did," Thomas said, "but he used Toby. That boy is unique. He has a power that I can't describe or explain. And it's not just me who thinks this about him. His mother believes in the miracles, and she knows him better than anyone."

"Are you saying he's a new messiah or apostle?" Pratt asked seriously. "Surely you can see the heresy in that."

"I'm not saying he can supplant Jesus," Thomas said. "I'll confess that I was leaning that direction when I first came to the CNJ. Everyone there thinks that way. It's encouraged, and at first it made sense. I've seen him work. Amazing doesn't even come close to describing it. I've studied miracles and the modern church. You know of my obsession with that."

"Obsession is a good word, Thomas."

"I've gone to countless healing services and watched them closely. Toby is different. I've seen cataracts disappear, skin lesions dissolve, deformities made right. Once I saw a child with a twisted spine stand upright. I'm not gullible, Dr. Pratt. I'm neither naïve nor stupid."

Thomas pulled a chair near the bed and continued, "But here's what puzzles me. He's not a spiritual leader. In fact, he's spiritually ignorant. He's never read or owned a Bible. He's never been in a church. He is just what he is and things happen around him—remarkable, unbelievable, inexplicable things."

"How does that fit into what you know of God?" Pratt asked. "What do you do with someone like Toby?"

"I was hoping you could tell me."

–*The Prodigy* by Alton Gansky, pg. 303

We won't give away the great answer to that question; dive into this one and come up with diamonds. This tale shows clearly where the lines of power lie, and who they lead to at the heart of the mystery of the supernatural in our universe. Anything supernatural, or beyond our natural realm of touch, taste, and smell, can be good.

Supernatural demons, spells, and sorcery conflict with right in every great fantasy, or they create a fantasy of dark power that we don't care to get into. But in the next wave, the allure of magick with a "k" is not easily defeated, locked in struggle with right.

Dive 10.5

The Allure of Evil in The Sword, the Ring and the Chalice

Magic—or power, control, and strength. Who has never desired these? Power is alluring to all of us who have felt the pain of helplessness, the pain of humiliation, or just the pain of our wanting. We yearn for many things. Many things we are not meant to control.

We *are* meant to control ourselves. Within the conflict of our avid desire for power and control and our holy yearning for strength, enchantment lies in wait for the unwary, and often the methods of magic in fantasy are diabolical.

> *Semi-crouched with Tanengard's heavy weight trembling in his grasp, Gavril kept his eyes closed and his teeth gritted. Sweat poured down his naked chest, and he heaved in another breath as he strained to hold the shaky spell he'd managed to weave.*
>
> *"Work with it. Feel its power flow through you," the Sebein priest murmured encouragingly. "Don't control it. Merge with it."*
>
> *Gavril struggled to obey. With his eyes closed against all distractions, it was easier to concentrate. He kept the five points of reference clear within his mind, and felt the abrasive, raw power of the magicked sword swirl through his consciousness. It carried lust and fury and the hunger for war.*
>
> *Soon, he promised it. Soon, I'll take you to war. Serve me!*

Become me, *the sword replied inside him.*

It had never spoken to him before. Amazed and exhilarated, Gavril felt the blade lift of its own accord. His heart lurched, and he grinned. "Look!" he cried. "Look at it! I have it! I have it!"

"Concentrate," the Sebein told him. After all these days of working together, Gavril still had not learned the man's name. "Do not speak. Stay with its force, and be what it wants you to be."

–*The Ring* by Deborah Chester, pg. 344

"Merge . . . be what it wants you to be . . ." the threads of context in this web are dangerous. Unlawful powers of magick subsume the one who wields it, devours the one who would master it. Under the guise of mastering magick, the practitioner is mastered.

There is nothing more horrible than to lose your very self, to become an empty shell, driven by magick, and every wave of desire that strikes, as Gavril was. When we are mastered by any *thing*, including our whims, we lose ourselves. But when we allow our Creator mastery, he gives that tyrannous self the kiss of death, and we die and rise, more ourselves than ever before. In his power we are at last able to master ourselves, destined to become our true self, strong and good. In losing our self, we find it. In our Creator, many seeming paradoxes meet.

In fantasy, true paradox exists between a method of magick and a gifting of power.

Dain frowned, backing up a step. "There is no magic."

"I know differently." Sulein picked up a stick and held it out. "If you hold this in your hand, will it sprout leaves and return to life?"

Dain held his hands at his side and glared at the physician. "No."

"I have talked to Nocine the huntsman," Sulein said. "You cast a spell and turned him into a tree to save his life."

"I created a vision, an illusion," Dain protested.

"You have mastery over the animals."

"No."

"You can touch the minds of men, read their thoughts perhaps. Oh, your abilities in these areas are not as strong as mine, but I have studied and practiced many years to learn the art of mind spells, while you do this naturally."

"I am not like you!" Dain said sharply. "I do not—"

"Wouldn't you like to increase your powers?" Sulein asked him. "Wouldn't you like to know how to wield them exactly as you wish, to use them for—"

"No!" Dain said. He hurried to the door, but it would not open. Frustrated, he tugged at it, twisting the ring this way and that, but it was locked. He gave the wooden panel a kick and turned back to face the physician.

"When you learn to put aside your fear, when you learn to open your mind to what you truly are, then you will have a future of limitless possibilities," Sulein said.

"I have no desire to be a sorcerel," Dain said defiantly. "Let me go."

"But you were so eager to come inside before."

"That's when I thought you might give back my bard crystal," Dain retorted. "Keeping my property from me is theft."

Anger touched Sulein's eyes, and the air inside the room grew suddenly cold. "I study, Dain," he said after a long silence. "I guard. But I do not steal. Remember that."

Dain stood there, mute and angry, his blood pounding impatiently in his veins. Sulein's words were all lies and trickery. Nothing he said could be trusted.

–The Sword by Deborah Chester, pgs. 343-344

Power from any source may seem the same—until it meets in antipathy and contradictive paradox, and its results become plain. Trustworthiness—or the lack of it. That is why knowing the source of power is so important. Something or someone that appears a being of light to our eyes may hide a heart of utter darkness, but its fruit cannot be disguised for long.

And darkness is out to destroy the light. There is no *balance* between them. It only appears so because the one who is Light has allowed the evil one's darkness thus far as well as our own, not wishing any to perish.

Fantasy reflects moral and immoral things that exist in our world in expanded exploration of the depths of evil and heights of good. Speculative fiction often contains real paganism and real humility, at times in the same story and the same person. Both must be recognized and acknowledged. Then the good may be followed, and the wrong noted and turned from.

As for Pheresa, Dain regretted he could not save her. He'd wanted to make her grateful to him, to turn her love from Gavril to him. He'd thought that if he could bring her a cure he would win her heart. But it was no good to force love from gratitude. Besides, he hadn't saved her, hadn't been the big hero he'd longed to be.

Nay, he'd done what his father had done—abandoned his people and vanished. Were they cursing his name now, while they were dying?

He would go back to them, he vowed. Although he returned without the Chalice, he would stand with them to meet his death in combat. In some ways, he'd been just as arrogant, foolish, and overconfident as Gavril. But he would go back to his people, empty-handed, and stand with them to the last.

Sighing, he forced himself to sit up. As he waited for the cave to stop spinning, he noticed a few scattered stones on the ground, as well as some sticks propped against the wall.

Another dim memory came to him. His father had knelt there once on the moist soil and placed those stones just so. Thia had helped him. Then they'd prayed together.

For his family's honor, Dain decided to do the same before he left.

Gasping, he crawled forward and slowly, one by one, placed the stones in a circle. The sticks had been peeled of their bark long ago. They had darkened with age and no longer gleamed white, but they were ash and therefore sacred. He ran his hand up and down their lengths, cleaning dirt and cobwebs off them, before he crossed them carefully. He had no Element candles to light, no bronze knives of ritual, no bell, and no green vines, but he did have salt. He took out a small handful from his salt purse and poured it carefully in a thin white line just inside the stone circle. When that was done, he knelt, feeling clammy and weak and very tired, and uttered the simple prayer that Thia had taught him when he was little. He even said the nonsense words they used to say afterwords, nonsense words that he now recognized as Netheran and sacred.

Then he lifted his gaze upward. "Forgive me, O Thod," he prayed simply, his heart pouring out its trouble. "Forgive me for the sin of pride. I wanted to prove to all men that I could do better than my father. I was angry with him for deserting us, and I meant to prove myself his superior. I am not. I am merely a man who tried but could not do all that I meant to . . . just like my father."

–*The Chalice* by Deborah Chester, pgs. 369-370

Wrong methods must not be called right, nor the immoral described as moral—despite Dain's good intent. Though we rightly still admire his good intent as a frame of heart that pursues truth. He has caught the scent of the track of truth.

The Sword, the Ring, and the Chalice series has a number of gods, and is one of those fantasies we must discern as to whether it is worth reading. It mentions adultery, since the king has a mistress, but does not paint immorality in a graphic or favorable light, rather as a hindering drawback of court intrigue. I find this trilogy a profitable study in magick and power terms, as an example of one of the most canny ways to discredit faith and the established church, and a potent picture of how lost we can get following ourselves. It is a fantasy of the best crafting but mixed ideology.

But there is hope for Dain. He pursues goodness much of the time, though in some areas he is deadly wrong. There is also a refreshing honesty in this adventure that makes me think, or at least hope, the author will not stop short of truth in her own journey.

Power, control, and strength—or magick. We must be careful what we truly seek. We will find what we wish for. Power to do right, or to do something else? To control our impulses, or control those around us? And strength to do what, to be what?

We pursue these truths into adventure: to investigate a world with inherent laws of magic.

Dive 10.6

Are Inherent Laws of Magic Paradoxical in a World including God?

Not always. Not if it is the law of God in that world that magic be a natural part of life. If magic carries a different meaning than "manipulation of power outside the law" in magick with a "k." If *wizard* means someone who honors the laws of the established order ordained by the highest authority. If the magic users follow the authority's moral law. Paradox is not always apparent at first glance.

Librettowit looked up from his mug. "A simple substance. Same three ingredients which make up all substances, only in different combinations. A wizard, with the right knowledge, can call together ozoics, azoics, and ezoics."

Fenworth harrumphed and glared at the librarian. "My lecture, I believe, Wit." He patted his beard and a slew of dots shot out from the grizzly curls to join the picture above the table.

"When a wizard," Fenworth cocked an eyebrow at Librettowit and continued, "places these zoics in close proximity with each other, they assume the positions that Wulder has ordained and become the substance they are meant to be."

Dar slurped his tea and ignored Leetu's frown at his manners. "Only Wulder can create the primary ingredients."

"Of course!" The wizard nodded. "And they can only be combined in a mode prescribed by Wulder. A wizard is only as great

as his understanding of the complexity of Wulder's established order. Within those parameters, a wizard can do almost anything."

He heaved a melancholy sigh and shook his head. His shoulders drooped. His gaze lowered from the busy image hanging over the table to the empty plates and scattered crumbs.

"Where Risto and his comrades have gone astray," Fenworth said, "is in the belief that they can create primary ingredients. And that they have no need of following Wulder's dictums."

–*DragonQuest* by Donita K. Paul, pg. 93

Here the paradox between a representative reflection of God and magic use is resolved, but another, larger paradox is revealed between the wizard named Risto who believes he can create life, and his blindness to the ramifications of the fact that he is himself a created being. Not one with the ability to make something from nothing.

Something created from nothing, now there's a paradox. And how about a heroine in a world among the stars of fantasy, who finds herself uniquely qualified to communicate by telepathy with an invading race, who wishes above almost everything to have the privacy of her own thoughts and the ability to make her own choices? Talents can be unwanted, and have far-reaching consequences for good and ill.

Dive 10.7

Telepathy is Pivotal to the World of *One Mind's Eye*

Talent is given that we may build and enrich ourselves and others. Is it any different in any other world where goodness is a factor?

Telepathy is something many of us would call a talent, especially if it was bred into us through the manipulation of other humans, without our yea or nay. Then we must agonize over whether to defy those who would use us against our will, or accept what has been done and use it, not as the gene manipulator would have us, but as our hearts and minds tell us is right, even against our sense of self preservation.

> *Warm wind tossed her hair around her shoulders. She looked small and delicate, unqualified to face an alien race . . . except for her courage. She nodded.*
>
> *Jahn quieted his mind and listened for the Sunsisan's inner frequency. Again he felt two phenomena. Winnow the human was alert and afraid and in pain. The other sensation was a high-pitched, warbling whine superimposed over her frequency.*
>
> *He pitched his inner frequency to the warble. Gently he gathered Llyn deeper into the nexus, synchronizing their shared frequency onto an oscillating rhythm that approached but didn't achieve the alien vibrato. This was like trying to block synch, but much more precise.*
>
> I don't think I can, *he admitted.*

Let me.

But you can't—

He was wrong. She could. She imaged a clipped height and an irregular downslope onto the oscillation. He matched it. She deepened its trough, and he matched that—

Thousands of voices shrieked inside his head. Her optimism surged . . . cautiously.

Can you hold that? *She seemed to modulate the vibrato like a transmitter superimposing information onto a radio wave. Where had she learned to do that?*

I can. I will.

Laying down control of a nexus might kill him, but that was a better fate than Gamal Casimir faced. He hid that fear from Llyn and backed down. She seized and held the frequency.

He didn't die. He wasn't even stunned. She'd done it.

He quieted all thought and effort, except what it took to support their inner frequency, now a wild—but controlled—oscillation.

. . .

Llyn, too, felt initial contact as a babble of shrieking voices, but an instant later it focused. Geometric imagery appeared where the stark Sunsisan landscape had vanished. She knew this music. This mindscape had inhabitants!

–*One Mind's Eye* by Kathy Tyers, pg. 352

We can be surprised, and surprise others when we use our talents well, from an unusual talent in a "what if" space fantasy tale, to those talents more common in our world, such as a talent with words, or numbers, or animals, or people. Empathy and everything else that stretches beyond what we imagine to touch those we live among, adds a mysterious wonder to our world and beyond.

Never underestimate the impact every person has on the realms. The impact you have. In our Creator, we hold much power to will and to do; we hold it as a cup holds water. We are the cup, discovering and working out the willing sparkle of Love's good pleasure in many things, all of them bubbling with the gift of clear, crystalline life for thirsty souls in the deserts of the worlds, including our own.

Watching the impact of a talent like telepathy in fantasy can make us feel a kind of awe of the supernatural, but often the true supernatural in our world feels every-day—at least to us. That is because we are rather blind to our Creator's power; we often do not recognize his unassuming, unpretentious, unobtrusive supernatural artistry.

Our talents may affect our world as quietly, steadily, and forcefully as any war-torn hero does the land of fantasy. The touch of the supernatural, if it is God's working, transforms gifts and talents, adding a dimension above the ordinary, or rather, revealing a dimension that was there all along, where we are called to defend the right with the paw of the lion and the voice of the lamb. In the next dimension, our definition of *ordinary* will stretch.

Dive 10.8

Unusual Gifts Transform the Supernatural in the *Cloak of Light*

It has been said trial by fire transforms talent; but talent may also lead us into fiery trial. Supernatural power in fantasy transforms what it touches, adding dimension and depth to evil or good. It does this by a deeper, higher, wider impact on our emotions, mind, and world—by pulling in another sphere altogether than we are used to dealing with.

The sphere where the spiritual touches the physical. Sometimes we feel it, but we almost never see it, other than with eyes of the heart. What if we were given the gift, or curse, of walking in both spheres at once?

Warning: A reader who has experienced a school shooting or a similar violent encounter may want to skip the following fantasy quote.

That's when he saw them.

Two massive alien warriors walked through the double doors into the building, swords drawn. The students strolled by them, headed to their next classes in complete ignorance. Drew froze, and the guy behind him slammed into his back. The student cursed, but Drew paid him no attention. His eyes were fixated on the warriors at the bottom of the stairwell.

They were looking for something. . .or someone. The hatred in their eyes spewed out onto the crowd of unsuspecting students. Drew's senses peaked and his mind began registering every sight and sound around him. A young man entered the doorway and stood next to the warriors. He looked human, but there was something different about him. The man turned his head from side to side, but there was a delay in his face as he turned, almost as if he had two faces and one lagged behind the other. It was a strange and deathly trio—two alien warriors and one two-faced human. Was this how an alien could take complete control of a human? Dread built within him as he realized what was happening. One of the warriors spoke something to the man, and he opened his coat to reveal a semiautomatic MP5 submachine gun with a least six thirty-two-round 9 mm clips.

Drew jumped back and screamed for the students to go back. Within seconds, there was absolute panic as the air exploded with the concussion of 9 mm rounds being fired. Shouts and screams sounded all around him.

–*Cloak of Light* by Chuck Black, pg. 135

An unusual talent is not given to be locked in a treasure chest or gloated over at a solitary table, but to gladly contribute aid to others, to spread a feast before those in need. An unusual gift usually also deals with a weakness in the wielder as well as bestowing strength. A talent, a gifting in our world or in fantasy, leads to testing and a fire of transformation that leaves us stronger if we do not shut our hearts to change. We are meant to grow.

Drew wondered at first if the gift he'd been given was good, and that tied into his questions about lawful power and authority between the United States and the two battling powers he saw in the spiritual realm. His questions and actions forced him into a transforming adventure not to be missed. What he did with his lawful power is inspiring.

The transformation of a person by the art of foreshadowing, simile, metaphor, and foretelling are a specialty of dream, vision, and prophecy, our next dive into imaginative fiction.

Dive 10.9

Dream, Vision, and Prophecy in Fantasy

Dream, vision, and prophecy lend themselves to story and to battle. They are also used for foreshadowing, metaphor, and foretelling, or in fantasy, a combination of the three, where meaning echoes between them.

Dreams in fantasy can reflect the hero or heroine's thoughts, fears, and enemies. Visions may seem interchangeable with dreams, except dreams come more often at night in sleep, while visions tend to be a direct message from a higher being, evil or good, and can occur at any time. Prophecy in our world is given from God by a prophet or prophetess, and sometimes angels are involved, as in the Book of Daniel. True dreams, visions, and prophecy are usually a direct word or message from God or the lawful authority of a fantasy universe, while other dreams, visions, and prophecies lean heavily on metaphorical meaning. We are not speaking here of the plethora of false oracles, sorcerers, and seers in fantasy who speak either half-lies or a false god's words to deceive.

In our world and the ocean of fantasy, dreams and visions make good use of metaphor or simile and pull us into their realm by various doors.

She fastened the recurve bow to the bay's saddle and dug a charcoal stick she had taken from their desert fire out of her sash. Alaina's face and soft hair blackened quickly. When Kyrin finished, Alaina smudged her face.

The dark wood reeked of burning, of her godfather's keep, of death. It felt smooth as her mother's cold, still face. Kyrin's hand tightened on her dagger and the falcon's beak pricked her wrist.

A growling cough came over the whisper of grass and wind across stone. The tiger crouched above them on the hill slope in the shadow of a bush, round ears pinned flat to his wide skull. His face wrinkled with a snarl, his lips twitched back over his teeth, and his tail was rigid. Kyrin froze. The tiger could not be there.

"Kyrin—?" Alaina turned her head carefully, her hand cool against Kyrin's cheek.

Kyrin's heart pounded. The tiger chuffed, uncertain, casting back and forth, as if they were hidden from him. His breath fogged in the first grey light, and he sniffed the ground before his paws.

The stick jerked in Alaina's clenching fingers.

Kyrin pulled violently aside and crouched, the falcon blade ready, futile as it might be.

Stripes of flame licked the stalking hunter under the old starlight, his stripes dark red, as of dried blood. No falcon's scream rang down the wind. The tiger raised his head and his ears came up. Even as his eyes fastened on Kyrin, his heavy shoulders faded. The bush grew starker behind his thinning form. The grass blades quivered. Then he was gone as if he had never been.

Fly high, see far, stoop fast. *Where was the queen of the air, the falcon who had driven him to the sand one wild night in the desert, taming him? But it was only a wraith of her heart that haunted her.* Kyrin let out her breath. Madness . . . *or her mind played tricks on her, as it so often did at the edge of sleep.*

Alaina threw the charcoal stick into the grass. "The shadows move, in this hour, and trick the eye. I didn't see the sand fox until it turned to go."

What fear had she seen?

–Falcon Flight by Azalea Dabill, pg. 73

So we see dreams can be metaphors or similes of our waking experience, as foreshadowing can lead to dream or vision.

Kyrin's dreams reflect her enemies and inner struggles, and lead her to battle. The falcon dagger is her symbol of courage, and the falcon itself, a sigil of freedom. But the tiger stalks them, a catalyst for evil, which God means for good. Kyrin's nemesis haunts her and her companions throughout her journey from slave to first daughter. She learns many things she would not, except for the tiger of her dreams.

But what of prophecy? As dream and vision bear inner conflict and messages from lawful authority, so prophecy relays truth, confers certainty, and teaches us humility.

Then Corradon looked up at Perena, his face pale. "This envoy, this strangest of figures, can you repeat what he said to you? His words were . . . ?"

Perena gave the tiniest of nods. "'Captain Lewitz, night is falling. The war begins.' The words will not easily be forgotten."

"Excuse me, Captain Lewitz," Clemant said, his dark eyes scrutinizing her, "can we be sure that this was an objective occurrence?"

Perena returned his gaze, her face revealing no emotion. "As opposed to a subjective vision? No. It could have been a hallucination. But as it preceded—and predicted—one of the most dramatic events in Assembly history, I think we ought to treat it seriously."

–The Shadow and Night by Chris Walley, pg. 305

True foretelling comes from outside ourselves, and is not a comfortable thing, whether it comes as prophecy, vision, or dream.

As The Lamb Among the Stars series relates.

"Where are they from?' Merral asked. "The north?"

Jorgio rubbed his bent nose with a heavy finger. "No. It's like . . . I don't know. . . . It's like someone has opened a door beyond the stars and all these things have come out and are running across the roof of the world." He made a grimace. "Like rats. And then I usually wake up and pray to the Lord of All Power and the noises go away. But then, the next night they come back . . .

–The Dark Foundations by Chris Walley, pg. 87

Foretelling by dream, vision, or prophecy, in the mode of simile, metaphor, or foreshadowing usually ends in battle, spiritual or physical.

The ties of evil, if we accept the threads of rebellion, selfishness, and despair, bind us to the spell of wealth, corrupt power, and futility, instead of the freedom to walk beside the Lord of All Power. They would bind us to the allure of magick rather than our gifts, would chain us to the authority of foolishness, and would see us destroyed rather than ever bow to wisdom.

Such power makes us pawns, without will or wit of our own. Though promising all, good twisted never gives us freedom to pursue goodness. Goodness, even in its smallest measurement, begins to grow us a backbone. Evil makes us prisoners to ourselves, chained by fear, by hate, by shame, by love of domination.

Darkness and the souls it drives never surrender, only fall, or flee for a time, to attack again. The battle of right against wrong is fought through many doors in fantasy, with the determination that faith, hope, and love bring to our hearts. The battles across far worlds and our own are often the same, at their roots, though fought numerous places. The power to fight evil in both comes from the same Person.

He grows the gifts of his power in us: the faith that our Creator's mercy blots out our dark deeds, the sure hope that He works goodness in us, the warmth of his love, and ours for him. These ties strengthen us with glints and gleams of another world, neither ours, nor fantasy, but better than both.

However small their beginnings, however surrounded by evil, such glints and gleams of goodness weave endless ties to our hearts. In the realm of fantasy, they are like threads, streaming through the depths to form strands of light, and then columns.

From the Father of lights they come, the weaver of all hope, loosing the fire of joy, beauty, and mystery in our inner beings. The three-fold strands of love, hope, and faith are a bright triple thread, a tie that will never be broken, stronger than any spell.

Dream, vision, and prophecy lend themselves to foreshadowing, to metaphor, and at times to foretelling; but this requires words, true words, which bind meaning to life, and to story, and battle. We must fight. Fight for the light, and for the life of others. Both in fantasy, and in our world.

Good metaphor, apt simile, and deft foreshadowing work to open the doors of fantasy so that gleaming threads of love, hope, and faith may lead us through the heights and depths of earth, wind and wave; to reveal to us what we are; and what we are destined to become. Selfish, or growing more selfless; honorable, or slipping into dishonor; fearful, or gaining courage; adrift in darkness, or safe in our Creator's hand.

Words embody many things and souls down to their tiniest detail. They reveal great powers, gifts, and talents in expanding glory, which pit them against evil, for *Fantasy Revives Relentless Ties and Direct Doors to the Spirit.*

Chapter 11.0

Fantasy Revives Relentless Ties and Direct Doors to the Spirit

Does not every book have a vision that beckons the reader to a door of feeling, meaning, and action that opens onto all kinds of paths among the worlds of fantasy? Choose well. For some paths and doors lead to joy, and some to doom.

When she opened her eyes, she saw a beautiful little creature with wings standing beside her, waiting.

"I know you," said Tangle. "You are my fish."

"Yes. But I am a fish no longer. I am an aeranth now."

"What is that?" asked Tangle.

"What you see I am," answered the shape. "And I am come to lead you through the mountain."

"Oh! Thank you, dear fish—aeranth, I mean," returned Tangle, rising.

Thereupon the aeranth took to his wings, and flew on through the long, narrow passage, reminding Tangle very much of the way he had swum on before when he was a fish. And the moment his white wings moved, they began to throw off a continuous shower of sparks of all colours, which lighted up the passage before them. —All at once he vanished, and Tangle heard a low, sweet sound, quite different from the rush and crackle of his wings. Before her was an open arch, and through it came light, mixed with the sound of sea-waves.

–*The Golden Key* by George MacDonald, pg. 21

Thankfully, Tangle's door led to a path of joy.

Fantasy doors call us to paths of the spirit, where words bring association of sound and sight and scent, and those things become more together than they were alone.

Among many paths, taste the sweet of Reepicheep's ocean at the End of the World and swim with all your heart and spirit to behold his last door. As Jonathan Rogers in *The World According to Narnia* relates,

> *"[Reepicheep] is the picture of pure focus. Aslan's country is his telos, his end, in every sense of the word: the end of the world, the end of his life, the goal and purpose toward which he bends his every effort.*
>
> *Reepicheep's desire is the same desire the apostle Paul speaks of: 'I press on to lay hold of that for which also I was laid hold of' (Phil. 3:12). In his singlemindedness, Reepicheep forgets everything, counts it as rubbish compared to the destiny that laid hold of him in the dryad's cradle song long before he was able to lay hold of it:*
>
> *Where sky and water meet,*
>
> *Where waves grow sweet,*
>
> *Doubt not, Reepicheep,*
>
> *To find all you seek,*
>
> *There in the utter east. ...*
>
> *That's what the overwhelming brightness of the sun in the Last Sea is about. It is glory, the light of Aslan's Country" (Time Warner Book Group, 2005).*

Reepicheep's door was blessed, and led through strange oceans to riches. Yet watch out. For some fantasy waters contain sirens aching to lead us to dangerous deeps, for treasures not worth the sand they lie on.

These flawed jewels are created by undersea volcanoes of swirling error, solidified in chilling waves of deception which tell us we are the sole masters of our destinies. When we dive in this ensorcelled sea we may be tempted to let the sirens encircle us, and tear our book of knowledge from our numbed fingers. And with it, our understanding of paths and doors, as they drag us to their own.

There we may risk our lives for flawed glass that sinks to the sand by the tinkling thousands of pieces, a rainbow of many colors beneath the waves, teasing our befuddled eyes, whispering in our ears, tapping in promise at our hearts. Will we leave our quest for true wealth for a broken fantasy of enchanted bits of glass?

The shadowed red promises fire—the ruby of sexual freedom that shatters into lacerating shards that cuts our hands the tighter our desperate grasp; the sparkling diamond of self-determination that holds power before our eyes—then cracks into crumbling carbon; the bright false jade that gives visions of prosperity—but conceals a poison-brew of bitterness.

For glass . . . glass is not gold, nor gems.

Fantasy that reveals flaws of unfaithfulness, selfishness, and betrayal as valuable assets, or as strengths, or unavoidable compromise—these fantasies betray us. If we insist on entering their doors of feeling, meaning, and action, and walk the underwater paths of the sirens, they bring our death in increments: death to trust, to courage, to joy. Never do false jewels fulfill the promise they hold out. At the last they drag us through doors of despair, where the sirens drown seekers in the weed-choked depths.

Instead, at first sight or sound of finned shadow or song, we must fling open our book of knowledge. Concealed no longer, the three-fold thread of hope, faith, and love blazes forth in words, illuminating the pages, the light twining together and weaving through the water to gently touch a curious fish. The rippling thread grows ever brighter and thicker. In the light of that tripling strength we see shades of glass, crumbling in the cold sea around us.

Our lungs burning for air, we see the flip of a departing siren's tail. Wiser, we grip our book of knowledge in our teeth and leap for the surface. We will dive again in another place, for real treasure. We will search out true doors, true paths, and jewels that do not disappoint.

Do not despise small beginnings. Great fantasies pull us toward change, build inside us what inspires us, what we will die for, and what we will live for. Every jewel of fantasy story we gather becomes a part of us in some small way—or large.

The pure ruby of *The Bonemender's Oath* may encourage the greatest romance, tried and true; the diamond of *The Broken Blade* may shape a life of courage; the jade of The Wingfeather Saga may draw us down a path of enriching mystery. As treasures brought to the surface, gleaming in the glory of a summer sun on the deck of our vessel that bears us bravely away from the siren sea, what worth do these true gems of fantasy bring?

The ever deepening ruby of royal love; the beauty of God-determined diamond, facets so strong and beautiful as to cut steel; the peaceful riches of jade, generous and wide as the enfolding heart that fashioned creation. And the pure gold of a vision rightly held, the door of meaning that touches all men: mending, enriching, and empowering.

The treasures of fantasy and the threads woven through them eternally beckon us to doors that lead to freedom on earth and under wave. Fantasy wealth shows us flawed paths honestly—as weakness, as wrong that harms—they also show us strength beyond ourselves, strength to become what we are not.

Or are not yet, for we are promised transformation, and the door of ecstasy. Hope of that door leads us to shore, away from dark depths, to further doors of destiny and paths of vision.

Auralia's Colors makes it clear that innocence can draw an indelible line of goodness in the hardest heart. Pandora's box is a door that can make or break the mind in *Hostage Run*. Laughter is a path that runs beside good tears in The Wingfeather Saga. The path of meaning hits hard in Children of the Blood Moon series, and strikes harder with the sure emotion of hope in *The King's Scrolls*. Intense truth faces powerful lie in *Dragonwitch*, *Ember Falls* true-names the world with spell-binding power, and *That Hideous Strength* withdraws the veil from goddess Nature to reveal her Master.

Dive 11.1

A Clear Truth—the Winning Appeal of Innocence

As we hunt for riches, exploring sea and land in the fantasy realm, many dangers encroach to choke the doors to life and laughter. Every realm but one has its places where lowering skies darken the way at some point. We look back and wonder, did we make a mistake, entering the door of Love? Envy and cynicism and rage and fear and the futile cry "it's useless," hedge us in—or out—seeking to turn us back or lead us astray.

But paths of truth and kindness make their way to and from that door, across all worlds, and however concealed from our eyes by en-spelled brambles, if cleared the littlest bit, the path of love blooms with color along even the steepest ways of the realm of fantasy. Every gem and jewel of imaginative fiction have further doors and continuing paths, branching from that which we are on, or driving ahead to further our upward climb.

But those walking through the door opposite Love, who choose paths of shadow, drain every world they walk through of color and life. They may hate the brightness of truth and kindness, for it threatens their control, their mastery, and they sneer at the perfume of flowers in a land of peace under the sun. They would have us join them in their pragmatism, in their refusal to be a hero or heroine, in greed, and in cynicism—by persuasion or by force, one way or the other.

But the scarlet flower of sacrifice, the yellow daisy of laughter, the green richness of truth, and the wild rose of kindness, once brought to life by the quickening dew of the Creator's Spirit in our dusty hearts, cannot be eradicated as if they never were.

Those who carry such blooms among us can only be banished from the world to the one without a shadow, transforming all they touch on the way with the power residing within them. Everything touched by light reveals its true color, or its lack. Blackness is absence of light, and therefore of color. Those who follow the paths of doom cannot abide the dark revelation of their heart. And the war is on—evil pitting itself against innocence and goodness.

Never in all his days as jailer had he seen a prisoner so young, so vulnerable.

He quickly put down the whip and blinked mole eyes at the flinching guards. "No one with any sense would bring. . .that. . .to Maugam. No one."

One guard escaped without reply, but Maugam's words stopped the other. "Auralia refused to respect the Rites of Privilege," he haltingly explained. "She is guilty of conspiring with an exiled advisor, an enemy of House Abascar. She is guilty not only of speaking deception but of inciting a treasonous riot. She has provoked the grudgers. And since she's arrived in the prison, she has made things worse. She has sought to deceive Prince Calraven and taunted the king by transforming the prisons through her strange powers." He glared at the shadows where the girl was almost visible. "It is. . .unfortunate."

"Unfortunate?" the jailer shrieked. "What do you mean, she transformed the prisons? Maugam rules the prisons."

"Her magic lit up the prison, Jailer, and enchanted the prisoners. She set the stones to shining. The place is full of color."

"But. . ." Maugam peered at Auralia out of one eye, then the other. "What Maugam will do to her she cannot endure. What is that she's holding?" Maugam reached for the girl, touched her trembling hand, and then recoiled as though stung. "Great bones

of Tammos Raak! She wears the prince's Ring of Royal Trust! If Maugam were to proceed, he would be. . .he would be arrested and sent. . .to Maugam!" The jailer began to quake, confused and distraught.

"Command of the king, Jailer. It overrules the Ring of Trust."

"Why didn't the king take the ring off her finger?"

"He also. . ." the guard clearly found his own testimony implausible. "He also condemned the ring, Jailer. Childhood fancies, you see. It's crafted in the shape of the Keeper. He wants it to vanish. Into the Hole. With the girl."

–*Auralia's Colors* by Jeffrey Overstreet, pg. 240

When faith in beauty, hope in goodness, and love for others blooms, and it is seen, and hated, and sent to disappear, those stout spirits are not bound by their fall into death's clutches. Though they may be struck down, they reveal their accusers. They carve a way for us, and the thickest snarl of thorns spread across our path edges back. Love is courageous; it overcomes. Even in its fall.

In every world where innocence is lost and yet that world is redeemed to goodness, strange as it may sound, that world is a part of our story. It is a facet of the fight to bring us back to life, of Love's sacrifice so we may walk through the great door of the universe into all it holds.

Goodness, innocent or redeemed, cannot be denied. It is itself in every world, and gives not an inch. The Creator approaches along Love's path, and brings with him justice for the afflicted and the helpless. And until the hour of final mending swallows death and danger and despair, and he comes with healing victory in his wings, the battle for life and liberty continues, fought even in our minds.

Even in a MindWar of virtual reality.

Dive 11.2

Think Your Way Around Pandora's Astonishing Box in *Hostage Run*

The mind has immense power. May we dare to discover ours—even to its limits?

When we meet our Maker, even in a small way, we discover how small we are and how great he has made us. How capable of losing all—quite by ourselves, and of gaining all—if we lose sight of ourselves in his greatness, where we finally see ourselves at last. It's another paradox.

Andrew Klavan has experienced similar things. As he says in *The Great Good Thing,*

> *I have lived two lives. That was the ending of the first: that screwdriver falling. Within days, I had made an appointment with a psychiatrist in Manhattan. What followed was a miracle of recovery, a swift, dramatic, and absolute transformation from one way of being to another. I sometimes like to joke that I've seen many men go mad, but I'm the only person I've ever met who has gone sane. It's not really a joke, though. Sigmund Freud is often quoted describing the psycho-therapeutic process as a journey from "hysterical misery to ordinary unhappiness." My journey was different: it was a passage from suicidal despair to a fullness of vitality and joy I had not even thought to imagine.*
>
> *While now I look back on this period and see Christ within it everywhere, at the time, on the surface, he was apparent only in*

hints and whispers. This was—or seemed—an entirely secular conversion. But it was this conversion that made my ultimate conversion to Christianity possible, and maybe inevitable, because it freed me to trust my own perceptions and reasoning. As long as I was in mental disarray, as long as my actions were self-destructive, as long as my outlook was deluded, any faith I thought to have, any idea of God I formed, seemed to me by definition unreliable, the comforting illusion of a mind in pain. As long as religion might even appear to serve me as an emotional crutch, I dismissed it as a form of weakness. It was only when I felt certain that my inner life was healthy and my understanding was sound that I could begin to accept what experience and logic had been leading me to believe. For others, I know it was Christ who led them to joy. For me, it was joy that led me to Christ.

–*The Great Good Thing* by Andrew Klavan, pg. 173

To gain all, to find joy, to lose and gain our selves in trusting him, we must uncover who we are. That is hard to do. The journey to self-discovery holds nightmares—yet also hope and help unforeseen—in our world and in fantasy.

He wasn't sure yet, but he thought it was possible he had fallen in love with her. Even though he had no idea who she was. Even though he wasn't even sure she was real.

It had happened like this. Two months ago, Commander Mars, the leader of the MindWar Project, had sent Rick into the Realm. The Realm was a bizarre country in cyberspace, a projection of the imagination of a mysterious terrorist named Kurodar. Kurodar had created the Realm by wiring his brain into a number of supercomputers. Through the Realm, he was hoping to infiltrate America's defense systems, its electricity grids, its business exchanges—infiltrate them through pure thought, unstoppable, and so destroy them and bring the country to its knees.

Until Mars and Miss Ferris had tapped him for this mission, Rick had been a broken man: his football career over, his legs crushed, his spirit in ruins. For months, he had locked himself in his room to play video games endlessly. And weirdly, it was that—his gaming skills, linked with his quick quarterback reactions and leadership ability—that had turned him into the perfect MindWarrior. Mars and his techs had projected Rick in avatar form into the online world of Kurodar's sick imagination. There, Rick had been able to stop the cyberterrorist from slaughtering thousands.

But it wasn't the success of the mission that had revived Rick's soul, that had inspired him to start working his legs back into shape, that had reignited his natural drive and ambition, and his pure macho fighting ferocity. No. It was Mariel.

How to describe her? She was a silver nymph who traveled through the MindWar Realm's metallic water; a mysterious Lady of the Lake who had armed and armored him for battle, who had taught him to marshal the power of his spirit so that he could sometimes change the very nature of reality in Kurodar's online world. And she was brave and wise and, yes, majestically beautiful.

And she was trapped in the Realm. And she was dying.

–Hostage Run by Andrew Klavan, pg. 15

Hope and the will to help another holds the beauty of a diamond, their facets held by the strength of our Creator, giving us another door of vision, opening to us a path of trust and courage. The worlds some villains make, as in *Hostage Run,* though twisted, are made to serve our Creator's ends still, for they are weak shadows of realities that he constantly holds in being. He upholds all things by the word of his power, in a sense creating them every moment. If he released them, they would cease. So would we, in every aspect.

He works through everything and everyone he makes. With him, we perform feats beyond our imagination, touching even the outcome of imaginative games in our Creator's power. Great fantasy on a spiritual level helps remove the cloud of hopelessness from one lens we see life through—our imagination. When our imagination despairs of hope he gives us himself, in many ways. He creates fun, and food, good times, and laughter, all riches of wisdom for our mind, soul, and body.

But freedom to enjoy them comes at a cost in every realm: sometimes the cost of disquiet instead of peace, of blood rather than water, of tears instead of laughter. But the cost makes the joy possible—and more treasured.

Some of the most wondrous paths of moral adventure are those of sacrifice. The Wingfeather Saga enfolds the value of sacrifice within a special family, a family at once common and significant. And full of mysteries.

This is an adventure we will never forget. Step onto the next path and follow the Wingfeathers through the door of a fallen kingdom that is ready to rise.

Dive 11.3

Learning With Fun and Laughter in The Wingfeather Saga

Can we agree mothers concoct the best surprises?

Take mothers in every world, mothers who care. Their loyal love lights the way through every danger. They add so much to our lives, helping us discern between paths good and bad. Some of us have not had a mother, or have had a bad one. But a mother who is a mother indeed, though not perfect—yes, there is something to smile at with her, or to laugh at together in joy, or to grin about in anticipation.

"Well! That's better." Nia folded her arms and tried not to smile at Janner. "I thought I'd see you with fresh grass growing on your face by now."

Janner blushed and shook his head as he took his seat.

Leeli and Tink tried to hide their giggles, as Nia pulled up a chair and sat with her elbows on the table and her chin in her hands, watching her children eat. Janner stared out the window, deep in his thoughts; Tink hunched over his plate like a buzzard, eating the hotcakes and sausage as if they might try to escape; Leeli watched her brothers and fidgeted with the hem of her gown, humming and bobbing her head back and forth while she chewed.

"Eat well, my dears. It's going to be a busy day," Nia said smiling.

The children's eyes widened. "The sea dragons!" they cried in unison.

Nia laughed and pushed herself up from the table. "The summer dusk hath split in twain the gilded summer moon, and all who come shall hear again the dragons' golden tune," *she sang.* *"Coming just like they have for a thousand years. Finish up your breakfast and we'll go on to town. The chores will wait."*

–On the Edge of the Dark Sea of Darkness by Andrew Peterson, pg. 17

The chores will wait. What a mother! She knew the treasures she held in her children, the worth they were, and the price they might be required to pay. She held them in hope, and strength, and prayer. And laughter.

Laughter, even through the tears brought by their adventures, always overcomes. That love, such a love between them all, lights the Wingfeathers's way through every danger and brings them to triumph. Their sacrifice of pain and tears and determination brings a quality to their victory that nothing else can. We cannot describe what that something is, but maybe after you enjoy The Wingfeather Saga series you will learn its name. Ties spring from it that overcome all, even paths of fear and hatred. Loyal, brave love threads a way through every sacrifice, and thrusts wide the door of right.

Dive 11.4

Children of the Blood Moon—Hard-hitting Fantasy

Love, or caring for another as we do ourselves, strikes blessedly at the level of our spirits. Such love is stronger than all our enemies. It endures. And by just so much as we love this way, by that much we are strong.

Love is not in us when we are born. Affection, yes, but a love that will put another's good above ours? That is not natural to us.

We are taught love: shown how to share, how to help others, how to put them before ourselves. Usually by mothers and fathers, but most of all, by the one who created us. He showed us love even while we killed him, and calls us closer, higher, and deeper into his heart. From his heart to ours, he taught us what we could not otherwise learn. Because he forgave and loved, we love, and a heroine can do the right thing.

> *Jayden trembled. If she didn't get the dagger in time, all would be lost.*
>
> *Lightning sparked. Warped flashes sped toward Jayden. The tension in the vine loosened. Jayden yanked her right hand up. The vine still clung to her arm but it was too weak to hold her against the wall. With her eyes squeezed shut, she focused on the feel of the lightning. Its presence pulsed through her every fiber. She placed the snakelike body of the plant in the lighting's path.*

272 · AZALEA DABILL

A jolt shuddered through Jayden's body and jerked her arm as the bolt blasted into the vine instead. The plant's hold withered and Jayden burst free. Eyes open, she dove toward her dagger.

The lightning left a black, gaping hole and the remains of a charred vine. She clutched her dagger. Its familiar hilt rested in her palm like an extension of her hand.

She looked up at her target and the skin behind her ears burned. Hatred flooded her—hatred so intense it made Jayden's chest burn—Idla's. No! What was happening? Why weren't the daggers helping her control her talent? She didn't want to act in hatred. She didn't want to become a monster like Idla. She couldn't do this. As she tried to push away Idla's emotions, fear choked her.

There is one thing stronger than fear: love.

Of course. A new emotion flared in Jayden's chest. Love. Love for everyone who had made a sacrifice so she could live. It grew hot, like a blue flame. Yes. She understood. Love fueled a righteous anger. It was not the same as Idla's. The queen's rage was thick black—like tar on Jayden's heart.

Idla sneered. "Oh, you'll wish you were dead, now."

Jayden embraced her own emotions and gripped her daggers tighter. The fog from Idla's hate cleared, leaving Jayden's senses sharp.

–*Scarlet Moon* by S. D. Grimm, pg. 366

There is always a choice. The dark path of hatred and rage clouds our inner sight; love cuts through the strangling murk, reveals the true path, *is* the path. But seeing and doing the right thing is not always easy. A heroine does the right thing—the good that is required by the moment.

What is a hero? Not necessarily the one who saves the girl, the day, or the world. But one who picks truth, who opens the door of right, no matter the cost. A hero or heroine does what is needed to bring into existence what ought to be. Here is love's triumph.

Dive 11.5

Anti-hero and Heroine or Realism vs. What Ought to Be

Heroism. Heroine. Hero. What is wrong with the word *hero* that we have felt the need to change it? Do we feel *hero* carries connotations of glory-hounding or narcissism? Why do we need the negative definition *anti-hero?* Must a heroine be pulled down to our level? Have heroes gotten too far above us?

We wonder. Are the words *anti-hero* a subtle attack on the thought that it is a great thing to aspire to be a hero? To aspire to goodness, strength, and sacrifice?

Heroism does not mean perfection; it never did. It does not necessarily mean success. It means when a hero or a heroine see evil they fight it. Because of what it is—and what they are.

A hero must have faith in right, and faith operates by love. A love that sees the loss that will come if it does not act, and sees the goodness that may be gained if it does. With that diamond of strength growing in their heart, heroes defeat badness in the end, either in themselves or in the circumstance, whether they live or die. In every way that matters, heroes and heroines overcome.

All the heroes I've had any acquaintance with will tell you of the negatives. They only did what needed to be done, and they were very scared, and sometimes not very good at it, but they just did what they could. That is a definition of a worthy hero that has nothing *anti* about it.

But many anti-heroes are not worthy of the *hero* part of the phrase that defines them. That word should not be in their name, it is too good for them. They pursue selfishness, pragmatism, whatever is needed in the moment to gain their ends. Which is the classic definition of a villain, except bad fantasy portrays the anti-hero as being rewarded for it.

An anti-hero glories in the flaws that degrade him; he is not at all the same as someone deeply flawed who is trying to do better.

Courage thrives in our Creator's smile of loving belief in us. If we have been washed we are also in the process of being cut, and he sees the jewel we will become. In his eyes, we are already that perfect gem.

We are called to be true heroes in fantasy worlds and in our own. And not by ourselves, for we do not always see evil clearly. It takes more than our self to defeat evil, or good twisted. It takes friends, family, companions—it requires love and learning—all of our Creator's gifts.

Good twisted can be hard for us to discern. Often we even follow wrong willingly, but others who love us will not let us become a self-serving anti-hero without lifting a finger. Those heroes fight to make us heroes. Their tenacious hope brings hope to us.

"What about Marcus?"

Her father sighed, and his expression sobered. "He needs your prayers too . . . maybe even more than Liam. I still don't know how to approach him."

Kaden broke in now, frustration edging his tone. "How can he not see what he's doing? How wrong it is?"

"I think he does, somewhere deep inside. I can see the conflict in him and how he struggles with his decisions at times. The problem is he truly believes he's doing the right thing. He's very much the way I was when I was his age. He feels an almost painful need to prove himself. For me, it was to prove I wasn't my father. For him, it's to prove his worthiness to the General and to himself.

Your grandfather has very high expectations, but I think Marcus's personal expectations are even higher. He fears failure. That's why he's so dedicated to succeeding, even when it means ignoring the part of himself that wishes things could be different."

Kaden grumbled, but Kyrin could see more similarities between her two brothers than her twin would ever admit. They both had their own stubbornness and were both dedicated to what they believed. They just happened to be on opposing sides.

She sighed and hung her head. As excited as she was about Liam, she was equally sad about Marcus. She longed to save him, somehow, from the emperor's grip, but how did you save someone who didn't want to be saved?

"Is there nothing you can say to him?" she asked, her voice small.

"I'm afraid veiled words won't penetrate," her father replied. "Especially as time goes on and he begins to make a name for himself. The only way may be to tell him the truth outright, but what he'll do with it . . . I don't know."

A cold hand seemed to grip Kyrin's throat, and she had to swallow to loosen it. "You don't think . . . he wouldn't turn you in . . . would he?"

Her father's hesitance put a hard knot in her stomach.

"No . . . I don't think he would, but it would trouble him deeply."

"Will you tell him?"

"Sometime. His eternity is far more important than my life here." He must have sensed Kyrin's rising fear at the risk involved and offered her a reassuring smile. "But we don't know what the future will bring. Right now, the only thing we have is to pray. We'll pray for guidance and the right circumstances. We can only guess what may happen or how Marcus will respond. Elom is the One working on his heart. He can bring about the perfect events to open it to the truth."

Kyrin gave a quick nod. Her father was right, and she willed hope to take hold.

–*The King's Scrolls* by Jaye L. Knight, pg. 150

Hope is won by the gifts of faith, and love, and inner heroism.

And we, seeking fantasy jewels on our journey, dedicated to the transformation of our fellow human beings as we are to our own, we cannot leave the realm of fantasy to our enemy. The enemy who throws dirt on all that is bright, weaving paths of darkness that lead to doors of doom. We must not leave any world to the harm and destruction of our archenemy's rule without contesting it fiercely to the end. Neither our inner world, nor our outer, nor any living thing.

If we immerse ourselves in stories that admire people and things that are not good, we are following a path of harm. Every path that our feet wears deep in our minds leads to a door. That door will sooner or later open into our own world.

Gene Veith puts it well in *The Soul of The Lion, the Witch, and the Wardrobe.*

If one believes that Darwin's "law of the jungle" is real, then one will write stories about ruthless struggles for survival. A despairing view of reality leads to despairing works of art. Invariably, a particular author's "realism" is a function of his or her worldview. Moreover, since every work of fiction is, by definition, a made-up imaginary story, every work of fiction, no matter how realistic it seems, is a kind of fantasy. ...

A realism that confines itself to descriptions of only those things that can be seen in ordinary life necessarily excludes that which remains unseen but which nonetheless gives ordinary life its meaning—namely, truths of morality, faith, and transcendent ideals. The challenge for a Christian writer or artist is how to get at these invisible truths. It is possible to show their effects in a realistic way or to go inside the heart of the characters to show their inner struggles. There are realistic Christian authors, such as Dostoyevsky, but another way to write about these invisible truths is to explore them symbolically; that is, through fantasy.

By definition, fantasy is wholly imaginary. It is not reality, but it can provide a way to think about reality (pg. 131).

We love good fantasy and the reality it holds, do we not? And even more, the people who walk beside us on our fantastic journey—enough to fight for the souls of both. Our enemy inspires bad fantasy adventures and imaginative fiction, false jewels and counterfeit riches. He spreads shadows, anger, and potent pain across the worlds, real and imaginary.

Those who revel in wrong doing, however small, in whatever realm, follow him in that moment as an anti-hero. Can we leave our brothers and sisters without a word?

No.

We cannot abandon our pens, our enjoyment in books, or our world to the desolate fate that so many good things have suffered through our neglect or cynicism. Far less can we turn from a seeking heart. A hero's victory is won in belief in the reality of goodness and the love that overcomes.

Within that struggle, we cross vast stretches of fantasy and time, step through the veil of this earth, and even walk among the stars of the future—until we cross the final boundary between our world and the next—and step through the door of the fate we have chosen.

It is hard to name the moment when our innermost journey began in the depths of our beginnings, but we may truly say, we are definitely shaped by the best and worst fantasy.

Dive 11.6

Intense Truth vs. Powerful Lie—Best Fantasy and Worst

The best fantasy contains the fire of truth, as a pristine crystal holds the bright heart of the sun. Do we dare bathe ourselves in that blaze after a long foray in the cold depths of the ocean has left us shivering, wildly clutching false treasure to our hearts as we drip on the deck? If we dare the fire, we may leave lit within.

> *The Chronicler drew a long breath. "I don't believe in chosen ones. In prophecies. In destinies."*
>
> *Eanrin padded into the room. "Neither do I," he said mildly. "On principle, I'm against them. Inconvenient, nonsensical things, and a cat does like to be master of his own fate, you know?" Then he put his ears back and gave the Chronicler a pointed look. "But what I believe or don't believe has little to do with the truth of the matter."*
>
> *The Chronicler ground his teeth. "I've fought against believing things I could not understand, and I laughed at those who clung to Faerie stories." His voice was bitter as black tea. "Faerie stories are the last thing the likes of me needs to believe."*
>
> *"Likes of you?" said the cat. "You mean, mortal?"*
>
> *"I mean like me," the Chronicler snarled, fixing a glare upon the cat. "Malformed. Disfigured. An accident." His face was like the old earl's in that moment, the face of a warrior, but a defeated*

warrior who had fought a long, losing battle. A face all the more terrible for its youth.

The cat sat silent, his eyes slits, his ears quirked back as though he was offended. When at last he spoke, his voice was silky soft. "What is it with you mortals and your fixation on size? Do you think your stature has anything to do with anything?" Then he spoke like a knife. "Look at me!"

Suddenly he stood up, and his cat form dropped away into that of a man. The Chronicler, though he had seen the transformation once before, fell back against the desk, clutching at its legs for support.

"Take a good look at me!" the cat-man said, indicating his tall, straight, golden self, clad in brilliant red. But when he turned his head, he was a cat, small and furry. Just as the Haven was both a structure built of stone and mortar and a woodland glade of trees and moss, the cat was all cat, the man was all man, and both were simultaneously Eanrin.

"Look closer still," said the cat-man. "Do you know what I am? I am Eanrin of Rudiobus, Bard of Iubdan, one of the little people, one of the Merry Folk. Do you see?"

And the Chronicler saw what he had not seen before. Even as a man, Eanrin was unbound by size. He could be small enough to stand in the palm of a mortal's hand; he could be tall enough to speak eye to eye with the great centaurs. But he was still, no matter his size, Eanrin.

"Do you understand, mortal?" Eanrin said. "We Faerie know it's the spirit that counts, and all else is malleable. Beauty or ugliness; brawn or frailty; height or the lack thereof—these appearances can be exchanged with scarcely a thought! But the truth . . . now, that's another issue. The truth of the thing, the person behind what you perceive with any of your paltry five senses . . . Creature of dust, it's the truth that counts! And you'll rarely find more truth than in Faerie tales."

–*Dragonwitch* by Anne Elizabeth Stengl, pg. 248

We can dare to bathe in the heat of that truth, to live in it, to stand within. Even in fantasy. For the air is often clearer there, that we may percieve truth better when we meet it again in the clouded atmosphere of our world.

Truth overcomes everything that stands against it, for the more lies flung at it, the more intensely truth is shown for what it is. Lies crumble to dust where they dare face it, flaming to ash in the diamond door of meaning, forged in love's light.

No lie deals with inherent meaning or with true-naming—with calling things what they are, and it does not set foot on the path to joy. Lies pepper the worst fantasy books with forced meaning and false-names, since a lie calls things what they are not. But true names are full to the brim with life, with the cutting knife-edge of existence. And everyone who names a thing what it truly is—as much as language can hold of it—follows a path that brightens more and more until the perfect day. Naming is a piercing, fiery truth, and its burn is not always comfortable.

A true name claims itself. To true-name also means to wear the cloak of responsibility: to order the world, ourselves, and everything else. To be a true-namer is a worthy vocation; to do otherwise is to deny what exists.

True-naming wields power and strength, for acknowledging what something is looses its power to interact, and ours to react and act again, to align ourselves in right relationship with both the named and the Namer. True-naming changes us for good, touching everything that exists. Truly naming a thing births further possibilities, expanding our ability to call other things that we have not fully seen or named into existence, in a sense. It was always there, we just did not see it until we breathed its name.

Dive 11.7

True-name the Fabulous World with Spellbinding Strength

Naming things gives us true boundaries and clear vision to act. In the realm of fantasy and that of earth, true-naming may often lead us to a door of forgiveness and the path of change.

And with every right name and subsequent right choice we refuse to be swept away by the tide of evil. Then, as we become more who we are meant to be, we give others courage, and hope, and strength, passing on what we have received—the power to true-name, to walk the path of change. Every person holds that power—even a rabbit.

Heather felt a cold weight fall on her, like early ice on an autumn garden. This all felt so wrong. She gazed at her friend, illuminated in torchlight, bravely resigned to her grim agreement. Behind her the great bird broke the bank of fog, beat his wings once and banked again, disappearing once more into the endless mist. Again his feathered wingtips cut the fog in a wispy furrow.

"It's all right, Heather," Emma said, a brave smile on her face. "I know how I'm going to die."

"I don't know how I'm going to die," Heather said, backing to the far side of the sixth standing stone, "but I know how I'm going to live."

Heather burst into a run—four stabbing strides—and then she leapt, covering the distance between the standing stones.

She landed, found her feet, and surged forward. The hawk began to emerge from the mist again. Heather shoved Emma hard, clutching the emerald at her neck. The princess fell backward, disappearing with a shocked scream into the fog below.

Heather bent to recover the fallen torch. She raised it high. In her other hand she held the Green Ember.

With a shriek, the hawk extended his talons.

–*Ember Falls* by S. D. Smith, pg. 322

The bravery to true-name the mistaken self-sacrifice of the princess, to protect a friend from herself, binds this friendship with love and hope.

That evil is strong needs no proof; that love is greater requires demonstration. The strength to restrain every spell of death whispered in our ears by the enemy lies hidden in many places among the worlds. Sometimes such strength surprises us, springing from the weakest, most rabbity hearts among us.

What do those hidden places contain? Names, names of meaning; and even the smallest courage to use them. Hope of change; of turning from false meaning to true, from our own falseness to the true-name bestowed on us by our Creator.

Names and more names boil within us, in every mind false and true, all fighting to be spoken, and birthed in action. Treachery or truth, hope or despair, worthy sacrifice or self-immolation. What lies within must be truly named, or we will be guilty of harm.

Naming our emotions, what we have done, and what others do, then acting rightly on it, helps us create a true picture of the world. Of course the world is always clarifying as we identify and gain new knowledge, then react and act again, changing and growing and naming. In this way we learn the world, and also begin to discover our Creator's name and nature. At least as much meaning as our words can hold of him. His qualities we can partially wrap our minds and hearts around.

But not every name or nature or power we find in the ocean of fantasy is true. In the far realms, will we find natural forces or God revealed? That depends on the true-naming of the fantasy we read: does it call things what they are? Does it imagine glorious, sparkling, true things and great persons outside ourselves who work high deeds within us, even if they are small? Or does it reveal a world of transient glory dependent on self, with nothing and no one beyond the grey borders of their solitary hearts, dry deeds, and shriveled souls who touch our spirits with chill, insatiable hunger for the unreality of false naming, descending into despair?

Name true. Be true. Take the path of change.

Ultimate Naming of the World—God Revealed or a Natural Force?

Don't names deal with meaning, by their very nature? The path of wisdom, leading to the door of life, may not be visible to us until we grip the truth of a name.

Wicca holds beliefs that place great emphasis on naming. They declare naming has power to change what exists. That naming something as we wish it to be can make our desire become real. This holds some truth and a lot of error.

The one who gave us all our names is God, the uttermost height of I AM, the Name who holds all names. He gave us the power to name creatures and things at the beginning of the world, through Adam. It is a kind of making, since naming gives linguistic shape to the meaning of something we perceive, by thought and word. But in true-naming, we try to discover the name that fits the meaning—to perceive the shape of the name that fits the thought, the creature, the thing best—to honor what it is—not to force anything to take shape against its inherent essence, or its non-existence. Morphing a name against what it is, trying to make something what it is not, always ends in destruction and the unmaking of the name, exposing its false root. And as for bringing something non-existent into being, we are not given that power.

We are given the power to imagine and carry out our thoughts within limits, but that is simply our working on the things our creator has made available to us in mind, spirit, and body, an adventure all its own. We never bring anything out of nothing, though from the beginning of time, we have tried.

Despite our history of misuse, our Creator still trusts us with the power to name. It is our privilege to name as truly as possible. And we want to mean, and deal with, and act on—things that are true, that are real. In the realm of fantasy, the spiritual realm, the wide world of ideas, and the realm we breathe in. This automatically means we oppose things that are false, because they are opposite what is true.

And two opposite things cannot be the same. Two opposites cannot mean the same thing, cannot hold the same nature, the same name. It is an impossibility.

If we try to merge two opposite things, bring them together, blend them, we get something un-nameable. Un-namable because the name literally makes no sense, it forms nonsense. White can change to black, or move toward it, but at that point it is no longer white. Just as Saruman found.

> *"For I am Saruman the Wise, Saruman Ring-maker, Saruman of Many Colours!"*
>
> *I looked then and saw that his robes, which had seemed white, were not so, but were woven of all colours, and if he moved they shimmered and changed hue so that the eye was bewildered.*
>
> *"I liked the white better," I said.*
>
> *"White," he sneered. "It serves as a beginning. White cloth may be dyed. The white page can be overwritten; and the white light can be broken."*
>
> *"In which case it is no longer white," said I. "And he that breaks a thing to find out what it is has left the path of wisdom."*
>
> *–The Fellowship of the Ring* by J. R. R. Tolkien, pg. 339

If we call something what it is not . . . we act on a lie. And then usually fall for it.

Following truth is the path of wisdom, leading to the door of life. True love, diamond-clear intent, and the jade of peaceful riches are tied to that path. The path of change and growth, however fantastic.

"Was it real, Sir?" she asked presently. "Are there such things?"

"Yes," said the Director, "it was real enough. Oh, there are thousands of things within this square mile that I don't know about yet. And I daresay that the presence of Merlinus brings out certain things. We are not living exactly in the Twentieth Century as long as he's here. We overlap a bit; the focus is blurred. And you yourself . . . you are a seer. You were perhaps bound to meet her. She's what you'll get if you won't have the other."

"How do you mean, Sir?" said Jane.

"You said she was a little like Mother Dimble. So she is. But Mother Dimble with something left out. Mother Dimble is friends with all that world as Merlinus is friends with the woods and rivers. But he isn't a wood or a river himself. She has not rejected it, but she has baptized it. She is a Christian wife. And you, you know, are not. Neither are you a virgin. You have put yourself where you must meet that Old Woman and you have rejected all that has happened to her since Maledil came to Earth. So you get her raw—not stronger than Mother Dimble would find her, but untransformed, demoniac. And you don't like it. . . .

–That Hideous Strength by C.S. Lewis, pg. 314

The horrible wrongness of things falsely named is rightly terrifying when we perceive them. Coming in many guises, Mother Nature, or Gaia, as she is called, is often falsely named a goddess. That is not who she is. *Goddess* is not her true name. She is not self-existent, if she has any aspect of personhood at all.

The one who gave her all the glory of the treasures and power she possesses is the one who rightly claims our worship, with all our awe, admiration, and grateful thanks. We want no name apart from truth, and claim no authority but that of our rightful King.

By true naming, and meaning, and walking, our knowledge deepens as we hold the wealth of The Wingfeather Saga, allow the light of *Dragonwitch* to cleanse our hearts, follow the brave deeds of *Ember Falls,* and taste the true springs of power in *That Hideous Strength.*

Those true paths lead us beyond or through nature, to a deeper experience of the *supernatural.* That true-name ties us to reality beyond our usual mode of vision in our world, though it is common elsewhere. Which leads us to wonder; *Supernatural Fantasy—Is It in This World or Out?*

Chapter 12.0

Supernatural Fantasy: Is It In This World or Out?

Is it not a relief to know that what we see with our eyes is not all there is? That what we see and touch is only a small part of what exists? That is most exciting—in a terrifying, encouraging way. For fantasy widens the unseen door to the spiritual arena, and there we find the supernatural beckoning us.

We've touched on supernatural fantasy before, but there are a few more gems to explore. In these fair realms the very earth and air, wind and wave and fire of wonder influence us—and we impact our world, which stands in dire need.

Supernatural beings and events, good or evil, strike our imaginations hard. I think this is because we sense at once that the supernatural is not human, that each being is completely *other*. And they are usually greater in power. Not to mention that what they do tends to be outside the ordinary.

But here is a curious thing. We readily hang the word *unusual* on the supernatural, which is humorous in a way, for supernatural manifestations of power are common in our world, where they often go unrecognized. The life that stirs in a seed and grows—the shifting of the tide under the influence of the moon—it's all supernatural. Only our senses are dulled by the false name *natural law*.

We also tend to become numb to anything familiar or ordinary, glossing over spectacular things rather than coming more awake to their intricate dance of power. To the play of sunlight and shadow that powers an oak leaf to grow and our bodies to thrive in the mind-boggling abundance of our plant and animal world—to the moon and the tide, and the growing seed. Every law and every bit of power that holds them in their state of being is orchestrated by Another.

Because our society tends to assume natural laws are not upheld by supernatural power, we now define *supernatural* as anything infernal or divine that suspends or shortcuts natural laws. In reality, our natural laws are still God's, and so are supernatural to their roots.

So supernatural beings who hold power in fantasy rightly fascinate us. But be wary, the realm of the supernatural is also dangerous, from demons, to Satan, to angels and God, to representations of them among the worlds.

To Lucy Pevensie's mind, Aslan never was a tame lion. But he was good. However, if we choose to align ourselves with spiritual beings who oppose and hate humans, we've just about signed our death warrant, as Nikabrik did.

Evil is selfish by nature. Selfishness tends to spread, and is quite non-selective of who or what it destroys in its full flower. It luxuriates in pain, in using others, in everything bad because its overwhelming desire is to direct everything toward itself. Love, the opposite of selfishness, luxuriates in giving, in healing, in sharing everything good.

In representational worlds besides ours there are supernatural beings who align with the supreme ruler of their universe for good, like the envoy in The Lamb Among the Stars series. There are others who follow our enemy and what they want at the cost of their very beings, as Atol does in *The Wounded Shadow*. Supernatural persons can even call us to humor, like Eanrin, Bard of Iubdan in *Moonblood,* and then there are fantasies that verge into horror, which we won't name. Our search for supernatural fantasy doesn't get into the chill of horror. I will not say all horror has no value, but it is too cold and fear-inspiring for me.

Rather, we pursue the call of heroism that leaves us breathless, the clarion cry of sacrifice that leaves us in cleansing tears, the trumpet blast of love that reaches from the lowest child to the highest king. We grasp for fantasy adventure in all its facets, for understanding, for laughter, and for joy—even in the face of death, struggle, and challenge.

In our world, cold-hearted cynicism and hopelessness are growing. Symptoms of this disease of despair spreads from tainted fantasy pages to our spirits in often purposeful ink. These enspelled speculations, pernicious imaginations, and monstrous thoughts struggle to break through the reflective mirror of fantasy, where they hold a feast of death in a hall of shades.

They lie in wait for us like crouching beasts deadlier than any depicted in story. Death without hope, achievement without meaning, struggle without end, life without aim. Even though this feast is only a fantasy, when we make those insatiable thoughts our own, such fare eats us from the inside out.

Our imaginations, our very souls, seek for existence beyond physical death, for achievement that matters, for rest after struggle, for a strong life of love, kindness, and meaning. And mercy that ends in victory, in triumph over our just hour of judgment.

For we cannot escape the knowledge we require much mercy. We know our failures. Unless we have blinded ourselves, our treacheries, small and large, stare us in the face, or lurk in the shadowy corners of our spirits, however deep we dive or far we roam.

But our Creator waits to forgive, to extend the right hand of friendship, if we will turn from our determined journey into darkness, if we will change our allegiance. When we walk with him, our imagination as well as the rest of us orients toward the strength of his love, as an unfolding bloom toward the summer sun. And a new story begins in a sure hope.

Every jewel of fantasy points to that story, either vaguely or clearly. To tales of weak hearts become strong, of death that gives way to the courage of life, of torches held high against the dark, of the victory every living creature will know after the last war is won. Of the rise of a kingdom overflowing with good, with no taint of evil left anywhere.

The light of excellent fantasies reflect that shining road more and more until the brightest day. For the glimpses we've seen and heard of truth and judgment and holiness in imaginative fiction are real in our world. Those seeds grow and bloom in our sphere and in fantasy alike.

The invigorating story of our redemption is true, as is the supernatural account of the one who brings us into his marvelous light. If we are scribed in his book of life, he directs everything, seen and unseen, for our every good. The full flowering is coming.

Much that was foretold of him has come to pass, some things are coming to pass this moment, and some are yet to bring conflict and restoration. Our Creator's rule declares far better things than that of Arthur.

That good king now heralds a bright memory of humanity's highest dreams and yearning for what we cannot name. But when the one who made all worlds reigns, we will be home, living in the days of the King.

His true story of the supernatural we too rarely read. Truth sets us free if we have the wit and will to seek it. The best inspiring fantasy is but a weak offshoot of that adventure, a faint reflection, a current amid the waves that points to the fountain of waters.

Every good deed large and small is breathed into being by someone driven by an imagination that has feasted on heroic fantasies in the spiritual arena, on brave ideas among the wide worlds, and who has fought for victory in all worlds—not fed heartily on false tales mirroring twisted shards of reality that bring monsters to life.

Even as evil reveals its hideous power in The Lamb Among the Stars, its nemesis comes. *The Wounded Shadow* reveals startling influences where evil opposes good, and demons and angels in *Cloak of Light* are far different than we might expect. The decay of darkness consumes every hiding place and shreds every mask of the hunted in *Moonblood*—until the light rises.

Dive 12.1

Divine Authority and World Powers in Spectacular Fantasy

Is it true that going against the wide current of common thought in any world leads to our testing? The supernatural can be both dangerous and good, or dangerous and evil, with eternal impact.

We are involved in a dance of treachery and trust that is tempering our steel, refining our hearts, enlarging our spirits, and polishing us into jewels. In a dance where the treacherous one takes as many down with him as he can, we must walk by faith in the faithful one when our eyes are temporarily blinded by our own reason that does not see.

> *Confused and angry, Merral turned to the envoy. "You've left him alive!" he protested.*
>
> *"And why shouldn't I?"*
>
> *"Because he will kill . . . thousands."*
>
> *"Far more than that. But what is that to you?"*
>
> *"You could end the war. Just like that."*
>
> *The envoy seemed to scrutinize Merral. "How human! You are delivered and yet you complain! Be warned: to criticize me is to criticize the One who sent me."*

Merral realized that the energy his fears had generated now fueled his bitterness, yet he could not rein in his words. "You could have spared the Assembly! Just taken one more life!"

The envoy put his glove back on his hand. "You are an ungrateful race. Instead of thanking the Most High for his mercy, you question his will."

The sound of the chiming from above was louder now, the notes urgent, angry, and restless.

"It makes no sense!"

But it was Nezhuala, not the envoy, who spoke next. He gave an icy laugh that was almost a cackle. "Go on, Commander! Ask on! That's how I started." He pointed sharply at the envoy. "Ask him! Query the One who sent him. I'll tell you what you will find. You'll find that he doesn't care for you. You are just little pawns in his great game. Pieces he moves about, hither and thither, just to do his will. You think I am merciless, cruel, and capricious?" He pointed upward. "Oh, I'm nothing compared to him."

–*The Infinite Day* by Chris Walley, pg. 282

We can be staring at the truth before us and at the same time open our ears to lies. We either serve good wittingly, or evil unwittingly.

The sleepless malice bent against us wields weapons we must recognize: the sword of unworthy question, slashing good character and proven intent, the bow of intrigue that shoots razor-edged arrows of distraction, the ragged-sharp dagger of veiled threat, the nagging, slow poison of painful fears. The battlefield in our minds is all too real, as is our weakness before the powers we face and their arsenal. Until we reach the victorious position of the one who leads us—and take up his armor—then the battle changes.

The inner and the outer battlegrounds are inextricably linked. Often, a conflict won in the inner arena means victory on the outer battleground. For fantasy affects our thought, and thought our motive, which affects our action. Then our decisive action reinforces, or redirects and affects our motive and mind, and again we are poised to act. The arena of the spirit, the battleground of ideas, and the sphere we breathe in are linked inextricably, and so fantasy impacts us on every level, for good or for ill, though it may admittedly begin in small ways.

For renewed imaginations thrive on epic stories, on moments of virtue written in the small and ordinary, as well as on larger acts splashed across the page of the extraordinary. An imagination with a taste for greatness in all its forms is a gift that requires care. A care and discernment that watches carefully how dream and vision thread through prophecy and truth, until at last they touch us with a startling influence, inside and out.

Dive 12.2

Dreams and Startling Influences in *The Wounded Shadow*

Who would not be shaken when beings we thought were part of super-natural dreams are revealed as living creatures? When one is good and one evil, of near-equal power, the potential for our startled fear, sorrow, and anger is vast. Yet hope remains. Especially when one of the two is a friend.

The vision stopped, and I was Willet Dura once more. My com-panions wore the same expressions of shock as I. Tears coursed down Custos's cheeks and Mirren wept softly. The remnant of Ealdor stood among us, his stole still draped over his shoulders, but his appearance had changed, the last impression of solidity dropping from him as though he'd become a dying memory. And it continued. My friend became more insubstantial with each passing moment. "Aer forgive me," I choked.

He looked down through his body with no more concern than if I had told him he had a spot on his stole. "I chose to break the binding, Willet. I chose, not you. Aer told us to cleanse the earth, but we—I—wanted vengeance. We buried Atol and those he'd taken unto himself, binding ourselves with our power, constrain-ing our actions with vows that couldn't be revoked."

I shook my head. "I don't understand."

"We held eternity and power that would have made us gods among men." Ealdor nodded to himself. "We had seen what Atol

*and the rest had become, and more, we knew the long dark of
loneliness that awaited us. We had no intention of wasting our
victory by becoming god-kings in his place."*

*"The children's rhymes," Gael said. "You couldn't appear un-
less you were called."*

*Ealdor nodded. "We wanted to give you the chance we squan-
dered." He smiled at me.*

–*The Wounded Shadow* by Patrick Carr, pg. 326

Friendship involves love. Love takes joy in the truth, love endures
flaming trial, love does not fail in the hour of need. Love mixed with
selfishness will fail. There is our constant conflict.

The one who loved us to the end when he walked among us, who
loves us now, is the one who will not fail.

Thankfully, the Creator of all good and the spirit of evil in our world
are in no way equal in power. The contest is not directly between Satan
and God, but between our evil nature and the prince of this world. He
would use us to wound our Creator. And this mortal cannot battle im-
mortal evil alone. Nor do we need to.

We are called to battle beside him who took up the sword for us even
unto death, and we are summoned by the Spirit of truth. By fantasy, in
the use of our imagination, our Father helps us in so many ways. He
draws our familiar, jaded, earthly battleground within another sphere
and there enables us to see issues of right and wrong more clearly, to
discern with fresh eyes as we go through struggle and adventure, even
take part in it.

Sorrow and joy, decay and accomplishment, defeat and victory
reach us more easily in fantasy, piercing our inner hearts, which are
sometimes grown world-weary. Cynical or not, when we come upon an
unexpected friend in our innermost sanctum, the arena of the spirit, it
can be quite startling, and strangely comforting—though even good
may shock us, when it wears an unfamiliar face. But wakeful shocks
can be good for us.

Dive 12.3

Shocking Demons and Angels in *Cloak of Light*

Often good and evil wear cloaks. They do not appear as we expect. Is not evil always supposed to have horns and a tail, or wear a fair bit of red? Is not good supposed to be a bit pale and willowy, with a hint of condemnation in its eyes, though its face is so gentle it judges nothing? But battle leaves no time for weighing appearance, supernatural or otherwise.

In the case of one young man, beings that no one else can see intrigue, scare, and appall him.

> *Drew scrambled for control over the man, but it was not necessary—the gunman was unconscious. The alien inside him, however, was not. The being was writhing about as if trying to force his unconscious host to rise up. It unnerved Drew to no end. He grabbed the gun and aimed it at the man, not sure whether to pull the trigger. He chanced a quick look over his shoulder just in time to see the light alien thrust his sword through the dark alien's chest. Blood spilled from the wound, and the alien fell to the floor.*
>
> *Drew felt like he was in some bizarre science fiction movie, and he wanted it to stop, but the oddity continued. As the dark warrior clutched his chest and gasped, his body dissolved just like the gun, but this time, the wisps of green vapor fell down through the floor. Everything about him dissolved, including his spilled blood, until there was nothing.*

Drew shook his head and refocused on the gunman and his writhing invader. What should he do? Just then the white-dressed alien came and knelt down over the gunman. There was a brief and obviously contrary verbal exchange, and then the light warrior slammed his fist into the head of the gunman . . . and the alien. The gunman's body jerked, and both he and the alien invader became perfectly still. The light alien warrior turned his head and looked up at Drew. Drew forced himself not to look into his eyes but continued to stare at the face of the unconscious gunman. The moment hung forever. The light alien tilted his head, and Drew knew his suspected something.

–*Cloak of the Light* by Chuck Black, pg. 142

Drew is appalled until, in the course of the Wars of the Realm trilogy, he finds out what the light aliens are. But he doesn't need to know *what* they are to realize one side is trying to protect humanity, and the other to destroy us. But why do the dark invaders target small children and encourage random, disgusting acts of no great destruction, instead of focusing on larger scale annihilation, such as the school shooter he confronted? A curious question—what form of destruction was their goal? To discover that answer, we must dive deeper, into another fantasy.

Dive 12.4

Oppose Hideous Evil in *Moonblood*

What kind of destruction do we face, walking along the path of darkness? Death of the body, death of the spirit, or something that goes deeper? Walk on . . . the face of evil is hideous beyond imagination.

The tug of the river is powerful, and Lionheart almost falls. "I don't belong to you!"

"Oh, don't you?" The Dragon's smile grows. "It wasn't enough, was it, little Lionheart? All your guilt. All your noble resolve. You gave your life for the girl you betrayed, but you did not succeed in rescuing her."

"I . . . I stopped the beast."

"Only for the moment." He comes nearer, the shadow of his cloak drawing a blackness around them that is deeper than nightfall. "Did you really think, pathetic mortal, that you could earn atonement? Did you really think that your own sacrificed life could begin to repay the evil you have worked?" Fire flickers in the recesses of his eyes.

Lionheart turns and runs into the river.

The current catches him like hands on his legs and drags him under, and the water is cold as it closes over his head. He wants to scream but cannot, for the air is knocked out of him as he is pulled, struggling, down and down. But the Dragon's laugh penetrates even there, filling his head as water fills Lionheart's eyes, his nose, his lungs.

Then, though darkness overwhelms him and water blinds him, he sees a hand. Desperate, he reaches out and takes hold.

The next moment he is on the shore again, gagging and spitting black water. Someone holds him and thumps his back until he has coughed everything from his lungs. He sits for what seems a long while, shivering, gasping. Then he turns.

And meets the Prince's gaze.

"No," Lionheart whispers, crumpling into a heap, his hands clutching the back of his head. The mist is cold. He'd not thought he would feel anything in the Realm Unseen, but he is frozen straight through to his bones. "No, don't look at me."

"Lionheart," says the Prince, "will you come with me now?"

"I'm worthless," Lionheart says. "I couldn't save her. I couldn't redeem my honor."

"You never can," the Prince replies. He takes Lionheart by the shoulders and forces him to sit up, to face him. "But do you think my grace insufficient to forgive you?"

Lionheart cannot bear to meet those eyes, but neither can he look away. Water drips down the stubble on his face and meets in a stream from his chin. The Prince gazes at him with eyes that see to the very truth of his soul, every unacknowledged cowardice, every sin glossed over with excuses. But in the Prince's eyes is no condemnation but rather an offer.

"Come with me now, Lionheart." His voice is firm, but it is a gentle request, not a command. He remains kneeling in the mud of the riverbed, not caring that he dirties his fine clothes, and his hands hold Lionheart by the shoulders.

Still shivering, hunched over with shame, Lionheart nods. "I will come with you," he whispers.

The Prince rises and pulls Lionheart to his feet. He presses something into Lionheart's hand. When he looks, the dead man finds that he holds once more the bent and burned sword. He frowns and turns again to the Prince, a question in his eyes.

"Follow me," says the Prince. He starts walking back up the river.

"Wait!" Lionheart cries, desperate. "You know what happened last time! You know what I did! I am a worm before that monster. I cannot face him, not again! I cannot fight the Dragon!"

The memory of his failure engulfs him, and it is more horrible to face than ever before. He thinks he will collapse; the weight of the broken sword is too much to bear.

But the Prince stands beside him and puts an arm across his shoulders. "We'll face him together this time," he says, slowly turning Lionheart to one side.

To look into the Dragon's burning face.

—*Moonblood* by Anne Elizabeth Stengl, pg. 332

In the end of our weakness, at our uttermost depth of need, when the dragon of despair gloats over us and our useless guilt, our endless shame, and we writhe, our very self laid bare before our Creator, then we see him, walking toward us in strength. The son of the Father, who calls us in a myriad voices: by the taste and feel and sight of food, free air, and flowers; in the love of family, kindred, and a heart's mate; speaking in his ways to our mind, heart, and spirit.

Answer the call. Then in his power, with his sword, rise reborn—and defeat the dragon.

Our rescue is in sight.

New treasures are ours in Lionheart's knowledge of the unseen and *The Broader Realms From the Beasts of Hamlin to Star Pirates.*

Chapter 13.0

The Broader Realms From the Beasts of Hamlin to Star Pirates

Our voyage together through the realm of fantasy nears its end. Should we not rightly ask what desires and dreams the jewels of fantasy that we have sought and brought on deck bring to life before our wondering eyes? Each of us has gathered a chest of treasures on our own quest in the ocean, containing false glass or true gold, gems gleaming wet under the scent of salt and the sea.

Do our gems approach truth in the worlds? Do they bring to us a culture, a kingdom, a person—a universe—worthy of our admiration and long memory? Does the smooth or faceted jewel in our hand give us the gift of the unexpected, the courage of hope, and dreams of mysterious, beautiful possibilities?

In realms near and far, every real thing has at least one thread or gleam different than we expect. The best fantasies add worth to life, sometimes in ways we do not consciously know or understand. In every world, victory or defeat may not unfold as we think. On our choices hang our doom or joy.

Hear the cry of the hero and the call of the heroine, and follow the silver ring of trumpets in the soul of imaginative fantasy. That thrilling cry draws us within the perilous realm of the *Lord of Dreams*, where there is treasure to be had. *Falcon Flight* holds a key of vision forever altering a kingdom torn by treachery. From there it is but a step to King

Arthur in *The Legend of Lady Ilena*. Hamlin town conceals more than a mysterious stranger in *The Piper's Pursuit*. Explore the cosmos of Faery prophecy in Eyes of Everia, and cross worlds to find a lost father in the parallel realm of *Moon Daughter Rising*. *The Mapmaker's Daughter* and *Mardan's Mark* are a battleground of heroes and ambitious pirates in alternate realms. *Brand of Light* defies those who would subjugate a universe. Dive into a lost world in *Dreamlander*. Unravel the mystery, the beauty, and the adventure hidden in every last gem.

Dive 13.1

Wide Worlds of Dream in *The Lord of Dreams*

The world is wide, and the worlds are wider. Often each is larger within than they are without.

One such world of dream weaves more than wonder.

She murmured into her pillow. "I wish. . .I wish I could be the hero."

Her window slammed open, wind howling inside with a flurry of rain. Claire shrieked, clapping her hands over her ears as she fought free of the covers.

Terror made her heart stutter.

A shadow stood between her and the window. It stepped forward, and in the strobe-like flash of lightning she saw his face.

He waved a hand, and the window closed behind him, and the storm suddenly muffled.

With trembling fingers she flipped on her bedside lamp.

He tilted his head and looked at her, a faint, toothy smile lifting his lips. His clothes might have been leather, thick and dark, with a faint, unsettling texture across his chest. Tight, dark breeches were tucked into black boots. His hands were gloved in a similar dark material. His cloak (who wears a cloak?) swirled and set- tled behind him, the edges ragged, made of feathers or perhaps tattered cloth. The exaggerated collar spread around his angular face, making it appear narrower and paler. High, sharp cheek-bones caught the light below glittering eyes of an indistinct color, blue and gold and silver all at once. His hair was long and white blond; it stuck straight out and up from his head, unaffected by gravity, fine as dandelion fluff.

He let her study him, his smile widening slowly as he watched her fear rise until it nearly choked her.

"Come." He held out a gloved hand to her so dark it seemed to suck in the light around it.

Her breath squeaked, and she gasped, "Who are you?"

His teeth gleamed, sharp and predatory.

"Your villain."

–*The Lord of Dreams* by C. J. Brightley, pg. 10

There are night dreams, there are daydreams, and then there are dreams worth fulfilling, as Claire discovers.

Dreams also weave mystery and battle in fantasy within the mists of Britannia when a medieval first daughter returns from slavery in Araby sands to learn the nature of courage and the naked combat of body and soul.

Kyrin shrank back, buried in pain, where every living thing she loved was dead or lost. Turning her head, she blurted, "Nothing, I'm fine—"

"Don't say that. You haven't been well for days." Talik's grey eyes were narrow.

Kyrin clenched her jaw. It did no good; tears gathered and fell.

The stone bench shifted as Talik sat on the end and stared at the red, pink-streaked blooms of the rosebush. Abruptly, he gripped her shoulders.

Kyrin flinched, and he released her. She couldn't look at him.

He lowered his head till his eyes found hers. "What is it? What grieves you so?"

"The tiger. It hunts me." She gulped. "I thought it was gone."

Talik frowned.

"I—there's a tapestry—in my chamber. There was one like it on Ali's ship. The beast has followed me in my dreams since my mother died. I haven't even told my father that—or that the sword that took her did this." Miserably, Kyrin slid the fish aside from her scar. "So I was afraid of blades, and the tiger came. But I broke the fear that gripped me in ice when any blade came near me. And I thought the beast was conquered too, when I freed the falcon in Araby. Our chains shattered."

"What do you mean?" Talik's eyes were gentle.

"I gave it up—vengeance. And fear. And somehow I and the falcon were loosed." She kicked one restless foot back and forth under the bench. "Vengeance was empty, dead ash. Mother did not want that, nor did the Master of the stars, nor I, in the end. I fought it, the hate, and the falcon and I flew free of our chains. I did not dream of the tiger anymore." She lifted her head with a small smile. "But the tiger has come back, nearer since the wazir sent me home." Scorn like a hot wind erupted, burning through her restraint. "I have come back, but still I fear, and so the tiger comes." Her voice was hard. "To wield a blade with my body is not the same as wielding it in spirit."

"Besides this tiger, do you blame yourself for your mother?" Talik asked softly.

"At times. Though I know it was not my doing." Kyrin bit her lip. "Father is sad when he thinks of her."

"And so glad to have you."

She shrugged a shoulder. "I am not the first daughter they think me." She touched the ring in her ear.

"No. But they love you nonetheless." Talik grinned; then his smile faded and he shifted. "His word can be a blade for defense. What do you fear?"

"I—" she looked down. "As well as finding Hamal for Alaina and Tae, as first daughter, I must protect Cierheld and my family. Did I not say I was stronger than they dreamed?" Her mouth twisted. "They expect something more, and I fail again."

"All know you are not a coward, for you fought Keffer's men, and in Keffold. It is wisdom to avoid raising your blade until you see your target." Talik shook his head with a wry smile. "You know, courage isn't a question of strength or failure or gaining what we seek, but trusting the one who made us. Then we can go forward, whether we fall or rise."

Kyrin wished she had a sweetmeat to give him for saying "we."

–Falcon Flight by Azalea Dabill, pg. 288

With each jewel of another life, another land, another time than our own, we find ourselves eager to be a little kinder, a little more true, a little quicker to see the mysterious beauty in everyday things. These are some of the rewards of moral fantasy adventure. There are yet greater wonders to gain.

Dive 13.2

King Arthur and Hamlin Town for all the World

We have wondered, at times, what it would be like to walk beside one of our heroines or heroes, such as King Arthur.

Arthurian fantasy at its best, this is a glimpse of Arthur as we never saw him before, a man inspiring Northern Britain against ruthless invaders, and with him Lady Ilena, a warrior who discovers what it means to lead her people.

> *"Wait, Ilena," Gillis says. "Consider carefully. This is a dangerous time in Britain. Your father and your friends will not know where you are or how you fare. If you choose exile, you might well be choosing death."*

> *"I . . ." I start to say that I am sure, but I think of my father. He still grieves for my mother and sister. If my staying would bring him peace . . . I turn and face him. "Father." It is hard to get the words out, but I must. "Do you want me to stay?"*

> *He looks at me sadly for a few moments, then says, "Of course I want you by my side, Ilena, as would any parent. But you are a warrior. The way of a warrior is a dangerous path and an honorable one. I would not ask you to forsake your life's calling. Go with my blessing."*

> *I blink and try to smile my thanks. I look at Gillis and repeat, "I choose exile!"*

"If you are sure," he says, "you must leave tomorrow. You may return when your deeds of valor can be told in this hall."

I hesitate for a moment, then bow to him and to my father before I turn back to my people. "I thank you all. I pray that your judgement is right and that I will deserve the mercy you have shown me."

I walk along the crowded aisle as proudly and as slowly as I can manage.

–Lady Ilena: Way of the Warrior by Patricia Malone, pg. 82

In lands other than ours, life can be very brief, and it teaches us to consider well, to live with honor, and to leave a blessing for those we love. But the blessing we give to others in our present moments speaks of the active book of knowledge we write in our heart's blood. It is a more worthy legacy, and a far greater treasure to the living.

Remember what the wise who went before us scribed in our book, in bold, glimmering hue of opalescent green, pink, and blue? The secret of imaginative fiction lies in how evil is portrayed, and in what is said, and not said, especially around Hamlin town.

She retrieved her other arrow—the one that she had shot at the beast and missed. When she came back, Steffan was still staring down at the animal.

"There's something about it." He squatted beside the mangled animal. "It doesn't look like a normal wolf. Or a normal anything." He stretched out one of its legs. "It's so large, it must be the Beast of Hamlin. And yet the second one looked exactly like it."

Kat knelt on the other side of it. "It's a wolf. Look at its head. But you're right. It doesn't look normal. The legs are longer and the body is bigger than any other wolf I've seen, but it's also so skinny."

"As if it was starving. Maybe that's why it was so aggressive. But why would it be starving? There are plenty of hares and squirrels around these woods and fields."

"And rats." Hundreds and hundreds of rats. "But the rats all seem to be in town."

"You live in a strange place, Katerina Grymmelin."

"My name is not Grymmelin." Katerina's body tensed at hearing Hennek's surname applied to her.

"Oh, yes. Forgive me." He looked chagrined.

"My name is Katerina Ludken. And I thank you for . . . not letting the wolf . . . that is . . ." Why was it so difficult to say, "Thank you for saving my life"? All the breath had left her lungs. She just couldn't.

Finally she said, "Thank you for helping me kill the wolf." There. If he turned out to be a wolf himself, she wouldn't hate herself for thanking him, as he had helped her kill it.

–*The Piper's Pursuit* by Melanie Dickerson, pg. 59

The blazing secret of the Zircon of purely great fiction is contrast. And there is more to find in amorphous Faerie-land, a place nearly between earth and air.

Dive 13.3

The Cosmos of Faery From Beauty to Ugliness

In the world of Faery not all is as it seems. Near the beginning of our journey, on our list of gems to watch for, one emerald was this: Good and evil, beauty and ugliness are drawn into battle in great fantasy, and there they show their differences in a way that make us want to stand up and cheer or knuckle down and fight with all we are.

This is one of those emeralds. A fairytale retelling that grows from what we think we know, but do not.

> *"Killing me will not stop what has already begun,"* the creature said. *"For two centuries the Cobelds have hidden in the mountains, waiting and watching for the prophesied child. My curse,"*—oh, he loved that it was his!—*"will stop the child's heart before she takes her first breath. My curse,"* he claimed it again, *"will usher in our opportunity to finally take the Kingdom that should have been ours from the beginning!"*
>
> The knight's knuckles, wrapped about the hilt of his sword, whitened. *"Tell me where I can find the cursed hair and how to destroy it."* His voice was quiet now, but lethally so. *"If either the child or mother is harmed we will wage a war the likes of which your kind hasn't imagined since the days of Lady Anya,"* he said. *"But this time we will finish you."*
>
> *"You will not succeed."* The Cobeld's eyes shone with pride, for surely the curse was, even now, speeding through the woman's

blood and finding its way to the child. He could almost taste his triumph. "Not without the child of the prophecy."

He felt it then, a freezing tingle of cold light expelling from the recently emptied follicle on his chin: the curse, delivered.

–*The Ryn* (Eyes of Everia) by Serena Chase (ebook edition)

A birth. Prophecy. Destiny. What we know, and do not know, but must discover.

From birth we yearn to fill our journal of knowledge. But knowledge by itself can cut both ways. It can protect or destroy.

In the worlds of fantasy and speculative fiction much is possible—even discovering deeper facets of who we are. And also who others are in relation to us—which leads us to who our Creator is—to us and for us, and through us.

At the beginning of our voyage Oswald Chambers gave us a jewel of wisdom: "The author who benefits you most is not the one who tells you something you did not know before, but the one who gives expression to the truth that has been struggling in you for utterance."

John Eldredge puts into beautiful, fierce, world-shaking story what we have been trying to say. Watch the DVD *Epic,* or read the book. You will not stand unchanged—in the best of ways.

Fantasy is adept at showing us worlds within worlds, and riches of meaning. It is a weaving of power that transforms a tapestry into a tale, a mirror into a portal, a string of runes on a page into a living, breathing world of mysteries.

Dive 13.4

Mysteries of the Universe in a Parallel World

Fantastic journeys invite us to search beyond what we see for truth, to dig deeper for courage. Never underestimate the power of anything we invite inside our mind and heart. False or true, foolish or wise, corrupt or honest, it transforms our inner world and colors all that we become.

Especially when we must cross worlds to find the truth and solve the mystery.

She'd sworn she would stay close, but she really wanted to find out what was by her window that night. What if she could find her dad out there somewhere? Her curiosity outweighed her promise, and she hurried up the hill.

A shallow dale dipped beyond a small hill. Annalee fought through the low tree boughs until she reached it. A soft rustle sounded past a wide cluster of fir trees at the far side of the clearing. She paused, straining to hear any other sounds, heart thundering against her chest. A humming filled the forest air. Plum-colored fog seeped around the trunks toward her. It gathered into a wispy cloud as tall as her waist and halted ten feet away. Two balls of light gleamed from the center of it and floated forward and upward until they rested at the edge of the haze. Then they solidified, and Annalee realized they were eyes, entirely focused on her. . . .

"Wizz biz muzz muzz?"

No mouth could be seen, but its eyes begged for an answer. It somehow repeated the same sounds. Annalee didn't snap out of her shock until it eased a foot closer.

Lurching back, she asked, "W-w-what do you want? What are you?"

Two white paws and two furry legs appeared on the ground below the cloud, and the creature thump-thumped the soft earth with one ginormous hind foot. It reminded Annalee of the rabbit Thumper from Bambi.

She smiled. "Are you what made those tracks near my window?" Annalee edged closer, unconsciously toying with her dad's camera.

The creature shuddered violently and two blue wings the size of a turkey's came out of either side of the cloud. Covered in scales that came to three points on the shoulder edge, they shimmered like gems. Annalee didn't realize she was holding her breath until the animal fluttered its wings and hopped toward her. She gasped, glued to the ground under her hiking boots. It leaned left then right as it shifted from one set of paws to the other.

The amorphous creature stopped about a foot from her, and a small pink nose and thin whiskers emerged below its eyes. Where there are whiskers, there must be a mouth, she thought. Was it going to eat her out here in the woods? Was it tricking her by acting nice?

It hesitated, like it might be scared, too. Then part of the purple cloud stretched toward Annalee's empty hand. It paused, all the while gazing at her with soft, quizzical eyes. She lifted her hand and stopped. Was it about to bite off her fingers? Annalee snickered at her own fear. How could a cloud do that?

Finally, she touched it, expecting her hand to fall through a cold, moist space. Instead, her fingers entwined in hair so airy, it must be magical.

The humming started again as the bunny (that was the only thing she could compare it to) pivoted, fluttered its wings, and hovered about ten feet away. Turning once to look at her, it made the zuzzing noises again and moved ahead.

"You want me to follow you?" Annalee asked, but she held back, unsure whether she wanted to chase it.

After all, it's not normal for a magical cloud bunny to exist, let alone lead someone deep into a forest. Did it do this to my dad before he disappeared too? She wondered.

"Where are we going?"

−*Moon Daughter Rising* by Emily Moore, pg. 18 (Not yet published)

The best fantasies are about change by conflict, where powerful mysteries transform the familiar. Where do we gather these excellent fantasies so we don't waste time on fool's gold and flawed stories? How do we sort adventurous, inspiring fantasy from the insipid, the bad, and the destructive?

We dive deep into the waves of the sea, climb the highest mountains, and read a page or few of our prospective wealth before we spread it on the heaving deck, bring it home to heap it on the table, or fit it into place in the walls of our castle.

Beware, pirates haunt the seas of fantasy, searching for the treasures that have eluded them.

Dive 13.5

Pirates of Sea and Air That Are Not Quite of Earth

Pirates of airships and sea-waves, never quite of earth, miss the untold riches that heroes and heroines strive to protect, and especially the jewels of great worth that the old salts steer by. They seek to possess by force the riches of change and truth, to steal transcendent beauty for themselves, to capture our sense of mysterious wonder, and to destroy the very vessel of our adventure that is beneath our feet. They seek every good thing, but they seek it the wrong way, taking what belongs to others rather than diving for their own jewels.

After we embark on our vessel again, excited at turning our prow toward our last port of call, we are becalmed. Our gazes turn toward the horizon, and the very air is dead and silent, without the flap of a forlorn sail. And then another ship rows into sight, the dread skull and bones at its masthead.

Without enough sailors or warriors of our own, how do we fight the pirates shaking their fists, raving to board? How do we defeat our dire circumstances, and the dreary, empty wind and sky? We must defend the treasures we have found, jewels of great price, for we protect more than ourselves.

As we dash across the wood, searching quickly among the imaginative riches glittering in the deep leather-bound chests we have gathered beside the forward hatch, we find ourselves beckoned higher up into the liberating power of wonder, deeper into the kind of beauty that imparts strength, and fully awake to the rallying call of an adventure beyond compare. Freedom is worth our very life.

As freedom always is.

One final map and no more. To bring the land closer so she wouldn't have to swim as far.

She fixed the parachute to her back before she pulled out the parchment. The airship lurched to port and starboard every time she let go of the ship's wheel. She threaded her arms through the rungs to hold the wheel steady as she drew. It was the only way she'd make it out of this alive.

And she needed to live.

To finally live, instead of sleep most of her life away.

To find a place where, if it was ever possible, she'd be accepted for who she was, not demanded upon for what she could do.

She opened the box of pens and nearly spilled the ink in the turbulence. Dipping one of the pens into the ink, she dabbed the extra drops against the edge of the inkwell.

How destructive a single, misplaced blotch could be when employing her magic!

Even though the airship shook, her hand stayed steady. She held her right hand firmly with her left as she drew the coastline, expanding it just enough.

That was as much as she dared to do. If she didn't pack up the pens and ink now, she'd go down with the ship.

−*The Mapmaker's Daughter* by Precarious Yates, writing as Joanna Emerson, pg. 12

We all search for destiny. It is known, but not by us. One thing is ours to do. Decide.

Are we an adventurer or a pirate?

Have we grasped the ruby of faithful, royal love, or do we gloat over the faithlessness that leads to bleeding hearts and hands? Does the diamond of our true destiny grow in our dreams, or is our blackened soul enamored with the glitter of glass? Does the thoughtful jade of generous deed hold our gaze, or does the bitter green of the miserly pirate choke all our pleasure?

We must deal with what we find, and choose every moment. Will we be forced into piracy?

"Bring her about, north by northeast. Look alive, you worthless curs! Scar! Get those sails trimmed." Rozar didn't quit giving orders until he'd set every hand to work. "Aldan, come here." He lowered his voice. "Get me down the ladder. Don't know why I ever touch wine."

Aldan half-supported, half-carried the captain to his cabin. Rozar hummed a tune under his breath and settled onto his berth with a muzzy smile. "Ish good you've grown up a bit, or I'd be . . . hmm . . . hmm."

Aldan stared at the captain, who'd fallen asleep the moment his head hit the pillow. "It's a good thing I'm the same size as you, or you'd have broken your neck coming down that ladder."

He stole a moment to watch the waves through the porthole. Ca-thartid's hull vibrated with life under his hand. The ship possessed a soul of her own, an evil soul set on destruction.

Cathartid made the most of the wind in her swept-back sails, slipping through the waters of the Great Gulf like the deadly predator she was, barracuda swift and shark hungry, the fastest ship in King Dzor's pirate fleet with a captain and crew to match her ruthless nature.

A short nap later, Captain Rozar took the helm. Aldan took his normal place — out of reach but near enough to take orders. Rozar summoned him with a snap of his fingers.

"Find Sam and clear out the cabin across from mine. Tell the cook to make a fresh batch of the sleeping potion. Don't make me wait."

Aldan found Sam in the galley. No surprise there. His best friend had long ago discovered he could earn extra food scraps if he acted as cook's drudge. Sam needed all the help he could get maintaining his extra-large form.

Mirza, the ship's resident witch, was in the galley too, preparing some unspeakable sacrifice of fish entrails, strong spices, and spoiled eggs for Azor. The stench was unbearable.

Aldan's stomach rolled over, and he tried not to breathe through his nose. He relayed the captain's orders to Biscuits in one breath.

"Sam. Come with me." Swallowing a gulp of air, Aldan raced through the narrow space to reach the fresh breeze flowing through the hatch overhead.

Sam emerged a few moments later, munching on a stale piece of bread. He held more pieces in his other hand.

Aldan stared as Sam popped another crust into his mouth with relish. "How can you eat when she's making Azor's stew? That's disgusting."

"Mirza's disgusting, but the bread's pretty good. I'm hungry. Besides, it's not even moldy."

Aldan snorted. "I'm so glad the bread isn't moldy. It's your ability to eat around Mirza that's disgusting. Hurry up."

Sam walked at his side, bumping Aldan's shoulder with every other step in the narrow passageway. "I have two more pieces. Want one?"

Aldan looked at the bread. His stomach rumbled. "Oh, all right." He snatched a crust from Sam's hand and stuffed it into his mouth. "Thanks."

"Do you have to walk so fast?"

"Just hurry," Aldan said. "If Rozar decides to check on us, we'd better be done."

–*Mardan's Mark* by Kathrese McKee, pgs. 9-10

To every adventurer worth his salt, every pirate must be fought.

So we will fight. Back to back, against flashing dagger and sea axe and scimitar, howling war cries of our own against tanned corsairs with gold rings winking in their ears, we lift blade and book. Courage sees us through a stiff brush with the pirates. At last we send them packing back over the rail. And then the wind picks up, and our sails fill.

We watch the pirate ship disappear behind us, and rather shakily open our book of knowledge, and write. "No matter how small, doing the right thing brings freedom." We must feel out the courage, the wit and will to act. Have we grasped the ruby of love, the diamond of destiny, and do we hold the jade of generous deed?

Here near the end of our journey, life beyond jewels and dreams awaits us.

Dive 13.6

Brave New Stars and Lost Times in *Brand of Light* and *Dreamlander*

We have opened many books to find the elusive gems under the sea. We have hunted by land and sky through many dangers, we have gained a deeper grasp of truth, a stronger hope in life, and a joyous wonder in the treasures heaped on endless shores.

We have seen the naked combat of body and soul, we have written with our heart's blood in our book of knowledge, and stretched our spirits to encompass wide universes. But have we felt the terrifying beginning of each new journey, each *Brand of Light,* even to the stars?

"No more." Gold cords swung across the stranger's chest.

*Achilus stepped back with a choked breath. Widened his eyes. He knew—*knew *what that meant. A master hunter!* A Kynigos. *But what was he doing in Kardia? May and true, they had authority everywhere, but here? In the castle?*

Clicking the device back onto the wrist strap, the stranger stalked to Achilus. Clamped a hand on Achilus's shoulder and bent, staring through a terse brow. "You are brave, yes?" Dark eyes seemed to stab at the fear within Achilus.

Mutely, he nodded.

"Then you will ride strong and fearless."

"Ride? In this storm?" Achilus looked to Father. "Where are we going?" He recalled Father and Uncle speaking of sending him away for protection should war come. "Is there war?"

Ma'ma pushed away, stifling a sob with the back of her hand. "Mercy ..."

A bitter burst of sadness erupted from behind. Achilus glanced over his shoulder. The stairs. Silvanus came flying into their mother's arms. The two embraced as if their lives would end. It was not comforting or helpful.

Father moved between him and the master hunter, then led Achilus to the foyer. "Remember the night you were able to ferret out the servant boy who had stolen your bow?" His grip tightened, the pressure almost painful. "No one could find him, but you did—said you could smell his fear."

"I'm not sure I could really smell ..." An unfamiliar rush pelted his courage like iced-rain in winter. Suddenly he understood why the master hunter had come. It seemed appropriate that he would arrive on a night like this. Tales spun over feasts and large fires colored them as haunting. But ... how? How could this be? He shifted his gaze back to him. "You've come for me."

"I have."

The doors swung open with a bang, jerking him around. Black night poured in, rain splattering the floors. Destriers stamped in the inner bailey as the storm raged. Guards worked to steady the war horses, who seemed impatient to be on their way rather than stand still. Achilus could relate to their restlessness.

"Achilus." He father knelt before him. "The Ancient has blessed you with gifts that will help bring justice to the lands. Ride with Roman."

Going with the Kynigos meant one thing: those who went never returned. Achilus bit his trembling lip and tightened his fists. He would be strong. Yet never again seeing Ma'ma ...? His gaze wandered to her and Silvanus. "Is the journey long, Father?"

Hands squeezed his shoulders. "A lifetime, my son."

Swallowing hard, refusing to be weak, Achilus lifted his chin and followed Father and the master hunter into the bailey. The hunter mounted and Father lifted Achilus easily onto the horse. "Be strong, Achilus."

A tear defied his will and dashed to his cheek.

"Vanko Kalonica, Father."

The beard twitched, rain dancing on it. "Vanko, Achilus." Forever.

They rode out of Kardia, his family disappearing in the inky, rainy night. The hunter's arm held him tight as they raced through Lampros City and out toward the raging sea. There, beneath the cliffs, hummed a large metal ship. It was bigger than the royal carriage and horses. Waves crashed behind it and swelled over the sleek hull as if to swallow it.

The master hunter reined in the horses.

–Brand of Light by Ronie Kendig, pg. 3

A journey begins, as ours is about to end. Your hands overflowing with jewels, lay them carefully in your treasure chest, and follow us on a last dive, even into the magnificent allure of a new world, for we have dropped anchor at our port. Sometimes we overlook the wealth closest to home.

Dreams weren't supposed to be able to kill you. But this one was sure trying its best.

Chris Redston floated in water up to his neck. Cold pounded through his bones, and fog shrouded his vision. He fought to move, but the sludgy water felt like slow-setting concrete. He gritted his teeth and tried to drag his hand free, but it barely shifted. He strained harder.

From out of the mist in front of him rode a woman on a black horse, rifle in hand. She was tall in the saddle, the flow of her white gown accentuating her height. A braided crown of mahogany hair piled atop her head, studded with matching white blossoms.

She drew the horse to a halt. It slid, hind fetlocks buried in the grass, then reared. With her hand on its shoulder, she quieted it. And then she looked up.

She didn't smile, didn't even blink an acknowledgement. She just stared at him, the thunderstorm blue of her eyes never flinching from his face. The sharp angle of her jaw above her neck and the straight slant of her nose exuded a survivor's fierceness. But it couldn't mask something softer and more vulnerable, something almost desperate, in the compression of her mouth.

Her expression bore recognition. She knew him?

Of course not. She was a figment of his imagination. All he had to do was wake up, and she and her gun and her black monster of a horse would disappear.

She pulled back the rifle's bolt lever and thrust it home.

–Dreamlander by K.M. Weiland, pg. 1

We gather a decisive sky-blue Topaz—and the beauty of truth, the conflict of good versus evil, and a hint of the sword of justice that weaves through the best imaginative fiction—they call us to leave desolation behind. Those bright threads wind through strongholds of deepest evil, but never on a journey of deception, muddling through injustice to exalt despairing fate. Rather, they call us to fight despair in the light of a sure hope. Goodness shines the clearer as it beats back darkness. It holds for us an often shapeless longing.

After diving in waves of salt, rising breathless from the deep coolness to the hot sun glinting across the surface, what is more natural than that we should be thirsty? Jewels, even topazes, though they stream through our fingers in a river, are not water.

Unlike fantasy wells, charmed or otherwise, we can drink the water our Creator gives, without price and without cost. What is the price of *not* drinking? Drink deep of his word and his truth, my friends; drain the sparkling cup, ever fresh and full.

Dip the cup in the fountain again, for that water also cleans away ocean muck, revealing what we hold in our hands, from gold to glass.

Fantasy can be beautiful. Fantasy can be ugly.

It can bring out the child in us: the sense of wonder, the openness, the enthusiasm. It can deepen our love: love of family, of friends, of life. And deepen our love of Someone more precious than any treasure in any world we can imagine.

Fantasy can make us laugh, or rage, or despair. It can make us cheer, or cry, or gather hope. The soul of fantasy transforms the spiritual arena, the wide world of ideas, and the sphere we breathe in.

It conveys life deeper than sand and sea, breathes into being lands nearer than we know, shows us the adventure of love in all its facets. Imaginative fantasy holds for us an often shapeless longing, real as the water we drink.

What we take in impacts us for good or ill, and *we* touch our world. Fantasy adventure transfers truth from thought and experience to our heart's grasp. In the light of story we have found that which is the wealth of souls. Freedom.

Behind and within that elusive joy, our Maker whispers.

AfterWords

... one moment more ...

When an adventure comes to an end,
we might linger for a last look.
Or a heart-felt touch and a few words
before we look ahead,
anticipating an adventure to come.
And so, we offer ...

AfterWords—a space to savor.
Thanks for reading!

Turn the page for ...

- **An Author Q&A Interview, About the Author, Acknowl-edgements**
- **A Sneak Peek into permafree Falcon Chronicle I: Falcon Heart**
- **Discover 35 Fascinating Fantasy Genres**
- **85 Epic Fantasy Authors Book List**
- **Join My Fantasy Fans Team**
- **Bibliography**

Note from the Author: Reviews are gold to authors! If you've enjoyed this book, would you consider rating it and reviewing it on www.Amazon.com?

Author Interview Q&A

Our first question is: How has fantasy impacted your experience of the world?

Answer: It would be easier to say how it hasn't influenced me.

Great fantasy adventure has been a lifeline, an inspiration, a joy, a teacher, an expander of my world. During illness it has been a comfort and enjoyment when I couldn't get out. Imaginative stories gave me the gift of adventure, and do today. Both good and bad speculative fiction inspire me, in the sense that the good shows me moral possibilities of the heart and mind and body, while the bad has shown me how far off track we can get, and identified evils that need fought in the spiritual arena, the wide world of ideas, and the sphere we breathe in. Fantasy shows me heart-thrilling new realms, including the inner world of minds I have not known, places I have not gone, and kingdoms yet to be won.

Question: Why do you think clean fantasy adventure is important to us as human readers?

Answer: Because moral adventure shows us a picture of admirable action, with a sense of the mystery, beauty, and courage we need to live well. It gives us a picture of goodness, not alone, or always unstained, but goodness as it opposes evil. It helps us sort out ourselves, and where we fit in life in the universe. We learn by inner experience what it means to be inhuman and human.

Question: In what ways are great fantasy and imaginative fiction vital to our future?

Answer: The moment we cease to imagine, an exercise in possibility and a kind of creation, we begin to die, in spirit if nothing else. And it is vital to create good, to think of virtue, to be a witness of its thriving existence. If we imagine evil things and live in them, we misuse our gift of sub-creation. We are not here to make the world worse, but to encourage, help, and inspire every person in the great race of life.

About the Author

I grew up in the California hills with four siblings, building forts in the oaks.

The fuzzy-sweet scent of acorns and moss rounded the strong, delicate perfume of lupine and golden poppies under the summer sun. We didn't have TV in the evenings but listened to the night-song of crickets and dreamed of our day's adventures. We hunted ground squirrels with our home-made bows - but never got any, rode our Red-flyer wagon down our mountain, and roamed far and wide.

I learned to read early and entertained my brothers and sisters with many stories I read aloud. Words hold so much power. They loved *Narnia*, *The Young Trailers*, and extraordinary fantasy. Robin McKinley's *The Blue Sword* enthralled me. I have never found enough imaginative fiction with threads of beauty, mystery, and wondrous adventure. Now I enjoy family, old bookstores, and hiking the wild.

Follow me on my Amazon page: https://smile.amazon.com/Azalea-Dabill/e/B00VPO8P9S?ref=sr_ntt_srch_lnk_1&qid=1598721892&sr=1-1

Or go to my website: www.azaleadabill.com **and sign up for new adventures.** Don't forget to check out the Speculative Fiction and Fantasy Q and A Author Roundup (almost 30 authors) on my blog.

Facebook: https://www.facebook.com/azalea.dabill

Twitter: http://twitter.com/AzaleaDabill

Pinterest: http://www.pinterest.com/azaleadabill

Join me on Goodreads: https://www.goodreads.com/user/show/10067218-azalea-dabill

Email me at: fantasticjourney.dynamospress@gmail.com

Crossover – Find the Eternal, the Adventure – Thank you for joining the journey!

Acknowledgements

Few great adventures are accomplished alone. This book is no exception.

CJ and Shelley Hitz's Christian Book Academy, Derek Murphy's CreativIndie ideas and courses, Nina Amir's blogging advice, and Derek Doepker's audiobook and marketing training took this book places I never dreamed.

Derek Murphy inspired the 100 blog posts in a 100 days idea, and without him the book cover would exist in a sad state. Nina assisted with her *How to Blog a Book* (though it shaped itself into a book before much of it was blogged). Through Christian Book Academy, Shelley and CJ Hitz provided courage, know-how, and the gift to see the adventure God gives. Derek Doepker taught me a sustainable marketing angle in Fans on Command and Audio Book training. Adam Houge coached me on a great launch plan.

And to all my writerly friends and encouragers – your help was so invaluable.

I thank God for you all!

Azalea Dabill

Derek Murphy: derekmurphy@creativindie.com

Nina Amir: www.ninaamir.com

CJ and Shelley Hitz: https://christianbookacademy.com/

Derek Doepker: https://bestsellersecrets.com

Adam Houge email: adam@thefanbaseformula.com

Website: http://www.thefanbaseformula.com/

Chapter 1

Pursued

The snares of death. ~ Psalm 18:5

With a deep breath, Kyrin shook back her long hair. She had not thought to watch the sea from her god-father's tower without Celine this leaf-fall. Falcons were true—but friends cut sharp as a treacherous blade. Lord Fenwer's tower gave her a high eyrie from storm for the second time in two years.

Another gust of wind batted shorter locks about her face. A chair creaked. Her mother padded across the stone behind her. Kyrin heard the sigh of a tunic dropped to the floor, the rustling of a dinner tunic donned. Rain spattered the window sill and misted on the floor, a breath of coolness wafting against her ankles.

Father was not here to tickle her mother's ear with a kiss and a low laugh on the morrow—to seal her freedom for a day in the woods, thick now with yellow-clad willow and birch and green pines. He could not tell Mother she would be safe outside Lord Fenwer's stronghold despite the sea-mist and the cliffs, flying her hunters of the air. The sea-thunder boded ill. The moaning wind around the tower would batter any hawk or falcon to a bolt of wet feathers hurtling to ruin under the trees.

"What do you think, Kyrin?"

Kyrin started and turned, with a swift smile.

Her mother's tunic, the rich ochre of autumn, flowed to the tips of her doeskin shoes. The saffron sleeves of her over-tunic brushed her girdle, and from the braided linen swung the key of Cierheld. A beautiful, handspan-long, angular piece of iron.

Kyrin stared at it grimly. Before many more sunrises she would hand her own key to a lord. And she had not yet found him.

"Are you well?" Lady Willa sat, her crippled fingers gripping the arm of her chair, living wood curling about a tree-knot. *She can be hard as a knot too, when she settles her mind on a thing.* Her concern enfolded Kyrin with the warmth of fur in winter. *She said I had until fifteen summers to choose.* Kyrin shivered. Her mother's grey gaze sharpened. "What is it?"

"Nothing, Mother. You will bring honor to Father this night, and Calee's tongue will wag in the kitchen—the sleeves are most becoming." Kyrin moved to the bed and dropped her tunic, which smelled of Aart, around her feet. She dug for a clean one in her mother's saddlebag. "Do not think of me, I'm well, truly. It was a long ride. But Lord Fenwer is as kind as ever."

She tugged at a strand of hair that had escaped the bonds of her leather circlet. Mother said her hair shone with glints of honey in the sun. It was not "drab as a draggled wren just in out of the rain"—as Myrna of Jornhold declared once, with a disdainful sniff.

Kyrin's fingers tightened. Wren or not, she had time to show Esther and Myrna that hunting a falcon was about swift beauty, about something of use in her hand, and something she could not name that rose inside her on their wings. Esther, the nearest stronghold first-daughter, would not laugh at her again. And Mother must never know what Esther whispered of her hill-blood.

Everyone in the three strongholds knew Esther was the beauty among their first-daughters, with hair of gold and straw-flower eyes.

Round faced Myrna was winsome in her ways, and cried over the rabbits that Kyrin's hawk, Samson, hunted for the stew.

But Kyrin of Cierheld was too small, with all the sharp angles of her blood, as apt to stumble into one with a scowl as to curtsey and smile.

An orphan and the stronghold daughters' companion, coltish, red-haired Celine was a born mimic—sure to find her place despite a rough beginning—if she stayed close to the others. So Aunt Medaen said. "High blood will call to blood."

As if old Medaen knows anything about high blood, or those of the blood of the hills—she followed Father from peasant to mercenary, and despised Lord Edsel until he repaid Father's protection with Cierheld. Now the other lords look at Father and Edsel's wall with suspicion. And Medaen can't see past her long nose. She insists I ready myself for Lord Bergrin Jorn. That I guard his suit as I can against Lord Edsel.

But Edsel makes me laugh. And he is as old as Father—and Lord Fenwer. With Edsel I am safe.

Kyrin smothered a grin. *Fenwer's stone* did *ward me well. Old Medaen need not fear. I will not hand-fast any but a true lord. Though I have not found one.*

But Esther—she could not wait for the lords or their sons to seek her out when she came of age. She sought them with wile and wit, and always Kyrin was the one caught stumbling over her feet, or missing the proper greeting and conversation. Kyrin clenched her hands.

Along with the usual bards' songs and tales, the scops brought to Cierheld the rumor of short, slant-eyed master horsemen from the Steppes—archers without compare—who drove all before them on the far side of the world.

Father would give a field for one of their bows. He said in battle their arrows fell like rain. Their horse-archers could strike a man's spine at two hundred paces as his mount galloped, and topple him from the saddle.

Capture by the Steppe barbarians *might* cure Esther. Hauling endless loads of dried horse dung to barbarian fires would bend her mind from the men's glances she drew behind her at every feast. After she escaped, with due trouble, (for not knowing how to ride astride or anything useful) she would gather with Celine and Myrna in Kyrin's room, and humbly ask Kyrin how she came to be so sensible. Kyrin smiled.

Myrna would wring her hands and cry over Esther's ordeal and take a cake from the platter on Kyrin's table for comfort. Celine would listen wide-eyed, but soon beg Kyrin to show her how to fly Samson as she had promised.

The tower shutter rattled. Esther was not here. Kyrin grimaced and fished her wrinkled tunic from the saddlebag. She would be a lady for her godfather tonight, though at her first guest-cup two seasons agone he'd caught her between a man's bow and a curtsey. Following guest-cups and another leaf-fall had taught her better. She was no longer so awkward in manners, though Esther seemed able to make her stumble with one cool lift of an eyebrow.

The pine-green tunic Kyrin held slid soft over her shoulders. Cut high above her breast, the soft wool fell to her ankles, secured by the girdle that held her pouch and Cierheld key, twin to her mother's. She could shoot and ride better than many of the lords' sons. She shook out her wide sleeves, edged with blue thread.

No matter what Myrna said of her fitted sleeves, they made shooting a bow possible. No wind could swell them like blown glass, to startle her hawk or her falcon. She never told Myrna of her riding trews and running through the grass below her hunters of the air. She donned her trews alone, when she reached the friendly trees. She flopped back on the bed and twisted the beads of her necklace.

The delicate carved fish of green-and-rose seashell leaped amid oak beads that she liked to think were peat-dark river bubbles. Her father's gift for her fifteenth name-day went well with her green tunic. Kyrin sat up to slip off her shoes. Rain drummed on the slate roof and in the window.

Mother would have something to say if the wet dampened her tunic—though she wanted the shutter open for the fresh air. She said storms made her feel alive.

In the morning the sun might be shining. Who can tell? I will fly with Lord Fenwer's falcons, high and far. Wind ripped the shutter around and slammed it against the outside wall.

A winged shape hurtled past the sill with a shrill cry. Was it one of Lord Fenwer's birds? Kyrin leaned out and twisted to stare up, blinking against the almost dark and the rain.

"Kyrin, your tunic—"

Again the call came—the harsh echo of a lone gull. Kyrin saw nothing but wind-blown rain.

"Yes, mother." She wiped her face and reached for the shutter. The wind pulled at it, and she struggled.

Along the east side of the out-wall a small door opened onto the cliffs. It flapped in the wind, a crow's wing. A torch bobbed through it. All else along the wall was dark.

A shout came, far and distant. Flames licked up the side of the stables and grew swiftly, as if fed with invisible fuel more potent than wood. Pale-robed figures crossed the yard below in a rough line. The spikes on their pale mushroom-like helms glowed silver and red in the firelight. Kyrin caught her breath.

None of Lord Fenwer's men had spiked helms. Raiders from the far Steppes? Had her wicked wish for Esther called them? No, no bows shone among the silent rushing shapes, flickering in and out of shadow. They streamed toward the servants who carried splashing buckets and pans from the hall door.

Kyrin gripped the sill, her breath frozen.

Falcon Heart, Falcon Chronicle I is permafree and you can find it on Amazon here (I added the entire link in case you have to enter it manually if you are out of WiFi):

https://smile.amazon.com/Falcon-Heart-Chronicle-Medieval-historical-ebook/dp/B00VOEQXIO/ref=sr_1_1?dchild=1&key-words=Falcon+Heart&qid=1598734288&s=books&sr=1-1

35 Fascinating Fantasy Genres

1) Alternative History or Historical Fantasy ~ is a story that is either built around a twist on established history or a time that might have been, either past or after a future cataclysm. Such thrilling adventures include Terri Luckey's dystopian *Kayndo: Ring of Death,* and Christina Ochs historical fantasy *Rise of the Storm.*

2) Anthropomorphic Fantasy ~ is a tale where animal characters reflect human characters in their adventures in a multitude of worlds. Find this entertaining genre in S. D. Smith's heroic *The Green Ember,* and M. I. McAllister's heart-deep saga *Urchin of the Riding Stars.*

3) Arthurian Fantasy ~ is a story that involves the legend of King Arthur in some way. An excellent example is Patricia Malone's historical robust adventure *The Legend of Lady Ilena.*

4) Christian Fantasy ~ is any story that mirrors the greatest story in the universe. Inspirational themes often include judgment, sacrifice, love, or redemption. This covers a wide range of literature, where Christian facets may be subtle or mention Jesus directly. From Patrick Carr's riveting first book in his Darkwater Saga trilogy, *The Shock of Night,* to Chuck Black's trilogy Wars of the Realm, and *Cloak of Light.*

5) Comic or Humorous Fantasy ~ this kind of fantasy adventure may have its serious themes, as all great adventure does, but if you vector into space with Timothy Zahn's The Dragonback series, *Dragon and Thief* will leave you pleasantly sore with laughter and your soul lightened, despite the dangers.

6) Coming of Age Fantasy ~ is about young men and women thrust into whirlwind events to become a hero or heroine and discover who they are in the midst of adventure. This is where Azalea Dabill's *Falcon Heart* begins, with a kidnapped first-daughter stolen away to the sands of medieval Araby.

7) Court Intrigue Fantasy ~ is where Court intrigue signals the rise and fall of kingdoms, as heroes strive for their people with a blend of wit and wisdom, not to mention underdog heroism, as Sherwood Smith's* *Crown Duel* does so well.

8) Dark Fantasy (not Grimdark) has themes of horror ~ such as Ted Dekker's The Lost Books series, beginning with *Chosen.* These are horrific enough to make your hair stand on end, literally.

9) Dragon Fantasy ~ as a genre, it is rather self-explanatory. These beasts range from the wise and good Sapphira in *Eragon,* to the evil and cunning Smaug in *The Hobbit* and Dennis McKiernan's Sleeth in *Dragondoom,* to both evil and good dragons in one series, along with a third dragon, an adorable type of miniature beast, all in Donita K. Paul's DragonQuest books, beginning with *DragonSpell.*

10) Epic or High Fantasy ~ tends to be a story that takes place on an original continent or world with entirely original cultures, usually medieval. Setting and world-building are key in this genre. High fantasy's bar was set with Tolkien's Lord of the Rings, and Anna Thayer's Knight of Eldaran trilogy added to that bar, revealing a riveting new world in *The Traitor's Heir.*

11) Fable or Mythic Fantasy ~ for this genre, *A Midsummer Night's Dream* by Shakespeare has been cited, but I would add George McDonald's *The Golden Key,* and Megan Whelan Turner's *The Thief.*

12) Fairytale Fantasy ~ is a delightful blend of fairytale retellings and new worlds of faery. Great examples are Cameron Dokey's *The Night Dance,* and A. A. Radda's *Numin U'ia.*

13) Gaslamp Fantasy ~ is a Victorian or Edwardian tale set in Regency England, usually with a hint of mystery and magic. Kathleen Baldwin's *A School for Unusual Girls* and KM Weiland's *Wayfarer* fit in these entertaining ranks.

14) Grimdark Fantasy ~ is a story that focuses on violent, immoral successes, for any who have heard the term and are curious. I will go no further with this one.

15) Gunpowder Fantasy ~ is a story where weapons utilizing gunpowder are used as a main part of the technology that drives cultures and characters. KM Weiland's *Dreamlander* is a great example, though other fantasy tropes come into play in the book as well. This is one general rule of fantasy – it weaves together worlds out of the imaginative ether, and likes to confound definers and definitions alike with extravagant beauty and strength.

16) Hard Fantasy ~ is a fantasy that is bound by its own intricate systems of power – magical, technological, or a blend. It resembles hard Sci-fi in this respect. These *laws* both constrain and free its out-workings of power, which are logical and able to be followed by the mind into mystery. Rachel Neumeier's The Griffin Mage trilogy follows *laws of power* in an awesome epic beginning in *Lord of the Changing Winds*.

17) Heroic Fantasy ~ is any story, edda, romance, myth, tale or legend of fantasy set in a non-tech civilization where a hero or heroine goes on a quest to save the world and is born through fire. Deborah Chester's series The Sword, the Ring, and the Chalice bear a strong thread of this throughout the epic adventure of *The Sword*.

18) Juvenile Fantasy ~ is not usually juvenile in scope or depth. It can be better than much adult fantasy in my experience. The Door Within series beginning in Wayne Thomas Batson's *The Door Within* is one prime example.

19) Low Fantasy ~ has everything to do with cultural and historical timeframes as far as I can see. If high fantasy is medievalish, low fantasy deals with magic in our contemporary culture, as J F Rogers does in the Ariboslia series, though *Astray* also crosses genres into shapeshifter fantasy.

20) Magical Realism or Mundane Fantasy ~ is a fiction that magic is so usual it is worked by every human as if it were common as sunshine, with its solar power to be harnessed as the user desires. A beautiful romance series set in Austen's times that is well worth reading, by Mary Robinette Kowal, is her first book *Shades of Milk and Honey*.

21) Mermaid Fantasy ~ this genre is what it says. A wonderful adventure beneath and above the waves is Melanie Cellier's *A Princess of Wind and Wave*. Don't miss the rest of her series.

22) Military Fantasy ~ in this kind of fantasy adventure, warfare methods and soldierly doings are central to the account, from medieval cultures to futuristic. A beloved trilogy that comes to mind is Elizabeth Moon's Deed of Paksenarrion, where Paks begins her career as a recruit in *Sheepfarmer's Daughter* on her way to becoming a legend.

23) Modern Fantasy ~ is a narrative of magic and mayhem in a world similar to our own times, though details vary. Karen Hancock's *Arena* takes place here, though the power comes from outside these brave adventurers, besides the spiritual power born within.

24) Noblebright Fantasy ~ was born in opposition to grimdark fantasy. Hope, nobility, honor – in some way goodness is its trademark. CJ Brightley's *Lord of Dreams* is a brilliant light.

25) Paranormal Fantasy ~ makes up any story that contains scientifically unexplainable power, leading to unheralded or strange events. Mary Stewart's *A Walk in Wolf Wood* is an entertaining romp in this mysterious genre.

26) Pirate Fantasy ~ this tale is – Ahoy! er, ahem – set on any sea where a piratical vessel or person is central in some way to ensuing deeds of derring-do. Kathrese McKee's *Mardan's Mark,* and Joanna Emerson's *The Mapmaker's Daughter* bring unexpected pirates to life.

27) Portal Fantasy ~ is any fiction where the adventurer steps into another world, universe, or realm from our own, where the hero pivotal to the plot operates on another plane of existence. The Another Kingdom series, beginning with Andrew Klavan's *Another Kingdom* is a great one to start with.

28) Quest Fantasy ~ is where a quest drives the plot, the characters, the story, and sometimes even the magic. Beyond every

horizon, every obstacle, every villain, there lurks victory. Andrew Peterson's Wingfeather Saga sets this stage in *On the Edge of the Dark Sea of Darkness*.

29) Romantic Fantasy or Fantasy Romance ~ is a story as varied as the setting. From Robin McKinley's *The Blue Sword* with its atypical warrior heroine, to Holly Bennett's *The Bonemender* where the heroine in her series is strong though not a warrior, and the romance is superb, with a touch of mystery.

30) Science Fiction or Futuristic Fantasy ~ is a story set in a near-future or far times that might be. A stellar example of this universe of fiction is Chris Walley's The Lamb Among the Stars trilogy. The war for our future begins in *The Shadow and Night*.

31) Space Fantasy ~ is any story in space, or between other worlds in another universe. Many novels in this genre are a combination of technology and powers beyond tech. This is quite natural, since the same partnership frames our world, where spiritual power (which tends to operate on a less visible plane) and technological power drive life on the seen and the unseen planes. This genre is growing, from Kathy Tyer's books, including the *Firebird* trilogy, to Chuck Black's The Starlore Legacy series in *Nova,* and Ronie Kendig's The Droseran Saga in *Brand of Light*.

32) Superhero Fantasy ~ this genre says it all. We all want to be saved at times, and at other times, we want to do the saving. Andrew Klavan's The Mindwar trilogy is an adventure that gives power to a crippled ex-football player in *MindWar*.

33) Supernatural Fantasy ~ is a story that bears similarities to paranormal fantasy because it is driven by a power not quantifiable by science, though this genre leans toward divine power and divine or divinely touched beings. Alton Gansky's *The Prodigy* is an example of both the mystery of power and a solid knowledge of its ways in our world.

34) Urban Fantasy ~ is a story with elements of magic, fairies, or otherworldly forces at work in an urban setting. Again, these kinds of stories cross genres in magnificent abandon, yet form

beautiful adventures full of mystery and danger. RJ Anderson's No Ordinary Fairytale series, and the Flight and Flame trilogy light up our armchair world, beginning with *Knife,* a fairytale extraordinaire.

35) YA Fantasy ~ is generally accepted as any story where a hero or heroine is a young adult, which encompasses a vast amount of the sea of fantasy. It is a rather loosely defined category and stretches into middle-grade, where some exceptionally mature young adventurers are found, and even into the adult realm, where they stretch their wings, climb high, or dive deep as the case may be. From DM Cornish's *Foundling* in The Monster Blood Tattoo series, to Jaye L. Knight's *Resistance* in The Ilyon Chronicles, through Morgan Busse's *Mark of the Raven* in The Ravenwood Saga.

85 Epic Fantasy Authors Books List

1) Shelley Adina, Magnificent Devices series, *A Lady of Devices*
2) RJ Anderson, No Ordinary Fairytale trilogy, *Knife,* Flight and Flame trilogy, *Swift*
3) Lloyd Alexander, *The Marvelous Misadventures of Sebastian*
4) Kathleen Baldwin*, The Stranje House series, *A School for Unusual Girls*
5) Wayne Thomas Batson, The Myridian Constellation series, *Sword in the Stars,* The Door Within Series, *The Door Within,* The Berinfell Prophecies (with Dennis Hopper) *Curse of the Spider King*
6) Holly Bennett, *The Bonemender, Bonemender's Choice, Bonemender's Oath*
7) Lisa T Bergren, The River of Time series, *Waterfall*
8) Chuck Black, Wars of the Realm trilogy, *Cloak of Light,* The Starlore Legacy, *Nova*
9) Nadine Brandes, Out of Time series, *A Time to Die*
10) C.J. Brightley, *Lord of Dreams*
11) Sigmund Brouwer, Merlin's Immortals series, *The Orphan King,* standalone *Clan*
12) Morgan Busse, The Ravenwood Saga, *Mark of the Raven,* Follower of the Word series, *Daughter of Light,* The Soul Chronicles, *Tainted*
13) Sharon Cameron, *The Dark Unwinding*
14) Sandy Cathcart, *Shaman's Fire*
15) Melanie Cellier, The Four Kingdoms series, Beyond the Four Kingdoms series, *A Princess of Wind and Wave,* Return to the Four Kingdoms series
16) Patrick Carr, The Darkwater Saga trilogy, *The Shock of Night,* Staff and the Sword series
17) Serena Chase, Eyes of Everia series, *The Ryn*
18) Deborah Chester*, The Sword, the Ring, and the Chalice series
19) Katie Clark, Enslaved series, Beguiled series, standalone *The Rejected Princess*
20) Eoin Colfer, *Airman*
21) DM Cornish, The Monster Blood Tattoo series, *Foundling*
22) Azalea Dabill, The Falcon Chronicle series, *Falcon Heart, Falcon Flight, Lance and Quill,* last story collection in the series coming 2021, *Falcon Dagger.* Companion poetry *Falcon's Ode,* and coloring books available on Amazon.

23) Melanie Dickerson, Fairytale Romance series, *The Peasant's Dream,* A Medieval Fairytale series
24) Cameron Dokey, Fairytale retellings, *The Night Dance*
25) John Eldredge, *Epic,* DVD and book. Non-fiction about the power and purpose of story, and fantasy in particular
26) E.J. Fisch, Ziva Payvan series, *Dakiti,* Ziva Payvan Legacy series
27) John Flanagan, Rangers Apprentice series, *The Ruins of Gorlan,* The Brotherband Chronicles
28) Susan Fletcher, *Shadow Spinner*
29) Lindsay A. Franklin, The Weaver Trilogy, *The Story Peddler*
30) Alton Gansky, Perry Sachs series, standalone *The Prodigy*
31) S. D. Grimm, Children of the Blood Moon series, *Scarlet Moon*
32) Shannon Hale, Princess Academy series, *Princess Academy*
33) Karen Hancock, The Guardian King series, *The Light of Eidon,* standalone *Arena*
34) Victoria Hanley, *The Seer and the Sword*
35) Sharon Hinck, The Sword of Lyric series, The Dancing Realms series, *Hidden Current*
36) Andrew Klavan, The Mindwar trilogy, *Mindwar,* The Homelanders (not fantasy, but excellent YA special forces type series), see bibliography for non-fiction, Another Kingdom series, *Another Kingdom, The Nightmare Feast*
37) Ronie Kendig, The Droseran Saga, *Brand of Light*
38) L. A. Kelly, *Tahn, The Scarlet Trefoil, Return to Alastair*
39) Jaye L. Knight, The Ilyon Chronicles, *Resistance*
40) Mary Robinette Kowal*, The Glamourist Histories, *Shades of Milk and Honey*
41) C. S. Lakin, The Gates of Heaven series, *The Wolf of Tebron*
42) Stephen Lawhead, The Song of Albion series, *The Paradise War,* King Raven trilogy, *Hood,* The Bright Empires series, *The Skin Map*
43) Tosca Lee*, *Havah*
44) C. S. Lewis, Chronicles of Narnia, The Space trilogy, *Out of the Silent Planet, Perelandra, That Hideous Strength*
45) Terri Luckey, Kayndo series, *Kayndo: Ring of Death*
46) Ashley Maker, *Under the Trees*
47) George McDonald, *The Golden Key, The Princess and the Goblin, The Princess and Curdie*
48) Patricia Malone, *The Legend of Lady Ilena, Lady Ilena: Way of the Warrior*
49) M. I. McAllister, The Mistmantle Chronicles, *Urchin of the Riding Stars*

50) Kathrese McKee, Mardan's Mark series, *Mardan's Mark*
51) Dennis McKiernan*, *The Iron Tower* trilogy onimbus, The Silver Call Duology, *The Brega Path,* Hel's Crucible Duology*, *Into the Forge, Into the Fire,* standalone *Dragondoom.* (The later books I have looked at are not sexually appropriate)
52) Robin McKinley, *The Blue Sword, Rose Daughter, Beauty, Deerskin** (caution, rape scene in *Deerskin*)
53) Tricia Mingerink, The Blades of Acktar series, *Dare,* Beyond the Tales series, *Dagger's Sleep: A Retelling of Sleeping Beauty*
54) Elizabeth Moon*, Deed of Paksenarrion trilogy, *Sheepfarmer's Daughter*
55) Rachel Neumeier, *The Floating Islands,* The Griffin Mage trilogy, *Lord of the Changing Winds*
56) Christina Ochs, The Desolate Empire series, *Rise of the Storm*
57) Jeffrey Overstreet, The Auralia Thread series, *Auralia's Colors*
58) Andrew Peterson, The Wingfeather Saga, *On the Edge of the Dark Sea of Darkness,* non-fiction about writing and creating, *Adorning the Dark*
59) Donita K. Paul, Dragon Keepers Chronicles, *DragonSpell*
60) A. A. Radda, The Numin U'ia series, *Numin U'ia*
61) Paul Regnier, The Space Drifters series, *The Iron Gauntlet*
62) J F Rogers, Ariboslia series, *Astray*
63) Jonathan Rogers, the Wilderking trilogy, *The Bark of the Bog Owl*
64) Rachel Rossano, The Novels of Rhynan series, *Mercy*
65) R. A. Salvatore*, The Dark Elf trilogy, *Homeland*
66) Sharon Shinn*, *Summers at Castle Aubern*
67) S. D. Smith, The Green Ember series, *The Green Ember*
68) Sherwood Smith*, *A Posse of Princesses, Crown Duel*
69) H.M. Snow, The Last Book of the Kings series, *The Keeper House Unending* (series may end unfinished with book two, *The King's Brother*
70) Anne Elizabeth Stengl, The Tales of Goldstone Wood series, *Heartless, Dragonwitch*
71) Mary Stewart*, *A Walk in Wolf Wood*
72) Anna Thayer, The Knight of Eldaran trilogy, *The Traitor's Heir*
73) J. R. R. Tolkien, *The Lord of the Rings, The Hobbit, Leaf by Niggle, Smith of Wooten Major*
74) Megan Whelan Turner, The Queen's Thief series, *The Thief*
75) Kathy Tyers, Firebird trilogy, standalones *Shivering World, One Mind's Eye, Crystal Witness (revised version just released)*
76) Gene Veith, *The Soul of the Lion, the Witch, and the Wardrobe* non-fiction

77) Chris Walley, The Lamb Among the Stars series, *Shadow and Night, The Dark Foundations, The Infinite Day,* this is a futuristic Christian Sci-fi/fantasy you don't want to miss

78) David Weber*, Honor Harrington – Star Kingdom trilogy, *A Beautiful Friendship* (The Honor Harrington books I have looked at outside this YA trilogy are not sexually appropriate)

79) KM Weiland, standalones *Storming, Dreamlander, Wayfarer*

80) Jeff Wheeler, The Kingfountain series, *The Queen's Poisoner*

81) Charles Williams, *The Place of the Lion*

82) Thomas Williams, The Seven Kingdoms Chronicles, *The Crown of Eden, Bride of Stone*

83) Jill Williamson, The Blood of Kings trilogy, *By Darkness Hid,* The Kinsman Chronicles, *King's Folly*

84) Precarious Yates, writing as Joanna Emerson, *The Mapmaker's Daughter*

85) Timothy Zahn, The Dragonback series, *Dragon and Thief*

Note: As a general rule, I have listed at least the first book in each series for your convenience. By no means is this an exhaustive list of each author's titles. It's meant to get you started.

Crossover – Find the Eternal, the Adventure

Join My Fantasy Fans Team

Are you interested in getting ARC (Advance Reader Copies) of new books in exchange for your honest reviews or endorsements? Please email a brief request to fantasticjourney.dynamospress@gmail.com for your application to join. This is the fan team for all my upcoming books, fiction and non-fiction.

I look forward to meeting you. Thank you!

Azalea Dabill
Crossover – Find the Eternal, the Adventure

Bibliography

Abanes, Richard. *Harry Potter, Narnia, and The Lord of the Rings: What You Need to Know About Fantasy Books and Movies.* Eugene, OR: Harvest House Publishers, 2005.

Anderson, R. J. *Knife.* Orchard Books, 2009.

Alexander, Lloyd. *The Marvelous Misadventures of Sebastian.* New York: Young Reader's Press, Inc., 1973.

Baldwin, Kathleen. *A School for Unusual Girls.* Tor Teen TR, Reprint edition, 2016.

Batson, Wayne Thomas. *The Door Within.* Nashville, TN: Tommy Nelson, 2005.

Bennett, Holly. *The Bonemender.* Custer, WA: Orca Book Publishers, 2005.

Bergren, Lisa T. *Waterfall.* Colorado Springs, CO: David C Cook, 2011.

Black, Chuck. *Cloak of Light.* Multnomah, 2014.

Brandes, Nadine. *A Time to Rise.* Phoenix, AZ: Enclave Publishing, 2016.

Brightley, C. J. *The Lord of Dreams.* CreateSpace Independent Publishing Platform, 2017.

Busse, Morgan. *Flight of the Raven.* Bloomington, MN: Bethany House Publishers, 2019.

Cathcart, Sandy, and Diana Shadley. *Shaman's Fire.* Needlerock Press, 2015.

Cellier, Melanie. *A Princess of Wind and Wave.* Glen Osmond, South Australia: Luminant Publications, 2019.

Carr, Patrick. *The Shock of Night.* Bloomington, MN: Bethany House Publishers, 2015.

_____. *The Wounded Shadow.* Bloomington, MN: Bethany House Publishers, 2018.

Chase, Serena. *The Ryn (Eyes of Everia # 1).* Candent Gate, LLC, 2013.

Cherryh, C. J. *Foreigner.* New York, NY: Daw Books, Inc., 1994.

Chester, Deborah. *The Chalice.* New York, NY: The Berkley Publishing Group, 2001.

_____. *The Fantasy Fiction Formula.* Manchester: Manchester University Press, 2016.

_____. *The Ring.* New York, NY: The Berkley Publishing Group, 2000.

_____. *The Sword.* New York, NY: The Berkley Publishing Group, 2000.

Clark, Katie. *Shadowed Eden.* Pelican Ventures Book Group, 2014.

Colfer, Eoin. *Airman.* New York, NY: Hyperion Books, 2008.

Cornish, D. M. *Factotum.* New York, NY: G P Putnam's Sons, Penguin Group, USA, Inc., Speak/Penguin, 2011.

_____. *Foundling.* New York, NY: G P Putnam's Sons, Penguin Group, USA, Inc., Speak/Penguin, 2007.

Dabill, Azalea. *Falcon Flight.* Chiloquin, OR: Dynamos Press, 2015.

_____. *Falcon Heart.* Chiloquin, OR: Dynamos Press, 2015.

Dickerson, Melanie. *The Piper's Pursuit.* Nashville, TN: Thomas Nelson, 2019.

Eldredge, John. *Epic.* P.O. Box 141000, Nashville, TN: Nelson Impact, 2005, DVD.

Fisch, E. J. *Dakiti.* Transcendence Publishing, 2014.

Flanagan, John. *Ruins of Gorlan.* New York, NY: Puffin Books, Penguin Young Readers Group, 2005.

Fletcher, Susan. *Shadow Spinner.* New York, NY: Atheneum Books for Young Readers, 1998.

Gansky, Alton. *Prodigy.* Grand Rapids, MI: Zondervan Publishing House, 2001.

Grimm, S. D. *Scarlet Moon.* Phoenix, AZ: Enclave Publishing, 2016.

Hale, Shannon. *Princess Academy.* New York, NY: Scholastic, Inc., 2005.

Hancock, Karen. *Arena*. Bloomington, MN: Bethany House Publishers, 2002.

_____. *The Light of Eidon*. Bloomington, MN: Bethany House Publishers, 2003.

Hanley, Victoria. *The Seer and the Sword*. UK: Scholastic, Ltd., 2000.

Hartman, Rachel. *Seraphina*. Doubleday Canada, 2012.

Klavan, Andrew. *Hostage Run*. Nashville, TN: Thomas Nelson, 2015.

_____. *The Great Good Thing*. Nashville, TN: Amalgamated Metaphor, Nelson Books, Thomas Nelson, 2016.

Kendig, Ronie. *Brand of Light*. Phoenix, AZ: Enclave Publishing, 2020.

Kelly, L. A. *Tahn*. Grand Rapids, MI: Fleming H Revell, Baker Publishing Group, 2005.

Knight, Jaye L. *The King's Scrolls*. Living Sword Publishing, 2015.

Kowal, Mary Robinette. *Shades of Milk and Honey*. New York, NY: Tom Doherty Associates, LLC, 2010.

Lee, Tosca. *Havah*. Colorado Springs, CO: NavPress, 2008.

Lewis, C. S. *That Hideous Strength*. New York, NY: Macmillan Publishing Company, 1946.

_____. *The Lion the Witch and the Wardrobe*.

_____. *Perelandra*. New York, NY: Macmillan Publishing Company, 1944.

_____. *Prince Caspian*. New York, NY: Macmillan Publishing Company, 1951.

_____. *The Silver Chair*. New York, NY: Macmillan Publishing Company, 1953.

_____. *The Voyage of the Dawn Treader*. New York, NY: Macmillan Publishing Company, 1952.

Luckey, Terri. *Kayndo: Ring of Death*. Terri Luckey Books, 2014.

MacDonald, George. *The Golden Key*. Grand Rapids, MI: Wm. B. Eerdmans Publishing Co., 1980.

_____. *The Princess and the Goblin.* Elgin, IL—Weston, Ont: Chariot Books, 1978

Malone, Patricia. *Lady Ilena, Way of the Warrior.* New York: Delacorte Press, 2005.

McAllister, M. I. *Urchin of the Riding Stars.* Miramax Books, 2005.

McKee, Kathrese. *Pirate's Wager.* Word Marker Books, 2018.

McKiernan, Dennis. *The Brega Path.* New York, NY: Doubleday and Company Inc., 1986.

_____. *Into the Forge.* New York, NY: Penguin Group, 1997.

_____. *The Iron Tower.* New York, NY: ROC, New American Library, 2000.

_____. *Trek to Kraggen-Cor.* New York, NY: Doubleday and Company Inc., 1986.

McKinley, Robin. *The Blue Sword.* New York, NY: Green Willow Books, 1982.

_____. *Deerskin.* New York, NY: The Berkley Publishing Group, 1993.

_____. *Rose Daughter.* New York, NY: The Berkley Publishing Group, 2008.

Moon, Elizabeth. *Sheepfarmer's Daughter.* Riverdale, NY: Baen Publishing Enterprises, 1988.

_____. *Divided Allegiance.* Riverdale, NY: Baen Publishing Enterprises, 1988.

Moore, Emily. *Moon Daughter Rising.* Coming fall 2020.

Neumeier, Rachel. *The Floating Islands.* New York: Bluefire Random House Children's Books, 2011.

_____. The Griffin Mage Trilogy, *The Burning Sands.* 237 Park Avenue, New York, NY: Orbit, Hachette Book Group, 2010.

Overstreet, Jeffrey. *Auralia's Colors.* Colorado Springs, CO: WaterBrook Press, 2007.

Peterson, Andrew. *On the Edge of the Dark Sea of Darkness.* Colorado Springs, CO: WaterBrook Press, 2008.

_____. *Adorning the Dark.* Nashville, TN: B & H Publishing Group, 2019.

Paul, Donita K. *The Dragons of Chiril.* Colorado Springs, CO: Water-Brook Press, Revised edition, 2011.

_____. *DragonQuest.* Colorado Springs, CO: WaterBrook Press, 2005.

Radda, A. A. *Cairns of Numin—U'ia.* Grants Pass, OR: Indrinia Press, 2014.

Rogers, J. F. *Astray.* CreateSpace Independent Publishing Platform, 2016.

Rogers, Jonathan. *The Bark of the Bog Owl.* Nashville, TN: Broadman and Holman, 2004.

_____. *The World According to Narnia: Christian Meaning in C. S. Lewis's Beloved Chronicles.* New York: Warner Faith, 2005.

Salvatore, R. A. *Exile.* Renton, WA: Wizards of the Coast, Inc., 2004.

_____. *Homeland.* Renton, WA: Wizards of the Coast, Inc., 2004.

Shinn, Sharon. *Summers at Castle Aubern.* New York, NY: The Berkley Publishing Group, 2001.

Smith, S. D. *Ember Falls.* Story Warren Books, 2016.

_____. *The Green Ember.* Story Warren Books, 2014.

Smith, Sherwood. *A Posse of Princesses.* Winnetka, CA: Norilana Books, 2008.

Stengl, Anne Elizabeth. *Dragonwitch.* Bloomington, MN: Bethany House Publishers, 2013.

_____. *Heartless.* Bloomington, MN: Bethany House Publishers, 2010.

_____. *Moonblood.* Bloomington, MN: Bethany House Publishers, 2012.

Thayer, Anna. *The Broken Blade.* Oxford, England: Lion Fiction, 2015.

_____. *The Traitor's Heir.* Oxford, England: Lion Fiction, 2014.

Tolkien, J. R. R. *The Fellowship of the Ring.* New York, NY: Ballantine Books, 1965.

_____. *The Two Towers.* New York, NY: Ballantine Books, 1965.

Turner, Megan Whelan. *The Thief.* New York, NY: Green Willow Books, 1996.

Tyers, Kathy. *Firebird* (Trilogy). Minneapolis, MN: Bethany House Publishers, 1999.

Veith, Gene. *The Soul of the Lion, the Witch, and the Wardrobe.* Colorado Springs, CO: Cook Communications Ministries, 2005.

Walley, Chris. *The Dark Foundations.* Carol Stream, IL: Tyndale House Publishers, 2006.

_____. *The Infinite Day.* Carol Stream, IL: Tyndale House Publishers, 2006.

_____. *The Shadow and Night.* Carol Stream, IL: Tyndale House Publishers, 2006.

Weiland, K. M. *Dreamlander.* PenForASword Publishing, 2012.

Wheeler, Jeff. *The Queen's Poisoner.* Seattle: 47North, 2016.

Williams, Thomas. *The Crown of Eden.* Nashville, TN: Word Publishing, 1999.

Yates, Precarious, writing as Joanna Emerson. *The Mapmaker's Daughter.* 4Radience Publishing, 2017.

Zahn, Timothy. *Dragon and Thief.* New York, NY: Tom Doherty Associates, LLC, 2003.

www.ingramcontent.com/pod-product-compliance
Lightning Source LLC
Chambersburg PA
CBHW020518260626
47156CB00006B/2045